Purple
Hearts

Purple Hearts

Tess Wakefield

Based on the story by Kyle Jarrow

EMILY BESTLER BOOKS

—

ATRIA

New York   London   Toronto   Sydney   New Delhi

An Imprint of Simon & Schuster, Inc.
1230 Avenue of the Americas
New York, NY 10020

Copyright © 2017 by Alloy Entertainment, LLC

First Emily Bestler Books/Atria Paperback edition April 2017

EMILY BESTLER BOOKS / ATRIA PAPERBACK and colophon are trademarks of Simon & Schuster, Inc.

For information about special discounts for bulk purchases, please contact Simon & Schuster Special Sales at 1-866-506-1949 or business@simonandschuster.com.

The Simon & Schuster Speakers Bureau can bring authors to your live event. For more information or to book an event, contact the Simon & Schuster Speakers Bureau at 1-866-248-3049 or visit our website at www.simonspeakers.com.

Design by Laura Levatino

10   9   8   7   6   5   4   3   2

Library of Congress Cataloging-in-Publication Data is available.

ISBN 978-1-5011-3649-8
ISBN 978-1-5011-3650-4 (ebook)

To Kim, at the CC Club

Cassie

Today, August 2, at 5:34 p.m. on the South Congress Bridge, also known as the South Congress parking lot, I accepted my true form. The windows of the Subaru were down, *Queen's Greatest Hits* was at full blast, and this was it, I was no longer a woman shackled to a cubicle, I was a bandleader, scream-singing with Freddie Mercury. The cars ahead were braking. I followed suit, holding out my hand to make sure the box on my front seat didn't slide. Inside was a picture of my mom and me at Disneyland when I was five, a coffee mug with David Bowie's face emblazoned on it, and three stale granola bars I found buried under some old depositions. My personal effects.

A half hour ago, my boss, Beth, had called me into her office. She'd reached over and taken my hand, the slime of her lime-scented lotion rubbing my palm, and fired me. I'd looked down at my thighs sticking out of my boxy navy dress, my cheap ballet flats, and felt this odd buoyancy. It was the feeling I got every single day at five, walking through the parking lot, but magnified ten times. Like at some point, I'd hear the clap of a director's slate and everything in Beth's office would get brighter under studio lights and someone would yell, "Okay, that's a wrap on *paralegal*! Nice work, Cassie."

And that was today. I had walked off the set to start my real life, hopefully one that involved not just car singing. Despite the fact that Beth's drawn-out, fake-sympathetic "I wish I didn't have to do this" speech had made me late for my second—now only—job, I had already realized being laid off from Jimenez, Gustafson, and Moriarty wills and probate attorneys was meant to happen. Not a blessing in disguise, not a wake-up call, but an actual pure-as-sugar good thing, a thing I had wanted and wished for: to be rid of the endless hours of licking stamps and finding typos, and, more often than not, quickly tabbing out of Hiatus Kaiyote performances on YouTube when I sensed Beth behind my desk.

I switched lanes to get ahead of the Pathfinder. This was it. I would announce it. I turned down Queen, put my phone on speaker, plopped it in the cup holder, and dialed.

"Yello." Traffic hummed in the background. Mom must have been on her way home from the Florien residence, where she cleaned on Fridays.

"Hi," I said. "I was fired."

Silence. The traffic inched forward. "You got fired?"

I blew out a breath and smiled. "Yes."

"You got fired?" she repeated.

"Yes, Mom," I confirmed.

"For what?"

"They said that business was down, and they were combining my job with Stephanie's, and Stephanie had been there longer, so, *wah-wah*." I made a sad-horn sound. "Good-bye, Cassie."

"I'm sorry, *mija*." I could picture her face, her lips smashed together, her brows knit. "I'm very sorry this happened. What are you going to do?"

I thought of Nora's smoky basement, of Toby swiveling on the stool behind his drum set, of pressing my ear to the wood of the old upright piano I got off Craigslist, of never having to end band practice at ten p.m. so I would be awake enough for a daily purgatory of Excel spreadsheets. I could find out what it feels like to be an actual musician. I could wake up tomorrow, and the next day, and the next, knowing the whole day was mine for The Loyal.

My voice was light. "I'm on my way to The Handle Bar, so, go to the next grind, I guess."

"You're taking this well."

"Yeah," I said, softening my voice so I sounded sadder, since it was what she expected. "I'm trying."

"What about your health insurance?"

A truck blared its horn nearby. I yelled over the noise, "There are government programs."

"What about your rent?" my mom interrupted. "I'm worried," she said, and, as if the word "worried" were some sort of password, a coiled spring released and she began to rant. I hoped she was still driving slowly. She tended to wave her arms a lot. She spoke of a severance package. The enrollment deadline for state-assisted health care had passed, she said, but they better make an exception.

I waited to tell her about my full transformation as she spoke, breathing deep, trying to calm the hard, twisted kernel of worry in my stomach.

I had learned to pay close attention to my stomach, more so than most people, I was pretty sure. We had to be on the same team, my gut and I, because for the past few months it'd been off, cranky. I pictured it as a wise, old, talking anthropomorphized object, like a character in an animated movie. What my gut communicated was usually limited to things like *I do not care for these Flamin' Hot Cheetos,* or *Good effort with the bean soup, I'm going to expand and sit with this for a while.*

Now it seemed to be saying everything my mom was saying, but in a nicer, less shrill way. *Cassie,* it rumbled, sending waves of nausea. *You're not facing reality.* She was still going.

"Stop panicking!" I interrupted, loud enough for the woman next to me in a VW to look over. "This is a great opportunity."

"You're right, Cass," she said.

And for a wonderful moment, we were all together, the three of us—me, my mom, and my gut. The traffic moved a whole twelve inches forward, and a breeze sailed through my open window.

Then she said, "You can use your free time to study for the LSAT."

My gut flared again, and I avoided hitting the bumper of the Honda in front of me by an inch. I wanted to slam my head against the steering wheel.

With her accent, anyone who wasn't me would have thought she said "El Sot." The dreaded El Sot. It wasn't as if Mom were going to smash my Yamaha and force me to enroll in UT Austin by gunpoint, but ever since I graduated prelaw four years ago, the law school seed had grown roots. Now she could bring it back into the sun, water it, talk it into growing until it strangled me. I wanted to play music. Not just any music, but my music with my bandmates, Nora and Toby, somewhere between Elton John and Nina Simone and James Blake. It was the only thing that made me happy. *But you can't eat happiness.*

My mother reminded me of that every chance she got, and now that I'd lost the paralegal job, I had nothing to point to in order to distract her.

"The LSAT, yeah," I said. I took a deep breath.

"You know what, I know you're going to be short on money," she continued. "I'll pay for the prep course."

The mass in my stomach was taking over my whole torso.

"I have to go," I said.

"Okay, I'll start looking for courses nearby."

I swallowed. "You don't have to do that."

"Why shouldn't I?"

"Okay, love you, Mom! Bye!"

The mass had spread through my whole body, throbbing, dizzying me. This happened a lot. Like, twice a day, thereabouts. Hence the gut intimacy. I usually chalked it up to student loan–related anxiety, and tried to nail the source of this particular spell: Deeply hungry? Too full? Did I have to pee? *Let's go with hungry,* I told my gut. I grabbed a granola bar and bit into the stale oats, trying to keep my head from spinning.

My phone buzzed. I expected a harried text from Mom, but it was Toby.

Plans tonight?

I smiled. A text on a day we didn't have band practice? And before midnight? This was new. When the traffic stopped, I started replying, *Maybe I'll come over after work,* but stopped. I'd let him wait. Toby was a tall, long-haired Cat Stevens lookalike who played a musical instrument. In Austin. He'd be fine. I was probably one of three women who received that text anyway.

My phone buzzed again. It was Nora, who was working bar-back. *Where are you?*

Traffic, I texted back. *Be there ASAP.* Also, whatever, Nora.

I got her this job, so she can't pretend like she's all responsible. If it wasn't for me, she'd be on her couch three bong rips in, trying to figure out the bass part to "Psycho Killer."

I needed to show Mom I was serious. An album by The Loyal, perhaps. As yet unnamed. Maybe a color. Toby had suggested naming it *Lorraine*, after his cat. We'd have to record it first. The rest—the health care, the money—would fall in line after that. My gut rumbled again, disagreeing.

"What do you know?" I asked it aloud, turning up the music to full blast. "Just eat your granola and be happy."

Luke

Fort Hood was its own little clockwork town. Equipment boomed and creaked. Gridded roads led to dried-out lawns, to shooting ranges, to seventies-era dormitories, to huge red gateways where vehicles of varying sizes and killing capability filtered in and out. They'd watered the grass, I noticed. Behind our line, family and friends sat in folding chairs, fanning themselves with *ARMY STRONG* flyers.

Earlier today, when we'd packed up, the blankness of our bunk hit me. Every trace of us was gone. Clean for the next set of recruits. Not that there had been much in the first place—my yellow army-issued towel tossed over the chair, the picture of Frankie's girlfriend, Elena, in a frame on his desk, the little legal pad where I recorded my running times. But this wasn't camp. This wasn't even basic. It was infantry training. The point of being at Fort Hood was to leave Fort Hood. And now we were.

"So relax and enjoy this time," Captain Grayson was finishing. "Use it wisely. Remember you represent the Sixth Battalion, Thirty-fourth Red Horse Infantry Division, and the United States Army. When you return to duty, you'll be in a combat zone."

"No shit," Frankie said under his breath beside me.

In fourteen days, our company would fly to an unknown base in southwestern Afghanistan. Antiterror unit. Eight months minimum, indefinite maximum, most likely a year. Going to the combat zone was kind of the point of the whole "congratulations and good-bye" ceremony. We clapped.

Across the field, happy people found one another. I watched Clark pick up his kid and spin her around like he was in an insurance commercial, setting her down so he could take his wife's face by the cheeks, pressing his lips to hers. Gomez jumped on her husband, wrapping her legs around his waist. Frankie had disappeared.

Davies came up beside me, holding his hat. Armando, too. The orphans, drifting together.

"Y'all got people at home?" Davies asked. He was a pimply kid, just out of high school, one of the youngest of us, as dumb as a bag of hammers. He could barely identify the letters on the vision test. Good heart, though.

"My main girl. My sister. They couldn't get off work," Armando said, crossing his arms across his wide chest.

"I ain't got no one," Davies said. "I hate this part."

Over their heads I found Frankie, watched him wrap his arms around a curvy woman in a yellow sundress. Elena. She'd brought flowers. *Atta boy, Frankie.* His parents watched, their arms around each other's waists.

Armando ran a hand through his clipped black hair, bringing up a spray of sweat. "I just want a cold Bud, dude."

I licked my dry lips, watching Gomez and her husband laugh and press their foreheads together. "I feel that."

"You taking the bus, Morrow?" Armando asked.

"I guess," I answered.

Davies put his gangly arms around both of us. "What y'all doin' tonight? Wanna get turnt?"

"Hell yes," Armando responded. "Now get off me, Davies, it's too hot."

Davies nodded at me. "Morrow, come on. What else are you gonna do?"

I checked my phone. At least Johnno hadn't called yet today. "I don't know."

Armando shook his head, looking at me. "You're one of the weird, quiet types, huh?"

"No," I said, proving their point.

Maybe I was weird. So what. I wasn't here, willfully getting my ass kicked, preparing to roam through the Middle East with a hunk of hot, deadly metal in my hands, because I got bored with my fantasy football league.

"Cucciolo!" Davies called.

Frankie and Elena approached, followed by his parents. His mother was a beautiful woman with Frankie's big brown eyes, wearing white linen pants, and his father was pure Italian, with curly black hair and thick eyebrows and skin that glowed. Elena kissed Frankie's cheek. He clapped his hands, approaching. "Anyone else going to Austin tonight? I want to get sloppy."

"Chyeah," Davies said. "I'm in."

"Where should we go?" Armando asked.

Frankie turned to me. "Dealer's choice."

"I'm out for this one."

"Aw, fuck that."

I gave him a look. "I gotta go to Buda."

"Tonight?" When I didn't answer right away, Frankie's smile faded. He lowered his voice. "Something wrong?"

"Nothing specific," I said, feeling my chest tighten. "You know, just family stuff. I'll find a motel on the way."

"A motel?" Frankie stared at me. "What about your brother?"

I paused, and stepped aside. Frankie followed.

"I have some other stuff to take care of. I don't want to—yeah." I should have just said *good point* and let it drop. "My dad and I don't get along. And Jake's got a wife and a kid. I don't want to burden them."

Last time I had seen Jake, I had brought him a list of apologies I had written on St. Joseph's stationery, where I had just spent ten days detoxing. He'd shut the door in my face. I still had the piece of paper folded up in my bag a year later, as if I'd never be able to write it again.

"Come on, you're about to go overseas. Someone will let you sleep on their couch," Frankie said. "Crash with me for a while."

"It's all good. I'm gonna get a hotel. Thank you, though."

He shrugged. "My parents have a big house. You'd have your own room."

My heartbeat sped. In the fight between spending the next two weeks in a bed in a home in Austin versus a room off Highway 49, staring at shitty TV, trying not to relapse, the air-conditioned bed would win. But I liked Frankie. He'd become my friend. I didn't want to bring my shit into his house.

His large, comfortable, air-conditioned house.

"For the whole two weeks?" *Don't look desperate.*

"As long as you need," Frankie said, glancing up at me, giving me a nod.

Luke Morrow was not the kind of person you bring home to people like this. Even before all this shit went down, I wasn't a shake-your-hand-and-ask-about-the-weather kind of guy. I never had a mom to teach me how to be a gentleman, how to offer to do the dishes after dinner. More like smoke on the back porch until everyone went to bed.

But no one here knew that. I could do the dishes and whatnot. I could call everyone ma'am and sir, I was good at that now. The air felt cooler for a second. I took a deep breath.

I lifted my hand. Frankie took it.

"I'd appreciate it."

"Morrow's in!" Frankie yelled.

My phone vibrated in my pocket. I checked the screen. There was Johnno. I silenced it.

And it wasn't like I was going out to snort powder off a dirty counter. This would be a bar with music and light and friends, ice in a glass. Frankie's smile was wide and open, carefree. We started walking back to his parents' car with the rest of the families, with everyone else.

Cassie

When midnight rolled around, The Handle Bar had cleared. Bittersweet air from the smoking patio was drifting through the high windows and over the pool tables. A few sweaty Lana Del Rey lookalikes were posing for selfies under the twinkle lights and Lone Star posters, a man with a man bun balanced a full-to-the-brim pitcher over the heads of hipsters playing Scrabble, but other than that, no money coming in. Everyone was drinking, but no one was refilling. I wet my dry mouth with the rest of a Gatorade, retwisted the kinky, black mass that used to be my hair before the humidity got to it, and reviewed the list I'd made on a cocktail napkin:

> get a spot at Petey's open mic
> get another amp
> get more hours at bar / make more $$$

Nora breezed past in jeans as tight as a second skin and a cropped Stones T, glancing at my list. "Big plans?"

I tapped the list. "No more block parties where we get paid in gift certificates. We need actual gigs, at actual venues, opening up for touring bands. That's how we get real money."

She looked around toward where a group of office workers stared at us, huddled at a high top. "No opposition from me! But—"

"Yeah, yeah." I waved my hand. I knew what she was going to say. "I've been too obsessed with getting the EP perfect. I see that now. We just need to go for it. A whole album of new songs is better than four, like, perfected songs, right?"

"I agree!" Nora glanced behind her at the table again. "And now that you've—"

I finished her sentence, feeling my giddiness rise. "Now that I don't have the office job, we can practice more, and I can work during the day on getting us more gigs! Right?"

"Right, but—" She pointed behind her.

"No more 'buts.'" I threw up my hands. "But what?"

"I need three gin and tonics and a Lone Star for the high top."

"Oh." I started to scoop ice into three glasses.

"You're on a tear, huh?" Nora said. "I like it. Jobless Cassie waits for no man."

Yes. My true form. "I just think a couple years of fucking around is long enough."

"As long as we can still have Fleetwood Fridays."

"Of course." I pretended to cross myself. Every Friday-evening practice, Nora and I wore witchy outfits and warmed up with songs from *Rumours* and Fleetwood Mac's self-titled album. Considering Toby, our drummer, had been around for only six months, he hadn't yet opted to participate, although sometimes he wore a vest.

A sudden wave of rumbling laughter hit the door, growing as a big group of buzz cuts walked in, already pretty hammered judging by the level of comfort they had when touching one another.

"Firefighters?" I said to Nora as I filled up a pint glass with amber.

"Soldiers, I think," she replied.

"Yes, ma'am," I said in an exaggerated accent, loading more drinks on her tray. Then I lowered my voice and leaned toward her. "I'm gonna make us some money."

"Go for it."

"Hi, fellas!" I called, opening my arms. "What can I get y'all?"

The soldiers stood behind the row of barstools in formation, their gazes drifting from me up to the TVs showing *SportsCenter*.

"Cassie!" I heard a man's voice call.

I looked around. Wedged between two muscled men, with a buzz cut and cheeks that were losing their roundness, was a face I recognized. He extended his arms across the bar. "I know her!"

I laughed in disbelief as I stared into his big brown eyes.

Frankie Cucciolo, Blue Power Ranger to my Pink. The closest I had to a brother growing up. Mom cleaned his neighbor's house while we shot water guns at each other and watched *Free Willy* over and over.

I came around the bar to hug him. He smelled the same way he did when he used to pour sand down my shirt—like potato chips.

"How the hell have you been?" I asked. We were close a long time ago, before I left for college, closer than close, but I hadn't seen him in a few years.

"Great! I'm on leave right now," he said.

I took him by the shoulders. "On leave? You're in the army?"

Frankie, a soldier. I stopped myself from asking him if he was for real. I got back behind the bar.

"Yeah!" he answered. "We'll be shipping out in two weeks." At this, Frankie slapped the shoulders of the guys who had inserted themselves into the spots next to him. I counted fifteen or so and braced myself. They lined up at my bar. I made conversation with each one, trying not to sound too much like a friendly robot:

"Fort Hood, huh? Wow, neat." *I have no idea where that is.*

"What am I? I'm Puerto Rican." *I'm human. Oh, you mean what* ethnicity *am I?*

"Oh, thank you! So sweet!" *Sure, my shirt is nice. Especially since my breasts are inside it.*

Toward the end of the line was a shorter, young-looking guy with a barrel chest and high cheekbones. He stuck out his hand. "*Soy* Armando."

"*Soy* Cassandra. What are you drinking?" I said over the noise, glancing at the guy next to him.

"Budweiser's good," he answered, but I was already distracted.

Armando was cute, they were all cute, but the guy next to him had broad shoulders and dark hair barely visible on a close-shaved head. Built like a wire. Long-lashed eyes and pouty lips. Sun-browned skin, almost as dark as mine.

When he realized I was looking at him, he took his eyes off the Rangers highlights.

"Hi," I said, out of flirty phrases. "What can I get you?"

"Oh, um. Not beer."

I laughed. "What kind of not beer?"

"Uhh . . ." He looked over my shoulder at the posted list, then to my right at the taps. "I actually don't know. Sorry, it's been a while since I was the sober one."

"What do you like?"

"Um." He stared at the surface of the bar, as if he were contemplating the makeup of dark matter.

"Here." I pulled three small glasses from a stack, and mixed a few virgin cocktails. I pointed to them in turn. "Soda with lime and bitters, Shirley Temple, and a spicy ginger ale."

He sipped on each, keeping his eyes on me above the rim of the glass. When he was finished, he waved his hand over all three. "I like this. All of this is good."

"Oh, you met Luke!" Frankie said, wandering over, his cheeks pink. "Luke, Cassie."

Nora squeezed between Frankie and Luke and ducked under the bar.

"That's my bassist, Nora," I said to Frankie, nodding at her while I scooped three glasses full of ice.

"Hi-lo, Nora," Frankie said, tipsy sounding.

"Nora, hello, wow," Armando said. He barely noticed that I had put the Bud in front of him. "I'm Armando."

"And I'm working," Nora said with a big, lipsticked smile, squeezing a tallboy in the crook of her elbow. Armando's eyes followed her as she dropped off the drinks. He moved away from the bar to a group of soldiers swaying to "This Is How We Do It" near the jukebox. Standard fare. They wouldn't find anything made later than 2005.

Good luck, I mouthed when she caught my eye. She rolled hers.

Luke, I'd noticed with a wave of pleasure, had not moved.

Frankie and I shot the shit while I poured another round for his friends. Luke's eyes were silver-blue. While I turned my back to make Frankie an old-fashioned, I heard him mutter something.

Then Frankie's voice, loud. "Cassie? No, she's like my sister. But soldiers aren't really Cass's type. At least that's how it was in high school."

I struck a match. My ears pricked. Idiots were my type in high school. "Let's not get into that."

"What *is* your type?" Luke asked.

I turned, holding the flame up to an orange peel. "Mythological creatures."

"Any of them in here?" he asked, raising his eyebrows, looking around.

"No," I said, feeling my mouth twitch at the corners, mirroring his.

Nora set her tray on the bar. "Could I get another round for the high top?"

Armando had joined us again, this time accompanied by a ginger guy in an unfortunate striped shirt and glasses. "Soldiers not your type, huh," the guy slurred, gesturing to me as he slumped on the bar. "We can fight for your ass but we can't touch it?"

"Davies," Frankie said. "Dude."

I took a deep breath. Asshole number 2,375 of my two-year bartending career. I filled a glass. "Have some water, buddy."

"Not water, come on!" the redhead said, and pushed away the cup with force, spilling it.

I picked up a rag and soaked up the puddle, my face burning. "I think you're good."

"Oh, come on," he called. Then, lower, to Frankie, "Your friend's being a bitch."

In a second, my belly was against the bar, my nose two inches from his. "Get out," I said. A lopsided smile grew on his skinny face. His lips were chapped, his eyes wet and red.

"Whoa, whoa, whoa . . ." He backed up, holding up his hands, still smirking. His eyes were starting to widen. "It was— I was just—you know."

Every vein in me was pumping. "Get out or our bouncer will get you out," I told him, my face impassive.

Armando took the redhead by the waist and wove with him toward the door. I picked up another tumbler and began to pretend to wipe it down, waiting for my heartbeat to return to normal. I blew out the dark strand of hair that had found its way into my mouth.

"Was that really necessary?" came a voice from the bar. Luke.

"Excuse me?"

Luke shrugged. "You didn't have to kick him out. He's about to ship out—of course he needs to blow off a little steam. He could die."

"Oh, God," I muttered. "I didn't ask him to do that. And for a war I don't even believe in, so, no, I'm not going to give him a break."

He stared at me, suddenly serious. "No, you didn't ask him, because he volunteered to defend our country. Which includes you."

"It's not just us who needs the defending. But, whatever." I raised my hands in surrender, and glanced around for Nora. The patriot could have this one. I just wanted to go back to making money.

I heard his voice closer, more intense, leaning over the bar. "Do you know what's going on over there?" I paused, turning back to him. "With the Islamic State?"

Did I know what was happening with the Islamic State? As if I didn't know how to read. I shouldn't have kept going, but I couldn't help it. He was so smug. "ISIS is a fundamentalist response to the U.S. fucking up that entire region of the world out of greed." His mouth hung open, shocked for a moment. "And you all seem to think it's a good idea to just keep on coming back and messing with them. That's what's going on."

Luke looked indignant. "We're not just 'messing with them,' Cassie."

The sound of my name in his mouth made my gut flip. "Oh, yeah? Luke?"

"The army also builds roads and hospitals and schools. We protect civilians. We protect aid workers."

I threw up my hands. "Well, good for you!"

He stiffened, pulled out a few bills, threw them down on the bar.

"You grew up with Frankie, right?" Luke nodded toward Frankie, who had meandered over to the jukebox.

"Kind of."

He stood up, draining the last of the water. "Then it makes sense."

"What makes sense?" I hated that I had to look up at him, hated that despite my rush of anger, I could still feel some part of me being pulled.

Luke waved his hand toward me, dismissing. "Tattoos, bumper stickers, indie rock, blah blah. Probably a Prius your parents pay for."

"All right. Number one, you don't know me. Number two, I wasn't shitting on you, personally. Or your choice to do whatever it is you do in the military. All I was doing was stating my right to not be called a bitch by your friend."

Luke jumped on the end of my sentence. "You're right, we don't know each other, and what we do know is that you didn't give a scared kid a chance to sober up, apologize, and spend the night with his buddies, because, what? You want world peace?" He tapped the bar. "Correct? Just so we're clear."

"I do know how he acted right here, right now, soldier or not." I was almost yelling, breathing hard again. "And you can vacate as well."

"No problem," he told me, stepping back from the bar. "Have a nice life."

A few minutes later the whole group stumbled out, Frankie offering a sad wave over his shoulder as they went. There went the possibility of any more tips. I felt my apron. Even after I'd served them two rounds, the wad of bills and receipts was thin.

Frankie stuck his head back in the doorway, giving me a sad wave before disappearing again.

Shit.

Nora sidled up, holding a colorful brochure in her hand. She looked at Luke's payment. "You gonna take that?"

"Yeah. But part of me doesn't want anything from that asshole." I wiped down every inch of the bar where he sat. "Can you get me another Gatorade?" I asked Nora.

"Sure. How many is that? Five?"

I shrugged. I was thirsty. I was always thirsty.

"Anyway, I don't want this, either." She handed me the brochure. *Go Army*, it read. *Count the Benefits.* "It came with a proposal from Armando."

"A marriage proposal? Seriously?"

"As serious as a drunk warrior on the eve of battle."

I shoved the brochure in my apron and pulled out the wad of receipts. "How many more rounds until we can buy another amp?"

"A lot." She sighed, before pouring two shots. "Cheers!"

"Get back to work," I said, lifting the little glass to clink with Nora's, laughing but barely feeling it. I chased the shot with a sip of Gatorade, and tried to shake off a feeling of dread. I wasn't sure where it was coming from. Maybe it was that soldier, or maybe it wasn't until now that my unemployment was sinking in. I was really cut loose, a flailing kind of freedom. As I finished clearing the bar of receipts and straw wrappers and soaked cardboard coasters, I found myself suddenly shooting my hand out from my waist, trying to catch a piece of paper as it fluttered in the air. My napkin to-do list, crumpled and disguised, had almost landed in the trash.

Luke

I woke up in Frankie's guest room under a comforter made out of feathers and the usual invisible elephant sitting on my chest. The lady who led our group sessions at St. Joseph's had said the "elephant sensation" might be anxiety. The idea of having anxiety just made my chest tighter, so I'd ignored her, but, yes, the elephant made things that were easy for most people hard for me. Things like being nice, enjoying substances or food in reasonable doses, believing the plots of movies, sleeping, making decisions. Never been able to get the hang of those things, even when I was a kid, and maybe never will.

Then again, some things that are hard for most people are easy for me, like waking up early, and running.

I found Frankie's room because the door was posted with FRNKIE on a Texas license plate. I cracked it open. He grunted. I glanced at the photos on his dresser.

Frankie and his mom and dad, squinting at the Grand Canyon.

Frankie as a toddler in a cowboy hat.

Frankie and a little girl closer to his age, maybe a cousin, sitting in a sandbox.

I looked closer. The expression on the little girl's face looked familiar, those full eyebrows, and the color of her skin, a shade darker than mine or Frankie's. Cassie, the bartender. *Huh.* I didn't realize she knew him *that* well.

"Running?" Frankie half whispered when I told him, lacing up my gray-green Brooks.

"Yeah, leave your back door open, okay?" I said, backing out of his room. I'd do six or seven, depending on the heat.

West Lake Hills was all downhill, dark, smooth pavement and giant, quiet mansions trickling by.

I was also good at thinking about things that didn't necessarily mean anything. And thinking about them a lot. The thoughts usually began with a random phrase I'd heard during the week, passing through my head. *Nice shot, Private. Nice shot. Nice shot.*

Today it was, *Well, good for you!*

Well, good for me. That bartender had gotten under my skin. For once it was good, for me and for everyone. Frankie and Davies and Armando and I were out here pushing ourselves to the brink, about to face death, and it meant nothing to her. To people like her.

I realized I was running in the middle of the road. I veered back onto the sidewalk.

Why did I care what one of Frankie's bleeding-heart friends thought of me anyway? Cassies were everywhere, especially in Austin.

The smooth pavement of Frankie's wealthy neighborhood soon gave way to the cracked concrete of furniture stores, used-book shops, public schools. Three miles.

In sync with the sound of my feet in this thin space, lacking oxygen, my thoughts shifted. The washed-out yellows and browns of Buda rose up behind my eyes and I started hearing the voices of the people who always seemed to run with me.

Dad's face pulsing with my breath, over and over, *you dumbass, you dumbass, you dumbass.* I couldn't help comparing the Cucciolos' spicy fresh pasta sauce from last night's dinner to the little balls of meat he used to slap on a sheet pan. But they were hot, and they came at the same time every night. Mess-hall precision at six p.m., not one minute late. Burgers and A.1. between store-brand white bread, or nothing.

Nothing, I had started to tell Dad when I was fourteen, on my way out the door. *I'll just get something from the gas station.*

On mile four, when the sun was fully up, I thought of Jake, sitting at the table alone with Dad after I'd left, night after night. I thought of Mrs. June, the history teacher who'd failed me, Coach Porter, the clerk at Mort's.

I thought of seeing them now, what they would say. *Wow, you've changed, Morrow. You've got your shit together.*

Except for Jake. The door shutting in my face. I could show up in a limo as a fully ordained priest and he wouldn't believe I'd changed. And until now, he had no reason to.

I looped back toward Frankie's house, back up the hills, past the sprinklers turning on, past a French bulldog and a retriever and the women in spandex who walked them.

My muscles twinged but they pulled out of the grip of the sticky air. Weeks of carrying fifty extra pounds of gear, hauling my limbs over walls and under spiked wires, pushing off the ground for hours, splitting seconds until I threw up—after that, this was nothing.

Between breaths, I made my case to Jake.

I wasn't a lazy, doped-up loner who passed out on Johnno's couch anymore. I knew how to execute. People relied on me. I knew how to take risks and put the good of others above myself. I knew how to push away fear and do whatever it took to get the job done.

Prove it, his voice said back.

Frankie's Spanish-style house came into view. I tapered my pace and checked my watch, panting. Seven and a half. Cut my fastest time by two seconds. The pleasure was white hot.

I'd go back to Buda as soon as I could.

Cassie

Playing at the Skylark was like playing in the basement of a surreal little house. The whole place was painted dark red. Soft disco lights made patterns on the unfinished floors and pipes snaked across the black ceilings. Nora and I had pooled our tips to get her a used amp that didn't sound like total shit. We'd played Petey's, and from Petey's we got picked up by the manager of Les RAV—one of their openers had dropped out and they needed a last-minute replacement.

We were on our second to last song, our newest song, the first I'd written for the album, and I never wanted it to end. Mom was here. She was sitting in the back, stone-faced, her purse clutched on her lap, but she was here.

My fifth Christmas, Mom bought me a small, plastic Casio keyboard, and I couldn't stop playing it. After about a year of telling me to shut up, she had a headache, she had converted her sewing room into a music room and left me to it. My big vocal cords must have been from my dad's side of the family, whatever Euro-clan they came from. All I knew is that he grew up in Iowa, had freckles and brown hair like me, and fell in love with Marisol Salazar in the checkout line at the San Juan Public Library. Beyond that, there's a wall in Mom that I don't get to cross. And believe me, I've asked, wheedled, interrogated.

Nora plucked, almost inaudibly, and the crowd whooped like it was over, but at the bottom of the quiet we shot again: *"Give me too much, give me too much, give me too much."*

I stepped back from the mic and banged out the bridge. The lights felt brighter, splitting my vision. I looked sideways at Nora. *Whoa*, I mouthed. I was smiling bigger than I had in months.

Then the good got too good. My gut jumped, warning me. I felt my skin crawl with shivers. But if anything, the lights felt too hot. There shouldn't have been shivers.

"You give me too much," I sang back for the chorus, *"I didn't ask for it, / You're heavy enough, / I didn't ask for it, / I got big bones, / I'll play you for it."*

I hit the D chord, waited for Toby's triplet. Nora switched keys and I was right there with her on a slight delay, like an echo, with the words I had written on the back of a receipt during a slow night.

While the last notes faded, I drooped with exhaustion. I could barely press the keys.

Shit. I hadn't had anything but a sandwich since lunch. Maybe that was it. I had meant to get something on the way over, but I'd gotten caught up trying to fit the amp and keys in the backseat of the Subaru.

"Thank you," I called, chest heaving. I stepped back from the mic, grabbed Nora's wrist. "Be right back."

Nora swallowed, stepped up to the mic next to me. "We've got EPs for sale back at merch, and thank you to Les RAV for having us . . ."

Panic struck. Darkness rimmed my eyes as I left the stage, holding on to whatever I could to stay steady as I found the door to the greenroom.

"Are you okay?" Toby's voice sounded behind me.

I didn't answer. My legs started to give out, so I knelt, too hard, bruising.

"Whoa, whoa, whoa." I heard him step closer, and he held my shoulders. "Are you okay?"

"I'm not feeling good, T," I tried to say, the words slurring together. I crawled toward the wall.

"Should I get your mom?" He was next to me again, kneeling, too, soft blue jeans. I was covered in cold sweat.

"No, no." I flopped my hand, dismissing, embarrassed. "It'll pass. Go back out there."

I opened my eyes—when had I closed my eyes?—to Toby's face in front of mine, in a haze. *He looks like white Jesus*, I thought. How had I never noticed this before? Brown hair, reddish beard, blue eyes. *Not Cat Stevens.*

He felt my forehead. He had taken out his phone. "Should I call 911?"

"No, no, no, no, no," I said. The room tipped again. *No money for the ambulance.* "Just stay here for a second."

Toby scooted next to me.

Through the wall, I heard Nora tell the audience to have a good night. What was happening? This seemed like more than skipping lunch. This was serious. I fought the urge to cry.

"I'm calling 911," I heard Toby say. I saw black rain, felt my neck go slack. I couldn't answer.

• • •

Mom had ridden with me in the ambulance. I'd blinked in and out until I was awake enough to drink some orange juice. The paramedic had said it was likely a blood sugar issue. Now we were at Seton Northwest, waiting for the doctors to release me.

"You used to be such a good eater." Mom sat next to me between blue curtains in the ER. She took her thumb and scraped under my eyes, frowning.

"I'm still a good eater." I was grateful she wasn't there to see the worst of it.

She clicked her tongue. "Your makeup makes you look like a streetwalker."

"That's not nice."

Considering my mother dropped out of college to live in Austin with my father out of wedlock, she was three thousand times less Catholic than most Puerto Rican mothers, but she still had a mean streak.

She tucked a strand of loose hair behind my ear. "You're making yourself sick. You need a stable job."

"I want music to be my job. That's why I invited you."

"Oh, boy. Cass. Come on. You should have been in bed," she said, shaking her head. "Not out in the middle of the night. It's ten thirty."

"That's all you have to say?" Any good feeling I had gotten from the crowd, from Toby's surprising attentiveness, had faded. "I poured my heart out onstage and that's all you have to say."

"*Ch, ch, ch.* Don't get riled."

A nurse walked by. We both looked up. She passed. Not for us.

"Your drummer was nice to call," Mom said, a tone in her voice.

"Yeah," I said, and stopped myself before saying more. It wasn't worth the hassle. She was already on my case about the band. Might as well save what "friends with benefits" meant for another time. Toby and I had a history of landing in all sorts of situations, many of them involving a bed, but fainting was a first. He was probably freaking out. Nora, too.

"You've got to take it easy." She took my hand, stroking my forearm. "You've got a brain. This is a good *hobby*. You haven't signed up for the LSAT course, you haven't dropped by to pick up the prep books that I bought for you. Instead you're doing this, passing out all over the place. I can't help but wonder *why*, Cass."

I pulled away and bit my thumbnail, because if I didn't, I'd start yelling at her. Finally, I muttered, "I'm trying to *show* you why."

"Sorry." She sighed. "I just don't see why you can't do a good job singing and go to law school at the same time."

I was forming a retort, but a doctor in a white coat entered.

Mom took a breath and pursed her lips. I took her hand again. We weren't *stay mad* people, Mom and I, we were just *get mad* people. We learned this as we grew up together—it's hard to stay angry at the person who is also your only entertainment.

"Cassandra?" the doctor asked, adjusting her glasses as she looked at a clipboard.

"Cassie," I corrected.

"I'm Dr. Mangigian. So we're here today because you lost consciousness?"

"Yeah. I got all shivery and blacked out."

"Mm. Yeah. I'm looking at your chart here . . ." She paused and looked at me. "Do you find yourself having to frequently urinate?"

I thought of moments in traffic, or at band practice, when I would have to leave in the middle of a conversation, practically sprinting up Nora's stairs. "Yes. I've always had a small bladder."

"Do you experience thirst and hunger at a high degree?" I recalled chugging two Gatorades the other night, craving a third.

"Sometimes." What was she getting at?

"Do you have a history of diabetes in your family?"

Mom and I looked at each other. I didn't know. She rubbed my back. Her father had it, she told the doctor. And his sister.

"Well, we're still waiting for the full workup to come back." The doctor looked at both of us from behind her glasses. "But I believe we're looking at a diagnosis of type two diabetes."

Diabetes. The messages from my gut. I looked at the ceiling. "Okay. What does that mean?" I asked, trying to keep back whatever was snaking up my chest, the tears burning at the back of my eyes.

"Well, basically your pancreas doesn't know how to break down sugar in your blood, so you might need to take insulin to help you do that. But insulin can also work *too* well. So you watch what you eat so you don't get hypoglycemic. Or, like you might have done tonight, pass out from low blood sugar."

"Is this—?" I blew out breath, trying to slow my speeding pulse. "Is this what it's going to be like all the time now?" I thought of smiling at Nora, banging on the keys with everything I had. How I finally thought I'd had it, and it was being taken away.

"It will be a couple of days until the test results come in," Dr. Mangigian continued. "And if that is the case, we'll start you on treatments. With diet, exercise, and proper insulin intake, diabetes is totally manageable."

I didn't really do "managing" when it came to my body. As long as it let me fit into my jeans and have orgasms and sleep every once in a while, I let it do its thing. But hypoglycemic? Pancreas? I couldn't even point to my pancreas. All this time, I thought my gut was my friend, and instead it was trying to kill me. "Any needles?"

The doctor laughed. Mom and I didn't. "Occasionally. You may just have to monitor. And as I said, we still don't know."

"But it's diabetes. That's likely what it is?" Mom asked, her voice faint.

The doctor nodded. Mom squeezed my hand.

"The nurse will be back in to check on you and get your insurance information, and we'll go from there."

My throat seized. I didn't have insurance. *My true form.* I was so stupid. "I might have to pay out of pocket."

Mom sighed. "Just have the nurse give me the paperwork. I'll cover this."

I sat up in the bed, still dizzy. "No, Mom."

"It's okay, Cass. You're not insured. What other option do we have?"

"No!" She still cut coupons. She was still paying off her leased Corolla on janitorial wages. She couldn't afford an ambulance and an emergency room visit any more than I could. "No," I repeated.

The doctor cleared her throat. "I'll give you a minute." She left.

"I've got the money," I said to the ceiling. I wondered if Mom could tell I was lying. There was my final paycheck from the firm, and the money from tonight's gig, but my share wouldn't be nearly enough. It was supposed to go toward a studio session anyway. I lay back and closed my eyes. My insides were boiling. My body ran me now. As the tears rolled down, I could feel Mom reach over and wipe them away.

Luke

I kept the Lexus I borrowed from Frankie at forty miles an hour, even on the freeway. No music, no air-conditioning. I wanted it to be like I had never been there. The sooner Jake and I could talk, the longer we had to get to know each other again before I deployed.

I entered on Old North Loop 4, down to Main Street, pulling past Bolero Pharmacy. I was surprised Tim wasn't smoking Newports in the back, his red vest uniform hanging over his shoulder. He was the one who scraped OxyContin off the stock at Bolero, sold it to Johnno at a fixed rate. An AT&T had replaced the video store, and they had put up a new sign, but everything else in Buda was the same. The grass was brownish green from drought or the remains of a drought. Minus the cement and parking meters, the curlicue roofs and red brick could have been a film set for a Western.

I rolled down the window and smelled the dust.

Jake and Hailey's house was just down the block from where we grew up on Arikara Street, a cobalt-blue single-story behind a patch of woolly butterfly and Gulf Coast penstemon, native plants we'd learned about working landscaping for a summer in high school. A swing set made of fresh lumber peeked from the backyard. It was Sunday, and I knew the garage would be closed. Unless Jake and Hailey had started going to church more than just on Christmas and Easter, they'd be home. Still, I should have called.

I parked and walked across the street, up the sidewalk, toward the door. I'd shaved my face raw and bought clothes. Nothing special, just stiff, generic denim and a checkered button-up that still smelled like the factory. In my hand, daisies for Hailey. Under my arm, a LEGO Star Wars set for JJ. In my pocket, the letter for Jake.

Neighboring kids screeched as they ran through a sprinkler. A dog barked. I ran my hand down my face, then knocked.

Nothing.

I knocked again. No one stirred in the house. I stepped back from the door, considering tucking the letter under the mat, which was shaped like a Dallas Cowboys logo. Then I heard laughter—JJ's, high-pitched and raucous. I held the gifts tighter, and followed the sound around to the back. When I got to the edge of the yard, I stood, unable to go farther, as if I'd hit a force field. An electric-blue shape darted into the sunlight, making loops. Jacob Junior. He'd shot up like a weed.

Hailey followed him, wearing a pink sundress and sporting a sweaty blond ponytail. She'd filled out a little since they married, and her face was wide and sun soaked. When she saw me, she stopped.

I lifted the flowers. "Hey, Hailey."

She looked toward the house, and then back at me with a small smile. "JJ, come give Uncle Luke a hug," she called to him.

He wrapped his arms around my legs. I put my hand on Jacob Junior's platinum head. For a minute, my muscles relaxed.

"How old are you now, thirty-five?" I teased.

He giggled, running away. "I'm four and a half!"

Hailey smiled at me. "Hi, hon. Come here."

Her body against mine was medicine, warmth and softness I had forgotten existed.

"Where've you been?" she asked into my shoulder.

"I've been around," I started, but the sound of their back door opening and shutting made me pause.

Hailey let go, giving my arm a squeeze.

We turned toward Jake. His expression shifted to anger. "What's going on, Luke?"

His dark hair was pulled back into a Cowboys cap, his sunburned shoulders bare under a clean white tank. A little chubby, hair a little curly. More of our mom in him, where I got my dad's hard features.

"I came to talk—talk a few things over. Apologize. I'd love to sit down with you and Hailey, if you have a minute."

Jake folded his arms over his chest. "I don't think that's a good idea."

Hailey crossed the yard, lowering her voice. "Babe, I think—"

"He should not be here," Jake argued. "That's what the counselor said. Hard lines."

They were probably referring to the clinic volunteer who came to meet with them shortly after I missed their wedding a few years ago, when they realized how serious my dependence was. I was supposed to be at that meeting, too.

"Hard lines when he's—" She cut off and looked at me. "She said if you're using, we don't contact you." She turned back to Jake. "You're not even giving him a chance."

Jake looked at JJ, who was now still, listening to the volley. "JJ, inside, please."

"But I want—" He had spotted the LEGOs, and was pointing at them.

Jake said louder, "JJ, one, two—"

JJ snapped his hand down with an angry little grunt, and ran inside, pulling the door shut.

I stepped closer to them. "I'm in the army now. I've been clean for almost a year."

Jake folded his arms. "Then why do I see that fuckhead on our street once a month?"

I tried not to show the rage that rose up. He had to be talking about Johnno. I let up my grip on the flowers, took a deep breath. "He's crazy. I don't know why he's around because I'm not buying from him. I'm not buying from anyone."

Jake shook his head. "But you're still in the shit, Luke. You may be off pills, and if that's the case, congratulations, but wherever you are, that asshole will follow, with my wife and kid around. I can't have that."

"Well . . . ," I started, then trailed off. I thought of the calls, the voice mails, but I wasn't here to talk about Johnno. That was another problem. "All I can say is I'm clean, and I can't control where he goes. That part's not my fault."

Jake exploded. "It's never your fault. That's the problem."

My insides twisted, but I stood my ground. My hand moved to my pocket. The letter could say it better than I could. "Can I read you something?"

Jake's face looked pained, like I had punched him. "Jesus, Luke—I don't know, man."

"It'll take one second. You don't have to say anything or forgive me or—whatever."

Before he could object again, I pulled it out. The paper was stiff with wrinkles from being folded and unfolded so many times over the past year. The ink had almost faded. My hands shook.

"I'm sorry I stole money from the garage, and from you." I glanced at Jake. His eyes were on the ground.

After I had flunked out and the government student loans had stopped coming, I had started scraping twenties off the safe in the Morrow Garage office, Johnno idling in the Bronco outside.

"I'm sorry I missed the birth of your son."

Hailey had gotten pregnant when they were twenty-one, after Jake had completed the mechanics certification at Austin Technical College—the one I was supposed to have done, too.

My voice was shaking now. I held back tears. "I'm sorry I was intoxicated on what should have been one of the happiest days of your life, your wedding."

I remembered my phone vibrating on the bedside table while a girl named Jen and I had snorted Oxy off the bathroom counter in her studio apartment. I had barely made it for the photos after the ceremony, wearing the only clean shirt I had, my long, stupid hair piss yellow and unwashed. The photographer had asked me to hold JJ, then just a toddler, in the family photo, so Jake and Hailey could wrap their arms around each other.

My dad had stepped in.

No, he'd said. *I don't want him touching my grandson.*

When I finished reading, I swallowed, composing myself. I looked Jake in the eye, then Hailey, and back to Jake. "I take full responsibility for all of this. And I don't want to disappoint you again."

"It's a little late for that," Jake said.

I took another step in their direction, gesturing toward the house. "Can we just sit down and—talk or something? Hang out? I'm only on leave for another week."

"I'm not ready," Jake said, immediate.

"What can I do?"

"Nothing!" Jake raised his voice. "I covered for you when you went out and got messed up. I didn't report you. I make you best man at my fucking wedding, you don't show. We try to help you, you don't show. I'm done giving you chances."

Hailey put her hand on Jake's back, rubbing it, calming him. In an even voice, she said, "I have to say I agree, Luke."

"I promise, Johnno is out of my life. I can prove it to you. Dad, too."

Jake and Hailey looked at each other. "Have you talked to Dad?" he asked.

"Not yet. No." And I doubted I would. At least Jake had stood and listened. If I went anywhere near Dad, I wouldn't have time to say hello before I was put in the back of a squad car.

Hailey looked back toward the house. "I'm going to check on JJ."

She stepped inside with a glance backward, offering me a sad nod.

It was just Jake and me now. "I'm deploying in a week. So. I guess I'll see you when I get back."

Jake was silent. For the first time that day, I felt he was looking at me closer, seeing me like a brother, not as an enemy. Then he turned back to the house. "I'll be the one to make that choice," he said.

The door shut. I was alone again. I made my way back around the house, left the flowers and LEGOs on the front stoop.

Even when I tried to do things right, to be normal, nothing could be normal anymore. I had missed the window where it would be all right to waltz into their backyard, talk about football, JJ's year in school. All my "thank-yous" and "sorrys" had grown too big. I bent behind the passenger side of the Lexus.

Something was cracking in my middle now, right behind my sternum, spidering through my gut.

The sobs came out in a horrible, retching sound, folding me. I remembered Hailey's hug, the hope it held, and the heat of JJ's small hands. It was almost too much, too much kindness, and I doubled over again, wanting to get away from this feeling. I wanted to stop trying, so I could stop failing. I wanted it to be over.

Oxy could give all that to me. OxyContin had given me a space in the world above what was actually going on, where it seemed like I was too high in the clouds for any of my actions to actually reach anyone. I could fall in and out of people's lives, leaving no trace.

I wanted it now.

I let myself want it. I let it hit me, over and over and over, pummeling me harder than anyone's fists ever could, the blows landing deeper than my skin, into my organs, into my nerves, my veins. I waited until it passed, and made my way around the car.

A Ford Bronco revved from down the street, squealed out from the stop sign. I thought nothing of it until it swerved, curling into a U-turn at the end of the block, and came straight for the Lexus.

My heartbeat sped. *Damn it.* I knew that Bronco.

I scrambled out in front of the Lexus, blocking the grill. The Bronco's bumper screeched to a stop and tapped my waist. Johnno got out of the driver's side, his pale white skeleton drowning in a huge Wu-Tang shirt, followed by Casper, who called himself Kaz, a bigger guy I had met a couple of times who would look like one of those pink-cheeked baby angels if he wasn't half the size of a whale. Johnno glanced at the SUV, and lifted his shirt to scratch his stomach, revealing a handgun in his waistband. *Subtle.*

"Sup, Morrow?"

"Not much," I said. My pulse was in my ears. I looked at Jake's house, praying they wouldn't come to the window.

"Heard you were back," Johnno said.

"Where did you hear that?"

"I just know these things, brother."

Kaz said, "Someone tagged you online."

Johnno glanced daggers at him. Kaz shrugged. I thought of Frankie on his phone. He must have posted a picture, something about being on leave. *Damn it, Frankie.*

"We got details to discuss." Johnno lit a Parliament, his mouth sucked back and his cheeks sharp out of his skull. Somehow he always looked like he was fifteen, eyes squinting.

"No," I said. "Not here."

Johnno nodded at Kaz. I wondered why, until I saw him come for me. A point-blank uppercut, knocking my jaw out of its socket, and another blow to the temple, too quick to feel any pain before I was out.

Cassie

"This sucks. This straight-up sucks, Nora."

We were sitting across from each other on my floor, our laptops open to healthcare.gov. Scattered around Nora's leggings and stockinged feet were her snacks: Flamin' Hot Cheetos, birthday cake Oreos, and a ginger beer. Around me were my snacks: three different types of nuts.

"I told you I didn't have to eat them in front of you! I can eat nuts, too," Nora said, staring at her split ends.

"It's not the snacks." It was partially the snacks. It was also the forms. And the awkward call to Jimenez, Gustafson, and Moriarty, wills and probate attorneys, asking them to access my W-2. The secretary, Elise, had recognized my voice and asked me how things were going. *Could be better.* The suck factor increased when I had to drive not once, not twice, but three times to the Kinko's six miles away to print out 1099s for catering gigs I had done through The Handle Bar. I had to send them as proof of my projected income, even though my guesses probably wouldn't be accurate, because I wasn't sure what my income would look like next year now that I had no full-time job.

"And this terrible, terrible hold music is killing me," I added. From its spot on the floor, my phone on speaker piped a tinned synth version of "Young at Heart."

Suddenly, the music clicked off. "We're sorry. We are experiencing a higher rate of customers than usual. Please hang up and go to healthcare.gov, or remain on the line and we will assist your call as soon as possib—"

"WE'RE ALREADY AT HEALTHCARE DOT GOV," I yelled. I was answered by another rousing rendition of "Young at Heart."

Nora ate a Cheeto. "This would be a lot easier if it were two months from now," she said. "Because then you wouldn't have to qualify for the special enrollment period."

"Yet another reason to finally invent that time machine," I muttered.

Nora snorted, still chewing. "Oh, you should call Toby," she said.

My gut did something flip-floppy, unidentifiable. Then again, it was doing a lot of that lately. "Why?"

"He texted me just now."

"Why doesn't he just text me?" *And what's with the sudden concern with my existence outside of band practice and our respective beds?* I wanted to add, but Nora never liked to hear about us hooking up, no matter how infrequent.

Nora pointed to the still-serenading phone. "He probably couldn't get through."

"Oh, yeah. Well," I said, feigning apathy, "tell him how much fun we're having."

I'd been on hold for two hours. I had found out that people who wanted ObamaCare in Texas could sign up only from November 1 to January 31. It was September 27. In the meantime, I would have to buy temporary private insurance, and my special enrollment period application had not gone through after a week. Nora and I were calling today to see if they actually received it.

Either way, there was no doubt I would be paying out of pocket for the ambulance ride, the emergency room visit, and the hour-long visit with Nancy, a diabetes nutrition expert who was unsettlingly cheerful and whose every sentence sounded like a question.

It didn't look like my glucose levels varied enough to have to take insulin yet?

So for now, we would try meal planning and exercise?

Here were some good on-the-go meals?

For a snack, Nancy recommended nuts?

The nuts weren't that bad. And neither was Nancy. She was just trying to help. But damn, eating greens and whole grains had tripled the cost of my last two trips to Central Market.

And over time, my insulin production would be worse. Once my insulin was gone, it would need to be replaced to keep my sugar levels safe. And that meant injections. And injections meant paying for all the items on the list I'd taped to my fridge reminding me why I was eating tasteless, boring foods like lentils: vials of insulin, needles, syringes, alcohol pads, gauze, bandages, and a puncture-resistant "sharps" container for proper needle and syringe disposal.

"Hand me that pen, Nor." She tossed me the one in her hand. It was covered in Cheetos dust. I wiped it on my pants, then started to write it all down.

My total costs, just for diabetes, added up to $650 a month. On top of rent. On top of student loans. At The Handle Bar, I made about $2,000 a month, if I was lucky enough to get good hours.

I was in bad shape. Even if I qualified for a low monthly premium, I wouldn't be above water because of the previous out-of-pocket bills. And until I reached the yearly deductible, I would pay hundreds of dollars each month for the insulin. And all of it just to live like a normal human being. Not even normal. A human being who would be alive enough to pay her debts.

I lay spread-eagle on the floor and tried not to panic. I'd read somewhere that cursing has a chemical effect on your brain, alleviating stress. "Fuck, fuck, fuck, fuck, fuck," I chanted.

Nora crawled over and lay next to me, the whiny drone of the hold music serenading us.

I handed her the paper on which I had written the costs.

She cursed with me, and crumpled it up, throwing it across the room. "What are we going to do?"

"About what?"

"All of it." She gestured to me, to the laptops, to where my keyboard was set up over by the living room window.

"First thing is to marry a wealthy patron," I started, putting out a finger.

"Get on their health insurance," Nora continued. We put out two fingers.

"Then we convert one of the rooms in their mansion into a recording studio, and we write a hit record."

"I'd marry you if I were rich," Nora said.

I tapped her stockinged foot with my bare one. "Me, too."

She looked around. "You'd have to be a little cleaner."

"Whoops." The floor we lay on was dusty. Three different shirts graced the futon like throw pillows. Old magazines were stacked on the shelves next to the knickknacks. My bartending apron was tossed over my keyboard, its contents falling out. I really had to take more care. In every way. "I'd try," I added.

"I wish we had rich friends who we could marry for their benefits," Nora said.

"Yeah, well. We need new friends."

As we spoke, my eyes landed on my bartending apron again. Sticking out of the pocket of the apron was the corner of a colorful brochure.

The army brochure.

Luke

I opened my eyes to the Bronco's ceiling, head throbbing. The interior smelled like sweat and cough medicine.

I'd met Johnno at a party at his house four years ago. When all the gin and whiskey bottles ran dry, he had started handing out pills. He was one of those kids who were always on the Austin Community College campus, but never in class. No one knew how old he was. The day after the party, I'd come back for more. And the day after that.

He'd never asked for money, only that I ride with him to someone's house, or play him in *Fallout*, or answer the door when cops came. Our friendship had turned sour when I tried to go back to school. He'd pull his gun on me when I told him I was going to class, then joke about it later, after we'd snorted more pills.

That's the kind of asshole he was. Pure chaos. And I was back in the epicenter. I sat up.

Before I could register Johnno next to me in the backseat, he landed another blow to the back of the head. My nose ground into the seat in front of me, spotted with grease and sprinklings of white powder. He was holding the back of my head in place.

"You thought you'd just lay low for a couple of months and get out without paying for all the shit you dumped? You don't answer my calls," Johnno muttered, digging his long nails into my neck. "You getting smart, motherfucker?"

I said nothing, even as his nails broke my skin and involuntary tears leaked from my eyes.

Kaz's pink cotton torso loomed in the periphery, one hand on the wheel, the other scrolling through his phone. He sighed, bored.

Johnno pressed my face harder into the seat. "If you don't talk, I'm gonna take you out and curb stomp you."

Kaz made a sound like a snort, still not looking up from his phone.

"I've been in training," I said, trying not to shake.

"One night we're having a good time, watching *The Wire*, then you disappear and get on a boat to Afghanistan."

Kaz let out another snort. "Afghanistan on a boat. Motherfucker, do you know where Afghanistan is?"

"Man, fuck you, Kaz," Johnno muttered, and suddenly his mouth was close to my cheek, stinking of menthol. "Ten."

"What? No."

"Five for all the shit you threw out, five for interest."

I blinked against the fabric, trying to ignore the throbbing behind my eyes. "How much does Tim want?"

"No, you don't talk to Tim. You talk to me." Out of the corner of my vision, I could see Johnno put his other hand to his lap, where the gun was tucked.

"Let me up," I said as calmly as I could. "I'm not going to pull anything, Johnno."

"Do not fuck with me," Johnno said, his voice tense and high.

I rose with my palms open, near my shoulders. *Nothing. I got nothing. I'm not a threat.* A thought flashed. *I wonder if he would give me a bump. Just to get through this.*

No. Stay here. Stay straight. "I don't have the money," I said.

"No shit," he said. "So you have a week to get it."

My palms became fists. "What the fuck, dude?"

"You got some vision while you were balls-deep high and wiped out my supply, dumbass. Just because you were feeling righteous one night."

I had flushed it down his toilet while he was in Orlando. He had returned home to no pills, all my stuff gone, and a vague note I had written, something like, *I'm okay, I'm just never coming back.*

Johnno pounded the seat. "Return to Earth."

I stuttered, glancing at the piece. "Yeah, b-but a week? You couldn't have pushed that much in six months. Is Tim after you?"

"That's none of your fucking business."

That meant yes. This was the same answer Johnno had given me back when we shot the shit on the futon, and I had asked him if Tasha, the girl he was seeing, had broken up with him. *None of your fucking business, bro*, he'd said, his upper lip twitching.

Still, it didn't add up. I opened my hands again, trying to sound casual. "Five K is nothing to what Tim makes. What's the rush?"

Kaz cleared his throat, eyes still on his phone.

And then I realized. "You got yourself into some other shit, didn't you?" Someone was after him, too. So he thought he'd shift the load.

Instead of answering, Johnno reached for the cup holder, grabbed a bottle of Sprite, and took a swig. Johnno had always drunk Sprite like it was water.

With a jerk he palmed my head and whacked it with the butt of the gun, Sprite spreading in the air like a fountain. Pain streaked through my nerves, my teeth, my spine.

"I need more time," I slurred, lemon-lime pop in my eyes. "I'm serious. You can kill me but I don't have it."

"If you don't have it, I'll come for your family, too."

I broke out in a cold sweat. "What am I supposed to do?"

Johnno chugged the rest of the bottle. "Not my problem."

"Half in three months," I said, blinking against the knives in my skull. "Half when I get back."

"Fine."

I tried not to shake. Johnno spit out the crack of the window. Kaz pressed a button to unlock the doors, and I staggered out, dripping blood.

The squeak of a door opening sounded from across the street, and my breath caught. Jake stepped out on his stoop. JJ's little blond head poked out from behind him.

He caught sight of me, and paused.

Go back inside, I silently commanded. Jake's gaze turned to Johnno through the open window, then to Kaz. His face hardened. I knew what he was thinking. We were double-parked in the middle of his peaceful street. It would look the same way if we were pulling some other shit. If we were high. He turned away to shuffle JJ back inside.

This wasn't the plan. The plan was to say sorry, to show him I'd changed. Now it looked like I had lied to his face. It looked like I was the same fucking idiot I'd always been.

Cassie

I was sweating through my Kinks shirt, biting a hangnail off my thumb, pacing up and down a block in West Lake Hills next to the Gopney Playground. After Nora had left, I'd brooded all last night, scheming, and drove over an hour early so I wouldn't miss him. I'd had to turn back once because I'd forgotten my phone at home, then I'd gotten in and out of my car three times, and almost made it down the block before turning around and parking again. Frankie and I used to dangle off the monkey bars here, kick in sync on the swings, play TV tag, freeze tag, bridge tag. Inside the little plastic cabin near the sandbox, we used to set up a house. Then we'd run around the borders and pretend we were fighting aliens, protecting our progeny. While my mother cleaned his house, Frankie was my day care.

I stood on the curb, waiting for him, the pads of my fingers sore, just like they used to be from playing piano. But now my fingers hurt because I had pricked them with a glucose meter. Now I waited for Frankie ready to play a different kind of game. Now, in my head, I was proposing to him.

Frankie, please fake-marry me.

Frankie, we both love snacks, and we are both from Texas. I think this could work.

Frankie, remember that time that you stepped on an ant and cried? I do. Who else knows you better than I do?

Before we lost touch, Frankie and I were best friends. He had started hanging out with the football players, and though he ignored me in the hallways, here on the Gopney benches he'd told me that I was better than all the guys I had crushes on, congratulated me when I'd made our high school's jazz ensemble on the keys as a first-year, listened to every story I exaggerated, affirmed every vague, ecclesiastical notion I had about music.

For a time, at least.

Can I come over and see ya? I had texted him.

Yeah!!! Eating lunch with parents but will be done at 1ish, he'd replied.

Here's what I figured: According to the army website, if Frankie and I got married, he'd get two thousand dollars more a month, for a housing allowance and subsistence benefits.

We would each get one thousand dollars a month, I'd get on his health plan, and I'd up my hours in bartending. This would still cover my student loans and copays and blood sugar checks. Frankie could do whatever he wanted with his share of the money. And in the meantime, I wouldn't have to get another day job. I could spend my days writing an album.

And most important, if something went wrong, if my blood sugar got too high or low, that one-thousand-dollar ambulance ride that isn't covered by insurance, and all the other bills—the hospital visit, and overnight stay—wouldn't be sending Mom or me into poverty.

Then there's the other part of it, the whole faking-a-wedding endeavor. No problem. Frankie and I would go to the courthouse, claiming we'd loved each other since childhood. It wasn't far from the truth, and hell, I know how to be in love. I'd done it a few times.

Frankie had been first, probably, but so innocent. A kiss on the cheek or the lips before the streetlights turned on. Next came Andy, the upright-bass player in the jazz ensemble. We spent Saturday nights in the backseat while Charles Mingus played in the CD player, convincing ourselves that our hands down each other's pants while listening to the best upright-bass player of all time was somehow different than regular hands down regular pants. I mean, how do you not fall in love with the first person who wants to touch you that way? I thought we were magic. Two jazz prodigies, entwined.

But we weren't prodigies. We were kids. Me, especially. Once, I'd flown three hundred miles to watch Andy's college showcase. Instead of surprising him after the concert, I witnessed him making out with a willowy, freckled flute player in the wings.

It was past one thirty, and Frankie still hadn't texted, which was weird, because he used to call back within seconds. Then again, that was years ago.

I started swinging to pass the time. The hard rubber dug into my hips. This was a terrible idea.

After Andy, I'd stopped playing piano altogether. I'd confined myself to antimusic, listening to No Wave, Kraftwerk, BauHaus, Joy Division. I was alone, and I liked being alone.

That's why I thought James had been perfect. James didn't believe in love, and neither did I. James believed in rational hedonism. I believed in secular humanism. We "fucked like animals," as he would put it, and ingested every drug available on campus until we burned out, fought, and made up again. We enrolled in the same seminars so we could spend our nights comparing notes, editing each other's papers, pushing against each other's viewpoints so hard that we would have to rip our clothes off in the private study room on the fourth floor of the library. We didn't think it was love, but of course it was.

I dragged my feet on the ground to slow the swing. I checked my phone. No word.

After I graduated from Pomona, I was surprised I didn't run into Frankie again. I moved back in with my mother, applied to paralegal jobs. I started riding my bike. I started baking. I started wearing colors. I spent hours plunking out ragtime versions of Katy Perry and Rihanna. In my headphones, I pumped Elton John, Billy Joel, the Carpenters.

And Tyler loved all this about me. Tyler told me he wanted to marry me on our third date, a late showing of *Sabrina* at Violet Crown Cinema. Tyler was in law school, Tyler brought my mom chrysanthemums the first time he met her. Tyler regularly got his hair cut by an actual barber. I bought toys for his niece's birthday, I decorated the apartment we found in North Loop with large vases full of dried reeds. I got a job at the firm full time, with every intention to get into law school once Tyler had passed the bar. I was twenty-three, I had gotten my wild years behind me, and I had it all figured out.

Then, something started to crumble, but in a good way. A hard shell falling off. I started to avoid Tyler by going on long walks, listening to album after album, any artist, any genre I could find, as long as I'd never heard it before.

I had realized the only times I felt sad, tired, inadequate, were the hours spent at the firm, or in that sterile, empty apartment. When I was out in the world, by myself, I felt free.

I'd moved into Rita's attic within a week.

That was a year ago. I'd been making minimum payments on my student loans, trying to keep my mother happy, teaching myself to hone my rough voice into something listenable, collecting synthesizer equipment, working fifty to sixty hours a week, and now learning how to cook food that wouldn't kill me.

And with the exception of exchanging occasional booty calls with the drummer of my band, I'd been doing all of it completely, gloriously, and sometimes terribly alone.

Now I needed help.

Finally, Frankie texted. *Sorryyyy, on our way.*

Frankie would get it. He was still there, still willing and kind, at least. He could go overseas, I would stay here, and by the time he got back, well, I would have had my shot. If I wasn't making a living from music then, and if Frankie was ready after deployment to pursue actual marriage with someone else, we'd break it off. I'd go back to having shitty jobs with crappy health insurance and figure out another way. Until then, we could just be two independent people in a mutual agreement.

I took a deep breath and started walking toward his house. My gut was burning, but on my side. I'd fed it expensive quinoa for lunch. That always helped.

After a few blocks, I looked up at his enormous house, hearing the door of the Lexus shut. People were laughing.

Up the driveway, three people got out of the car: Frankie. Luke, the asshole from the other night. And a woman in a turquoise dress, maybe Luke's girlfriend.

I nodded at the woman and pretended Luke didn't exist.

"Frankie, can I talk to you for a second?" I said, holding the army brochure like a weapon, smiling big and scared.

"Sure, Cass," Frankie said, his brows furrowing. "Be right there," he called, and Luke and the woman made their way into the house.

"First of all, hi," I said, and laughed for no reason, nervous.

"Hi," Frankie, said, laughing with me. "Good to see you after an 'eventful' night."

"Right, about that . . ." I had bent the brochure into a cylinder.

"Sorry. Again. Also, please tell me we're going to get to see you play before we ship out."

"Yeah!" I swallowed. "I mean, no, but that's also kind of why I'm here."

"What's up?"

"I found out I have diabetes, and—" Frankie's face twisted in concern. I stopped him. "No, it's okay. I'll be okay. Hear me out."

"But that's so scary," Frankie continued, softer.

"It is. And I just lost my day job." Before Frankie could pity me further, I said quickly, "So here's what I'm thinking. With your army contract, married couples get two thousand dollars extra a month, and the spouse gets covered under your health care. So, like—" I paused, smiling with my teeth, my gut sloshing. "So what are you up to tomorrow?"

Frankie squinted, smiling. Then an expression of understanding passed over his face. "Wait, is this a proposal?"

"N-not like that," I stammered. "We go to the courthouse. We get a marriage certificate. I'm your legal spouse. We split the money."

"Cassie," he said.

I handed him the brochure. He flattened it out of the crumpled mess.

"It'd be so easy," I pushed, on the verge of pleading. "We wouldn't even have to pretend for that long, because you'll be overseas."

"Housing and subsistence benefits for married couples?" Frankie laughed, incredulous. He stared at the paper. "Where did you get this?"

"Armando gave it to Nora that night at the bar."

"Fucking Armando." He shook his head. "Cass—but, like, why? Why are you even considering this?"

A knot of regret was already forming. This wasn't how I'd pictured this going. I pushed through it. "My health insurance is fucked, and if something were to go south with my diabetes, I couldn't afford it. Especially on top of my student loans."

Frankie exhaled. "Why don't you just get a new job?"

A flat laugh escaped me, thinking of the hospital room. *This is a good hobby.* "You should talk to my mother."

"There just has to be another way."

"I've been living the other way, Frankie," I said. I felt the desperate edge to my voice. "It sucks. I did everything right. I went to college, I paid my own bills, I took care of myself. I had a career. Even when I was doing everything right, things went wrong. They're going to go wrong again, especially now that I'm sick. So I might as well pursue my passion instead of grinding away at some buffer job that will get me nowhere anyway."

He stared at me, opening his mouth to speak, then closed it.

I lowered my voice. "All you would have to do is sign some papers before you deploy. When you come back, I will get divorced, anything you want."

Frankie handed me back the brochure, and crossed his arms over his Captain America T-shirt. He kept looking back at the house as I spoke, as if he were afraid of someone inside. "Cassie," he said, then pushed air out of his mouth, shaking his head. "I want to help you. I really, really do. You're like blood. I would do anything for you."

"Those are things people say when they're about to say no." I could hear it in the air, his refusal. I was already thinking of ways I could pull it off as a joke. But if it were a joke, I wouldn't be getting tears in my eyes. *Damn it.* I just asked someone to commit fraud so I could afford to have a disease.

"If things were different, I would," he said, reaching a hand out to touch my arm. "I've got Elena to think about now."

"Elena?" I asked, swallowing the lump in my throat.

"My girlfriend," he said, jerking his head toward the house.

"Oh, of course!" The woman in turquoise. "Of course. Well."

"We're pretty serious."

"Makes sense. That's awesome," I said, hoping I sounded happy for him.

Clicking heels sounded on the pavement behind me. I turned to face Elena, a woman around my age with sleek black hair in styled waves. Her makeup was visible but tasteful, her dress bright and flattering.

"Hey, baby!" she said to Frankie, cheerful. Then to me, "Hi, I'm Elena."

"Great to meet you," I lied.

As I shook her soft hand, some sort of chasm broke beneath me, pulling me down, spiraling around my gut and squeezing like a python. Elena appeared composed, loving, in control of her life, and of course Frankie didn't want to upset that. Of course not.

"How'd y'all meet?" I forced out.

Frankie's face lit up. "Through my mom. She came over here for a work thing last year. I always thought she was cute."

"We're moving in together when Frankie gets back," Elena said, and they exchanged nervous, adoring glances. "We're so excited."

I could feel myself falling deeper into the chasm as they took each other's arms.

"That's awesome," I repeated. "Congratulations."

"Hey," he started. "What if I give you a loan?"

Elena tilted her head toward him, confused.

"No, no, no, no." I put up my hands in embarrassment, then realized I was still holding the brochure. I stuffed it in my purse. "I gotta go to work. I just, um. It was nothing. I'll figure it out."

"Hey," Frankie said again, and opened his arms.

I hugged him hard, pinching my eyes against tears.

"Frankie?" I whispered. "Could we keep this between us?"

I felt him nod. We let go.

"It was great to see you, Cass."

"You, too, Frankie." It was. "Good to meet you, Elena."

She waved and I walked back toward the playground to my car. The tears came, quiet and thick, putting out the fire of nerves I'd felt earlier. They also dissolved the positive heat I'd felt, the sizzling *go for it* feelings that had lifted me through the events of the past week.

Nothing was any different from before.

I started to see my future. It wasn't too hard to picture, really.

I would wake up and test my blood sugar.

I would go to my shift at The Handle Bar, pass out, wake up, do it again.

I would keep pushing to make The Loyal a real band, until I got too tired or broke or both.

If I got lucky, I would find a new, mindless desk job, listening to musicians who were better than me on my commute.

Maybe if things got a little better, I would get a cat or a dog, or maybe if things got a little worse, I would move in with Mom. I would probably be paying off my medical bills and student loans until I had gray hair, or until I gave in and finally went to law school.

And, hey, no fake marriage meant I wasn't doing anything illegal. Everything was the same. No harm, no foul.

I reached the playground, but I couldn't bring myself to get into my shitty Subaru just yet. I looked at the swings where I used to pump until I was flying, looping at 180 degrees, positive in my little girl head that any second I would float off the swing and into the sky.

Luke

We'd pulled into the Cucciolos' driveway, and Cassie had walked up in her jean shorts and unlaced Converses, with her hair falling out all over the place, her eyes on Frankie. She'd looked different from the woman I'd met behind the bar, the woman who knew exactly what she was doing and fuck you if you didn't like it. She reminded me of a photo of her I'd seen on Frankie's wall the other night, a little girl in a watermelon swimsuit, building sand castles. She was saying something like *two thousand dollars extra a month*, and at the mention of money, I couldn't help it. I stayed next to the garage door and listened.

I still didn't know how I was going to pay Johnno five thousand dollars in three months, and I was losing time. I had considered a loan from the bank, appealing to their patriotism by pretending I needed it to put a down payment on a house. *Help a poor soldier out.* Hell, I'd pretend I was married for that one thousand dollars extra a month.

I started running after her after she turned out of the driveway, toward a little playground down the street. Her words struck a note. After detoxing, it took me months to find a minimum-wage job with regular hours. Even then, it wasn't enough to cover a life. It was half of why I enlisted. I had two years' tuition to repay. And now I had Johnno to consider. When I caught up with Cassie, she was wiping her face, her shoulders hunched, about to get in her beat-up white Subaru.

"Hey!"

She kept her head down, bringing out her keys with one hand. With the other, she lifted a middle finger. She must have thought I was catcalling her.

I started over. "Er—excuse me, Cassie?"

She saw me approaching, narrowed her eyes, recognizing my face. "Oh, hi."

I put a hand on my chest. "Luke."

She draped her tattooed arms on her door. "Yeah." She looked me up and down, pausing at my broken face. "Did you run here?"

I nodded. "I wanted to say, uh—" I stopped. Now that I was able to see her face more clearly, I noticed she'd been crying. "I'm sorry for what happened the other night. At the bar."

"Thanks," she said, and glanced at her keys.

I took stock. Why had I come? Her plan. A wedding.

Frankie was focusing on the risks, the alternatives. He wasn't considering the benefits at all. I guess one thousand dollars meant very little to someone whose parents would pay his way through law school, whose family home was worth seven figures. It wasn't like Frankie couldn't be compassionate, but until you've wondered how you're going to feed yourself, there's a wall between you and everyone who does have to worry about that.

I'm still on the other side of that wall, and apparently I wasn't alone.

"Well," she said, sniffing, trying to wipe away the traces of tears still left. "Bye. Enjoy building roads and saving lives."

"I also wanted to ask you more about your proposal," I said quickly. "The one you just made. To Frankie."

She stared at the ground, scrunching her face. "You heard that?"

"Kind of."

She looked everywhere but at me. "It was crazy. I don't know what I was thinking." She sighed.

"But it's actually a thing?"

"It says so right here in your beautiful little propaganda booklet." She handed me an army brochure.

"'Propaganda' is a bit dramatic," I muttered, shaking my head at the stock photos. I couldn't help myself. "This is about as harmless as IKEA furniture instructions."

"IKEA instructions aren't harmless," she deadpanned. I looked up. "It's well known that the little stick-figure guy is a socialist."

I found myself smiling. "Ha ha."

I paged through it, focusing on the spousal benefits sections. With every mention of money, I saw myself writing my signature on a check. I saw the taillights of Johnno's Bronco fading, never to be seen again. And then Jake, laughing next to me on the couch while we watched the Cowboys. My dad sinking into a chair beside us, the hint of a smile, proud. I swallowed, then handed it back to her, noticing for a moment how the sun made her eyes spark gold. "This is a genius idea."

"You think so?"

"If you could find the right person, yeah." There it was again, my signature. *Good-bye, Johnno.*

We stood in silence. My heart pounded. Finally, she gestured at me. "Are you recommending yourself, or are you just making vague, positive statements?"

Before I could think, I pushed out the words. "I think I am."

She raised her eyebrows. She stepped out from behind the car door, and shut it, muscles visible in her legs from her Converses all the way up to the edge of her cutoffs. "I'm very serious about this."

"Me, too." I felt my chest tighten. I was saying the words before I could comprehend what they meant. But it felt scary and correct at the same time, like in an animal way, a primal way, like sprinting down a hill or waking up suddenly after a long, sober sleep. We were both trapped in a corner of our lives, snarling and biting until we got out.

She closed her eyes, shaking her head. "I don't know."

I tried to make my voice softer. I wanted her to open her eyes again. "What are you worried about?"

"First, I don't know you. I think we made that pretty clear the other night."

Well, duh, I resisted saying. "We only have a few days that we have to get along. We don't have to actually like each other."

We caught each other's eyes.

She bit her nail and spoke, quiet. "I don't mean that, I mean. Well, maybe I do, but whatever. I mean, how am I going to know you're not going to fuck me over?"

I tried to resist the anger that rose, heating my skin. I knew it wasn't for her. The anger was for a past version of myself, running down Arikara Street with twenties in my pocket. "How do I know that you're not going to fuck *me* over?"

She looked at me like I was stupid. "Because it's my idea. I'm the one with the medical bills."

"Right." I nodded in the direction of the Cucciolo house. "We tell Frankie. Frankie holds us to it."

"Yeah, but then what?"

I shrugged. "We get . . ." An image flashed of Jake and Hailey outside the church, grabbing hands as people flowed around them. "We get married."

Cassie squinted. "So, wait. What's in it for you?"

The image of Jake and Hailey again, the phone vibrating, a razor slicing a pill. I tried to look her in the eye, to let her know how deeply I meant it, how much I needed it. Less detail, more truth. "I'm in the hole, too. I need to get it paid off as soon as possible."

"What are you in the hole for?" she asked.

My lungs tightened. Would she get it? No. She'd think I was unreliable. She'd think I'd blow the money on pills. "That's not something I want to discuss."

"Uhh . . ." She narrowed her eyes with a sarcastic half-smile. "It feels kind of important, Luke."

I put up a hard line, hoping I wasn't sweating. "I guess you'll just have to trust me."

"Great." She gave me a pointed look.

"Hey," I said, stepping away from her, steeling myself. "You're the one who had the illegal idea. We're par for the course here."

"Yes, it's very illegal," she said, sighing. "If they find out, you'll be court-martialed and kicked out of the army. We both could go to jail."

"I know that." I didn't know that. But if I could get Johnno paid off before they found out . . . Jail was better than Johnno going after my family.

She began to walk. I followed her. "We'd have to convince everyone," she said, turning her eyes on me. My heart leaped. She was getting back on board.

"Right." We were walking side by side now.

"It wouldn't be that hard, I guess," she mused. "I'm not close to that many people. And you're about to ship out. We go to the courthouse, we don't make a big deal." She was speaking fast now. "Then you come back and we get into a fight. I mean, not really. But irreconcilable differences. That kind of thing."

"You could cheat on me, or something," I suggested, using air quotes.

She stopped in the middle of the block. "Do I look like someone who cheats?"

I turned to look at her, confused. "No? I don't know."

"I'm not a cheater," she said, as if I had accused her of it.

"Whoa, hey! It was just an idea. Sensitive topic?" It came out more biting than I'd meant it. I'd meant it to diffuse. It ignited.

"Being cheated on? Yes," she snapped.

"I only suggested it because it's the most clear-cut breakup."

"Not gonna happen," she said, shaking her head. "I'm not going to play the villain to the poor, upstanding soldier. If anything, you'd be the one to break it off with me."

"But how am I supposed to cheat? With someone in my company? No."

"Then no cheating at all," she said loudly.

I raised my voice to match hers. "It can't be out of the blue, though. We need a reason."

"Don't yell," she commanded.

"I'm not!" I yelled. "I'm not," I corrected, quieter.

"Why are we talking about this? We're getting ahead of ourselves," she said.

We continued walking, silent for a moment. Two women passed, chatting, one of them pushing a stroller. I kept my mouth shut. *Irreconcilable differences* seemed more feasible than the marriage. The divorce would be the easiest part.

"I promise henceforth I will always try to get along with you," I said.

"Mm." She walked faster. "You're going to have to try harder."

My chest had started to get tight again. Cassie could be harsh at the drop of a hat, but at least I would always know where she stood.

"All right," she continued as we turned a corner to circle the block, "when do you want to do it?"

Relief. "So you're still in?"

"Yeah, guy. I'm not a quitter."

I tried to keep from smiling too big. "Tomorrow?"

"That soon?"

"We need time to put on a little bit of a show before I ship out. So it looks real to everyone I serve with."

"Yeah, we do." She grimaced. "I'm not much of an actor."

I clenched my teeth, sucking in air. "Yeah. Me, neither."

She checked her phone and sighed. "Okay, I gotta go. You fill Frankie in. I'm free all day tomorrow to, you know, nail down the details."

"Okay." My skin was buzzing, ready to take action. I was ready right now. I wanted Cassie to be, too. I gestured for her to hand me her phone and punched in my number. She hesitated again before she got in the car.

"Hey, what's your last name?" she asked, putting up a hand to shade her eyes.

"Morrow," I said, glancing at her, my eyes traveling down the tattoos on her arms to the CD cases on her dashboard to the granola bar wrappers at her feet. "You?"

"Salazar," she said, smiling against the sun.

The quiet was surreal. A breeze licked one of the swings in the playground behind her. My heart was full of something like gratitude, something big and scared and shaking, but my mind kept getting slammed into Johnno's Bronco. Jake, slammed into Johnno's Bronco. JJ watching.

No, Cassie was going to help me. She was annoying as hell but she was fierce, and she was going to help me protect them. I wanted to shake her hand or hold her. It seemed absurd that we would just go off in our separate directions, like we had talked about the weather.

But that's what we did. I glanced back over my shoulder when she reached the road. Though I couldn't be sure through the afternoon glare, I thought our eyes met, and I waved. She lifted her hand and waved back.

Cassie

Someone was knocking on my door. I looked up from my keyboard, the remains of three joints on a saucer next to me, the shells of pistachios scattered under my feet. Pistachios were an expensive but type 2–friendly cure for the munchies, I'd found. I had been pacing, crunching, going back and forth between contacting Luke and telling him we had to call it off and playing piano to calm my nerves.

I checked the peephole. It was Rita, my landlady.

Uh oh.

I opened the door a crack. "Yeah?"

Rita was holding her dog, Dante, who was panting, cross-eyed. Rita sniffed, her eyes as pink and puffy as her robe. "I noticed your lights were on all night. Just wanted to check if you were all right."

"Yeah, yeah, I'm good."

She sniffed again. "Were you smoking weed in here?"

My pulse quickened. "No."

"Yes, you were." I prepared an excuse, something about buying the wrong incense. Then she said, "You have any left?"

Phew. "Of course."

It was an unspoken agreement that I could get away with a lot in Rita's attic if I wasn't stupid about it. There were a lot of unspoken agreements. I didn't say anything about her loud weeping, for example, or her occasional parties where it sounded like people were making animal noises at one another, and she didn't say anything if my rent was a few days late, or about the fact that my subwoofer shook the entire house.

"Nothing like a good wake-and-bake," Rita said, settling herself on the couch.

Wake-and-bake? I looked at my phone. Six. *Shit.* I hadn't realized it was so late. Er, early. I was supposed to meet Luke and Frankie in an hour before we went to city hall. And I was supposed to have written a "biography" of sorts for Luke, a collection of facts about my life that he could have reasonably retained in the week or so we'd "known each other and fallen in love." It was a good idea—he'd suggested it on the phone last night. He was writing one for me to read, too.

Instead, I'd started writing a song. When I feel something I can't quite understand, like when I felt smothered by Tyler, or when I found out I had diabetes, or now, for instance, I'd look for the feeling in notes.

Writing a song is like walking through a forest, foraging for food. You start at the edge, at the organ sound in C major, or E, then you see color somewhere through the trees, maybe a more synthy F-sharp, and you pick it up but it's not quite right. Not quite the right berry to eat, so you venture further, touching E minor in a vibraphone like you would a familiar leaf, feeling its texture, playing it fast or slow, and there it is. You take it and you start picking more notes nearby. Nutty G chords and back to F, now that it's ripe.

I never quite found the right notes for *I'm getting legally bound to a person I don't know*. The feeling went in too many directions. Disbelief. Fear. Skepticism. But I found the notes for hope, a bright shapeless thing far off in the woods. I focused on this feeling in particular. Hope, though I didn't know what it looked like, was leading me forward.

Playing all night had been a sort of ceremony before the ceremony. A big nod to whatever force had decided to make me fall in love with music enough to do this in the first place.

Rita handed me the final tip as Dante sniffed around at the empty Accu-Chek boxes and the clothes, in varying shades of denim or black, that covered every surface.

"My life's about to change today, Rita," I said, blowing out a puff.

"Yeah?" she replied, standing up to call Dante with a whistle. "Good. I try to tell myself that every morning."

An hour later, I was ready. I had checked my blood sugar, and eaten a potato and white bean spicy scramble. I'd found my phone in a pile of laundry. I'd even put on a little mascara and some lip color. It wasn't until I got in the Subaru that I realized what my wedding clothes would be: the same Kinks T-shirt and jean shorts I wore yesterday. My hair was in a bun that would probably fall out soon. My Converses were unlaced.

I ran back upstairs and found a heavy cotton black sleeveless dress with a deep V-neck. A bit revealing, and it smelled a little like old beer, but it didn't have stains on it.

"Shoes, shoes, shoes," I whispered to myself. Then I remembered I had a pair of red heels from when I was Marge Simpson for Halloween. I slipped them on and looked in the full-length mirror on the back of my closet. *Fine, no bun*, I decided, and took my hair down.

It took me a second to find myself in the feminine figure.

Then I realized that in this dress, the antler tattoo just above my left breast was visible. A protector.

Oh, there I was.

Luke

Apparently, to the hair-sprayed, aging waitress, it seemed totally normal for two men in tuxes to be eating eggs Benedict at seven in the morning, one of them flipping the box of a Walmart-bought wedding ring, the other furiously taking pictures of his companion, of the menu, of the ring, of the row of empty booths, and, within full view of the waitress, of the waitress herself.

Once she got here, Cassie, Frankie, and I were going to lay down the details of the nine months to come. Frankie was documenting everything as evidence just in case, God forbid, the legitimacy of the marriage ever had to hold up in court.

"They'll pick apart every detail," he was saying, showing me the time-stamped captions to each photo. "How you met, the proposal, everything. So I'm your witness. Look excited," he finished, pointing the camera at me.

I raised my eyebrows, tried to open my eyes wider.

Frankie reviewed the photo. "I said 'excited,' not like someone just stuck their thumb up your butt."

"Shut up."

"There's a smile." He took another photo. I pulled my Moleskine out of my army bag and set it near my empty plate, ready to exchange lives with Cassie. Or "Cass," as Frankie said I should call her. That still didn't feel right.

The door to the diner opened, and Cassie walked in. My eyes were drawn toward the antler on her breastbone, visible in her low-cut dress. Her black hair flowed in waves from her face, blending near her shoulders with the S-shaped silhouette of her body under her dress. It made me nervous, how beautiful she was. Beautiful people had one-track minds. You learn that in adolescence, when looks start to matter. Everyone steps out of the way of beautiful people just for the pleasure of watching them pass. They never have to learn how to make do, how to compromise, never have to learn how to find their way into the back doors of places. And this was definitely a back door.

"What?" she said, approaching the booth. I realized I was staring at her.

"Nothing."

Frankie stood. "Cass!" He stood to kiss both her cheeks. He looked at me, jerking his head.

I stood, too, towering over her a bit. I bent to kiss her cheek. Frankie snapped a photo.

We sat. Frankie and I on one side, Cassie on the other.

"Just coffee. Black," Cassie said to the waitress. She turned to me. "You get that?"

I opened my Moleskine, finding a blank spot to scribble it down. Then it seemed ridiculous. "You really think we need that tiny of a detail?"

"Maybe not, but you'll need this one," she said, leaning forward. "I have diabetes. Type two. Hence the medical bills."

I remembered that. "And what exactly does that mean?" I started. "If you don't mind me asking."

"Well, basically my pancreas doesn't know how to break down sugar in my blood. So I have to watch what I eat so I don't get hypoglycemic. Or, I guess, pass out from low blood sugar. Like after I eat a meal that has a lot of simple sugars." She pointed to a piece of pie in one of the display cases. "Or if I don't eat snacks regularly, or don't eat a full meal, or if I eat later than usual." She was putting out her fingers. "Or if I drink alcohol without eating any food, et cetera."

"Wow."

"It's a lot," she said. "It's going to take some getting used to."

"Do you have that written down?" I asked, holding up my notebook. "For our biographies?"

We paused when the waitress returned.

Cassie gave me an apologetic smile as she took the steaming cup.

She waited until the woman left to start speaking again. "I'll be honest." She looked back and forth between Frankie and me. "I'm kind of ill prepared."

"What do you mean, ill prepared?" I rested my hand on my notebook, where I'd spent an hour trying to make my handwriting neat enough to read, combing through all my memories and mistakes, trying to decide what was relevant and what was not. We'd decided e-mail was not a good idea, because it left a record.

Cassie looked chagrined. "I, just, didn't write it all down. I'm sorry."

My chest clenched. "Come on. We're doing this today. What else took priority?"

"I'm sorry!" she said louder. "Until, like, an hour ago I wasn't sure I could go through with this."

"Okay," I said slowly, feeling my heart bang. I tried to breathe. I was getting angry, but that wouldn't help the situation.

Frankie put a bite of eggs Benedict in his mouth. "Y'all could just talk," he said with his mouth full. "Like normal humans."

Cassie and I looked at each other. She appeared to hold the same sentiment that I did: *No, thank you.*

"How about you just read what you have, and I'll respond? Here," she said, gesturing for the pen and notebook. I tore out a page for her. "Go ahead with your first one."

The heat was starting to subside. I cleared my throat, and read. "My name is Luke Joseph Morrow."

Cassie started writing her answer as she said it. "Cassandra Lee Salazar."

"Lee, huh?" Frankie said. "I didn't know that."

"It was my dad's mother's maiden name, I think." She looked at me, her brown eyes stone. "Oh, um. I don't have a dad."

"Are you going to keep your last name, or—?"

She knit her eyebrows together, looking back up to me. "Of course I'm going to keep my last name."

I held up my hands. "Just asking."

She smiled at me across the table, closed red lips, sarcastic. "I will pretend to be married to you but I'm not going to sit at home knitting a blanket until you come back."

"I never said anything about knitting."

"He's just trying to be cautious, Cassie," Frankie said, in a much nicer voice than I could manage right then.

"Then how about you take my last name?" she muttered.

I couldn't tell if she was serious or not. "I don't want to do that, no."

Frankie looked at his watch. "We should keep this moving if we don't want to wait in a long line at city hall."

I read, "I am a private first class in the Sixth Battalion, Thirty-fourth Red Horse Infantry Division, United States Army."

From all that, I watched Cassie write the word "private."

She looked at me, sipping her coffee. "I play keys and sing lead vocals for The Loyal, a band I started here in Austin." She smiled a little, glancing at Frankie before she wrote it down.

I looked at my sheet. "My favorite food is salami on crackers."

She giggled. "Sorry. I don't know why that's funny. Mine"—she wrote—"is my mother's *tembleque*."

We went back and forth.

I run six miles a day.

About twice a month I sign up for yoga classes then cancel.

I like RPGs. Fallout *and stuff.*

I like to read critical theory and trashy magazines about celebrities.

I don't really like to read. I wasn't good at school. I liked Huck Finn, *though. And* Where the Red Fern Grows.

I like records. Vinyl.

Me, too. My dad had some growing up.

Things as big as *My mom died* to small things Cassie said couples know about each other even after a short time, like *I wear boxers to bed.* Cassie preferred a tank top and underwear. She pointed to all of her tattoos. Right forearm, some sort of lion with wings. *A sphinx. Traditionally female in myths. Symbol of wisdom.* Left forearm, the cycle of the moon. Upper right arm, flowers, apparently the same kind that grew in her mother's yard. Upper left, a black star, for David Bowie.

I showed her a scar on the back of my head. I told her it came from my father, by accident. I didn't elaborate.

We'd decided that whenever anyone got suspicious, we would start acting in love. Touching each other, laughing together, whispering secrets in each other's ears. That would distract the person asking questions; either they'd think it was cute and understand the timeline more, or they'd think we were disgusting and understand the timeline more.

We would Skype every two weeks, hopefully during times when other members of my company were present, in case they had to serve as witnesses as well.

I gave her my health insurance forms to sign. We exchanged e-mail addresses.

We agreed that my paychecks would be direct-deposited into a joint account we would set up later today at Austin Credit Union. She would withdraw her cut on the first of every month.

Cassie's leg had started to twitch under the table.

"And now," Frankie said, holding his camera, "is the perfect time to capture your proposal."

I looked around. "Here?"

"Why not?" Frankie said. "It's perfect. It's in public. There are witnesses, but nobody to hear our conversation. And we can say you were so overcome with love you insisted on going immediately to city hall."

Cassie glanced at the fake velvet box Frankie and I had picked out from the Walmart Supercenter off 290. "Oh, lordy," she said, and picked it up, unclasping it.

"Don't!" Frankie said, glancing in fear at the waitress. Cassie dropped it on the table.

Frankie jutted his chin at me, speaking with his eyes. *Do it.* I guessed it was better the less staged it looked. We couldn't rehearse this one. I looked at Cassie. She wrinkled her nose.

I took her cool hand and pulled her up to a standing position. I made sure the waitress had paused behind her counter, watching. *Here goes nothing.*

I cleared my throat, and got down on one knee. Cassie laughed, a genuine laugh that I felt move through her body. I laughed, too. "Look me in the eyes," I muttered.

She did. I started smiling, tried to stop myself, and realized I didn't have to stop myself. I was supposed to be smiling.

"Cassandra Lee Salazar, will you marry me?"

She said yes.

Cassie

City hall broke the skyline of downtown Austin in angles, all slanted brown tile and sweeping glass. Frankie parked on the street, but I didn't realize we weren't driving anymore until the white noise of the talk radio had bleeped off and the car was quiet. I spun the too-tight gold band on my finger, trying to remember the chords I had found this morning, a rhythm for my heartbeat to follow so it would slow down a bit, stop jumping around.

"Before we go in," Frankie said, looking at us with sentimental eyes, like we were prom dates, "I have this idea. My parents do it in couples' therapy."

"Your parents go to couples' therapy?" I asked.

George and Louise Cucciolo were the most in-love couple I knew. They were always making out in the kitchen when one of us went to get more snacks. They went to Italy every year on their anniversary.

"Yeah, they like it. Helps them 'grow,' they say."

Luke and I glanced at each other and shrugged. I wondered if he was thinking the same thing I was, which was that it was probably easier to "grow" as a couple when you had disposable income to throw at marriage experts and trips to Europe.

"Anyway," Frankie continued. "When they're having a disagreement or whatever, they start off the session by staring into each other's eyes for thirty seconds."

"No," Luke said, scoffing. "No way."

"Frankie," I said, touching his arm. "I appreciate your effort. And you doing this. Everything. But we're just going to go in there and sign some papers, take some photos. Okay?"

"I'm not letting you get out of this car until you do it. Seriously. Elena and I do it, and it's amazing. We can talk about anything."

"We don't need to talk about anything, Frankie," Luke muttered. "Except for financial stuff."

"As your future lawyer . . ."

I couldn't help it, I snorted.

"Seriously," Frankie said, and he started to raise his voice, which didn't seem to be a familiar sound to either me or Luke. "You need to take this seriously. Because if anything goes wrong, they will bring a body language expert into that courtroom. I swear to God."

Silence. The idea of a courtroom infected our thoughts. The consequences that lay there. Jail. Money gone. Future gone.

"Okay," I said.

"Luke, get in the backseat with her."

I watched Luke come around the car, the black suit a little too short at the arms and legs, but cutting his form in all the right places. Wide, wiry shoulders, a runner's waist, long legs that he shoved behind the front seat. He smelled like sharp, wet wood and herbs, probably Frankie's cologne, too.

At least everyone would understand why I'd be attracted to him.

"And what are we supposed to be thinking about, anyway?" Luke asked.

"Whatever comes to mind," Frankie said.

"Like what?"

I almost said *sex* as a joke-not-joke but decided against it. I mean, we were in a backseat together. It was kind of funny, but not the time. I popped my knuckles and tried to focus.

"All right," Frankie said. "Look at each other in the eyes. Don't break. Don't laugh."

I laughed immediately. But then I took a deep breath. *Do this for Frankie. Do this for Mom. Do this for the album.*

"One one thousand, two one thousand . . ." Frankie began to count out loud, but then fell silent. *Three one thousand, four one thousand, five . . .*

I looked at Luke. I remembered those eyes from when we met last week, before he became an ass. The blue and gray, with long lashes under delicate brows. He had light purple circles underneath them.

I could smell his breath, mint toothpaste and a hint of something else, not unpleasant, just warm. Lungs and nerve endings and bones, that's all Luke was. Just like me, just like anyone else.

He'd said he ran six miles a day. He must like to push himself. Yet it seemed like he'd been taught that *man body* must go with *man thoughts*, must be strong and never show otherwise. I didn't envy that.

In the corner of my eye I saw his hands, wide palms, smooth, thick fingers, resting on his thighs. Occasionally, they tensed.

He had done something to his body that he was trying to undo, I could sense that being next to him now, and from the way he carried himself.

Believe me, I told his sad eyes silently, *I can relate.*

Luke

*T*wenty-four one thousand, twenty-five one thousand, twenty-six one thousand.

After *this is stupid* had drifted through my head a couple of times, I noticed Cassie had a freckle under her left eye, and some of the hairs in her eyebrows, full and dark, were lighter at the tips.

The freckle was a tiny island on the otherwise uninterrupted skin of her cheek.

It was strange that I probably could have gone the whole year of knowing her, being "married" to her, without seeing it.

I watched her blink and keep hold, and, goddammit, Frankie was right, maybe I grew a little more trust in her ability to stick with the whole situation. Not ability, I suppose, but desire to stick to it. I was thinking about earlier, about her being beautiful and breezing through every opportunity.

She was, but the way she was looking at me now, eyelids almost twitching with the effort of staying put, I could tell she hadn't let that be the thing she used to get by. If her appearance was how she defined herself, she probably wouldn't be here, at the back door. She'd be at the front door with whatever person she wanted.

Looking at her, though, erased every other possible life out of my mind. She was so unquestionably *here*.

Cassie

"Time's up," Frankie said, and all the sounds of the street and world came crashing back. The spell was broken.

Luke cleared his throat, and grabbed his army-issued bag. "Let's do this."

Our footsteps echoed in the foyer along with all the other footsteps of people Making Things Official everywhere—permits, lawsuits, licenses. I ducked into the bleach-streaked bathroom and pulled out my glucose meter. Who knew the next time I would be able to check my blood? I had no idea how long a city hall marriage would take. I had a weird vision of it being like Ellis Island, mile-long lines of women who looked like old pictures of *abuela*, flared skirts and rolled hair, their arms hooked around the arms of D-day survivors in uniform.

When I emerged, I paused, watching Frankie and Luke mutter to each other. I took a deep breath, and walked toward them. The Travis County Clerk's office was on the second floor.

We shared the elevator with a woman and a man about our age, dressed in formal clothes. They had their arms around each other. The woman was holding a bouquet of daisies. Oh, God. These people were *actually* getting married. Luke and I stood with our shoulders barely touching, Frankie humming quietly along with the Muzak version of "Goodbye Yellow Brick Road." We were such a sham.

As the elevator doors opened, the woman turned to me. "Y'all getting hitched, too?"

"Yep!" I said, putting on a big smile. "This guy," I added, slapping Luke on the back.

Shit, shit, shit. Did people who love each other slap each other on the back?

"That's me," Luke said. His swallow was audible. "I'm the guy!"

"Say," Frankie said to the couple as we exited to the wood-paneled hallway, pointing in both directions, "where is the room where the ceremonies are held?"

"You already got your license?" the man said.

"Right," Luke said. He looked at me, his eyes searching. "The license."

"The license," I repeated, looking back at him. *Shit.* "Not yet. We should do that."

"So cute," the woman said. "You two look so nervous. Wedding day jitters!"

"Because you can't get married by an officiant until you've had a license for three days," the man said. "Maggie and I learned the hard way last week," he added, and they looked at each other, giggling.

"Fuck" dropped out of my mouth. Luke was leaving the day after tomorrow.

The couple's giggle turned into nervous laughter, then faded altogether. The woman looked at me like I was bleeding out of my eyeballs. Her eyes traveled the length of my body, stopping briefly on the antler tattoo, then over to Luke.

I grabbed Frankie's arm. *The Normals have picked us up on their radar. They know we're not like them. Abort, abort.*

"But not for military, hon!" the woman said suddenly, pointing at Luke's bag. "You in the service?"

"Active duty," Luke said, eyes on the woman, as if willing her to explain.

"Actually," she started, looking at her fiancé, "I think there's an exception for the seventy-two-hour waiting period for active military?"

"Yeah?" I said.

There was relief, but part of me had kind of wanted it all to be over, some clear obstacle that barred us from pulling it off. Up until now, it had felt like a harebrained scheme, just on my shoulders, which meant that if it didn't work out, I shrugged it off and found another way. Now it was spilling into the wide world, with Luke and Frankie and clerks and strangers named Maggie.

"Well, if you'll excuse us," Frankie said, putting on his most charming smile. "Thanks for your help."

The license was the easiest part. Blank spaces for names and social security numbers, and a line to sign. *Cassandra Lee Salazar.*

I watched Luke sign *Luke Joseph Morrow.*

Frankie snapped a photo of us standing at the counter, our hands barely touching each other's backs.

"Well, that's it," I said to Luke, and he nodded, glancing at me for a moment. He had been quiet through the whole thing. A lot of "yes, ma'ams" and "no, sirs." He kept checking his phone, rubbing the back of his neck, like it was painful to be here.

"You're not even going to pretend to be happy?" I asked him.

He shrugged. "No one's watching here."

I lowered my voice. "Yeah, but aren't you relieved that it's almost over?"

"It's not over for me. I'm on my way to Afghanistan, Cassie."

I stepped back. "Right."

Our officiant was a volunteer notary, a man who either knew God personally or had drunk three espressos that morning. He towered over Luke and Frankie and me in a hunter-orange polo, with a balding head and visible gold teeth. Frankie held up his phone, filming it all.

"Any preference for prayers?" he asked.

"Sir?" Luke asked.

"Jewish, Christian, Muslim, Pagan, I got 'em all. I got the widest variety of Christian prayers. Catholic, too." He counted on his chubby fingers, listing them in his deep accent as if he were giving us options for video game consoles at Best Buy. "Serenity Prayer, Hail Mary prayer, the Lord's Prayer, 'The Lord is my shepherd' prayer, any psalm, really, and that Corinthians one is popular, the one that goes 'Love is patient, love is kind'?"

I couldn't wait to tell Nora about this guy. But then I realized: How the hell was I going to explain any of this to Nora?

"There's also the no-prayer option, being we're in a government office. I'm happy to merely officiate over the proceedings."

"That'll be fine—" I started.

"Maybe the Serenity Prayer?" Luke said, his voice cracking just a bit. He looked at me for permission. "My mom used to like that one."

"Sure." I shrugged. Next to me, Frankie nudged me with his elbow. "I mean, sure, sweetheart."

While the officiant dug behind his podium for a Bible, I remembered Luke saying in the diner that he had lost his mom. I couldn't imagine. Well, I guess I could, considering I never had a father, but he was never mine to lose. For a second, I wished that my own mom could be here. Fake or not, she had always wanted to see me get married.

"As you embark on this marriage— Wait, y'all gonna look at each other, or hold hands, or what?"

Frankie nodded, encouraging us with a wave from behind his phone.

I took Luke's hands. I smiled at him like in-love couples do, with my eyes, a serene upturn of my lips, as if I had never been more sure of anything. He smiled back. It frightened me, how easy that was. As if all love was just fooling oneself until it was real.

The officiant ahemmed, making a big show of closing the Bible and reopening it, as if he were starting from the very beginning.

"As you embark on this marriage, God grant you both the serenity to accept the things you cannot change, the courage to change the things you can, and the wisdom to know the difference."

"Can't disagree with that," I said quietly.

Luke squeezed my hands. I couldn't tell if it was a friendly squeeze or a warning squeeze.

"Do you, Cassie, take Luke to be your partner for life? Do you promise to walk by his side forever, and to love, help, and encourage him in all he does?"

I opened my mouth to say "I do," but the officiant kept going.

"Do you promise to take time to talk with him, to listen to him, and to care for him? Will you share his laughter, and his tears, as his partner, lover, and best friend?"

I lifted my chin, waiting. That sounded like a lot of jobs for one person. If the real thing ever came along, I think I could be good at two, at best.

"Do you take him as your lawfully wedded husband for now and forevermore?" The officiant looked at me expectantly.

"I do," I said.

As the officiant asked Luke the same questions, I watched Luke listen, his eyes down, eyelashes brushing his cheek.

"I do," Luke said when the officiant finished.

"By the power vested in me by the state of Texas, I now pronounce you husband and wife."

For a thick second we stared into each other's eyes, as we had done in the Lexus, but this time we knew what the other was thinking. *Shit.*

"Go on and kiss her, son!"

The officiant was directing Luke to kiss me, as if I were his property now. Screw that. I took Luke's face in my hands and brought his mouth to mine, hoping he would take it from there. Long peck or actual make out? Open mouth?

Somewhere in between, it turned out. His lips were quite soft, yielding.

After a long moment, he tried to pull away, but my hair had snaked its way around one of his suit buttons. The result was a painful yank of my entire head.

"Ow!" I yelled. "Fuck!"

"What happened?" Luke said, touching me in a genuine way for the first time that day.

"That's hair! That's attached to my head!" I cried.

"Wait, hold still," he said, trying to disentangle the strand but pulling too hard.

"Careful," I scolded.

"Sorry!" he snapped.

Frankie put down the camera with a sigh. The next couple and their friends gathered near the entrance of the ceremony room, their made-up faces expectant and curious. I heard titters and frowned.

This was a sign, I was pretty sure. Our marriage was doomed. Either that, or it was time to cut off all my hair.

Luke

We walked out of the city hall chapel, onto the elevator smelling like everyone's perfume, and out the doors to the sidewalk. The wind was whipping hard through the buildings of downtown Austin, smacking my tie into my face, and Cassie's hair was billowing up, catching her earrings. No one said a word. There must have been a storm coming.

Cassie and I kept glancing at each other, not hostile but not nice, either, more like we were checking to see if the other was still there.

I couldn't stop thinking about this neighbor kid I knew growing up. I couldn't remember his name because it seemed like there was always some neighbor kid Jake and I were running around with in the summer while Dad was at the garage, Mitch or Mark or whoever, but he was the kid you always had to watch your mouth around. He'd pick up any word and poke at it until it seemed like the dumbest thing anyone had ever said. Jake and I could never say we loved anything, like Power Rangers or our dad or Ritz crackers, without the neighbor kid spitting, "Oh, yeah? If you love it so much then why don't you marry it?"

It wasn't like that, Jake and I would always tell him. We didn't love crackers in the same way we loved people we would marry.

And yet there I was, married, and when it came time for the sake of the marriage to tell Cassie I "loved" her, even though I didn't, there would still be a part of me that choked on the words, waiting to be taunted for them.

And there would also be another ounce of little kid logic that would want to point to someone as beautiful as she was right then, pushing the wild hair out of her face, and answer the taunts back. *Well, I did marry her, motherfuckers. See? I did.*

Cassie

Nothing in the Florien house needed cleaning, but here we were. Mom worked for Green Team, which meant she used tea tree oil and Dr. Bronner's and vinegar on the tables and toilets of executives at Dell and IBM who decided their offspring should not inhale Lysol fumes. I had come here to talk to my mother about Luke, but there seemed to be no good time for that. How would I tell my mom I was married while I knelt next to a toilet bowl?

My phone buzzed. Toby, again. I ignored it.

And how would I tell my hook-up partner that I was married? Scratch that. Did I have to tell Toby anything about this, for that matter? I supposed not. And why was Toby calling me in the middle of the day? Was he trying to up the *fuck* portion of the *fuck-buddy* equation to include quickies in the afternoon? Was he trying to up the *buddy* and remove the *fuck*? I had no idea, and I didn't want to find out. I had enough on my plate.

"Cassie," Mom said. "Hello. Are you losing it?"

I looked up. I realized I had been scrubbing one spot on the sink for several minutes. "Whoops."

She stood next to me in the kitchen, looking out the window above the sink to the Floriens' sprawling backyard. A cast-iron table and chairs stood under the shade of a Texas ash. Beyond that, a large swimming pool.

"How's your blood sugar?" Mom asked. She snapped on a pair of blue latex gloves.

"I checked it this morning, like I do every morning," I replied. It was starting to become like second nature, this organized thing amid the chaos. Check blood sugar. Prepare healthy meal. Set phone timer to make sure I had an afternoon snack. Walk at least thirty minutes a day. Not that my mother trusted me to be on top of it.

"Have you cracked open the LSAT prep books?"

"I've been busy." I picked at a piece of lint on my sponge.

"With what?"

Marriage. "Music," I said.

There'd be more forms to fill out. IRS forms, direct-deposit forms, and Luke had called today about more army paperwork. There was the wedding, and that was it. There were no winks across rooms or fake briefcases or secret handshakes. Unless our "honeymoon trip" to Chili's this evening was actually going to be a *North by Northwest* case of mistaken identity, this whole thing was unsettlingly easy.

Mom picked up a bottle of Windex and headed to the breakfast nook. "If you're going to stand there, at least polish the silverware."

I picked up a fork from the pile near the sink. "We're probably going to play again at the Skylark."

Mom sighed as she stepped on a bench to reach the high windows. "When I was your age I was doing the same thing, going to the bars with my face painted, different places every night, going on dates, trying to find another daddy for you. And look how that worked."

I rubbed a butter knife, tense. "It's not the same."

"Nights in bars. Looking for something that isn't there."

"It *is* there," I called. "You heard it. And it's something I'm passionate about."

Mom shook her head, laughing to herself as she made small circles on a pane. "What do you mean, passion?"

"Doing anything else besides it sounds like hell. That's passion."

She stepped off the bench, scooted it to the left, and stepped up again. "Life is hell, Cassie. We do what we can to make it manageable, and we wake up and do it again."

"That's terrible."

"I know. That's why you can't just say 'I want, I want, I want' and hope something happens to you. You don't waste time following. You get into a position where you don't have to *follow* anything."

"Aren't you 'following'?" I asked. "I mean, is this what you want?" I picked up my polishing rag from the counter, shaking it at her.

She scratched her flushed cheek with the back of her wrist, and resumed scrubbing. "I want to earn my pay, go home and put my feet up, read books, and tell jokes with MiMi."

"Is that it?" I pressed. If Mom and her sister lived a reasonable distance from each other, they would be inseparable. Now they just purchase wireless plans for the pleasure of chatting about Rosario Ferré novels, their gardens, and the various ways the weather has failed my mother.

She stepped down from the bench. "It will be hard to ask myself that question until I know my only daughter has a safety net."

Deep down, I had known this all along. Mom couldn't do so much as think about looking for a different job, going back to school, moving back to San Juan, until she was no longer the person who would catch me if I failed. If I was broke, if I was sick, I still relied on her. But not anymore. Luke and I were married now. Sham or not, I had his extra income and health insurance. And maybe that was something she needed to hear.

"Don't freak out," I said, as quiet as a little girl. "But I might have one now. A safety net."

"Like what?"

I swallowed, and lifted my hands. "I got married."

"What?"

I found myself stepping away, scared, though the top of her poufy black hair came only up to my chin. Her cheeks flared red. "To who?"

I stammered quickly, "His name's Luke Morrow. He's a private in the army. We're not in love, we did it for the benefits."

Her mouth dropped open. "Are you serious? How long have you been planning this?"

I extended the time period, though it hardly made it seem more reasonable. "A week."

"A week." She stood frozen for a moment, staring at the floor. Then she started peeling off her latex gloves.

"It's one thousand dollars extra a month and free health care! You saw the hospital bill after all that diabetes testing."

More silence. She started fixing up the rolled sleeves of her polo. My gut burned.

"Wow, Cassie." She gave me a closed-lip smile, and turned away. "Wow. Every day you surprise me."

"Sorry I didn't invite you. It was yesterday, kind of quick."

She tossed her gloves in the trash, and slammed the lid closed. I jumped. "What the hell were you thinking?"

"I'm doing this for you, so you don't have to help me."

"What you could do for me is get a stable job."

"It's health care and extra money every month. And it's happening *right now*. Do you know how long it took me to get that paralegal job in the first place? And then it took three months for my crappy benefits to kick in."

"But, Cassie, you're lying to the army!"

"Couples do it all the time. We've got a story . . ."

She laughed, bitter. "What did you do, find him on the street?"

"He's Frankie's friend."

Mom stepped toward me again, saying through clenched teeth, "Frankie *Cucciolo*?" I nodded. "Do George and Louise know?"

Mom still got together with Frankie's parents for dinner every once in a while. I was tempted to tell her yes. Maybe if Louise approved, she would go easier on me. But I couldn't lie.

"Why would I tell George and Louise?"

"Thank God."

I started speaking to her like the doctor had spoken to me when I was diagnosed. Like someone being talked down from a ledge. "It's very temporary. We have a schedule. We have a shared account. We're going to get divorced when he comes back from overseas."

Except now I felt like I was the one on the ledge, trying to convince my mother it was a good idea to jump. She'd never reacted this way before. Not when I told her I was going to college in California, not when I told her how much I was going to take in loans, not when I told her I was moving back in with her with nothing to contribute but a manic postgrad bitterness and a critical theory degree.

Mom sat down at the kitchen table. "This is insane."

"Well, so is drowning in debt," I said, shrugging her off. "Even when I was a paralegal. Even when I wasn't sick. You can't blame me for trying something different."

Mom shook her head, breathing deeply, like she was trying to cleanse herself of what she just heard. "Not if it lands you in jail."

"It's not going to." I tossed the polishing rag on the table, realizing I had been twisting it into a rope. "I just need a little help right now. I won't waste this time, Mom. I will make it. I just need a little support to get there."

"I will absolutely not support this." She buried her face in her hands, and then looked up at me. "You're crazy. You need to get real."

I set my jaw. "Well, I did it."

She rolled her eyes and stood. "Then you'll have to fail on your own."

"I'm not going to fail," I said, swallowing. Hoping I believed it. "That's so dramatic," I added, but didn't know if she could hear me.

She opened the sliding glass doors that led to the backyard, stepped through, and closed them again. I watched her spray and wipe in wide loops.

I cupped my hands around my mouth, pressing them to the pane. "How can I prove to you that I'm not crazy?"

Mom narrowed her eyes, her reply muffled. "Who knows."

I watched her work, remembering the looking-for-a-man days she had talked about. I was a toddler. I remembered the cat-piss smell of our neighbor Mrs. Klein's house. Of weeping and weeping until I fell asleep, waking up in the middle of the night and crying again until a grumpy, exhausted Mrs. Klein handed me a dusty juice box and a handful of stale crackers from her bathrobe pocket.

I remembered the relief when Mom was the one to wake me up in those days. Mom with her dimples and big, soft chest and constant, quiet tongue clicks, like a train slowing down. She wore Lancôme perfume, from a beautiful bottle with gold-plated lettering spelling *La vie est belle.* I used to sit in her room, tracing the letters with my finger.

Mom tapped on the glass. *Look*, she mouthed, pointing to the tall wooden fence that surrounded the Floriens' pool.

On the far corner sat a big bird with a green head and a white breast.

Mom slid open the door, letting in the warm, humid air. "It's a green heron!" she said, her voice clear and bright, anger lingering at the edges. "The only advantage of working for people with pools."

All this talk of dreams and passion. I didn't know exactly what I meant, either. It was like foraging for notes in the forest. Always *not that, not that. Not Mom's life. Not law school.* But it was as if I could never say *that, that's it.* I had it briefly at the Skylark, after we'd played, that I knew.

I would find it again.

I pointed to the heron, nudging Mom's shoulder. "Maybe it's a good sign."

"Don't be stupid, Cass," she said, wiping her forehead with a blue-rubbered hand as she looked on. "That's just a bird."

Luke

"Chili's. Ugh," Cassie said as we approached the decorative door flanked by cacti. "We're in one of the culinary capitals of the United States," she continued. "Why did your friends choose Chili's?"

"They're not foodies, Cassie. They're just hungry."

After Cassie had picked me up in her Subaru, the entire car ride through suburban Austin had been a stream of criticism. Or "just questions I have," according to Cassie. *Why didn't you tell me we were supposed to dress up? All the army wives are going to look like Jackie Kennedy, aren't they? Do you guys think drone bombs are taking your jobs, or are you all for drone bombs? Do I salute, too?* I had tried to answer her as best I could while the annoyance pressed on my chest. I didn't realize tucking in my one button-up shirt was "dressed up," I'd told her, and I didn't know anything about drone bombs, I was infantry, and, no, for God's sake, please don't salute. I assured her we'd be in and out of there, then we'd follow them to the hotel near the airport that Frankie had booked for us and a few other couples, then we would be done.

Inside, Chili's was full, loud, smoky from fajitas. A teenage hostess with a too large headset greeted us and held up a *one second* finger. We nodded.

"I'm just saying." Cassie leaned close to me and muttered, "What about barbecue?"

I sneezed in response.

"Are you getting sick?"

"No, your perfume makes my nose itch." Her car smelled like someone lit a match to a field of herbs. Not unpleasant, just *spiky*.

"I don't wear perfume. Remember? I told you that at the diner."

I hadn't remembered. I was probably too busy being pissed about all the stuff she forgot. "Okay, then the smell of your car makes my nose itch."

"Are you allergic to my smell?"

"No!"

Cassie was laughing. "I'm sorry," she said. "The face you just made."

I realized my jaw was pretty much wired shut. I tried to loosen it, took a breath, and said quietly, "Can you handle this?"

"Handle what?"

"This is the last impression people in my company are going to get of you and me in person. This is, like, our *army* moment. For an *army* marriage. So."

"So?"

I was walking on the edge of pissing her off. A familiar place. "So. You know."

"What?"

"Just, don't ask them questions about drone bombs."

"Dude." Cassie gave me a relaxed thumbs-up. "I've been in relationships. Straight back, big smile, laugh at everyone's jokes. I'm a pro."

"And pretend you like me," I added. My stomach flipped. I've heard couples say that to each other, but usually they were joking.

"Duh," Cassie said.

She got quiet, biting her thumbnail, staring absently at one of those tacky black-and-white posters of Marilyn Monroe near the host stand. Reality was approaching. I sensed her nerves.

I nudged her shoulder. "Just pretend I'm that hot musician. Bon Iver."

She narrowed her eyes at me. "You don't look like—"

"Father Jack Misty," I tried.

"It's Father John."

"Father John Misty. Dressed like David Bowie. Holding a key-tar."

"Now you're just pandering," she said. But she smiled.

We followed the hostess toward the back of the restaurant, where there was a large room behind French doors. I could hear a burst of laughter, and Armando came into view, a couple of pounds on him since boot camp had ended, and Gomez, her lips painted, and Clark with a red beard he'd have to shave off before we deployed. Then there was Hill, a corporal I barely knew, and his wife. And Frankie and Elena, gelled and crisp, looking like they were about to sign a lease in an ad for expensive condos. Empty pint glasses stood along the table. We entered to a burst of laughter.

"Nobody told him drills were over!" Armando was saying, pointing at Frankie, out of breath.

Clark noticed us and stood up, putting a heavy hand on my shoulder. "Morrow! And who's this?"

The room got quiet.

"Hi, y'all," I said.

"I'm Cassie, Luke's wife," Cassie said beside me.

"Luke's *wife*?" Gomez asked, her eyes widening with surprise.

Cassie wrapped her arm around my waist. I hadn't thought about this part. I was ready to eat mozzarella sticks, put my arm on the back of Cassie's chair, point at her with my thumbs, and refer to her as "this one," like I'd seen friends' dads do. I wasn't ready for their shock. Nor for the possibility that shock might morph into disbelief. *You're going to blow it. And even if you did blow it, no one would care. None of these people know you. They don't care about you. They'll turn you in.* A bump of Oxy would have really mellowed things right then. I pushed the thoughts away.

"When did you get married?" Gomez gasped.

My veins pumped. Cassie looked at me with dewy eyes, squeezing. *Ouch.* I swallowed and said, "A couple days ago."

"It was love at first sight," Cassie added with a bright laugh. Her voice didn't sound like her own.

"How wonderful!" Gomez was saying.

Armando's eyes traveled the length of Cassie's body and he shrugged, approving. I gave him a warning look.

I led Cassie away from Armando, to the opposite end of the table. As we sat, Cassie leaned close to me, her breath in my ear. "Remember the plan."

That's right. The plan. Whenever anyone seemed skeptical, we were supposed to act in love. "We can't get all hot and heavy right away," I whispered back. "It's weird."

Cassie leaned closer, rubbing her hand up my thigh. "You know what else will be weird? Jail." Hot blood rushed from my head to a place it should not go, not right now.

"Fine," I said, making sure to take her hand and put it on the table, where everyone could see.

Our server, a skinny younger guy with gages in his ears, shouted over the din, "What can I get y'all to drink?"

"Water's fine," I called.

"Me, too," Cassie said.

"Seriously?" Hill, the corporal, was looking at us, his blond eyebrows raised with surprise. "Water, Private?"

"Come on, Morrow," Armando said, lifting his beer. "Last night of freedom!"

I could go for a bump, I thought again. The same thought, like a record player. I shook it off and looked at Cassie, as if for approval.

"You've got an early morning, babe," Cassie said, bright, unnatural.

"We all have an early morning, sweetheart," Corporal Hill said. "Come on."

I saw Cassie's lip curl.

"I'm good, sir, thanks," I said, trying to sound like I meant it.

Gomez's husband knocked over a glass with a bang, and Hill's attention went elsewhere.

One round down, I couldn't help thinking. We were only two people out of eleven. There was no way they could care about us for long. Beside me, Cassie was listening to Clark's wife tell her about their honeymoon. Cassie cooed and *aww*ed at a description of mosquito curtains. Under the table, her leg was twitching.

While the rest of the group ordered another round, I checked in. "Why do you have that voice on?"

"What voice?"

I looked at her like, *you know what I mean.*

"I thought it seemed nice and . . . wifely."

I almost spit out my water, laughing.

She shrugged, looking panicked. "What? I don't know."

"It's cute."

She rolled her eyes. "Don't even."

"No, I mean, cute, like the sound of a music box in a horror movie cute."

"Gross."

Suddenly, my name rose from the other end of the table. *Shit.* Another gauntlet. Cassie straightened her back.

"And over here we've got Morrow, the king of romance." Armando was gesturing toward me, shaking his head. "Cassie," he continued. She tensed next to me. "Cassie, right?"

"Right," she said. Her voice was clipped.

"How the hell," Armando said, his words stringing together. "How did you guys get from arguing about Davies's drunk ass to a wedding chapel?"

All other conversations at the table died. Cassie cleared her throat. I felt Frankie's eyes burning the side of my face, willing us forward. The story. It was time for the story. The story would make everything better. We had talked about this. Something about a walk by the river. "I took her for a walk by the river," I said.

"He came . . . ," Cassie started, and Armando whooped, interrupting her. "He came *back*," Cassie continued, trying to keep her voice light. "To ask me out."

"Exactly," I said, almost too much like I had just remembered the answer to a question on a game show.

"And, and . . . ," Cassie stumbled. I could feel her trying too hard to pick up the emotion I had dropped. She put her hand near her breast, for emphasis, like a soap opera. "And since he was deploying so soon, we wanted to make sure we had each other when he got back. I'm his rock."

We hadn't said anything about rocks. "She's my rock," I repeated, trying to make it sound like it wasn't a question.

I couldn't even look at Cassie, but I had to. *The plan.* The tip of her tongue hit her lips, waiting. I knew what I had to do. I resisted nervous laughter. I leaned in, open mouth landing on hers, which was closed. It wasn't so much a kiss as it was just *wet*, and off target. We had done a much better job at city hall.

"Ow-w-w-w! Slow it down," Armando said. "No, wait, I'll just watch."

Clark cleared his throat. "Still hilarious, though."

"What is?" I could hear Gomez asking as we unlocked our lips.

"That y'all were at each other's throats one night, and proposing the next." Clark's expression was doubtful. *Shit.*

"Means there's a lot of passion, right?" I added.

"Sure." Clark shrugged. "Whatever works."

Cassie put her hand on mine. I leaned close to her face again, planting my lips on her cheek. I could feel her jaw harden. We'd pretty much fucked that up. I imagined Frankie was doing everything not to kick us under the table.

The food came. We repeated the story. We made out again, but better.

Elena stood with her glass of white wine, and the attention turned toward her. Cassie and I simultaneously let out our breath. This was almost over. We had almost made it through.

"Y'all, I'd like to say something real quick," Elena called out.

"Oh, boy," Gomez said, rolling her eyes at her husband. "Here come the toasts."

"Just real quick," Elena said, nervous, smiling at the group. "I just wanted to say that all of us wives and girlfriends . . ."

"And husbands," Gomez said, putting her hand on the back of her husband's neck.

"And husbands, of course. We're all going to miss y'all so much. We're going to be waiting every single night for you to come home safe. And until then, we're behind you one hundred percent. We hope you accomplish what you set out to do, which is keep our country safe. God bless America."

"God bless America!" the group repeated, lifting their glasses. They cheered, bumping the rims across the table, proud. I cheered with them.

"Hooah!" Armando shouted.

"Hooah!" we repeated.

Cassie looked at me, a glint in her eye. I gave her a steely look back. She was on the verge of a joke. I shook my head.

Hill stood, and started a cadence. "The Army Colors, the colors are blue . . ."

"To show the world, that we are true," we sang back.

"The Army Colors, the colors are white . . ."

Frankie smiled at me as we sang together. "To show the world that we will fight."

For every sidelong glance Cassie gave me, I sang louder. My heart lifted. This is the song we sang in boot camp on the track every morning when we ran. We'd sung this song as I discovered the feeling I could get from accomplishment, from dreaming.

When the song ended, Hill raised his glass, growling, "To bombin' some mothafuckin' Arabs!"

"Hooah!" Everyone cheered and drank.

"Holy shit," Cassie said, in her regular voice. I tried to catch her eyes. Maybe she hadn't realized it had slipped out. "Are you serious?"

My company members' faces turned toward me, silent. My mouth was dry. "What's the matter?" I asked.

"That's fucked up," she said, louder.

Hill sat down back at his place at the head of the table, leaning back. "Uh oh. PC police."

"I'm just, like, trying to digest the fact that you're celebrating taking lives. Do you always do this?"

Now she was looking at me. "Uh . . ."

"And where are the cheers about building roads and schools?" She was disgusted. She was mocking me. "Not to mention how phenomenally racist that is."

My face burned.

Hill put his arm over his wife's chair, a conspiratorial smile growing on his face as he looked at me, sighing. *Women, right?*

"Let's not get into this," I said, begging with my eyes. *Almost done.* She looked away and shrugged my hand off.

"Hey, sweetheart," Hill said, pretending to speak gently.

She tilted her head. "My name is Cassie," she said. "What."

"You might not know this, but that's our job. It's a hard pill to swallow, but you gotta do it." He gestured at his wife, who was staring at the table, with his beer still in his hand. "It's not easy being an army wife. Ask Jessica."

"I'm not a fucking 'army wife,'" Cassie said, sarcastic, and stopped midbreath. She pressed her lips together.

My stomach dropped. The one thing we were trying to prove. The one reason we were even here in the first place, she had knocked down. The truth.

"Cassie," I got out. I gestured to Cassie, confused, and to Hill. "Corporal, she doesn't mean it that way . . ."

The only sounds were the clash of forks on plates, the *ting-ting* of Top 40 over the speakers, and someone, probably Gomez's husband, saying, *"Yikes."* Down the table, Frankie stayed frozen, his eyes on Cassie. He wasn't indignant, though, or offended or surprised. He looked sad. Regretful.

Cassie stood, scooted around her chair, and folded her napkin in the center of her plate. I stood with her, my hands in fists. There was a pause, the table braced. Cassie opened her mouth, closed it into a serene smile, and walked out.

"Excuse us," I said. I swallowed.

I willed myself to follow her, though all I wanted to do was roll my eyes and watch her go. As I closed the door, I could hear the chatter of my friends rising again behind us, knowing whatever they were saying was full of relief that we were gone.

Cassie

I drove us to a motel, still seething, though Luke, staring out the passenger window at the car dealerships and gas stations whipping by, didn't seem to notice. *PC police.* Sure, whatever they wanted to call it.

And then I had all but blown our cover. Was it worth it? Depended on which part you were talking about. Was being around a bunch of xenophobic, oversized children worth the one thousand dollars a month? Was calling out a bunch of xenophobic, oversized children worth throwing away the health insurance? Either way, my mother was right. This was crazy. *And thank fucking God we were almost done.*

"Well, are you coming in or do you want to officially call this thing?" Luke asked as we pulled into the parking lot.

Instead of answering, I parked, and followed him out of the car. He was already bounding up the motel steps.

"It's 201," he called out to me.

We creaked up the metal stairs to the second-level balcony.

The room was a smoker's lung with a funguslike carpet and walls peppered with blurry watercolor prints by Thomas Kinkade.

Luke sat on the bed, unlacing his boots.

The bed. Bed, singular. There was nothing in our agreement about having to share a comforter. "Why the hell did you get a queen bed?" I asked.

He untucked his button-down and I felt my body getting hot with embarrassment, and a strange pang like lust, which I hated.

"Frankie said that's all they had available," he muttered.

"Oh, I'm sure." I took off the Walmart ring and flung it on the table next to a telephone from 1992, finally able to feel my finger.

He kicked off his boots. "Yes, I'm the one who did everything wrong. Blame me."

I slipped off my Converses and socks, switched off the lamp, and got under the covers. He slipped in next to me. It was strange to feel his weight, his breath on the back of my neck.

After a moment, Luke said, "Everything was going fine until you had to be a . . . fuckin' . . . social justice warrior."

"I'm not a social justice warrior." I kicked off my jeans, trying to keep the comforter in place. "I'm a sane human who got scared to be around, like, violent chanting."

He said nothing. I could feel him forming an opinion. "You're not the only one who's in this, you know."

He sat up behind me, leaning on his arm. "It's not the same, Cassie."

"How is it not the same?" Silence. My palms turned clammy from sweat, heart thumping. "Tell me exactly how it's different. If we're caught, we're both in trouble."

He swallowed. "You're going to be safe at home."

I turned to face him. "I wouldn't call diabetes safe. And that's not an answer."

He sat up, bare chested. "Can I get any respect from you?"

I sat up with him. His eyes went to my bare legs. I didn't care. "Talking about killing *motherfucking A-rabs*? I think you and I have a different definition of respect."

"I didn't say those things," he said slowly, emphasizing each syllable, moving his face closer to mine.

I imitated him. "But you let them happen."

"There's a culture, Cassie. I'm the one going overseas with these people." Then he muttered, "And you get to stay at home and reap the benefits. So a thank-you would be nice."

Okay. Enough. I took his face in my hands. "Oh, Luke, thank you, man."

"Stop," he said. He pushed my hands away.

I clapped my hands together in fake prayer. *"For all that you do for everyone. Thank you so much."*

He was quiet. The skin of his chest and stomach glowed from the motel neon. I realized that when he was still, like he was yesterday, like he was now, I could see him well enough to appreciate how beautiful he was. How easy it was to forget everything in the dark and light of his eyes playing, the line of his nose falling straight to the center of sad lips. Much simpler than whatever it was we were arguing about, much easier than remembering that we were stuck in this, no matter who won the fight.

Before all our words could rush back, I kissed him hard on the mouth. I expected him to push me away.

But he didn't. A current traveled from my lips to elsewhere, alighting my skin. When I stopped, I saw the rarest hint of a smile. It was unlike any expression I'd ever seen Luke make. "What the hell was that?"

I looked at his lips again. "I don't know."

This time, he kissed me.

While our mouths were still connected, I pushed him until he was lying flat, opening my mouth to his, placing my hand on his stomach.

He grabbed my leg and pulled me across until I was on top of him. His skin smelled like Frankie's house, like expensive soap, like the cool, dark basement where they did the laundry.

He grabbed me and I let him, but when his hands started to move down my sides and onto my hips, I pulled them off and pressed them above his head. We locked eyes again. His muscles tensed under my weight. Between my legs, I could feel the flesh of his stomach get harder. He could flip me like a pancake if he wanted to.

But he didn't move.

"You like this, don't you?" I heard myself say.

He raised his eyebrows. "And you don't?"

I let go of his hands. His tongue met my tongue. I tasted tap water and salt, felt his solid arms, moved my hands across his chest, down his stomach. While we kissed, the line his fingers made on my thighs reached the cloth of my bikini cuts. I curled my finger around the elastic, and felt his fingers follow mine.

I scooted back inch by inch until we could both see the brass button on his Levi's, his zipper.

His right hand made a slow path up my shirt to my left breast, scooping under the fabric of my bra, stroking my nipple with his rough thumb.

"Fuck it," one of us said.

He went to unbutton his shirt while I yanked on the waistband of his pants. When I looked up I found Luke sitting, pulling me to his lap, his mouth on mine, unable to wait. With his back against the headboard, I lifted my hips to meet his, and though we both knew what was coming, our eyes met, amazed.

Luke

I woke up to nothing, which was more jarring than waking up to a sound. My brain just snapped on, like an old refrigerator sputtering to life in the middle of the night. My arms were around Cassie, her thick, black hair loose all over my chest, under my chin, her hand resting on my stomach. The hours after we left Chili's snaked across the dark ceiling; the compressed silence of the car, losing my temper, and then on the bed, her eyes on mine as she pushed my hands above my head into the scratchy motel comforter.

The sight of her on top of me, unhooking her bra.

Looking down at her antler tattoo, lifting her by the small of her back.

My mouth in the crook of her neck, tasting her, propping her on the bathroom countertop as I found the space between her legs.

For a moment, I was at peace, remembering. Then the elephant of anxiety sat on my chest. Unrelenting, the sound of nothing but everything pulsing. Heart and skull in sync, too hard to hear or think, needles in my eyeballs, my tongue a bitter, foreign object.

What time was it?

I shot off the bed, picking up pieces of clothing off the ground, dropping them when I realized they weren't mine. Found my Levi's, my dead phone.

The motel clock said 6:00. I didn't trust that. What if it was just stuck on 6:00? I had to be at the airport to deploy at 0800.

Cassie stirred.

"Where's your phone?" I hissed, grabbing her jacket, her purse.

"Purse," she muttered, her voice hoarse.

I dug through lighters, cylinders, journals, pens. Found it: 6:01.

All right. I could get there if I left now. I googled *cab austin* with shaking hands. We'd had exactly three hours of sleep.

"What are you doing?" she asked, yawning.

"Getting a cab. I should have left an hour ago," I said, hearing the click and snappy voice of the operator after two rings.

Cassie pulled open the curtains, flooding the dingy room with white morning sun, dust lifting from the furniture where we had draped ourselves last night, hungry for each other, forgetting.

I'd be cutting it close. But TSA would let me through quickly if they saw I was active duty. I went into the bathroom, washed my hands, my face, wishing I could pierce a hole in my head and empty out the thoughts stampeding through. *You're late. You'll miss your plane. You'll slip up and use again. This woman hates you. She's embarrassed.*

Cassie appeared behind me, fully dressed. Her eyes still had puffy sleep in them, her hair matted at the ends.

An image hit of her unbuckling my pants. Half lust, half nausea shot to my gut.

That was not part of our agreement, what we did.

Whose idea was it? Had she come on to me, or had I come on to her?

We didn't even get along.

Maybe that's what we were doing. We were trying to fuck ourselves into liking each other.

"Do you want me to take you to the airport?" she asked, yawning again.

"No," I said. "Thanks," I added.

"It's no big deal," she started, then caught my eyes in the mirror.

I avoided them. "I want to go alone."

"When is the cab getting here?"

"Twenty minutes."

"I can take you . . ." She pretended to look at an invisible watch. "Literally now."

I let out a laugh despite myself. It made much more sense. And it dissipated two out of the thousand circulating thoughts. I wouldn't be late. She didn't hate me. "Thanks. It's probably better for appearances anyhow."

I took a swig of mouthwash from the tiny bottle near the sink.

"So," she said as I swished. "Last night."

I shook my head, keeping the mouthwash in longer than I needed to, hoping she'd drop it. Too many bad thoughts remained. I couldn't find the right ones even if I wanted to. *Everyone knows you're faking. You're not one of them. You're going to have no one. You'll be alone. You're going to die. You're going to die alone.* The liquid burned my gums.

I spit.

"I don't feel awkward," she said, leaning against the door frame. "I mean, we're married. Married people do that sometimes."

"Yeah." I walked past her in the doorway, still smelling the cucumber of her shampoo. I pushed it away. I found a pad of paper in a drawer in the bedside table, and lugged my bag on my back.

"Word," she said, grabbing her purse and giving me a winning smile. "Awkward silence it is."

"I don't feel awkward. I'm just focused."

"I get it, I get it," she said. "I mean, I don't fully get what it feels like, but, yeah. I get it."

I closed the door and we descended down the stairs. Cassie jogged over to drop the room key in the slot next to the lobby.

We got into the Subaru.

"Here," I said as we clicked our seat belts. I handed her the piece of motel stationery on which I had written Jacob's phone number. "You're my next of kin now."

She kept her eyes down, reading. "I know."

She put it in her pocket.

"If anything happens to me, they're going to come to you."

Cassie took a deep, shaky breath, backing out of the parking space. "Okay. Yeah, that makes sense."

The morning light shone through the windshield. So much

buildup for deployment, so much training for this day, and it was finally here. No turning back. Whether or not I was a coward, whether or not I deserved to make my life better, it was already decided for me. Either I would get through the next nine months, or I wouldn't. Starting today.

At the American Airlines drop-off, Frankie and Armando stood, their eyes on every car that passed. When they saw us pull up, they jogged over. I got out of the car.

"Damn, Morrow!" Armando said. "We thought you were going to miss the flight."

"Let's go, dude," Frankie said.

Cassie stood next to the driver's side, the car idling.

"Salazar, come here," Frankie said. Cassie came to the other side of the car, and they embraced, speaking quietly to each other. They parted, and Frankie and Armando made their way to the curb, waiting.

I took my bag out of the trunk, and as I passed her, I brushed my hand on her shoulder. "Well," I said.

"So your brother, Jacob," she said, touching her pocket. "I guess, have you made arrangements with him in case of, uh, emergency?"

I nodded, squeezing the straps of my bag. "Jake would take care of things."

"Jacob Morrow," she said. "In Buda, right?"

"Right." I got closer to her, speaking low into her ear. "You can tell him about us. Just make sure that you come up with a story for my dad."

She nodded. "Skype in a couple weeks?"

"If there's access, yes." A car behind Cassie's honked. We ignored it. A pigeon came fluttering down to her feet. We both glanced down, and when we looked up, we realized Armando and Frankie were still looking at us. As far as Armando was concerned, we were still husband and wife. Not only were we married, this would be the last time we saw each other for almost a year. And we were in love. Cassie took a deep breath. *One more time.*

I leaned down, closed my eyes, and this one was right on target. Soft. She took my face in her hands. My fingertips found her waist. For a moment, the world went quiet. We breathed each other in.

I lingered there until Frankie shouted. When I took a step back, I still couldn't quite let go, even as she got in the car and drove off. Even as I boarded our flight and I watched Texas and everyone I knew fade away.

Cassie

I was pacing outside Nora's house, eating handful after handful of raw almond slivers out of a plastic bag, wearing a fringed shawl and high, black witchy boots. Reality check: Every detail surrounding the last two days was very real, and yet did not fit together, like pieces of various jigsaw puzzles. Luke and I were married (the piece with the ring on a finger), we had consummated (hotel key), and I had his handwriting in my pocket in case I forgot his family name. We had woken up (his bare shoulder), gone to the airport (the plane icon), and I had made out with him in front of all of his friends like the nurse in that World War II photo, but with less back flexibility. We would now be thousands of miles apart for longer than we had known each other. Where did all of it lead? All I knew was that it was Fleetwood Friday, and my first deposit of one thousand dollars would arrive in two weeks.

"Come on, Nor," I muttered, checking my phone. I had asked her to meet me early before practice tonight so I could make sure I didn't invent all of this out of some delusional psychotic episode due to low blood sugar. I needed her to tell me everything was going to be okay.

She pushed open her screen door and made a fart noise, wearing her usual Fleetwood Friday–appropriate tunic, her long black hair feathered under her top hat. I ran past her inside and down to the basement.

She came clomping down the steps in platforms, eyeliner in hand. "What is the fuss, Cass?" she called.

I stood in the middle of her basement, hands on my hips. "I did it."

"Did what?" She had to step sideways because of the boots.

I took a deep breath. "I married an army guy."

She stopped in the middle of the steps. "Wait. What?"

"'Go army'? 'Count the benefits'?" I echoed the language of the brochure. "Remember when that Armando guy proposed?"

"Yeah, but—"

"I did that."

Nora came down the rest of the stairs, furious. "You married *that Armando guy*?"

I held up my hands. "No, not him—"

"Thank God."

"But that other guy. Luke. Frankie's friend. The asshole from the bar."

Nora sat on the bottom step, eyes wide. She opened her mouth to speak, but didn't. I couldn't tell if she was angry or confused or admiring me or all three. She set down the eyeliner next to her and folded her hands.

"Except he's not really an asshole," I said. "It's nuts. I can't even believe I went through with it myself."

"So it's done?" she said. "You're actually legally married?"

I lifted my finger. "The Walmart ring is at home, but yeah." My gut twisted, staring at her. She stared back. Nora was usually the *fuck yes* person in my life. When I asked her for a drink the night we met at a Father John Misty show, *fuck yes*. When I broke up with Tyler, a big *fuck yes*. When I asked her to form a band, *fuck yes*. Even when I told her that Toby and I hooked up behind a hay bale at the Harvest Festival shortly after he started playing with us, a minimal but present *fuck yes*. There was no *fuck yes* yet.

"Well." She shrugged. "You're insane."

That would bring the tally of important people in my life calling me insane up to two out of two. "Am I?"

"And yet." She held up a finger. "All things considered, it was kind of my idea. Remember when we were at your apartment and we were talking about rich people we would marry for benefits? That was me. This is a Countess LuAnn, Bethenny Frankel Skinnygirl margarita situation."

I didn't know what she was talking about, but I was pretty sure it was reality TV. And after the big leaps of the last couple of days, I was ready to listen to her talk about reality TV as long as she wanted to. I had my best friend on my side. I wanted to cry with relief. "Sure, Nor. It's all you."

"Okay," she said, concentrating. "Where did you do it, how did you do it, why didn't you call me, and what are you going to do now? Go."

I told her everything, still popping almonds. From the moment I'd formed the idea after she left my house to the embarrassing proposal at Frankie's to the shocking on-board-ness of Luke, to the day at city hall and the disaster at Chili's. When I came to last night, I paused.

I tried to make my voice casual. "So, yeah. Now he's deployed, and we'll Skype every once in a while, and that's it."

She stood up and got closer to me, narrowing her eyes. She smiled. She smelled like rose petals. "You slept with him, didn't you?"

I breathed in a mouthful of almonds, coughing, then laughing, then coughing more. Nora cracked up with me, patting my back. When I recovered, eyes watering, I said, "How did you know, you psychic?"

"I saw you two together, Cass. There was some *heat*, queen." I looked at her, suddenly confused. "Some real heat," she muttered, pulling her phone from her pocket to use as an eyeliner mirror. "And not just anger."

"I mean," I started, thinking back to last night. Thinking back to crying out as he pushed me against the wall. "I thought he was cute, but . . ." Thinking of this morning, how slowly our lips let go. "Whatever. We are so awkward together. We piss each other off constantly. He's, like, this conservative bro. Maybe I have a thing for bros."

"You don't have to justify it to me!" She tossed the eyeliner toward me. I missed it. It clattered on the floor.

Right. It was her idea. Kind of.

But Luke, specifically, was not her idea. And in any other circumstances, I would have never seen Luke again after that night at the bar. Maybe I would have run into him again through Frankie, but we would have never even remembered each other's names. And now we were entwined. There was another mismatching jigsaw puzzle piece: Luke's silver-blue eyes.

I heard the door open and close upstairs. Toby. It was time for practice. I got nervous.

"Okay, Nor, this is an absolute, military-grade secret."

"Ha!" She squatted near the case for her bass, flipping the levers on the lid. "Duh."

"Swear."

She did a budget John F. Kennedy impression. "'We hold these truths to be self-evident,' I solemnly swear not to reveal this classified information."

Toby came down the stairs, wearing a fantastically crisp white shirt over his broad shoulders, a red bandanna, and his dusty brown hair pulled into a ponytail. "Very festive Mick Fleetwood, Toby," I called.

He grinned. "Long time, no talk, Cass," he said.

"Sorry."

As we set up, Toby came near where I was bent, and plunked a few notes on the electric piano. "Oh, by the way."

I looked up. In his hands was a shiny, brand-new vegan cookbook. "I saw this and I was thinking about you today, so . . ."

Nora released a large cough. I looked over at where she was innocently plugging in her bass. I couldn't be sure, but I could have sworn I heard her say something underneath it. *Bad timing.*

Luke

My small, donated German laptop sat on the green tin table that also served as the place for cards, for clipping fingernails, for unwrapping milky British chocolate, for putting lotion on blistered palms after maneuvering a heavy gun all day, for setting up a mirror to shave. Our room at Camp Leatherneck was about half the size of our dorm rooms at Fort Hood. Fake wood paneling and exposed pipes that didn't keep the cold out at night.

We were in temperate country, in Helmand Province. The heat was bad, but the frigid nights were worse.

It was me and Frankie and a kid from the division we didn't know too well, Sam Adels, the only other redhead aside from Davies. Everyone called him Rooster.

Both Frankie and Rooster were over at the community room, the bass from someone's R&B shaking the thin walls, so it was kind of pointless to Skype with Cassie. We didn't have anyone to fool.

But we had said two weeks, so I was here, online.

In a lot of ways, this place was good for me. Sobriety was a gift I received every morning. Clarity. Blinding sun. Everything I had to fear was outside of me, and the ways I would fight it were established, unquestionable.

I woke up, I ate, I bent next to Clark over a huge engine, repeating his words, writing down parts and drawing diagrams, following his lead.

Then we'd load up and take the rickety roads up and down the Kajaki Dam into the villages, negotiating with the Afghan National Army (ANA) at checkpoints. The elders of the villages would speak to the translators, the translators to the captains. We'd hand out blankets to the women, licorice to the kids, passing through herds of goats and volleyball games. Still, we were on full alert at all times.

I watched for Cassie's name to go green in the Skype window. I looked closer at the icon she'd chosen as her contact photo. A man in red and gold robes, smiling and pointing. I realized it was the Dalai Lama. Spokesperson for world peace. Funny, Cass.

"Hi!" she said when the call came through. "Hello?"

Slight delay. We waited for the video to load.

"Hey. I'm alone, by the way," I said.

"Got it," she responded.

I took in her face. She looked different. Her hair just reached her jaw, framing her face with thick, black waves. "Did you cut your hair?"

"Yeah," she said, her voice a bit tinny through the speakers. "I look exactly like my mom now."

I laughed.

"Oh, by the way," she said, sighing. "I told Nora about us."

I felt my eyes widen. "Everything?"

"Yeah."

I realized I was holding my breath. I let it out. "Okay. Um. Why?"

She avoided looking at the screen. "It's just . . . I wouldn't not tell my mom and best friend I got married." She looked up, hard.

"All right. Just, maybe better to . . . you know. Keep it as simple as possible. Uh, so." She was wearing her wedding dress, the one that revealed her tattoo. "Are you dressed up?"

"What can I say? This is a special occasion," she said, giving me an exaggerated wink.

I coughed, trying to cover up a heat I felt on my neck. "For real?"

"Nah, I'm going out."

With a dude? I wanted to ask, but didn't. "So you got the money okay?"

"Yep, thank you," she said, biting her thumbnail.

I cleared my throat. "Everything else going good?"

She nodded, giving me a genuine smile. She was wearing lipstick. Maybe she really was going on a date. "Everything's going well, yeah. I'm playing another show next week."

"That's awesome."

"How are things over there?"

"Good." I looked behind me, gesturing at the room. "Pretty magical accommodations."

She snorted. "Living that army life. Are you promoted to a general yet?"

I matched her sarcasm. "Soon enough. Just have to get my nature badge."

We laughed.

When the laughter died, she started fidgeting. I picked up a deck of cards and shuffled it from hand to hand. I lowered my voice in case anyone could overhear. "I don't really know what to talk about. With you. Other than pretending to be married."

Cassie bit her lip. "Yeah, we should have covered that in the meeting at the diner, huh?"

"What if we try now?"

Voices came down the hall. Frankie and Rooster were coming back.

Cassie said quickly, "E-mail me. Tell me things that are important about your life, like some conversation we're picking back up on. Just be careful so that it can't be used as evidence we don't know each other."

I found myself smiling, surprised at her scheming. She gave me a nervous smile back, shrugging.

"Okay," I said, and jerked my head toward the makeshift door.

She cleared her throat, understanding. Frankie and Rooster came in, laughing.

"Not if I don't first, dude," Frankie was saying.

Rooster passed behind me, glancing at the laptop screen.

"So I guess I'll see you in another couple weeks, baby?" she said, leaning forward, putting on a pouty face.

I blanked, trying to stay casual. I had made a mental list of "married" things to say, but most of them were just normal things with the word "honey" tacked at the end of them. "I—I don't want to wait that long, either. Honey."

"Uh oh, are we interrupting?" Rooster asked, wiggling his eyebrows, leaning over my shoulder.

"Hi, I'm Cassie," she said in her high, wifely voice.

"My wife," I said, gesturing toward the screen as if he didn't already see it. *Ugh, idiot.*

"Hey, Cass!" Frankie said, taking the spot on my other shoulder.

At the sight of his face, Cassie's act broke for a second. "Frankie! You good?"

Frankie blew her a kiss. "Never better!"

My blood pressure rose. "Well, Cassie has to go. We've been at it for an hour, so."

"Girls' night!" she said, fluttering her hands.

"Bye-bye now," I said.

Frankie cleared his throat, muttering something that sounded like "love."

"Oh," I said, my hands up instinctively, telling her to wait. *Oh, God.* I looked to the left of her, hoping it appeared to Rooster like I was staring fondly at the screen. "I love you."

We caught each other's eyes. Hers were a little wide, panicked, like mine, her lips trying to suppress laughter. "I love you, too!" she cried, and the call ended.

I let out a slow, quiet sigh of relief as Rooster went to get something from his bag.

Next to me, Frankie snickered. "Nice one."

Cassie

I hung up with Luke and immediately pulled out my phone to cancel on Toby. Toby giving me the cookbook turned into him asking me out for drinks, and me somehow saying yes. But how was I supposed to move directly from saying "I love you" to my fake husband to going on a date-that-might-not-be-a-date? But when I pulled up his number, I reread our text message exchange again.

So what do you think?

After we had hooked up the first time, Toby had been the one to say he wasn't looking for anything serious. I had told him I was fine with that, and from then on it was an unspoken agreement that I would occasionally hook up with him after practice.

Why the sudden penchant for traditional romance?

He wrote back right away, *I've been wanting to hang for a while.*

Hang?

Date? Go on one?

So if I say yes, then what? I'd realized this could be read as a flirtation tactic. But I'd also honestly meant it. I had enough ambiguous male figures in my life. I was stalling.

I would say how about Thursday night?

He had basically saved my life. I didn't feel so much that I owed him a date, because that was icky, but more that I was genuinely curious. What the heck would we talk about? The album? Nora? The state of our country? Plus we'd already slept together and not talked about it. I'd doubted this could be any more awkward. *Ok*, I typed.

Rad.

Rad, I had repeated, not sure whether I was making fun of him.

I'll pick you up at seven, he'd texted. *Thinking we can eat like three steaks each, and then take naps, how does that sound?*

I laughed, as I had done the first time I'd read it. *Sounds perfect*, I had written. *Meat and naps. You really know the way to my heart.*

I hadn't been on a date for a while. I'd kind of forgotten how. When Nora and I went on "dates" we would usually spend the whole time talking across from each other with our mouths full at Mai Thai, fantasizing about ways we would murder John Mayer.

I called her. She picked up on the first ring.

When I told her, she screamed. "Toby Masters? Our little drummer boy?"

I sighed. "Yeah."

"But why?"

I thought of his long hair, his gap-toothed smile, his gushing compliments after shows. "He's nice. He's funny."

"So are lots of human beings."

"But most human beings don't ask me out."

She laughed. "Probably because you spend all of your time playing piano and scheming the army for benefits."

"Yeah, the timing isn't great . . ." I started.

"Uh, yeah, no," Nora said, her voice dry. "You get fake-married and all of a sudden you want to lock down your fuck buddy? Is this a contagious disease I should worry about?"

"No, no," I said, forcing a laugh.

I was quiet, trying to quench the fire in my stomach with a sip of wine. Of course Luke was a factor. *Maybe I'm trying to see what a normal relationship looks like so I can use my experience to fool the army police.* Is that what I was really doing? No. And what if I actually got hurt? I changed the subject.

"What kind of questions do I ask? Like, am I supposed to ask what his favorite color is? Or, like, what his relationship is like with his mother?"

"Ask him to come in earlier after the bridge on 'Too Much.' "

"Seriously, Nora."

"Seriously, Cassie," she echoed. "Do whatever you want. You're a queen. Toby's lucky to have you."

I smiled. "He doesn't 'have me' yet. But, yeah. It's been a while since I've been liked. Like, actually liked," I said.

"Awww—"

"I'm experimenting," I interrupted, feeling my face flush.

"K. Well, good luck, Dr. Kinsey. Don't fuck with our drummer. Seriously, Cass. Band comes first."

"I know."

"Promise?"

"Promise."

We said good-bye and hung up.

I checked my lipstick in the camera. I checked my blood sugar to make sure nothing would happen like in the greenroom at the Skylark. I put on Nicki Minaj. When I was full-on rapping along to "Favorite," Toby texted that he was downstairs. I turned off the music.

I opened the door and he smiled wide. "Hi, good to see you."

"Good to see you, too," I said. I slipped on my Converses, waiting.

He was still standing in the doorway, taking a big breath. "This is weird."

I laughed, covering a sigh of relief. "It's not that weird, but, yeah, it's weird."

"We'll improvise. I'm supposed to, like, present you with a gift from my people, right?"

"After we sing the ceremonial mating song, yes."

"Fuck it, let's go eat."

• • •

An hour later we were sitting on a curb outside of Lulu B's, talking with our mouths full of *bahn mi*. After dinner, we'd go to a show at Swan Dive.

He was telling me a story about a time when a venue manager in Tennessee accidentally double booked a night, and his old band got scheduled to play at the same time as a Christian rock band.

"We did the only thing we could," he said. "We played."

"You kicked them out?" I asked, laughing.

"No."

"Then what?"

"It's not very punk. It's kind of embarrassing," he said, looking away from me with a smile.

"No one said you had to be punk," I told him.

"Well, they were a Christian rock band, we were a rock band, so we decided to play songs we both knew."

"Which were?"

"Creed."

I almost spit out the bite I had just taken. Creed's success was baffling to anyone in music, probably even Creed. Their sound was basically constipated-Kurt-Cobain-meets-youth-pastor-trying-to-be-cool.

"I'm sorry, I'm sorry," I said, trying to keep it together. "I'm laughing with you."

"No one wants to admit they know all the words to 'Arms Wide Open.'"

I imitated Scott Stapp, the lead singer, and it was his turn to spit out sandwich.

I took him in, trying to match the drummer with benefits I knew against the guy I had yet to know, the guy who was taking me on a surprisingly good date. Toby had grown up in a country song in Arkansas. His dad was a trucker, his mother a waitress, and he had basically raised himself. He never went to college, opting to take an apprenticeship with a well-known sculptor instead. He became a drummer when one of his fellow line cooks at Denny's wanted to form a band. His car's name was Sergio, which Toby pronounced "Surge-ya."

Things going for him:

He didn't ask me if it was all right if we sat on the curb, he just went ahead and sat, a paper-wrapped, greasy sandwich in each hand.

He could wear the shit out of some boot-cut jeans.

The boy could talk music. Because we were always practicing or otherwise-ing, I'd never known how much.

". . . well, it's not that I'm opposed to Jeff Tweedy's sobriety, it's just that I don't know how you could ever make another masterpiece like *Yankee Hotel Foxtrot* without being completely messed up. I mean, think about it, even the songs themselves were drunk. Drony and rambly and full of this electricity that you don't get with the measured, composed country ditties in *Sky Blue Sky* . . ."

"Mm-hmm," I said into my sandwich. The thing was: He was right. Or rather, I agreed with him. We're never going to get another *Yankee Hotel Foxtrot* out of Jeff Tweedy. The world was different then. Alternative rock had been clamoring for anything with substance post-Nirvana.

And he could discuss, at length, Portishead's *Roseland NYC Live*, one of the greatest fifty-seven minutes of music that has ever taken place.

". . . it was the orchestra that did it, though. I mean, it would have been great with just the band, but, oh man, when it tunes up at the beginning."

"I get chills."

"Me, too."

I motioned for him to go on. I would wait to throw in my two cents once we circled back to Portishead. Or Björk.

I wasn't obsessing over aligning my opinions with his. I wasn't trying to prove myself, because he knew me. I wasn't performing. The only thing I had to prove to anyone would come in the form of the songs we were writing. The Loyal had played every night for the past two weeks and we'd started to record rough versions of our songs on GarageBand.

"Ready to see this?" Toby asked, crumpling up his sandwich wrapper. "It's going to be wild."

"Can't wait," I replied.

When we stood, he took my arm like we were British gentry, and we laughed.

As we parked on Red River Street, we could already hear the show beating through the entrance.

The duo was called Hella, and was more noise rock than anything I liked, but had the dynamic sound of a band of six. I closed my eyes, rocking back and forth with the dips and switches of the drumming. This drummer took me to the forest, but instead of foraging for notes, new plant life was sprouting in front of me, leaves and petals on fire with color: 9s, 7s, 5s, all over the place.

I opened my eyes to look over at Toby, whose eyes were closed, too, long brown hair behind his ears, unaware of anything but the music. For a second I thought of Luke, and the way he looked off into the distance somewhere, his thoughts in a faraway place. I wondered what he thought about.

"This is fun," I said into Toby's ear, calling above the noise. "Why didn't we do this sooner?"

He looked amused at the prospect, and brought my hand to his mouth, kissing it. Then he leaned close to my neck, his warm breath sending shivers down my back. "You tell me."

Luke

Sometimes, when we were high into the hills where the roads stopped, I'd jog ahead, my feet digging into the ground because of the fifty extra pounds of ammo on my back. It was mostly scrub and rocks, but when you're rolling through the landscape long enough, you start to notice the difference between light brown and dark brown and red brown, between opium and cotton, the difference between 100 and 105 degrees. Out of the city we'd hit tobacco or sugar beet or poppy fields. We'd pass donkeys or camels on the road, or other vehicles whose horns played a little song each time they sounded. Depending on who was driving or who was riding, we'd pause at prayer time. Our interpreter Malik would get out and face east as he bowed his head on the road.

It's hard to run when you've got to gear up practically everywhere you go, but I found ways. I started to get up before the heat hit to run around the makeshift track at the FOB that some hardcore marathoners had worn into the earth. A few of them did something called shadow runs, where they timed themselves running the same number of miles as a race back in the States. They got T-shirts and water stations and everything.

I preferred to run alone. Most of our days were hard and long, too hot or too cold, hours and hours waiting on the decisions of our superiors. Alone, running, was the only time when I had control. I could run for as long as I wanted. I could escape into my running dreams.

I imagined I had returned home to Texas, running at the high school track in Buda. I listed jobs in my head that I could do, as unrealistic as I wanted. Firefighter. Gym teacher. Radio DJ. I composed letters to my brother and his wife and my nephew, which I tried to remember as I wrote them later in my Moleskine and mailed them off.

I wrote letters to Cassie in my mind and then got nervous when I went to write them down. But I'd send one soon.

When I'd return to our room, Frankie would be Skyping with Elena, or in the community room playing video games with Rooster, or we'd have a briefing before a mission, and he'd have brought me some toast and a warm, dusty bottle of water if I didn't have time to eat before we had to go.

Sometimes we annoyed the shit out of one another. Sometimes Rooster snored and we had to throw pillows at him. Sometimes Frankie had to yell at me to get my laundry done because there wasn't enough ventilation to handle the smell of sweaty clothes.

But we did everything together. We got the same food poisoning, we hit the floor at the same time if there was an explosion close by, we went to the Hindu barber together in Lashkar Gah, watching the muted Bollywood videos while we got a shave.

It was like having brothers. Friends. It was like having a life.

Cassie

Behind me, Toby was wailing on 7/8. Nora and I got closer to our mics, poised, bouncing, looking at each other, waiting to come in. He paused, dipped into 6/8, and we stepped into the forest, breaking down a G-minor chord, hocketing like birds, until I opened my eyes and we hit the full F so hard I almost lost my breath. We'd been working on this technique for a month, and it came and passed as easy as water. It was October, four weeks since our last show, and we were back at the Skylark, sharing the bill with Popover.

Every day had crystallized. Every day I would:

Wake up, prick myself to check blood sugar.

Make something that wouldn't kill me. Crack an egg and whisk it with one tablespoon of milk. Sprinkle in some garlic powder and ground pepper.

A slice of whole grain toast topped with fat-free margarine and a plum.

A small bowl of bran cereal with a half cup of low-fat milk (or sometimes I'd use unsweetened almond milk or unsweetened soy milk, which had fewer carbs and calories per serving than regular milk).

Top the cereal with fresh berries if I hadn't spent too much on records at End of an Ear.

Walk at least two miles down to South Congress or to the university, sometimes with Toby, most of the time alone, listening to various playlists.

Midmorning, check my blood sugar.

Play and write.

Lunchtime, check blood sugar.

Mix together some cooked quinoa, white beans, chopped bell

pepper, carrots, and broccoli to make a grain salad. Toss with some olive oil, lemon juice, salt, and pepper.

Or canned tuna, light mayo, diced celery, lemon juice, and freshly ground pepper.

Or a whole wheat tortilla wrap with rotisserie chicken, hummus, sun-dried tomatoes, feta cheese, and greens.

Or a hard-boiled egg, with a peach if the blood sugar allowed, maybe some string cheese and five, count 'em, *five* whole wheat crackers.

Play and write.

Midafternoon, check blood sugar.

Before work, check blood sugar. Drive to work. Sling cocktails. Notice how I wasn't as tired by midnight. Notice how I wasn't as fazed by customers. How my car was cleaner. How I was beginning to form another layer of calluses on my fingertips from the needle.

Toby always helped me remember before I went to bed. Sometimes he brought almonds or a nectarine to rehearsal, just in case I forgot. He was so tender.

Tonight, The Loyal's set was so tight we had barely talked to the audience between songs, launching into new styles and tangents without explaining this was "something new that we were trying," not trying to make them like us but just releasing the sound that had lived in our heads like a hungry animal. Now people were crowding the stage, almost on top of the amps. We were a different band altogether.

"Dance!" Nora yelled on a downbeat, and we swung in again on the 6/8. Like a miracle, they did. The shadows jerked and twisted and bobbed their heads, spraying sweat and spilling their drinks. I looked back at Toby and he was in ecstasy, lifting shoulders up and down with the snare, eyes everywhere like a revivalist speaking in tongues. I signaled for him to loop around the last part of the chorus again. He read me, instinctively slowing so that I could extend the notes and growl the final verse again. *Yes. Exactly what I wanted.*

The bodies fell into a sway, and we thanked them. They screamed their approval.

Backstage, we descended into a damp, smelly hug.

"What the hell, dudes?" Nora said, out of breath. "What the hell did we just do to the masses?"

"We slayed them," Toby said, his arm sliding around my waist as we pressed our foreheads together.

"We did," I said, and kissed his cheek. "And with what's probably going to be our album."

"Yes," Toby said, pulling me closer. "Yes, yes, yes."

"And Cass survived this one!" Nora joked.

We laughed. Nora went to grab a celebratory beer. Toby jogged over to peek his head out to the front, to see if the crowd had cleared enough so we could take down our instruments.

I flopped down on one of the greenroom's ratty couches and took it in. I *had* survived. There wasn't a second when I felt too tired or too fried. I'd begun to think of my diabetes like one of my more demanding plants. One of those expensive, rare flowers you had to talk to and water and move in and out of the shade, except now I had no choice, because it lived inside me.

Toby crashed half on top of me, half on top of the cushions, and we kissed, the rush of the show still ringing in our ears. When we leaned back, we laughed a little. Toby picked a piece of hair off my shirt, suddenly shy. Being public was still new. But so good. I thought of his long arms bashing the beats, drawing the eyes of every woman in the front row. I kissed him again.

"We probably sold it out, huh," I said.

Toby nodded, face lifted, too happy for words. We sold out the Skylark. My diabetes wasn't a total monster. Everything was falling into place. I couldn't wait to tell Luke.

To: Cassie Salazar
From: PFC Luke Morrow
Subject: Hello

Hello Cassie
Just thought I would test this out. I don't see why this
wouldn't go through but it seems crazy that I can write this

from a laptop in the middle of [REDACTED]. shows you how good i am at the internet. You don't even want to know how long it took me to set even this up. Next thing you know I will be yelling at you to get off my lawn.

But yeah here's where you can reach me and we can set up skype dates. Feel free to also send me hot pictures. You know, stuff like you dressed up as a Ninja Turtle, you dressed as the Fonz from Happy Days, you know what I like. Kidding. But you are my wife so think about it. But seriously I'm kidding.

So remember how I was telling you about how my running times will go way down when I get home because I will be used to the elevation here? They are already going way down here, even though i didn't get to run for the first few weeks because we were getting adjusted. Must be the food. And by food I mean lack of food.

Anyway I bet they are going to be off the charts when i get home. Maybe I will train for a marathon. Maybe I will make you train with me. :)

Luke

•   •   •

To: PFC Luke Morrow
From: Cassie Salazar
Subject: Miss you!

Luke, It is I, your devoted wife. Things are as usual here. The Loyal played another gig at The Skylark and we smashed it. SOLD OUT crowd, everyone was digging it, and I can't even describe the feeling to you. Imagine you ran a four minute mile, every mile, for thirty miles, and everyone you ever knew was cheering for you the whole time. It was like that. (Is that what marathon's like? Because fine, I will do one with you, if so.) All of the compromises we have made in our short but very passionate marriage are paying off. Thank you for supporting me. Your support in words and gestures and knowing *a lot* about how much this means to me has been super valuable. :)

I thought about buying a bike to add to this very exciting eating right and exercising life I have begun and you would have definitely laughed me out of the store. I had a saleslady wheel one out for me to "try it on" but it was WAY too tall and I couldn't balance so I FELL OVER right on my side like someone had pushed over a statue or something. My friend Toby and I (you remember Toby, the drummer for my band) were laughing so hard and I was so embarrassed that I didn't try another one and left.

Everyone misses you, including Marisol (I know how you hate to call her Mom). I hope you are doing well and feeling healthy.

I love you very much, my dear husband.

Cassie

•   •   •

To: Cassie Salazar
From: PFC Luke Morrow
Subject: RE: Miss you!

Hi cassie! I was so glad to hear about your show! I cant wait to come to one when I get back. I havent been to see live music since I was in middle school when I thought death metal was cool. Remember when I told you about my death metal phase? It was probably when we were walking by the river and stuff. Anyway I never told you it lasted a week because I burst my eardrum at a metal show, but I had snuck out to see that show, so I lied and told my dad that I got in a fight, and when he asked me who it was I made up a name because I'm an idiot.

The name was Rick Richardson. Richard. Richardson. I am laughing just thinking about it. The whole time I was in high school my dad thought I was in this tough guy rivalry with a very obviously made up dude named Rick Richardson. i would get home and he would be like, did that kid Richardson give you any trouble? And i was like no dad, he doesn't mess with me anymore. At one point my dad even asked me to "point him out" when we were at Jake's football game and I pointed to some random kid and I had to stop my dad from crossing the stadium to yell at his parents. Like just imagine this big military dude in your face pointing to your kid, who's name is definitely not Rick Richardson, and him being like, RICK RICHARDSON, DON'T MESS WITH MY SON.

And all because I didn't want to admit I burst my eardrum at a metal show. And you think you're an idiot for falling over on a bike. Well you kind of are. We both are. I think that's pretty clear by now in our marriage. Anyway I remember that night I told you about my metal phase, the night we walked by the river like it was yesterday. That was when I knew I would marry you. :)

Things are good here. Had a bit of a cold when I first got here but Frankie had much worse. He was shitting his brain's out. He really likes to talk about it (like I'm actually serious, he likes to talk about it much more then most people like to talk about shit) so do me a favor and don't ask him about it next time we skype. I've heard enough.

Sorry about my grammar, btw. Community college never gave me many good skills, unless you count making up various funerals for relatives so I wouldn't have to go to class for a good skill.

Love your husband,
Luke

•   •   •

To: PFC Luke Morrow
From: Cassie Salazar
Subject: RE: RE: Miss you!

Hi Rick,
You don't exist, but you're real to me.

Your archenemy's wife,
Cassandra Salazar

P.S. See you on Skype next week, Tuesday at 11 a.m. your
time?! Will give you all the updates then.

Luke

We played volleyball every day. Everyone loved volleyball here. We played soccer, too, but volleyball brought in a more diverse crowd. Everyone from six-year-olds with Mickey Mouse shirts playing over a cord tied between two poles to ANA commanding officers with trimmed, British-looking beards to older men with inch-deep wrinkles on courts that had been up since the eighties. Wherever there was a flat enough space and a net, we played.

Our usual team was me, Frankie, and a gangly eight-year-old named Ahmad, against Majeed, another, college-age interpreter; Randall, a British captain; and Franson, one of the women from the Red Horse unit I knew vaguely through Frankie. Franson actually played in high school, so they'd beat us every time.

Today she'd offered to switch with Majeed, Frankie, or me. Ahmad didn't know much English but Franson put her Oakleys on her head and smiled at him, pointing to her and to me, making a rotating motion with her hand.

Majeed interpreted.

Ahmad smiled and grabbed our uniforms as we stood on either side of him, shaking his head. "No, no, no, no."

He said something to Majeed. Majeed said, "Ahmad likes to stay on a team with Frank and Luke."

Frankie and I shrugged at each other behind our sunglasses. Ahmad and I gave each other a high five.

"We may not be good but we're fun," Frankie said.

"It's only because you let Ahmad serve every time," Franson joked, backing up to her spot, tossing the ball.

Majeed laughed.

"Yeah, Morrow and Cucciolo don't know how to serve, anyway," Randall called.

"Whatever, dude," Frankie said, bending his knees to get in the ready position. "Watch what you say or Luke will break your nose."

"All right, all right," Franson said, stepping behind the line.

She served. The ball came fast to the far-right corner and I stepped under it, bumping backward to Frankie, who set it over the net. Randall picked it up and bumped it to Franson, who spiked it hard back over off Frankie's wrists. The ball went flying in a wide arc toward the FOB. Frankie and I stood and watched it until we realized Ahmad had jetted after it, his gray perahan barely visible against the dust and glare.

"Look at him get after it!" Frankie called.

"Go Ahmad!" I yelled.

He came back smiling, but defeated, with the ball in his hands. Frankie gave him a pat on the back.

Ahmad said something and pointed to his eyes.

Majeed said, "Ahmad said he almost got it but the sun got in his face."

Without a second thought, Frankie took off his sunglasses and gave them to Ahmad. Ahmad put them on, and I had to hold in a laugh at how much they dwarfed the rest of his face. But Ahmad just tossed the ball up and caught it, slapping it, ready for business.

"That's better," Frankie said, winking at me.

Franson served again, but this time the ball went out of bounds. It was our team's serve.

"Whose turn is it?" Frankie said pointedly, turning up his hands in exaggerated curiosity. It definitely was either mine or Frankie's. Franson was right, Ahmad had served every time.

"Hm, not mine," I said.

"Not mine, either," Frankie said.

Over the net, Franson and Majeed smiled, shaking their heads. Randall scoffed.

"It's Ahmad's turn, for sure," I said, and tossed him the ball.

He ran to the line, holding his sunglasses in place, and the game carried on.

Cassie

"It's *ba-da-da-ba-da-da ba duh-duh-duh be-dum be-dum* and *then* I come in," Nora was telling Toby.

"Uh uh." Toby wagged his drumstick like a finger.

I laughed. Nora did not find it amusing.

Toby continued. "It's *ba-dada-ba-dada ba duh-duh be-dum be-DUM*, you come in on the *DUM*."

"Cassie, tell him." Nora looked at me, flipping her pick between her fingers.

"Uh." I lifted a shoulder. Toby was right. But only this time, and I didn't want Nora to think I was taking his side. "Let's just play again and find out!"

We launched into "Merlin," and I went into the forest. This song was less about foraging and more about chopping undergrowth. Staccato blades, an easy rhythm, bossa nova–influenced. Toby really was at the heart of this one, keeping the beat driven forward but the overall mood of the song light. With the wrong production it could sound like the theme song to *The Jetsons*, but it was in good hands.

Nora stopped again. "I'm not feeling that, Toby. I can't pick that up. I have to come in *after* the *be-dum*."

"Mm," Toby said, and played a quick train beat. "Fine. Let's just call it. Cassie and I wanted to catch a movie anyway."

"Do you want me to pick this up or not?" Nora said, looking back and forth from me to Toby. I avoided her eyes, and popped open a can of sparkling water.

Toby said slowly, "I do, but I'm tired."

Nora said something like "poor baby" under her breath. "Cass? For real?"

"I'm good with giving it a rest," I said. "It's Thursday."

"What the hell does Thursday have to do with anything?" Nora checked her phone. "It's seven thirty! It's been an hour. We can't call rehearsal now."

Toby said, "I'll do whatever Cassie wants to do," but he was already standing up, setting his sticks in place on his snare.

"Um." I weighed the options. We wanted to catch a showing of *Tombstone* in Pease Park. "I've never seen *Tombstone*, and we wanted to get a blanket and a bottle of something. À la Paree," I joked. I turned off my keyboard.

Toby stepped over his set and wrapped his arms around my waist. "Plus I quote it all the time . . ."

I put my hands on his hands, running them up his solid forearms. "And I never know if he's quoting something or just speaking nonsense words." I looked up at him. He stuck out his tongue. I giggled.

"We can pick this up over the weekend, Nor," I told her. "I promise. It's just been a long week."

Toby looked at Nora. "You can come if you want."

"I'd rather die in my own vomit, thanks," Nora said. She lifted her bass strap over her head.

"No, come!" I broke from Toby, and hooked my arm in Nora's.

"Nah," she said, and gave me a small smile, freeing herself to put away her bass. My heart sank. I could feel judgment coming off her like heat. Maybe I wasn't spending enough time with her. Maybe she was feeling left out. It used to be Nora and me escaping from practice.

"Cassita!" Toby called, pulling out the keys to his pickup.

"Just a sec," I said.

"K, I'm going to get the truck and bring it around," he said, and jogged up the stairs. He paused at the top, and ran back down. He extended his face toward mine. I gave him a kiss, my face burning under Nora's eyes. "There," he said, and ran back up.

"Sorry," I said to her. "He's cute but he's a bit much."

She nodded toward where Toby had disappeared from. "So you guys are, like, dating seriously now? Like, going to public parks and holding hands and making out?"

I felt a smile creep over my face. Other than rehearsal and Luke's occasional funny quips, seeing Toby was what I looked forward to all week. "Yeah."

"Huh," Nora said, her face puzzled. Then she was silent. She took out her ponytail, letting her curtain of hair hang loose, picked up a couple of empty cans from the ground.

"What?" I asked. What was puzzling about that? I mean, other than the fact that neither of us had ever expected to call Toby my boyfriend.

She straightened, raising her eyebrows at me. "I don't know," she said, sarcastic. "Is it pretty common for army wives to make out with Gumby-looking hipsters in their spare time?"

She had a point. Technically, legally, I was cheating on Luke.

"I've considered that," I said. Of course I'd considered that. For a few disparate minutes between putting on and taking off my clothes and checking my blood sugar and all the other shit I was supposed to do, I'd thought about how I probably should be more careful. And then I thought about the conversation we'd had by the playground before Luke shipped out and wondered if it would help the divorce look real once he got back. If there was a way to spin it if we did get caught.

Nora continued, "So you know that if someone that knows both you and Luke sees you with another man, there will be questions."

I swallowed, my mouth suddenly dry. "I know."

"And the questions will lead to talking, the talking will lead to reporting . . ." Nora said.

"But Luke and I don't know any of the same people," I pointed out. I told her to recall Chili's, and how unlikely it was that our circles would intersect.

Nora shrugged. "Someone's always watching. Haven't you seen *House of Cards*?"

I let out a laugh, half because it was funny, half because she was making me nervous. I did not want to feel nervous. I wanted to lie on a blanket in Pease Park and listen to Toby drawl along to Val Kilmer and Kurt Russell in his raspy, Arkansas way.

"I see what you're saying," I said to Nora, nodding, trying to clench my brows to look serious. "I will definitely be careful."

I felt my pocket vibrate. Probably Toby, waiting out in the truck. We had to stop at the liquor store before we got there. And everything seemed to take twice as long with him. We were always laughing or teasing or forgetting why we came to the store in the first place. I started to take a few steps toward the door.

Nora followed.

"You're going to the park anyway, huh," Nora muttered next to me as we ascended the stairs.

"Yeah." I sighed. She could read me like a book. "I'm just having fun."

"Oh, Cassie," she said, a note of resignation in her voice. She patted my back. "Don't let anyone ever tell you you're afraid of fire."

Luke

Skype had gotten a lot easier. I was telling Cassie a funny story Hailey had written me about JJ, how he had taken his stuffed turtle named Franklin to preschool and got in trouble for taking off the toy shell and telling everyone in his class that Franklin was "naked." Cassie insisted that he shouldn't have gotten in trouble for that, that he was just stating a fact.

"It's a Presbyterian preschool in Buda, Texas," I told her as I sewed up a hole in one of my socks. "And he didn't really get in trouble. The teacher just told Jake and Hailey, that's all."

"Still. That shouldn't even be a thing."

Around Thanksgiving, after I'd sent three letters with no response, Hailey had finally started writing back to me. I got the first one last week: She'd said Jake knew that she was writing, that he appreciated it but wasn't ready to respond, but she'd like to keep in touch, make sure that they knew I was safe, at least.

Meanwhile, Rooster was behind me, cleaning his gun with shaving cream. Cassie had to stop herself from staring at it in abject fear. When he clicked the safety on, she jumped and let out a little scream, all the way from Austin.

I couldn't help but laugh at her. A moment later, she started laughing, too.

"What else?" she'd asked.

It had been three weeks since we last spoke. I told her about volleyball.

I had even started a letter to my dad. Hadn't gotten much further than *Dear Dad, I'm sorry* without crossing everything out, but earlier drafts had things like *I'm learning a lot, I'm becoming a better man. How are those Cowboys looking?*

I looked back at Rooster, who had moved on from cleaning his gun to doing sit-ups, conveniently in sight of the laptop's camera, of course. It was a small room, but he didn't have to make those grunting noises.

I looked back at Cassie. We were both trying not to laugh.

"So," I said, glancing at my notes. "Savages? The band?"

"Oh, good. Yeah. So underrated. They are going to blow up, I swear to God," she began.

As she spoke, I began to want a little more—I wanted to know what her own music sounded like. After a pause in her description of a "love-hate" relationship with something called *Pitchfork*, I asked her.

"What about you?" I said. "How's your music coming?"

"Great," she said.

"Can I hear something?"

She looked surprised, and then happy. "Yes, yeah. Definitely. Be right back."

I wasn't a connoisseur, but I was human. Everyone liked music. I liked the classic-rock station my dad played on a boom box in the garage. Led Zeppelin. David Bowie. Doobie Brothers. Moody Blues. The Doors. Janis Joplin. The ill-advised metal phase.

I snorted to myself thinking about the e-mail where I told her about Rick Richardson. I would have never thought to tell anyone about that—I'd hardly thought of it since it happened. There was something so unapologetic about calling and writing with Cassie that brought out parts of me that I'd forgotten.

Cassie was back, humming to herself, setting an open notebook beside her on the couch.

As she set up her keyboard, I found myself wishing I could tell Cassie about listening to classic rock in the garage. When I was a kid, I knew how much my dad loved the song "Spirit in the Sky" by Norman Greenbaum, so I used to call in to V100 and request it for him. I did it so much that they started to note our number on their caller ID and answered each time with "Hi, Luke. 'Spirit in the Sky'?"

"Are you ready?" Cassie asked. "This one's a little rough, but it's getting there."

"Go ahead," I said. Rooster had stopped doing sit-ups, I'd noticed, and was now lying on the floor on his back, listening.

"This is called 'Green Heron,'" she said, and played a chord. "And imagine this with bass and drums behind it," she added.

"Okay," I said.

"Okay," Rooster said from the floor.

"When I saw you, you were on the fence," she sang, and flourished the keys. *"They said you weren't a sign from God. I didn't know what that meant. But when I walked to you, you didn't fly away."*

After that introduction, she played a rhythmic, almost old-timey section. Every time I thought I knew the beat, it swept off to another. But it always returned, too. It wasn't off the rails or hard to listen to, like jazz. It made its own kind of sense.

The lyrics were about her mother, about not knowing what to do, about forgiving herself for not knowing what to do, and her voice was dramatic and sweeping, a combination of Billie Holiday, if Billie Holiday were one octave lower, and Freddie Mercury. She seemed to skip shame and go straight to forgiveness. I'd never learned how to do that.

"Man, that was good! Goddamn!" I found myself saying as she finished.

"That was really, really good," Rooster said from the floor. "I almost cried a little bit."

"What'd he say?" Cassie said, wearing a big smile, catching her breath. She had put her hair up into a little ponytail at the top of her head, and now it was almost gone, the strands having fallen as she played, nodding along.

"He said he cried a little bit."

"Almost!" Rooster corrected.

"Wow," I said. "Nice work. That's great. Really great. Honey," I added with a sideways glance at Rooster.

"Thank you," Cassie said, her cheeks reddening. Was she blushing? Or just flushed after singing? "Well, I should go. Gotta go to work."

"Okay, we'll talk in a few."

"Thanks for asking me to play for you, Luke. Baby," she said, scratching her head, embarrassed.

"You're welcome." I swallowed. Here it was. The time when we said those words. Before I could start, Cassie was scrawling something on a piece of paper, and held it up. *I think we did really well today.*

I grabbed my Moleskine to reply. *Me too. Keep the emails coming.*

"Are y'all showing each other your privates?" Rooster called from the floor. "I want to play online solitaire and Skype sucks up all the Internet."

"All right, all right," I said. I rolled my eyes at Cassie. "I love you, honey." It rolled out easier this time.

Cassie gave me a knowing smile, turning up one corner of her lips. "Love you, too, babe."

It was smoother from her end, too. Then she crossed her eyes at me, sticking out her tongue.

As the call ended and I pushed back from the green table, I realized I was smiling to myself.

To: PFC Luke Morrow
From: Cassie Salazar
Subject: What did you REALLY think?

So I know you were trying to be nice to your wifey in front of your bunkmate about my new song but I'm actually curious about what you thought for real, since you and Push-Up Rooster are the first people to hear that who aren't in a band with me. Nora said it's one of my best, and Toby said it was good, too. Your opinion also matters to me because not only are you my husband but you're someone who doesn't listen to a lot of current music, and if you actually DID like it, I would want to do more stuff like that, because I don't just want to play songs that appeal to obscure Pitchfork people (the blog I was telling you about, not a strange alien race of people with pitchforks for heads).

So when you get a chance between volleyball games, shoot me an email.

Love, C

PS Please please PLEASE tell me you wear spandex when you play and if so, pix or it didn't happen

•　　•　　•

To: Cassie Salazar
From: PFC Luke Morrow
Subject: RE: What did you REALLY think?

It was one of the best songs I ever heard. I was thinking to myself the whole time that your voice sounded like a combination between Billie Holiday and Freddy Mercury from Queen. I also really love how it changed up in the middle, fast and slow, fast and slow, but without seeming too jerky. It was natural sounding. Don't listen to Toby, it was better than good.

We're going out on a scouting mission so I can't skype for a while but to tide you over here is a pic of me and Frankie and Ahmad, who has one of the best serves in the entire world. Sry about the grainy quality of the pic. It's from Majeed's cell phone. #selfie <<<Did I do that right?

Love from your husband
Luke

Cassie

I got cut from The Handle Bar early, so I had asked Toby to meet me across the street at Tucci's. We'd eaten garlic bread and pretended like we knew something about wine.

Toby was signaling to the server for another glass, and pointed to my empty one. "You going to join me?"

I nodded then took another sip of water. "So, I'm thinking The Loyal needs to go on tour soon. If I can figure out a way to get off work for a month or so."

"I'm ready whenever you are." He took a strand of my bob and rubbed it between his fingers. My hair was longer again, brushing the middle of my neck. People say your hair and fingernails grow faster when you're in love.

Oh, God, that was ridiculous. I wasn't in love.

"We'll see how this next show goes," I said, taking his hand. He smiled at me, quiet, and a wave of warmth passed through me.

But I also wasn't not in love.

My boyfriend *got* it. He'd known me from the beginning of this little band. He'd been on tour, and he was ready to drop everything and go on tour again. He'd been in bar fights and played with church groups. He'd broken down on the side of the road, taken payment in the form of baked goods. All so he could play. He understood what music meant to me, because it meant as much to him.

Toby had even gotten us a show at the Sahara Lounge. And this time, we weren't splitting the marquee with anyone. It was just The Loyal, for an hour, playing the new stuff we'd put into our album.

"I want to take you home," he said, reaching to brush a thumb across my cheek.

"My home or your home?" I asked, already feeling the nerves alight in my thighs.

My phone vibrated in my purse. I reached in to turn off the ringer, figuring it was my mom or Nora. They could wait till morning.

"Ready for the check?" a black-clad server asked.

"Yessir," Toby said, placing his credit card on the table.

"Can I split it with you?" I asked.

He shook his head, folding his lips over that sweet gap of his, smiling with his eyes.

The phone vibrated again. Another call. I pulled it out and noticed it was from an overseas number, or what I figured was an overseas number.

"I better get this," I told Toby as we stood up from the table.

"K, I'm going to use the restroom real quick," he said, and walked away.

I answered.

"Cassandra Salazar?" a woman said quickly.

"Yes?"

"This is Captain Grayson, of the Thirty-fourth Red Horse Infantry Division. Ma'am, I'm calling because your husband, Luke Morrow, has been injured in the line of duty."

I stopped breathing. I blinked twice, mechanical and slow.

"Ma'am, are you there?"

"Yes." *Injured?*

"Your husband's been evac'd to an army facility in Germany. In two days, he'll be transferred to the Brooke Army Medical Center in San Antonio. I'm sorry to have to give you this news, ma'am."

I unlocked my jaw, sat down at the table, feeling tears hit my eyes. "Is he going to be okay?"

"He's in stable condition, but seriously injured. Bullets shattered his shin and kneecap. He should be ready for transfer very soon."

"Okay."

"We'll keep you posted on his status."

"Thank you," I said, because it was all I could think to say. Then, "Can he talk? Who— Who do I call for news?"

"He's unable to talk at the moment," she said. "We'll be in touch as soon as we can. Good-bye, ma'am, and God bless you." The line went dead.

My heart was beating so hard, my eyesight flashed red and black. He had told me in an e-mail that he might be on a mission. And it had almost killed him. Good lord, what about Frankie? Was Frankie okay? I should have asked. I should have asked more about both of them.

The sunlit hotel room came back to me. Luke had handed me the piece of paper, the number scrawled with a motel pen. *Your husband*, she had said. My husband.

Toby returned from the bathroom whistling, hands in pockets. When he saw my face, he stopped.

"I have to go home," I told him.

He drove me, though I was unable to answer his chorus of *Cassie, you can tell me. I'll help you. Just tell me if everything's okay. Cassie?*

Where was the paper? Where was the goddamn, stupid fucking piece of paper? I had put it in the junk drawer in the kitchen. Last month's Internet bill. Last month's electricity bill. A smaller, lighter paper. Was this it? No. A fucking take-out receipt. Why the hell had I saved a take-out receipt?

I emptied the drawer onto the kitchen floor.

Key from a bike lock I'd never used. Pennies. Bottle caps from when Nora's niece needed them for her school fund-raiser. More pennies. Nickels. A tiny gift bag from when one of Mom's clients had given their staff "Merry Christmas chocolates." No more pieces of paper.

I moved to my room, searching the drawer in my bedside table.

A leather journal to which I had contributed two lines. A pack of condoms. A guitar pick Nora and I suspected belonged to Jack White after The White Stripes had played The Moody Theater.

For three hours I searched, tearing apart my apartment, finding nothing. I sat on my couch around two a.m. The quiet was quieter than normal. I eyed the keyboard, thinking about playing something to ease my anxiety, but found I couldn't even touch the keys.

I heard a small tap on the door, footsteps on the stairs. I looked through the keyhole. It was Rita, holding Dante, who appeared to be half asleep. I opened the door.

"You moving out up here?" she asked, her pink bathrobe open to an oversized T-shirt reading JUST TELL ME WHERE THE CHOCOLATE IS AND NO ONE GETS HURT.

"No." I sighed. "I was looking for a piece of paper with someone's information. That I need really badly, like, right away."

"Someone's information?"

"Yeah, like their phone number. Anyway. Sorry to disturb you."

"Wanna smoke?"

"I don't have any." I'd stopped buying when I got diagnosed. Every penny I earned went to bills, medical supplies, or music now.

"I didn't ask if you did," she said, and pulled a joint from behind her ear.

"Thank God," I muttered.

We sat in our usual spots, not having to talk, passing the joint back and forth, letting the marijuana bathe the destroyed room in a haze. I put on Donovan.

After a while, Rita repeated, "Someone's information. Hm."

"Yeah," I said.

"Did you try Google? For this person's number?" Rita asked, coughing a bit as she exhaled.

The sharpness came back. Google. Fucking *duh*. Panic had scrambled my brain. Of course I should do a Google search. "Rita, you're a genius."

"Tell that to my job," Rita said. "They just fired me."

"Damn, Rita," I said. "I'm sorry."

She shrugged, stretching as she stood. "Everyone's losing their jobs these days."

I grabbed my laptop from the floor. Morrow, Morrow, Morrow. Now, what was his first name? The e-mails. Luke's e-mails with the questions I was supposed to ask during our Skype calls—Luke had written the name there. "Let me know if there's anything I can do."

"Just keep payin' your rent on time," she called as she opened the door. "I'll see ya later. Come, Dante." Dante clicked across the floor.

As the door shut, I typed. There it was. *Morrow Garage, Buda, TX.* If I called now, no one would answer. If I left within the hour, I'd be there at sunrise.

Luke

*C*ucciolo, I was saying. *Cucciolo.* But I was lying down and there were three suns and my mouth was made of rubber. Frankie wouldn't turn. I needed him to turn around because they were shooting at us. We had ducked behind the jeep and they were shooting. Rooster was on the ground.

The shooting wasn't bullets but beeps. Beeping.

But then for some reason we were back at my dad's garage. Why were they shooting? Get them out of my dad's garage. It was lunchtime. It wasn't time for people to shoot at my dad and my brother. I had to get up from this bed. I had to protect them.

Rooster was taking a nap under the jeep on a red pillow. *How can he sleep right now?*

I couldn't get up because the bottom half of me was a tree, a trunk where my legs should be. It was growing, cracking my skin, bark made of knives, stabbing.

I screamed because it hurt. *Someone cut this tree off!* I screamed.

Three suns were so bright. People were talking funny. I was, too. *Cucciolo.* No one was listening.

They put a piece of rubber on my face.

Blue and white and blue and white.

The tree grew again. I screamed.

"Goot, goot," they were saying. "Ess weird goot sign."

"Not goot," I said, but the rubber got in the way. "Frankie."

Frankie. Not good. Someone cut this tree off.

Frankie.

Cassie

Dads and I do not mix. Never had one, didn't want one, didn't need one. Didn't like them when they verbally abused my fourth-grade rec-league soccer refs, didn't like when they got too drunk at *quinceañeras*, didn't like how they rolled their eyes at my college friends' majors from their La-Z-Boys.

Dads and I especially did not mix when I was running off no sleep, three bites of tikka masala, and a joint with my landlady. I rumbled down the main drag of Buda, gas tank low, past the mom-and-pop stores and trucks parked in front almost as big as the buildings themselves, fast food trash skittering near the curbs. I scanned the buildings for the red-and-white sign I'd seen on the website.

When I found it, I got out, ready to knock on the door and see Luke's brother. A brother, I'd imagined, who would be a nicer version of Luke. A younger, jumpsuited guy looking like an ensemble member of *Grease*, with a cherubic toddler hanging on his pant leg, who'd usher me into an office with leather chairs next to a sorority girl wife with moist eyes. They'd all listen and tell me what to do.

Instead, the garage was closed. *Back in five. If it's an emergency I'm at Morts getting coffee*, a handwritten sign had read.

So I waited. I waited for five, then five more. I called the number that had called me last night in hopes there would be an update on Luke's condition, but I couldn't get through. I gathered my dress and sat in the middle of a cement square bordered with weeds, watching the tricked-out cars pass at fifteen to twenty miles an hour. Mothers pushed kids in strollers, blowing smoke from their cigarettes away from their babies' lungs as they complained into their phones about someone who had done them wrong. I sent a text to Toby, telling him sorry, and that I'd call him soon.

Then Luke's dad came up the walk with a Styrofoam take-out coffee in hand. Legs up to the chest, triangle jaw, but with ghost-white hair and a stooped back. Unmistakable.

I thought about getting up and walking away. Luke had talked about his brother working for the garage, so I figured I'd see him first. I figured the dad would be puttering about in the back somewhere, running the books.

It occurred to me that Luke had given me his brother's number. That Luke had told me to contact him first.

"How can I help, ma'am?" he asked, pulling out his keys. His hands were thick and strong with gray, wiry hairs.

How could he help? "Uh. Well." I stood, brushing gravel. "So," I began.

He pressed a lever to the side of the door, creaking open the wide garage.

"Is that your car?" he said, pointing to my Subaru in a long line of cars parked on the street.

I tilted my head. "How did you know that?"

"Buda's a small town," he said, turning around and striding toward my car.

"Sir," I began again, following him. "Sir, I'm not here for car trouble."

"Is that so?" he answered, unhooking the hood, propping it on its metal stand. "Then why are you waiting outside my garage?"

I recognized his casual stride from the way Luke walked back and forth through a room, as if no one were there, as if he were alone in the woods. But he meant no harm. He was aggressive without the anger. Just matter-of-fact, grabbing on to something he could play with, like a kid goes for a toy left out on the table.

I let him unscrew something or other, making contemplative noises to himself. And then I took a deep breath.

"Sir, I'm married to your son Luke," I began.

He bolted upward, banging his head on the edge of the hood.

"Ma'am?" he said, holding a purple-veined arm to the back of his head, scowling.

"My name is Cassie Salazar and I'm your son's wife and he's been injured overseas." It came out as three facts. Another great thing about not having a dad is not really being afraid of dads.

He dropped his hand and the *how can I help you?* demeanor, taking a step toward me. "Overseas as in serving in the military? Luke Morrow?"

I was suddenly aware of my tattoos and tangled hair and red-rimmed eyes. I put my hands on my hips. "Yes, sir. His kneecap was shattered by bullets in Afghanistan."

For a second, he said nothing. I thought I saw his jaw twitch, but I couldn't be sure. "Is he coming home?"

"Tomorrow."

He looked back at the garage, void of customers, and pulled out an old brick-style Nokia cell phone, spitting on the ground. "That son of a bitch."

Luke

There are three kinds of pain. There's physical pain, handed to you in gasping, sharp doses. No rhythm to it. Just mad stabbing when the whim hits, like a steel rod into the flesh of a peach. That's the kind of pain I felt in flashes on the trip to Munich, watching the shadows of paramedics cross the cabin lights.

When Frankie and I had stepped out from behind the jeep, the pain had announced itself, bloody and throbbing. The bullets had pummeled my knee and upper shin until it was a useless sack, but the pain shoved me forward, pushing me to hold the gun tighter, stand straighter with the leg that was left.

"They're picking us off from the northwest hill," Clark had said between rounds.

It'd been so quiet. Wind had whipped the NATO flag on the hood.

"Let's get back in and get a better position."

"We can't," Clark said. "Probably mines ahead."

Everyone was breathing hard. In sync, in harmony, even then. My socks were wet, sticky, squishing in my boots. I shouldn't have looked down. Someone's boots had fallen off their feet, splattered red. Two other pairs of boots, on a pair of bodies on the ground, faces obstructed.

They had started shooting again.

Then there was the ache that had smothered me when I woke up in the hallway of Brooke Medical Center back in America. It covered me like a blanket, lulling me to sleep, calling me to some higher purpose, whispering in a sweet voice, *You don't have to worry anymore, your job is to suffer, and that's it. Don't get up, don't fight, all you have to do is bear it.*

I'd heard deep Texas accents answering phones. I'd looked at the hand holding the bars of my gurney. Each nail was painted with a tiny Santa Claus.

Between the physical pain and the ache, or on top of them, or all around them, is the third kind. I suppose you'd call it emotional or mental pain, but that would imply it was knowable, that it could be labeled and stored somewhere in the brain, and you'd just keep on living.

No. Every thought, from *my arm itches* to *what am I going to do now?* was suspended on hooks over a dark sea. There was what was happening, then it got snagged on what happened.

What was happening: Thirty steel pins in my leg the previous afternoon. An indefinite stay. A view of the parking lot.

What happened: *That morning Gomez showed the British officers that they were cleaning dishes wrong. They ended up squirting one another with bottles of soap.*

I might walk, I might not. Two more people in scrubs had looked over the doctor's clipboard when he said that yesterday, then to my leg, then back to the clipboard.

Our room with the crummy wood paneling, shaving mirror standing on the green table, the exposed pipes, blankets folded in the corner where we'd left them, would be empty.

Frankie was gone.

An army nurse in Germany had told me he was gone. There was a knock on the door frame.

Rooster was gone, too. The volleyball team would have to find new players.

The door was always open here. Just in case.

Ahmad, the eight-year-old who loved to serve and dive after wild hits, would be asking where we were today.

"Private Morrow?"

I turned my head on the pillow. A gray-haired man stood in the doorway. "Yes, sir."

"Lieutenant Colonel Ray Yarvis, Medical Service Corps. Welcome to Brooke."

I brought a stiff arm up to salute. He returned it. "Every new intake gets assigned a social worker, and I'm your guy."

He sat, bending over a paunch, and took in the damage. He had deep lines around his mouth and eyes, which were a silvery, pool-water blue. He had a two-packs-a-day voice, just like the guy who ran the lotto booth at Mort's, the corner shop in Buda. He was the first person here to look me in the eye.

"I do this job because I've been where you are. Served two tours in Vietnam, now walking on a titanium foot." He pointed to his left shin. "Anything you feel you can't ask your doctors, you tell me. You pissed at the army? You tell me. I'm your buffer."

I tried to bring some moisture to my mouth. "Did they tell you if I'm going to walk again?"

"I think you are."

"Yeah, but—"

He held up a chubby hand. "If they said maybe, they're just covering their butts. Judging by other men I've seen with pins, I bet you'll be up in a few weeks."

For a minute, I came up out of the haze. "That's good."

"We'll talk more, but there are people waiting outside to see you."

"What people?" I grew a dim, stupid hope. Someone from my company. Captain Grayson. Frankie, not dead after all.

"Your people." He nodded to the door. "Your kid brother and folks."

"Oh. Yeah."

"You sure? I can tell them you pressed the morphine button too hard."

A laugh escaped. "No. Thank you, sir."

He stood with a grunt. "Okay, Morrows," he called. "You can come on in."

The first to enter was Hailey, elephant-walking JJ, who was clinging to her leg, his light-up sneakers balanced on one of her sandaled feet. Then Jake, scooting past her holding a Dr Pepper and a *Sports Illustrated*.

I didn't know whether to be elated or just pretend I was asleep. I wasn't ready. I was still knee-deep in Afghan quicksand and Frankie's dead eyes and the horde of woodpeckers that were hacking at my leg.

"Got you a DP," Jake was saying. "They were out of everything except for that and orange soda."

Jake had gotten me a DP. He'd not only driven from Buda to San Antonio with his wife and kid, he'd stopped at the vending machine. I wondered if it was out of pity, or the desire for reconciliation, or both. Either way I caught his eyes as I took the cold bottle, opening it to find it was the best Dr Pepper I'd ever tasted.

"Thank you, Jake," I said, hoping whatever I was doing with my face resembled a smile. "It's so good to see you."

"You look like a stranger. Damn, they did a number on you, huh?" Jake replied.

"Just got out of another surgery yesterday," I told him. The bullets had almost shattered my leg in two. It was saved by a metal plate, and five screws to hold my knee together.

Then I noticed Cassie slide in against the wall, eyes down, clutching her purse with white knuckles. She made a beeline for the bed, leaning over me for a light kiss on the cheek, her chest pressing mine.

"I'm sorry," she whispered.

When she backed away from the bed, I noticed another body.

There, between Jake and Hailey, was my dad. Judging by the apology, I'm guessing Cassie had contacted him. Why the hell she decided to do that, I didn't know. I searched for what to say, wondering if he was just biding his time before he told me I owed him money.

He looked thinner, paler, than the last time I'd seen him. He was chewing sunflower seeds, spitting the shells into a paper cup. I was already starting to feel inadequate and stupid all over again, frail and dumb in my thin white robe and gimp leg.

"Hey, Dad," I said, the words like goo in my mouth.

"Luke," he said, glancing at me for a total of about a half millisecond before his eyes went back to the TV above my bed.

"So we met your—" Hailey took her hand off JJ's head to gesture at Cassie. "Your wife."

"Yep," Cassie said in her fake upbeat voice, nodding from the wall. "Great to finally meet y'all. Luke's told me so much about you."

"We don't know jack shit about you," Jake said with a half-smile.

"Babe!" Hailey scolded.

"What?" Jake shrugged, glancing at me with a *what the fuck?* face. "Guess out of everyone I know, it makes the most sense Luke would have a shotgun wedding. He's always been so fucking impulsive."

Cassie and I caught each other's gaze.

"When you know, you know." Cassie looked at Hailey, her head tilted as if she were overcome with adoration. "Right?"

Cassie then turned her gaze at me, urging me with a look only I could see. *Romantic phrases, romantic phrases, romantic phrases.* I couldn't think of a single one. I mean, Jesus, I'd been through a lot in the last forty-eight hours. Sue me if I wasn't feeling like fucking Fabio. My hands started to feel clammy.

I took the Dr Pepper from where I'd set it on the side table, and turned to her with the sweetest look I could muster. "Wanna sip, honey?"

"Thank you, darlin'," she said, and I could almost hear her teeth clench.

Yeah, sorry, I tried to tell her with my eyes. *Not my best.*

She took the tiniest drop, almost none at all. Then I remembered. *Diabetes, you idiot.*

"Well, I'm still pretty exhausted," I said. As much I wanted to talk to Jake, I was too tired to fake it with Cassie right now. She looked like she was on her last bit of fuel, too.

"We'll leave you to it," Hailey said, and she and Jake turned toward the door.

Dad spit another shell and stepped out of the room without a nod. But he had come. That said a lot.

"Are y'all—" I called, and Jake paused. "Are y'all gonna come back?"

Hailey looked at Jake.

"I'd love to have you back," I added, and tried not to sound desperate.

"Yeah, I mean, but we're not all roses," Jake said, his eyebrows knit together, glancing at Cassie. "I'm not gonna, like, change your bedpan."

"I wouldn't expect you to," I said.

"But, yeah, we'll come back," he said. Hailey nodded. "The fact that you got close to being taken." He paused, swallowing. "That puts a lot of things in perspective, doesn't it?"

At the doorway, Hailey whispered something in JJ's ear.

"Tank you for the LEGOs!" he called.

My heartbeat was still fast as they left, but I felt energized, hopeful.

Cassie was still against the wall, slumped, but her lips were turned up, watching them go. She pulled a chair next to my bed. "Any news of Frankie?" she asked.

The smiles left both our faces in turn.

Cassie

I'd gotten back from San Antonio a few days ago, after spending as little time as possible with Luke's family. It wasn't too hard. I still didn't know the whole deal with all of them, but no one seemed to want to really talk, anyway.

Frankie was dead. That was all I could think about. Just when I'd forget, something would remind me again. Right now it was the smell of potato chips. This kept happening. One moment I was fine, happy even, and the next I would burst into tears. Frankie had always smelled like potato chips because his mom put them in his lunch every day, and instead of eating them all at once, he had liked to carry them around with him in a Ziploc baggie. He'd do that thing where he'd position them in his mouth to make it look like he had a duck beak. Cassie, look, he'd say, and I'd look up from whatever sand structure I was building. Ha ha, I'd say, and roll my eyes, because he did that every day.

Now he was erased from the Earth. Every time I was reminded of this fact, I was shocked all over again, like my whole body had stepped on a tack.

I wiped my eyes on the sleeve of Toby's giant Longhorns sweatshirt. I was lying on his floor.

"Hey! Hey." Toby looked down at me. "Are you okay?"

"Just thinking," I said, swallowing what was left of the tears.

"Family stuff again?"

"Kind of." I hadn't figured out how to tell Toby any of it. It felt like explaining Frankie meant explaining Luke, and that felt so small compared to anything else. Where I knew I should feel guilt about lying to Toby, I felt only grief. I had never lost someone before Frankie.

"Well. Get up. Let me cheer you up."

I sniffed and sat up.

A dissonant chime echoed through Toby's apartment. Topy looked at me. My phone.

"I thought I'd left it at home again," I muttered, making my way down the hall. I found it sitting near the front door, on the table where he kept his keys. A number I didn't recognize lit up the screen. *Something's wrong with Luke.* My stomach dropped.

"Hello?" I asked, my fists clenched.

"Cassie?" It was a man's voice, unfamiliar.

"Yeah," I said, my mind flipping through the worst.

"This is Josh van Ritter, with Wolf Records."

Wolf Records? My brain was trying to catch up. Not Luke. Not bad. Good. Very good. "Oh, hi!" I said, trying to make my voice sound normal.

"Yeah, are you familiar?"

Was I familiar with one of the biggest indie labels putting out right now? Uh. Yeah. "Very. I mean, huge fan," I told him, padding as quickly as I could to Toby's room, and pointing to the phone, my mouth open in a joyful silent scream. I put the call on speaker.

"So Todd Barker, the manager for Les RAV, sent me your Bandcamp page and I'm interested to see what else you've got going on."

Toby had sat up in his bed and scooted, somewhat undignified, to the edge, and was now riveted. He glanced at me and said, loud, "Hi, Toby Masters here, also in The Loyal. I hope you don't mind Cassie's got you on speaker."

"Hi there, Toby. So I see you've got a few singles up. Do you have a full EP as well?"

"Kind of, but we have new stuff, too," I said, matching his quick words, pacing around Toby's room. "I can send you our first EP and we'll probably get more tracks out after the New Year."

"Tell you what, I'm booked solid until the end of the year, and it's kind of crucial that our bands tour anyway, so I'd love to see you live. I'm going to fly down for your show in March at the . . ."

"Sahara Lounge," Toby filled in.

"Right. You play me songs for a full album, we'll talk. Sound good?"

After exchanging contact info, we hung up happy. My head spinning around with which of the new stuff to play, heart fluttering, walking to the kitchen on the balls of my feet.

Toby followed.

"That was Wolf Records," I said to Toby, manic. "On the phone."

Toby's voice went high. "Cassie. That was Wolf Records as in *Wolf Records*. Holy shit."

"That's the one." I smiled, feeling my head shake, shocked.

He laughed, and began to talk logistics.

Suddenly, as had happened several times over the last forty-eight hours, my thoughts ran smack into a wall. I could barely move from room to room, let alone think about banging on an instrument in front of people.

I sniffed, trying to make my throat loose again.

"T, I need a second."

"Okay, no problem," he said, absent, still flipping through records. "I'll just find this real quick."

He held out the album, a preacher with a Bible. "You know how many bands would *kill* to be considered by Wolf Records?"

I sighed, pushing sleeves to my eyes, wishing his giant sweatshirt would swallow me whole so I could be in darkness and softness and nothingness. "Yes. I do happen to know that," I muttered.

"They're one of the only indie labels that puts out *Billboard*-level stuff. They've got great shit going on. And they want us!"

"I know!" I shouted. "I fucking know that!"

He stared at me, mouth open. Tears were coming soon. I clenched my gut hard, keeping them in. I hated feeling like a child, like a kid who'd gotten sick at a sleepover and was ruining the fun. I opened my mouth and took a breath, holding the small, rocky ocean that had started to occupy my stomach whenever I thought about the last few days.

Toby opened his arms. I went to him. Lorraine, Toby's cat, seemed to understand. She wound between our ankles, purring. "Remember my friend who was in the army?"

"Yeah," he said, and I could feel him tense under me.

"Well, Frankie died."

"Oh, my God. I'm so sorry, Cass," he whispered. "I didn't know."

"We've been friends since we were little," I said.

Toby said nothing, waiting, stroking my hair. I let myself remember Frankie as I'd last seen him, at the airport, looking at Elena with total devotion. I let myself remember how he looked when I'd first met him, wearing a Power Rangers shirt with his little belly always hanging out.

I breathed again, no longer able to hold back. For now, the present—the night and the floor and the cat and the feel of Toby's paisley chest against my cheek—these were the only sure things. I held him tighter, and let myself weep.

Luke

Someone was sitting beside my bed. The sound of the chair scraping on hospital tile had woken me up, and I could feel their heat near my leg. I kept my eyelids down, allowing a slit of light, but couldn't make out who it was. Must be visiting hours. If it was my nurse, Tara, she'd be pulling off the covers, lifting my legs with her cold, thin hands, chatting about her son, her feet, her car, whatever else came to mind to distract me from the fact that she'd be lifting my balls and ass into a bedpan.

This person was silent, still, maybe sleeping.

I wondered if it was my dad. He could do that, just sit in any chair and close his eyes. Long hours at the garage and taking care of two boys solo would wear you out, I guess.

I kept my eyes closed. It was a match of wills. Who would give in first?

We did not "ask questions." You were supposed to just *know*. You were supposed to just *know* how to change your brother's diaper, why the sky was blue, how to brush your teeth, if ghosts were real, how to switch the lightbulb that went out in your room, how to preheat the oven, how much shampoo was too much, who was pitching for the Rangers, how to shave your face, how to drive a stick, why your mom died.

And if you didn't know, you shut the fuck up and listened until you did.

The person in the chair shifted, sighing through his nose.

Apologies didn't happen, either. You broke something, you didn't weep and say sorry, you fixed it or figured out how to replace it. If you couldn't replace it, like I couldn't replace the goddess figurine he'd brought home for my mother from Vietnam after I'd knocked it over practicing karate, you fucked off for a while.

Forgiveness came in the form of "Rangers are playing," or an impromptu lesson in how to take out an intruder with a crowbar if he wasn't home: You run into a room and wait next to the door, and when the intruder opens it, you smack him in the balls. He let Jake and me practice on him with pillows. Probably one of the five times in my life I'd seen him laugh.

He never laid a hand on Jake or me. He signed our permission slips. He went to our football games, our parent-teacher conferences, dropped us off at birthday parties.

Maybe it was time.

Maybe I could tell him that I had fixed it, that I was sober now, that I had opted out of the stronger drugs for tramadol, even when the doctors said I could risk my spine "winding up" from too many pain signals.

Maybe him sitting here was the equivalent of him forgiving me after a few days, opening a Lone Star, turning on the TV, telling me to turn up the volume so he could hear the announcers.

Dad, I'd say, keeping it simple. Taking it slow. *How ya been?*

I opened my eyes and choked on a gasp, wishing I'd kept them closed.

Johnno turned, snapping his chin. A tobacco-stained smile grew. "Morrow! Morning, dude."

Fuck.

He stood, his windbreaker swishing, the smell of secondhand smoke washing over me. My heartbeat rose to my ears. "Welcome home, soldier. Happy New Year. They did an article about you in the *Buda Times*. I wiped my ass with it."

"Why are you here?" I asked, my tongue still slurring with sleep.

He narrowed his eyes. "Why do you think? To get paid."

I wished I had enough spit in my mouth to gather and hurl at him. After the initial shock, I had no more fear left. "I paid you. I had my bank pay you."

"You paid me half."

"We said the other half in nine months."

"We said the other half when you get back."

"I won't have it until I get severance. That will be months from now."

"Fuck that."

I pointed to my leg. "What do you want me to do?"

"You got money, I know you do. You figured it out before. I don't know what you did, but do it again."

I reached for him, just barely missing his jacket. He stepped back, laughing.

Then Johnno looked behind him at the open door, strode to it, and calmly pushed it shut.

"If you fucking try anything, I swear to God—" I started, my teeth clenched.

But my reflexes were slow. With one hand, he moved the call button out of reach, and with the other, he pressed on my leg. Softly at first, then harder, until the stabbing pain blotted out every other sensation. I tried to reach for him again, but he had moved to the end of the bed, hands moving up my shin.

"You're going to pay me half of the rest in a month, and half the month after."

"Agh!" I cried out, feeling tears come to my eyes.

Johnno let up for a second, looking behind him. The door didn't budge. He pressed again, harder. Slicing, burning, not sure if my eyes were open anymore, red, white, red, white.

He let go. Water rushed over my nerves. Eyesight returned. Johnno had pulled the newspaper out of his jacket, squinting at it, still standing over me like Death.

"'Wounded fighting at the Pakistan border with the Thirty-fourth Red Horse Infantry Division,'" he read aloud. "'Morrow will be awarded the Purple Heart for his sacrifice to the United States Armed Forces.'" He stopped, breaking into a cheesy, yellow smile. "Congratulations, Private Morrow!"

"Get the fuck out of here," I said, still reeling from pain.

"You know what else this article said, though? Said you got a wife. Little Boricua situation? Thinking I might need to look her up."

I didn't have the energy to respond. I just closed my eyes, hoping he'd go away, like a bad dream. When I opened them again, he was gone, but metal spikes were still grinding into my leg, relentless. The ache and the stabbing combined.

He was right, I guessed. I would get a Purple Heart. To be forever reminded of that moment at the jeep, of pulling Frankie's body toward mine, leaving a trail of blood in the road. The third pain, always there, always hooking me back.

Tara arrived in bright pink scrubs, her bangs freshly permed, strapping on her latex gloves and starting a story about the officer down the hall.

"Hey, Tara?" I asked, swallowing, trying to block out the semicircle of faces I'd seen at my last Narcotics Anonymous meeting at Austin Universalist, smiling at me with bright eyes. Telling me to *stay strong*.

"What is it, hon?" she said, bending my good leg.

"Tramadol isn't working. I'd like to up my medication."

Cassie

George and Louise Cucciolo held Frankie's memorial service under the hundred-foot-tall arches of St. Mary's Cathedral, dwarfing the fifty or so of us who were invited. Luke could stand with the help of a few nurses, but he could barely put any weight on the leg, and the cathedral's only wheelchair-accessible entrance was through a back door, up a noisy wooden ramp. I'd picked him up in San Antonio this morning, and we drove here in silence. It was like neither one of us knew what to say now. I hadn't really imagined what it would be like when he came home. I certainly hadn't imagined it like this.

As we rattled through the door, we realized that the ramp led not to the back of the church, where everyone was entering, but to the area behind the pulpit. We had wheeled right into the middle of an operatic rendition of "Ave Maria." We had to steer around the casket and a blown-up photo of Frankie as the tear-stained eyes of the attendees followed us in confusion. He would have found the whole thing hilarious, probably.

• • •

Once we were back in the van, Luke took off the leg brace he had to wear for certain time intervals throughout the day and asked me to hand him the bottle of painkillers. His second dose, at least since I'd been with him.

"Are you sure you should take two this close together?"

"It says 'as needed,' doesn't it?" Luke replied.

"I guess." I checked the bottle.

"Well, there you go."

"Trying to numb the pain?" I joked weakly.

"Of my leg, yeah," Luke said, his eyes out the window.

"K," I said. We'd joked in other serious moments. It was kind of one of the only ways we could communicate. But he'd ignored it.

"But seriously," I started. "Are you okay?"

Part of why I asked was to make sense of my own feelings.

Frankie was the one who brought us together, after all. I wanted to talk to the only other person who knew how it felt to lose him in the same way I did. I wanted to know that there was still a common goal, even if our link was gone.

I looked at Luke. He was resting his chin on his hand, eyes drifting. "Luke?" I said.

"Hm?" He blinked a few times. "Oh. It was sad."

It was sad? "Is that it?" I asked.

Luke's face transformed in an instant to anger. Angrier than I'd ever seen him. "What, you want me to cry? I can't just turn it on and off. That's not how grief works."

"I know. But Frankie was my friend, too. I mean—I can relate. Believe me."

He looked back out the window. "No, you can't. You weren't there."

That one got me in the gut. Of course I wasn't there. But I had been there in spirit, listening to him, writing to him. Bearing witness. If not being a true wife, then something like a friend.

I opened my mouth to respond, but stopped. This was bigger than this moment. I understood. He could stew. He could hurt. He could be angry at me now, even though I was trying to help. But not forever.

After the procession wove through Austin, Frankie was buried in Texas State Cemetery under a dull January sun. Beside me, Luke had remained hard-jawed in his dress blues. When the officers fired ceremonial shots, he twitched in his wheelchair.

Elena had tossed a turquoise necklace into the grave, one Frankie had given her before he left. Louise, a license plate that spelled FRNKIE and three white roses. George had dropped in a stack of Marvel comics. The three of them held one another and wept.

Christmas had been last week. I thought about standing up to speak with a few of his other friends, telling one of the many stories we'd shared as kids, but none of them was self-contained—if I was going to tell the story of the Barbie car, then I had to start with the Christmas of 1995 to give context, and if I told about Christmas of 1995, I'd have to compare it to the previous Christmas, the one where my mom caught us dressing in his parents' clothes.

The nurse who had driven us to the funeral waited in the van, hooking and unhooking Luke in and out like a kid to a car seat, popping handfuls of Corn Nuts. I thought I saw him crack a smile as I struggled to push Luke's chair through the grass of the cemetery.

"Bastard," I'd muttered.

Luke either hadn't heard or pretended not to hear.

Two hours later, Lieutenant Colonel Yarvis greeted us at the entrance to Brooke Army Medical Center, giving a cold nod to the nurse as he lowered Luke's platform to the ground. "That guy's a bastard," Yarvis said as soon as we were rolling back to Luke's room, out of earshot.

I decided I liked him.

"So," Yarvis said, wheezing a bit as he settled across from us. "How long have you been married?"

"Four months," I said.

"Five months," Luke said at the same time.

"We got married in the middle of August," I said, grabbing Luke's hand, burying my nails into it. That seemed to wake Luke up. *That's better, you jerk. I'm sad, too, but we have a job to do.* He cleared his throat.

Yarvis looked from me to Luke, back to me. "Well, I can't imagine the separation was easy. I know my wife and I couldn't stand to be apart in our first year, and it's clear that Cassie being able to visit you has helped a lot."

"I come when I can," I said, hoping he'd change the subject soon. The truth was I'd been there only a handful of times. An hour and forty-five minutes was a long drive, and when I did visit, we sat in silence while Luke watched the Dallas Mavericks on TV and I worked on mixing songs on GarageBand.

Luke and I tried to smile at each other. It looked more like we had gotten headaches at the same time.

Yarvis stared at his clipboard. "You've made significant progress, Private Morrow, and the doctors say you're ready to go home."

We were quiet.

Home. Okay. It took a while for what exactly that meant to set in. Luke didn't have a place, so "home" meant *my* home. What else could it mean? We were married. That was why people got married. Not to deceive the U.S. government into giving them money. Most people got married because they liked each other enough to share a home.

The silence stretched on until Luke cleared his throat. "Wow, we're obviously speechless, here."

"Yay!" I followed, lifting our clasped hands in a pathetic cheer.

"I'll be checking in on you every week or so," Yarvis said, "and of course you should be doing your physical therapy, but for now, you get to make like a tree."

"Great!" Luke offered.

"It'll still take a couple of days before we discharge you," he said. "We'll discuss your situation first, give you a chance to transition."

"Got it," Luke said, though his eyes looked glazed.

"I'll leave ya to it and let the doctor know."

When Yarvis had shut the door, Luke let go of my hand, putting his own to his forehead. "Shit," he said.

My stomach was churning. "Yeah."

"I could stay at my brother's," he suggested, but I shook my head. Both of us knew that would look too weird, unless I were to stay with him, and of course I couldn't. I had to work in Austin.

"Plus not a good idea to live near your dad, considering he's a *former army police officer*. When were you going to tell me that?"

I had overheard his father and Yarvis talking about Vietnam one day. Yarvis had asked what his dad's role was. The CID were the very people who busted illegal activity within the military. Rights violations, protocol violations, you know, stuff like *fake fucking marriages*.

"I honestly forgot," he said, shrugging.

I sighed, pinching the bridge of my nose. "What are we going to do?"

Luke put a fist to his palm. "We wait for my leg to heal, then I get an honorable discharge, then we make a plan to go our separate ways. We can get through this."

For a minute, he felt more present. It felt like we were on the same planet. The same hostile, hurtling-through-space-toward-a-black-hole planet.

Then I remembered Toby. Sweet Toby, who spent hours in my apartment, taking baths, cooking bland spaghetti, and going through a serious early-nineties hip-hop phase.

"What?" Luke said, studying my face.

"So, while you were gone, I kind of started seeing someone."

He crossed his arms over his chest. "You have a boyfriend?"

"What are you, jealous?" I asked, instinctively. But for a second our last night together flashed in front of me. I felt my cheeks burn.

He didn't respond, so I tried to make light of it, pushing him on the arm. The muscles there were rock hard.

He looked at the spot where my hand had been, and rolled his eyes. "No, I'm not jealous, but people see you have a boyfriend, then they see you have a husband, they start asking questions."

"Yeah, I know." I swallowed. "But it's not like you and I are going to be out in the same places I'm out with Toby."

"Toby?" Luke asked. "That sounds like a dog's name."

"Don't be mean."

He cleared his throat, sitting back. "So you guys are pretty serious."

Yeah! I was about to say, but it sounded off. Like I was forcing it.

I went with, "Serious enough that I don't want to break up with him because I've got a fake husband in my bed."

Luke held up his hands. "Uh, I'll sleep on the couch, thanks."

I blushed. "No, I meant you can take the bed. With your leg and all."

"We'll flip for it."

We flipped. Luke lost. I felt bad for a minute, then I remembered him comparing Toby to a dog. We sat, saying nothing, probably thinking about the same thing. Sharing a bathroom. Sharing a life. It would be different. This was real. This was sharing oxygen, and re-sources, and time I usually spent on my band, on my real boyfriend. And whatever it was that Luke would do all day. I didn't know if I could handle it. If Luke kept acting like he did today, like he was someone I'd never even met, I definitely couldn't.

Luke broke the quiet. "Are you going to tell him?"

Deep breath in, deep breath out. "Maybe when the time is right. We'll just have to avoid my apartment for a while."

"Damn, Cassie," Luke said, reaching for his pills, his lips lifting into a half-smile. "What the hell are you going to say?"

Luke

The morning of my release, I sat with Cassie in the fluorescent cafeteria behind weak cups of coffee. We held each other's sweaty hands, gazing at a quietly wheezing Yarvis, my surgeon, Dr. Rosen, and Fern, a young woman from the Quality of Life Foundation with glasses and black dreadlocks wrapped into a bun.

I had taken OxyContin this morning, and was resisting taking another one, though my leg was sore down to the bone from physical therapy and the doctor palpating it to check my progress. I wanted to be able to listen, to be present. The surgeon's jargon was making that hard, words like *distal third tibia* and *fibula* and *fractured patella* washing over me in a dull blur.

"Since we were able to fuse the patella, we'll just be looking to avoid nerve damage, atrophy in the quad muscle, and possibly cartilage fusing your knee in a straight position. But you've been progressing pretty well with flexibility, it looks like, so that doesn't seem to be too much of a risk."

That last part I understood. Yarvis muttered, "Atta kid."

"Now that your patella has begun to heal, we'll move on from the static quadriceps exercises you've been doing to knee flexion. The idea is to get you partially weight bearing with support, then gradually weight bearing once we see little periosteal callus on the twelve-week serial X-ray."

"Per— callus?" I asked, wishing I had paid better attention when they showed me the X-rays the first time.

"A mass of tissue that forms at a fracture site to establish continuity between the bone ends. So, basically, the mushy glue holding your bones together. We want it to start disappearing as your bones heal."

"So when that disappears, I get out of the wheelchair?"

"It depends." Everything depended. "We want you to be up now, but not fully weight bearing. We'll do a slower incremental increase in weight, bearing twenty-five percent, fifty percent, seventy-five percent, one hundred percent with a cane, then complete free bearing."

A cane? Like an old man. At least I could move around on my own then. "So how long is that total?"

"We're thinking twelve weeks initially, especially considering it's not just the tibia and fibula but kneecap as well, and you came in right after Thanksgiving? Now we're in week, what, six? Probably another eight for physio, just to be safe. Keep in mind if you are diabetic or if you smoke, you may be slower to heal, but . . ." He glanced at my chart. "It doesn't look like that will be a factor, right?"

"I quit," I said, avoiding his eyes.

"And I'm the only diabetic in this household," Cassie said with a wry smile. The doctor ignored the joke.

"Great. So. I wrote all this down, but I'll just tell you now, too, because this is important. Your knee will naturally tend to slip out of place, but we have to keep these distinct parts as close together as possible while they heal. To prevent slipping, don't experiment by putting more pressure on that leg than what the plan lays out here. Whenever you give more unexpected pressure, there will be more pain." Dr. Rosen tapped the table. "And with that in mind, stay the course with OxyContin but don't take more than prescribed."

I was quick to say "Of course." Dr. Rosen looked at me through his bifocals. My gut clenched. Maybe my answer was too quick.

"Not only because it's addictive, but because you need to know what your pain limit is. Pain is the alert system for slippage."

More like pain was the alert system for everything. Wake up: *Hey, this sucks.* Move: *Hey, this sucks, too.* Think: *Hey, did I mention how much this sucks?* "Got it. Thank you, sir."

He shook our hands and wished us luck. We turned to Yarvis and the woman, Fern, beside us, who were muttering together over another stack of paper.

Yarvis nodded and Fern began to speak. Very fast.

"So, a little about us. After a family completes a brief enrollment process which includes signing a few forms, providing contact information for their appropriate VA case manager—"

"Is that you?" Cassie interrupted, looking at Yarvis.

"No, I just work for the hospital. You gotta register down at the VA for one of their caseworkers."

"Right," Fern continued. "Anyway, we'd get a rundown on your financial situation. Then we assign a support coordinator. The SC then contacts the family caregiver and begins to develop an understanding of the family's unique situation."

"Do you have a caregiver lined up?" Yarvis asked.

Cassie and I looked at each other. "You mean, like a nurse?" Cassie asked.

"No," I answered. "We don't."

"Not yet," Cassie added.

"But all that sounds great." I swallowed, hoping that was the right thing to say.

Fern nodded. "Then we leverage available resources from government, nonprofit, and community organizations. The SC reaches out to the resource, describes the family's situation, ensures a solution is available, and then serves as an ongoing advocate until the solution is delivered."

Whoa, I wanted to say. *Slow down.*

Cassie spoke. "You say 'ongoing advocate.' How long does this process usually take?"

"It depends on how quickly the government resources respond. But we're pretty good about it in San Antonio. A month at best."

A month? Would I even need in-home help by then?

"Oh. We'll be in Austin," Cassie said. "Is that a problem?"

Fern looked at Yarvis. "Not at all. I'll print off a list of organizations in Austin."

Fern went across the hall to the small bank of computers and printers available for patient use. I took a deep breath, and gave Cassie a look that I hoped was reassuring. She pressed her lips into a small smile in return. Maybe Fern was overestimating the time it all took, just to be safe. Maybe all of this would be quick and easy. Fern returned with a big smile, holding a few papers before saying her good-byes.

"I'll be in my office until I have a home visit at two," Yarvis said. "Holler when you need me, and I'll help you—you know—navigate."

He stood, took another sip of coffee, and limped away.

Cassie pulled the list of options toward her, and then, after a moment, slid them toward me. I noticed she had painted her nails a vivid red, and they looked longer. Except for the thumbnail. It was still bitten down to a stub and the damage looked recent. Made sense.

"A month. And until then we just . . . deal?"

I shrugged.

"Well?" she said, gesturing to the stack.

I began to read:

A Million Thanks
Able Forces—Executive Level Jobs
African American Post Traumatic Stress Disorder Association
After Deployment
Aggie Veterans—Texas A & M University
Air Compassion for Veterans
Air Force Sergeants Association South Central Divisions
Airlift Hope

I scanned the *Bs*, the *Cs*, all the way through the end of the list.

"Most of these don't even apply to me," I said.

Cassie sighed.

"Wha—" I began, and stopped. I was about to ask, *What should we do?* but I looked at Cassie's eyes, reading the list with confusion, her leg twitching under the table. When we'd agreed to this arrangement, she hadn't signed up for playing nurse, or providing transportation to and from a hospital in Austin where I could do PT. "What do you think I should do?"

She shrugged, biting her thumbnail. "You're the veteran in question."

"Yeah, but it's your house."

"Apartment," she corrected.

"Right." God, I hoped there was enough room for a wheelchair to move around. I wanted to ask her, but it wouldn't make a difference either way. We'd still be living there.

She scanned the list, and looked back at me. "I don't think you're going to like my answer."

"What?"

She scooted her chair closer to me. I could smell her cucumber shampoo. She got quiet. "I say we avoid all this paperwork as much as possible."

"Go on," I said.

She looked over her shoulder and turned back to me, continuing. "I mean, if you're okay with it, I could just do the stuff you need until you're able to move around on your own. We have the exercises in your file."

I started to play with the idea. "We go off the grid."

"Exactly." Her gaze was intent on me. "That way we don't have a paper trail to deal with when we want to divorce. Like all these forms that she was talking about? I'm going to be registered as your spouse."

She waved her hand, dismissing that part, but my stomach still jumped whenever anyone, including Cassie herself, referred to us as husband and wife. Her face had gotten a little red, too.

"And if it all goes through, someone will be in the house with us. A lot. That's another person to fool. Then when we split, they're going to need a whole new round of paperwork, right?" She held up the list. "And then there might be some programs you might not even be eligible for anymore, et cetera, et cetera."

I voiced what I had thought earlier. "Plus I might be walking again by the time we even get enrolled."

"True!" she said. "So I say we say fuck it. Get through the next month or so until your discharge, we part ways, and then, if you still need help, you can apply for it then."

I nodded, considering. I was glad I hadn't taken another pill. This plan would have gone over my head, and I would have been happy to let it. "Yeah, why bring in more people and institutions that we have to lie to?"

"Bingo." Cassie leaned back, a contented smile on her face. "I'm glad we're on the same page." Her smile then turned into a quizzical look. "You're good at listening. When you want to be."

I tried not to let a smile take over my face, giving away the punch line. "I've never heard that before."

"Well, maybe because you weren't as good at listen—" Cassie began, then she got the joke. She bumped my arm with her fist.

As she stood, my muscles twitched on instinct to stand with her. For a minute, I had almost forgotten I was injured.

"You're an idiot."

"Whatever you say, *honey*," I teased.

She hated that nickname, above all nicknames we threw at each other. But this time she just smiled at me. "'Honey' doesn't make me feel awkward anymore. Nothing can make me feel awkward anymore. I mean, come on, I've seen your tibia."

I couldn't help but smile.

Cassie

L uke and I left the cafeteria. He had one last physical therapy appointment before his discharge, which was all the way across the hospital and on the third floor. He began to struggle a few minutes in, after we stopped joking. It wasn't until he was out of breath that he gave up trying to manipulate his wheels himself. I silently eased behind him and helped him push forward.

He was quiet when we reached the elevator. He had seemed fine minutes before. Another mood swing. This was becoming a pattern. When the doors opened, he muttered, "You don't have to come."

"I should, though," I replied. "To see what your exercises look like if I need to help you."

He didn't respond. *He was a runner*, I reminded myself. *He must hate not being able to move in the ways he used to.*

I wanted to remind him that he wasn't as helpless as he felt. Before he'd gotten tired, he'd been steering with a certain expertise, turning quickly around corners and moving at least as fast as anyone could walk. And he sat tall in his chair, still browned by the Afghanistan sun, face a little hollow but as handsome as ever.

Jake was waiting on the third floor for us; he'd wanted to come help see Luke off.

"Evening, Private," he said, hands on the hips of his oil-splattered jeans and Bruce Springsteen T-shirt. They looked like brothers in small ways—in the joints, in the eyebrows—but Jake was softer everywhere, from his rounder cheeks to his thick thighs and middle, to his curly hair.

I put my hand on Luke's shoulder. I felt him relax. The friendlier Jake was to him, I'd noticed, the happier he was.

"Hiya, Juke," Luke said.

Jake snorted, giving me an embarrassed look. "Haven't heard that nickname in a while," he said. "Hailey's getting something from the car, she'll be here in a few."

We continued down the hall past the row of windows behind which patients of varying mobility sat on exercise balls, balanced on beams, stretched bands with their shoulders.

"Well, maybe because you haven't juked in a while," Luke shot back.

"What's juking?" I asked.

"It's a fake-out move in sports that Jake used to be good at," Luke said over his shoulder. "Honey," he added, loud enough for Jake to hear.

Luke was greeted by a therapist in scrubs with a pixie cut and New Balances, who ushered him inside to show him some stretches. His left leg was two centimeters shorter than his right, the doctor had told us, but he would regain full mobility if he stuck to his routine. Jake and I watched from the windows.

"Y'all get everything sorted out with the social worker?" Jake asked.

The woman had Luke sitting on the floor, bending and straightening his leg. I had to look away every time his face contorted with pain. He could barely get his knee past 180 degrees.

"For the most part," I answered evasively.

"I'd love to say Hailey and I will help out, but"—he paused, sighing—"I'm just not ready to take that on. We got our little JJ at home. And Luke's got more problems than being in a wheelchair, as you know."

He gave me a look of camaraderie, like, *Am I right?*

I froze. He may have been right, but I didn't know what he was talking about. But it was probably something I was *supposed* to know. And it wasn't like Luke and I had the excuse of knowing each other only a week this time. We were five months into marriage now, almost six. So I gave him the same look back, raising my eyebrows, like, *Whew, you're telling me.*

"He wasn't always like this, though."

I offered the trait about Luke I was most sure about. "Moody?"

"Ah, no, he was always moody, just like our dad. But the good moods used to be bigger, more frequent. But then he took on a lot of responsibility right away after our mama passed. Our dad all but checked out. He practically raised me."

"He didn't mention that." At his words, some hard part of me melted, the stored annoyance dissolving with images of Luke as a boy holding his brother's hand as he crossed the street. "We have a lot to catch up on."

"You two are just in a whirlwind of—" Jake was at a loss for words, spinning his hands around. "Just going for it? Aren't you?"

"Yes," I said, and composed an adoring gaze as the nurse helped Luke prop himself up on a bar to stand, his face clenched with effort.

"He seems happy with you," Jake said, following my eyes.

"Does he?" I realized the tone of surprise in my voice a little too late. Luckily Jake didn't seem to notice.

"I mean, look." Jake nodded toward Luke, who was now raising his chin at us, lifting his hand with a relaxed smile, signaling *five minutes*. "Thank you for taking care of him."

"Hey, it's my job," I said, shrugging. "And my pleasure, of course," I added quickly. My heart started pounding. I thought of our plan to eke out the next few months on our own.

Being a bartender is practically half nurse, I figured. All that throw up? I'm used to long hours and demanding people with weird needs.

But looking at Luke, his face twisted in agony, his leg a spider web of red flesh and scar tissue, I wondered what the hell we were in for.

Luke

After Cassie left, Jake and Hailey got ready to wheel me to free-dom. I'd shoved the bottle into my bag just in time when I'd heard their voices down the hall from my room. Now, thank the-whoever-above, my evening pill was cushioning every moment in a hand-spun cloud.

"I packed my stuff in there," I said, reaching for my army bag. "If you could just hand it to me, I'll hook it on my chair."

"I'll grab it!" Hailey offered, hoisting it on her shoulder.

"Oh, okay. Thank you," I said, trying to be casual.

What if they found them and thought I was abusing again? Taking pills for pain wasn't abuse. But Hailey and Jake were counting on me to stay sober, all the way sober. I mean, we hadn't talked about it ex-plicitly, but I assumed that they assumed I was. Based on the fact that they were talking to me at all.

But if I stayed completely sober, no pills, no anything, I couldn't talk or think or move without feeling my leg wrung out like a sponge, my face twisting involuntarily, and the looks on their faces, the pity-ing, sad-eyed looks I'd seen them make while I did PT. I couldn't take those. With Oxy it was as if the knives were made of plastic, the memory hooks made for fish. And even Yarvis had said it was a good idea to take the pills.

One thing at a time, he'd always tell me when I left the PT room covered in sweat. Without Oxy, it was everything at once. *Johnno's gonna kill me, Cassie's gonna hate me, Dad already hates me, Frankie's dead.* Oxy made everything simple. One thing.

Get a haircut.

Get in the van.

Find some space in Cassie's house.

Make myself walk. Make myself run. Be someone new.

One thing at a time.

I called it "cloud head." My cloud head was carefree, dumb, sweet, like a kid. Cloud head didn't want too many details. Cloud head knew that everything was going to be okay. My regular head couldn't do that. My regular head would get caught up in everything that could go wrong, and lash out. I needed cloud head for tough times, so that they looked more simple and nice than they actually were, so I could get through them without worrying so much. And then when I didn't worry so much, people liked me more.

"So when are you expected to walk again?" Jake asked.

Regular head didn't like this question, because I didn't know. It depended on how well the home PT exercises worked. But cloud head stepped in. "Soon, I hope. They gave me a cane, too, for when I'm ready to move out of the chair."

"That's good to hear, man," Jake said.

"Who knows," I said. "Maybe I'll be better enough to shoot some hoops soon."

"We'll see," Jake said.

Hailey had brought clippers from home and started to give my hair a buzz. I let myself enjoy her fingers on my scalp. Jake's answer wasn't a no, and here I was, getting a haircut, just like I'd wanted. Cloud head was working.

See, that was my mistake before. That's why I had gotten addicted. Because I wanted *only* cloud head. That's no way to live. You couldn't be *too* carefree, because then you'd stop caring completely, and you sure couldn't care for the people you loved. I loved my brother and sister-in-law. I loved my nephew, JJ. I even loved my dad. I still needed cloud head to be happy, but this time I wouldn't let it take over.

When we were little, Jake and I used to dribble our basketballs down to the air-conditioned gym at the high school and shoot baskets. I was never very good, but he was great, so I signed him up for all the camps. We'd shoot hoops until it got cool enough to go back outside, where we'd hit ground balls to each other. We could escape and be content in our own little town and no one expected anything of us, except to be on time for hamburgers at six. That's kind of what cloud head reminded me of. That and running. Nowhere particular to be, just moving through the world. One foot in front of the other. Simple. Not great, not bad, just okay.

"Are you excited to start nesting with your bride?" Hailey asked.

Regular head would have gotten nervous at the very mention of Cassie, knowing that she was better at faking it than I was. Regular head wouldn't know what to say.

"Yeah, she's great," cloud head said. "She's a musician."

"Oh, my! I didn't know that. She always seems so shy."

"She's very creative," cloud head said.

Jake pushed me through the automatic doors toward the transport van, where a nurse would drive me to Cassie's house.

Regular head started to panic. "I'll see you in a couple weeks?" I asked. Jake was leaving again, and we hadn't really gotten a chance to talk, for me to explain what my new plan for life was once I healed. Or rather, to explain that I needed to come up with a new plan, because I didn't really have a plan yet. I guess I had been counting on the inspiration of nine months in the desert.

"Maybe pick me up for a Bears game once the season starts up again?" I continued. The Bears were our high school team; they played where Jake and I used to practice.

"We don't have a place to put a wheelchair in the Honda," Jake said, uncomfortable.

"Maybe we could rent a van?" Hailey asked.

Cloud head tried to reassure regular head that it would be fine. But I couldn't not care about the prospect of being alone in Cassie's apartment, in a neighborhood I didn't know, unable to tell anyone I was there without having to justify our situation.

"Nah, I'll be up and about soon," cloud head said, hoping I was right.

"Take care of yourself," Jake said. I shook his hand. Hailey bent down to hug me.

From the windows of the van, cloud head waved good-bye.

. . .

When I woke up, we were in East Austin, and the Oxy had worn off, leaving a headache and a beating in my joints. I started to dig into my bag to pop another pill, but before I could find the bottle, Cassie was sliding open the van doors.

"Hey," she said, her hair up in a tiny ponytail. "Let's get you settled."

The bastard nurse came around the front of the van, scoping out the little white house as he activated the platform. There were two front doors, one with a red *A* over it, one with a *B*.

"You're on the first floor, then?" he asked Cassie.

"No, um. Second, actually," she said, her tone uncertain.

"Second, as in upstairs?" I said.

I could barely walk for five minutes without collapsing in pain, let alone take stairs. Cassie hadn't mentioned this. I could feel my jaw clenching. It would take all the restraint I had to wait to explode at her.

"Yeah," she said. "I told you that."

Oh. I might not have been fully present during that conversation. *Shit.*

The nurse nodded toward the second floor. "You gonna need my help to get him up there?"

"Nope, we got it covered," I said.

"Suit yourself," he said, and pulled the lever to bring the platform back into the vehicle. Cassie looked at me, incredulous, and back at the nurse, but he closed the van door, turned the ignition, and drove away.

Cassie threw up her hands. "What do you mean, 'we got it covered'?"

I didn't want his hands on me, carrying me like a wet noodle. And maybe this was what I needed to start walking. No choice. A kick in the ass. "We'll be fine. You saw me today. I can probably get up there by myself."

She wheeled me down the sidewalk, my bag on her back. "Are you kidding?" Cassie paused, softening when she saw my face, and approached the door. She gestured toward her body, perhaps two-thirds the size of mine. "Look at me." She turned toward the door and knocked on A. "I'm gonna grab some help just in case."

"Wait, Cassie . . ." I clutched my wheels, still fuming.

A middle-age woman opened it, dirty-blond ringlets framing a kind, puffy face. She wore leopard-print leggings and a T-shirt that said WAKE ME UP WHEN IT'S OVER.

Amen to that. She looked down at me, her expression curious. I nodded hello.

"Hey, Rita," Cassie said, putting on a big smile. "This is Luke, my new husband I was telling you about."

The stairs swallowed all of my concentration. At least ten minutes later, we were still only halfway up, and I was soaked with sweat from the effort. My wheelchair was folded at the bottom of the steps, my bag on top of it, guarded by a yipping mutant of a dog.

"One, two, three," they counted, panting, and I pushed as hard as I could with my good leg, their bodies propelling me upward and forward, landing on the next step with less than a millimeter to spare. My bum leg trailed uselessly behind me, pins flaring with every movement.

Six more steps to go.

"This is a bad idea," I said for the fifth time. "We should just call the hospital. I should go back."

In the physiotherapy room mirror I'd watch myself hauling the limb in its droidlike, knee-immobilizing brace with the swing of my hips, or even my hands, like a cord of wood, an object that didn't even belong to me. Sometimes I could put weight on it, but tonight I could give it about twenty pounds of pressure before the pain would stab me enough to almost knock me out. Less than 25 percent of body weight, that's for sure.

Cassie and the nurse were right, and I hated them for it. I couldn't do this alone.

"We can do it," Cassie said, beads of sweat dripping down her red face.

"I'm game," Rita said, her breath thin. "This is the closest I've been in twenty years to a sweaty man under fifty years old."

Every step was harder than the last. By the end, I could see tears mixing with Cassie's sweat. I'd landed my full weight on her toes more than once.

I sat at the top of the stairs as Cassie and Rita went to fetch the wheelchair.

My leg was trembling, my stomach heavy, my face burning with shame. They shouldn't have to do this. I shouldn't have to do this. And if this was a sign of what was to come, then I would either be stuck at Cassie's place, completely frozen, or the equivalent of a two-hundred-pound toddler who'd throw a tantrum every time he had to get out of his stroller.

They held the chair steady as I dragged my lower half up to the seat, grabbing on to any available hold like some desperate, feral creature, slithering into a sitting position.

"Bye now," Rita said, holding an ice cube to her forehead. "Thank you for your service."

I could barely respond. The appearance of my creamy, sticklike shin peeking out of the bottom of the brace made me want to vomit.

"We did it!" Cassie said. "You want a glass of water or anything?"

My mouth was dry, but hell if I wanted her to serve me. "No, thank you."

"Chin up, dude," she said. "I wrote out my schedule for you so we can come up with a system."

While Cassie was in the kitchen, I wheeled to where she had put my bag on the floor, reaching with hungry fingers for the straps, hoisting it onto my lap.

On the sky-blue futon, which I assumed would be my bed for the foreseeable future, she had set a folded blanket and a pillow, and on top of that, a handwritten piece of paper reading *Cassie's Schedule*.

I could make out the phrases in her slanted hand: *Nine AM wake up and play for two hours, sorry, I'll be playing the same songs over and over. Doctor's appt on the 9th. Band practice every Tuesday and Thursday.*

I took a pill and closed my eyes. I hoped by the time she left the apartment, I'd be knocked out.

Cassie

"So it's basically like having a roommate," I was telling Toby. Cross-legged on the floor, I aimed the lance at the pad of my thumb and waited for the stick. I'd told Luke to text me if he woke up and needed something, and came here to take a shower, and to remind myself of why I spent the entire day carrying Luke's sweaty body around my apartment. When Toby asked me what I had been doing all day, I couldn't bear lying to him. The Loyal. I did this for The Loyal, and now not only was he my actual partner, he was the only member of the band who didn't know.

By now I had become good at telling the story. I would almost forget why I was telling it. It had become banal. Casual. A story about health-care premiums and city hall. But of course that wasn't true. I would have to leave his apartment and at some point I would put my arms around another man, if only for show.

He was walking in a circle around his living room, running his fingers through his long brown hair, Lorraine following him like a shadow. He threw up his hands. "Yeah, like a sexy soldier roommate who's also your, like, legal partner!"

I stuck my thumb onto the meter, and waited. Eighty. Good. Even though I'd been doing this for months now, I still waited on every glucose score like I was waiting on the lottery. But it was more like most tickets were winning tickets, and you were dreading when you lost.

"No, no, no, not sexy," I assured Toby, thinking of Luke as I had found him before I left, head lolling on his shoulder as he slept. I had wheeled him gently against the wall, putting one of Mom's old throw pillows behind his head. I would have moved him to the couch but I didn't think I could do it without him being awake. "Plus we barely know each other." I thought of our e-mails and Skype calls and wondered if my words were entirely true. There was the night before he deployed, too. . . . But, then again, I didn't know the Luke who'd come back, the man who would stare out the window for hours, not talking, bristling every time I approached.

"Then why would you trust him? That's what I don't get."

"T, I was desperate. You saw what happens when I get low blood sugar. It could happen again, and I just can't afford another visit to the ER or"—I held up my meter—"any of this stuff on my own."

He paused, picking up Lorraine, drumming her back. "Yeah," he said, staring into space. "Yeah, I remember."

"He also needs money, I think. I don't actually know."

Toby jumped on that. "What do you mean, you don't know?"

"I thought it was best that I didn't ask too many questions about his situation. Mind you"—I held up a finger, because Toby was starting to protest—"this was before I knew I had to live with him."

He glared at me, brows furrowed. "So you didn't *plan* to live with him."

"No! Toby, no. Like I said, we have to keep up the ruse until he gets officially let go from active duty. It's for you and Nora just as much as me," I added.

"Because you can use your extra time for the album?" Toby said.

"Exactly."

"I don't know, Cassie." His pace had slowed again. "I mean, we're serious, right?"

"Yes. And I like it a lot."

He smiled at that. I knew he would like that.

He set Lorraine down on the ground. "Honestly. Honestly, tell me something."

"Honest," I said, scooting forward on the couch, giving him my full attention. At least I could give him that right now. That seemed to be what he wanted. It was cute, almost childlike.

"You agreed to marry him," he said, putting one finger out. Then he put out another. "And now you have this guy sleeping on your couch, in your home. And you expect me to just believe that you two don't have a thing for each other."

My chest tightened. A thing? Sure, Luke and I slept together once, and now we did things like watch each other go through various medical procedures and fight at our best friend's funeral. We couldn't have a *thing* if we tried. "Um. No, no, we don't. How can I explain this?"

"Yeah, explain it." He stood in front of me. "Please. Before I start fantasizing about beating this guy up."

"It's not complicated," I said, even though it was. But there was no way to explain it that Toby wouldn't misunderstand. I swallowed. "I want you, and that's it," I said, knowing how vague that sounded, and stood up to wrap my arms around his neck, kissing him hard enough that he'd forget.

Luke

I was running through green hills on packed earth that formed a circular track. Up and down, up and down, and Jake was there in one of the valleys, lying with Hailey and JJ on a blanket. They called to me with faraway voices: *Yes, go, yes, go.*

Suddenly, Jake yelled and I could hear him better. "They're picking us off from the northwest hill."

Which one is the northwest hill? I shouted.

A gun sounded right next to my ear.

I opened my eyes.

I was lying on Cassie's couch.

Still dark. I reached behind me to the table next to the couch, feeling around the ashtray and roach clips and guitar picks and diabetic-candy wrappers for the edge of the lamp, working toward the lamp cord.

I needed distraction. I needed to slow my heartbeat down.

Cassie had stacked her magazine subscriptions next to me on the floor. *SPIN*, featuring a girl with buckteeth and braids—read that one; *Rolling Stone* from September, August, July, and June—read those. I knew more about the evolution of David Bowie's career than I'd cared to.

I clutched the couch cushions to pull myself up to sit, swinging my gimp leg around. I'd been here about a week now, and every day I'd try to get into the chair on my own. Mostly I could do it.

I rolled my chair in front of my legs, and locked the wheels. The scars winked at me. They looked like bad bruises that would never heal, with dark holes where the pins went in. I grasped the back of the chair and pushed with my good leg, up, up, up, and for a second it seemed like I could swing the momentum of my hips over to the target.

Then the slightest twist of my ankle on the floor and the pain came streaming back. And just like that I felt the bullets again. The metal spikes stabbing, stabbing, stabbing.

I was on the floor, rolling. Wetness on my cheeks. Stabbing, stabbing, up through the bottom of my foot and from the sides, my bones were made of pain. A gunshot sounded near my ear.

It's not real.

Footsteps.

Cassie knelt and bent over me, her hair on my face, smelling like sleep. "Did you fall out of bed?"

"No," I said, and I wanted to explain exactly what happened, but the stabbing dominated my thoughts. The red polka dots on the dust. A pair of boots. I pulled them toward me.

No.

Open your eyes.

"One, two, three," she whispered, and I was sitting upright on the floor in the pile of old magazines.

Her eyes were half open, her tank top thrown on backward and inside out, a strap falling off her shoulder. "Can you get back on the couch from here?"

"No," I told her, avoiding her eyes.

She put her hands underneath my armpits, the skin of her chest in my face. I turned my face away, blood rushing to my head.

I propped my hands on the edge of the couch, ready to push.

"Were you having a bad dream?" she asked.

"No."

If I told her what I saw, she might think it worse than that, but it wasn't. It was just a bad dream that happened to come when I was half awake, half asleep, sometimes all awake, mostly all asleep.

"Yeah," she muttered. "Right. One, two, three."

When I was back on the musty cushions, Cassie straightened, gave me a weak smile, and sat on the floor.

"You can go back to bed," I said.

She rubbed her eyes. "No I can't."

"Why?"

She looked up at me, confused, a little hurt. It must have been my tone. *Damn it.* I didn't mean for it to sound as bitter as it did. When the Oxy wasn't working, it was like the pain was a filter for everything I said, clipping it, spiking it.

She shrugged. "I just can't get back to sleep once my brain starts going. I'm supposed to get drowsy on metformin, but it never seems to work. God, I hope it's working in general," she mused.

Metformin was one of her diabetes medications. I'd peeked in the medicine cabinet on Wednesday while I was washing my hands. She had seven altogether. Even under my health insurance, that was a lot. A lot to pay for, and a lot to put down your throat.

I wanted to be kinder. "Sorry I woke you."

"You— I've kinda noticed in the past week," she began, then stopped, choosing her words. "Luke, you make noises a lot when you sleep. Like screams." She continued, slow, each word making me feel smaller, more compact. "Do you think we should rethink the plan? And maybe get you some help?"

Just like that, kindness failed me. I felt like a floodlight was shining. How was it possible to feel so exposed under the stare of just one person? Her eyes were still sleepy, gentle, but if this was her version of kindness, I didn't want it. It was too close to pity.

I tried to keep my voice level. It didn't work. "I said sorry for waking you. I don't know what else to say. If you want to go back on the plan, then that's on you."

"Hey, whoa," Cassie said, standing. "It was just a suggestion."

"Just say the word and I'll do it."

"Uh, okay." She picked up the pillow from where it had landed on the floor and tossed it next to me. "I'm not your boss, or your mother, or whoever. I was just trying to point out that something seems to be off."

Her gaze burned. Everything I wanted to say was cycling at once, up and down, like the hills in my dream, and I couldn't figure out which one to take hold of. I kept going toward anger because it was the easiest. But it wasn't the only thing I was feeling. Everything else was buried under my nightmare.

Jake, with Hailey and JJ, lying on the blanket. *Why hadn't Jake called me? What if Johnno had showed up in Buda again? Is that why Jake wasn't calling again?*

Running. *No, wheeling. Limping.*

The gunshot in my ear, sounding real. *Frankie's boots on the splattered ground.*

"I don't want to talk about this right now."

"Rad," she called over her shoulder. "I'm gonna go in my room and not sleep. Thanks."

"Fuck," I said, burying my face in my hands. The closest I'd get to another apology. I needed to condense everything into one thing. I wanted cloud head, but the stabbing pain had subsided. Technically I didn't need the pills.

I reached for them anyway.

Cassie

"Okay, like, when George Harrison was with Pattie Boyd, he wrote 'Something,' he wrote 'If Not for You,'" I was saying to Nora as I sat behind my piano in her unfinished basement, holding my hand out for the joint. Toby was sitting next to me on a milk crate.

She passed it to me, shaking her head while she held in the toke. "Nope, nope," she corrected, "'If Not for You' was written by Bob Dylan. George just covered it."

"Nora's right," Toby said.

"Of course I'm right," Nora said, not looking at him.

I sucked in, watching the fringe on Nora's vest sway as she got up to get her guitar. It was Fleetwood Friday, but Toby and I had both forgotten. So there she was, in all her glory, and I was wearing Toby's Longhorns sweatshirt. I'd never forgotten Fleetwood Friday, even before Toby was in the band.

I was realizing it was no coincidence that Nora had suddenly brought up the idea of musicians being sucked in by their relationships, ruining their art.

One forgotten Fleetwood Friday did not make Toby a Yoko. And besides, I wanted to remind Nora, Yoko didn't give enough of a shit about The Beatles to break them up. Yoko had just wanted to make badass conceptual art about clouds and scream into microphones. Toby and I both gave too much of a shit about this band to let our relationship get in the way.

And, damn, the real sucker of my life force was Luke. The fight we'd had last night stayed with me. Waking up to his screams. The rage behind every word. I knew not all of it was about what I had done. But I shouldn't have to take the brunt of it. I didn't say a single word to him before I left for practice. Which took skill, considering I was literally propping him up as he limped to the bathroom.

Toby reached for my thigh, giving it a squeeze.

"It was a collaboration between George and Dylan," I called to her, coughing. "And anyway, the point is the creativity. The creativity was unchanged."

"Especially if the artist's, uh"—Toby cleared his throat—"partner is in the same band. They work to make each other better. You know?"

"Show me a woman," Nora said, sitting back down on her amp. "Show me a female musician who didn't get swallowed by her relationship. Look what happened to Joanna Newsom when she dated what's-his-face. Or, okay, not musicians, but Frida Kahlo and Diego Rivera."

I thought, while I stared at the Patti Smith poster on the concrete wall, the only decoration we allowed in our rehearsal space, *Luke's the goddamn problem. Not Toby. And Luke is my fault.* It was on the tip of my tongue, but I held it.

"What about Kathleen Hanna and Adam Horovitz?" Toby chimed. "Bikini Kill only grew *stronger* even though she was living with a member of the Beastie Boys."

"Some might even say *in spite of*." Nora turned her heavy-lined eyes toward Toby.

"Let's play 'Rhiannon,'" I said, hoping this discussion was over.

"Okay, I'll say one more thing," Nora said, holding up one of her ringed fingers. "Artists with other artists is a proven disaster, especially when the woman is more talented than the man. He will try to . . ." She made a choking motion. "Lock her down and make her into his manic pixie dream girl."

The tension in the room swelled. "Are you saying we're more talented than Toby?" I finally asked.

Nora's voice got louder. "I'm saying that The Loyal was ours first. . . ." She stopped. "And now that we've got a good thing going on, you had to complicate it." She looked at Toby. "I just wish that you never asked her out."

Toby looked back at Nora, an apologetic smile on his face. "We can't help that we like each other."

"No offense, Toby," Nora said, meaning *all offense*. "You can like each other all you want, but if you break up and we can't play the most important show of our lives, I'm going to kill both of you."

"Why didn't you say you had a problem earlier?" Toby asked.

"Do you really want to know?" She looked at me, then at Toby, then back at me, her ponytail swishing on her back. Neither of us answered. "Because I didn't think Cassie would get this serious with you. All things considered."

"What are you saying?" Toby asked.

I could feel blood rushing to my face, my gut throbbing. "Toby's been with us one hundred percent from the second he auditioned, even before we, whatever. What do you want to do, kick him out so I can date him?"

"I have stake in this band, too, now, Nora. No matter what happens with Cassie," Toby said, glancing at me.

"Fine," Nora said.

Then she pressed her lips together, and she looked at me for several seconds, unblinking. Nora had been there when I'd pushed Tyler away, when I'd reconnected with music, when I'd come to the conclusions about myself that made me want to form The Loyal with her in the first place. *I need to make my own space from the ground up*, I'd told her. Dating my drummer, especially now that I shared my futon with my fake husband, was not exactly making my own space.

She began setting up her instrument.

"And for the record, I *did* tell Cassie that I had a problem with it. From the beginning."

"Why not me?" Toby asked.

"Because we're not good friends," Nora said. She gave him a look like *sorry, not sorry*. Toby held up his hands in surrender.

She was being paranoid. We had chanted *music comes first, music comes first* to each other for long enough that she was having trouble seeing what happened when something else—or someone else—was important, too. There was space for everything, right?

"We can talk about this later, Nor." I played the opening chords to "Green Heron" and sighed. "And I'm sorry I forgot Fleetwood Friday."

Nora wasn't looking at either of us, focused on hooking up her bass. "It's fine. Let's just play."

"Let's do 'Green Heron.' Toby's been practicing that hard switch after the bridge with me."

Plunking her bass, Nora said, "I don't doubt that he has."

Toby sat behind the drum set, banging out a few beats, laughing to himself. "Come on, Nor. There's no point in speculating what could go wrong. Let's just have fun."

"Let's see if you can keep up this time," she said. "Just make sure y'all don't break up before the Sahara."

Toby looked at me, winking. *No way*, he mouthed. My gut rumbled, defensive. I threw my lighter at Nora a little too hard.

Luke

Two weeks in and I was sitting next to Rita in my chair, bouncing a tennis ball on the east wall. We were supposed to be looking for jobs. But every job Rita read from Cassie's laptop either required a college degree, which I didn't have, or required the capacity for heavy lifting and movement, which I didn't have, either.

Johnno wouldn't stop calling, even when I answered and told him I didn't have my severance yet. So I'd turned my phone off. I'd learned to watch the sun as it moved across the floor, memorizing its path. Sun coming through the bathroom, hitting the mat, meant it was around eight o'clock.

With my phone off, I felt less of the gripping fear I had every time his name showed up on my screen. At least, I told myself, he didn't know where Cassie lived. At least that part of my burden wasn't on her shoulders.

I'd risked powering it up to call Jake a few times. He'd called back once and left a voice mail while my phone was off. The downside to the phone being out of commission was that I might have missed more of his calls, but luckily all the feelings—the guilt, the pain, the fear—went away when the pills did their work. I'd taken four already today.

Sun that hit the other side of the place, reaching the couch, meant it was around three in the afternoon. At the moment, it was near the wall, shining directly on the plants.

"Rita, I can tell you right now, it is exactly 11:58 a.m. Look at the time."

"Oh, 11:52. Close."

"Damn."

Rita, currently unemployed, had been hired to "look in on me" for one hundred dollars a week. It was cheaper and easier than a nurse, and it meant Cassie didn't have to worry about helping me get out of the chair when she had to work late, or go to her boyfriend's house, which she'd been doing more and more since I bit her head off nearly every time she tried to help me. When the pain went away enough for me to speak like a normal person, I would tell Rita about Jake, about JJ, wishing I were talking to Cassie instead, and then feel guilty and take another pill.

Rita and I would talk about her son, who was around my age, living in Louisiana and trying to be a chef, and then we'd sit in silence watching *Hell's Kitchen* for hours. Rita would order sesame chicken with broccoli to be delivered. Rita didn't make me do any exercises, which meant I didn't have to waste my time making my pain worse, and that was really all the exercises seemed to do. Somehow I could convince myself every time that the pill would make getting up a little more bearable, but it wouldn't. *There was slippage*, I would tell myself when I tried to put any weight at all on the leg. *The exercises make the slippage worse.*

Rita returned from the kitchen, where she'd warmed up today's plate of sesame chicken.

"Where's yours?" I asked her.

"I'm burned out on Chinese food."

Footsteps on the stairs.

Cassie entered, kicking off her Converses and socks, humming along to some tune in her headphones, smelling like fresh air. I wondered if I was excited because it was Cassie, or if I was excited because since I'd killed a fly earlier this morning, this was the most exciting thing to happen all day.

My tongue was feeling loose. Cloud head was descending. "Want some sesame chicken?" I called.

She paused in the path to her bedroom and looked at me, startled. "What?" She took her headphones off her ears and I noticed for the millionth time that everything was harder than before. I thought of our e-mails, our jokes. Speaking in code, poking at each other, but stopping if it hurt.

"Oh, I said do you want any lunch? You can have some of this," I said.

"I can't eat that shit," she muttered, and continued on her way. That's right. I always forgot. But how was I supposed to know? *I don't know, dumbass, maybe look it up.*

"Well, I should be going," Rita said. "I'll leave you kids to it."

"No, don't go—" I began.

At the same time, Cassie said, "No, Rita, you can stay."

"Nah, I gotta go let Dante out." Rita held up a peace sign. "See ya later, champ."

When she shut the door, the room got quieter. I could hear the music pumping from Cassie's headphones across the room. She kept them around her neck, pressed pause, and continued into the kitchen without a word.

As I ate, I could hear her take something out of the refrigerator, the sounds of a knife hitting the cutting board. Since I'd moved in, she'd begun to sort of vibrate.

Or else I just knew her now. Measured steps, water for tea, humming: she had either just played music or had sex with Toby, which I hated to think about. Quick steps and tossing her purse meant she was late and pissed, or looking for something she had lost, which happened a lot; she forgot her phone on her nightstand at least every other day. Slow steps meant she was tired or thinking hard or about to sit down and write music.

My empty, sesame-sauce-streaked plate sat in my lap. I was about to set it aside, but then I realized Cassie might think I expected her to clear and wash it. Rita usually took care of this part. *Well, not today,* cloud head said. Cloud head told me I should prove that I wasn't just an eating, sleeping blob.

But you are *just an eating, sleeping blob,* regular head said. *You couldn't keep Frankie safe. You can't keep yourself safe. What makes you think you're not going to fuck this up?*

With my good leg, I scooted the chair into the kitchen, plate and fork in hand. *Go ahead, try. See what happens when you try.*

Cassie was cutting tomatoes, keeping her eyes on her task. *Chop. Chop. Chop.*

Her kitchen seemed to shrink. I was having a hard time steering the chair in the right direction without the use of both hands. I started to sweat, from frustration or effort, I couldn't tell. Now I was in the middle of the tile, not one foot from Cassie, eye level with her back and ass. *Great.*

Either I would have to wait until she was done chopping, or ask her to move so I could get to the sink.

My thoughts were moving slowly. This was the problem with the "one-thing" function of OxyContin. It seemed to take about three minutes to move from one idea to the next.

I summoned more cloud head, trying to sound polite. "Could I get by here?"

She turned, glancing at the plate and fork. "Just give them to me," she said, reaching.

"No, no, it's okay," I said, moving them out of her reach.

"Luke, you can't reach the faucet—" she said, grabbing again, and the movement made me lose my grip on the plate. It fell to the floor and cracked in two.

"Shit," we said at the same time.

She stooped to pick it up.

"Please, let me," I said, and the room seemed to expand to normal size again, but too quickly, almost knocking the wind out of my lungs. I heard bullets—no particular sensation had reminded me, and yet I could hear them, just like I could hear the sound of the flag whipping. *They're picking us off from the northwest hill.* My voice was distorted again, shaking, this time by something other than anger. Something that came from the same place in my stomach.

As if sensing it, Cassie rose and stepped away.

I leaned over in the chair, folding my torso to its limit to grab the plate halves.

Why did these little things mess with my brain like this? Why couldn't I just let life pass through me? And of course, because I never left her apartment, Cassie was around every single time this happened.

I wheeled to a spot next to the counter and set the pieces near an avocado. "Or do you want me to put them in the trash?"

"Right there's fine, thanks."

She breezed past me. "Do you need the bathroom? I'm going to take a shower."

I stayed facing the wall, but I could feel her moving across the room. *Good fucking work, Morrow.* This was the problem with regular head. Regular head was worse. Regular head sent me nightmares during the day. Cloud head would take over most of the interactions from now on, I decided right then. *And I know what you're thinking,* I said in my head to no one. *You think it's because I like the OxyContin. No. That's not it.*

"Luke?" Cassie called. "Can you hear me?"

"No, I don't need the bathroom," I responded. I needed to defeat my own thoughts. I could be a new version of old Luke. "I mean, no, thank you," I corrected, reaching for another pill.

Cassie

I stayed in the shower longer than normal, turning up the hot water to pelt me raw. Luke was always there, hurting in the quiet, a dark cloud in the house. I felt bad for shoving him on Rita, but after two weeks in the same house, his moods were beginning to affect mine. I had started to write sadder songs, which didn't quite fit. I had a chance at a record deal, for Christ's sake. I should have been pushing out hits, or at least joyous, forward-moving songs, songs that bloomed with possibility. I had even started to get annoyed with Toby, as if he should act as a punching bag for my frustration with Luke.

Mom would have known what to say to lift my spirits, but she had no sympathy for me. When I called, her voice was strained, a cold kind of friendly, like a *how are you* to the guy who delivers her mail. She would make an excuse to get off the phone before I could tell her much about Luke. She knew just that he was home, and injured. Nothing about how hard it was, how bad things were with him. I'd gotten myself into this mess, I could almost hear her say, and I could get myself out.

The muscles in my back and arms were aching from holding Luke's weight. He was supposed to be able to put some weight on the leg by now, but he could still get to the toilet only if I helped him from the doorway, where the wheelchair wouldn't fit. This morning I had slipped on the wet floor, and my head missed the edge of the sink by centimeters. I had to be more careful.

I thought of the broken plate. *He* had to be more careful. Doubt was creeping into my thoughts every day, but I pushed it away. If it was this hard to care for each other when no one else was around, think of how difficult it would be to make it seem like we were a couple in the presence of a real nurse.

And I still needed his health insurance and the extra thousand dollars a month.

I thought about how strange it was that after two weeks, he hadn't asked me to get him anything. He ate whatever was put in front of him. He made sure to never be on my laptop whenever I came home. No requests for certain foods, no new clothes, no boxes from Buda he wanted to retrieve.

Maybe that was the problem.

All he had was the space that I had set up. My books, my records, the dusty trinkets from vacations Mom and I had taken. My schedule, my nonathletic arms to lift him. *I should get him a plant, or something*, I thought. *Something living to be around other than me and Rita.*

I stepped out of the bathroom, glancing at where he had wheeled himself next to the window. He turned to me, but quickly looked away, a tennis ball in his clenched fist. I disrobed in the bedroom, and got ready for work. I'd said I would go in early today to do liquor inventory, get some extra hours.

On my way out of the room, my eye caught a strange sight on my pillow. Two orange dots I'd never seen before. I looked closer, picking them up. They were small, cylindrical, and made of foam. Earplugs.

I smiled.

Luke had gotten me earplugs. Or rather, he had asked Rita to get earplugs for me, so I could sleep through the night without waking up to his muttering through the thin walls.

The hardness I'd felt toward him dissipated. The pain was not his fault.

On my way out, I noticed his head had collapsed. He must have fallen asleep.

"Luke?" I said.

No answer.

I approached him, reaching for his shoulder. The muscles near his neck were still hard, knotted now from controlling the wheels. I noticed his buzz cut was growing out into a dark amber color.

He should get a haircut. And maybe I could help him do some leg bends for a few minutes.

"Luke," I whispered, nudging him. He didn't move.

Fear cascaded suddenly, fragmented *what-if*s jumping to the front of my brain. *What if he took too much pain medication by accident?* And what followed almost brought tears to my eyes: *What if he did it on purpose?*

"Luke," I said louder, shaking his shoulder harder.

He snapped awake, craning to look at me. "What?" he said, his eyes hard.

"Oh, um." I took a step back, relief flooding. *I was worried about you*, I wanted to say. "I just wanted to thank you for the earplugs."

"Yeah," he said, resting his forehead on his hand.

"Sorry I haven't really been around."

He turned his sleepy eyes on me. "You don't have to say sorry."

"I know, but." I wanted him to know that I could tell that something was wrong. Maybe he needed to talk. Rita wasn't exactly an ideal conversationalist. "So, um, how's the physical therapy going?"

"Very good, Cassie, thank you," he said.

What was with this weird, polite tone? I almost preferred him sullen. At least that was closer to his real self.

I resisted the urge to bend over and pull his chair so that he was facing me. "Has Rita been okay at helping you up, or would both of us be better?"

He bounced his tennis ball. "It's fine."

"So you did your therapy this morning?"

He was quiet. "Yeah."

"Have you gotten hold of your brother?"

"A couple of times. But I didn't want to invite him over to your house."

"You can if you want to."

Luke sighed, as if he were tired of talking. "Sure, thank you for offering."

My sympathy was running out again. I was trying, I was giving him a lot to work with, I was making it easy, and he was pushing me away. "Is there something wrong?" I offered.

"Nothing's wrong. Thank you."

That politeness again. It was like a screen. I tried again. "Is it money?"

"Nope," he said, almost too quickly.

It wasn't like we were best friends or anything, but he was so different from the Luke whom I had Skyped with, who had stories to tell, or even the Luke who'd sat next to me at the hospital cafeteria, the eager listener, or the person who made me feel like my ideas were magic. "All right, so, then, what's going on?" When he didn't answer, I raised my voice. "What do you *need*?"

He groaned, turning jerkily to face me. "I need to have never gotten myself into this situation in the first place. How's that?"

"Well, I can't help you with that one." I grabbed my purse from the couch, heading toward the door. I needed out of this den of sadness, what used to be my haven. Where I was now apparently a situation.

"I didn't mean you."

"Right." Before I slammed the door, it slipped out. "Enjoy wasting away."

As I stomped down the stairs, I didn't know if the guilt in my gut was stirring because it was a mean thing to say, meaner than his silence, or because I knew that no matter what I said, no matter whether he would respond in anger or just ignore me, I would always have the upper hand. I would always be the one to move on with my day, to try to forget and move forward, to slam the door and stomp down the stairs and get in my car and go. Because I could.

Luke

Cassie was practicing that song again. She kept getting caught up on one part, where the notes jumped from low to high. It made it hard to concentrate on what Yarvis was saying as he sat across from me on the couch, his feet in a spot where, not eight hours ago, I'd pissed myself.

"You catch any of the game?" Yarvis asked.

Bum bum bum be dun, ba ding. Ba DING. Ba ding ding DING.

"Damn it," we could hear her say.

I didn't know which game he was talking about. No TV here. And faulty Internet. And even if I could watch sports, it pissed me off to watch clips of people running and jumping like it was nothing. "Um, no."

Yarvis had come over for a check-in, though it was supposed to have happened three weeks ago. He'd given us only about an hour's notice to get rid of the blankets and pillows on the couch, put the overflowing bag of my stuff out of sight, throw away the sweatpants I'd pissed in because I couldn't get to the bathroom in time. I was supposed to be able to hold a certain percentage of my weight by now, but I hadn't been doing the exercises. So I could hold zero percent, and fell. That was when I'd hated having cloud head. Regular head knew I should have just yelled to Cassie to help. Cloud head told me no, it was the middle of the night, I'd be fine.

Bum bum be dun dun.

I wasn't fine. I'd peed on the floor. That was the tough part about cloud head. Cloud head was calmer, but maybe a little too calm.

Ba ding DING ding. "Damn it!"

"Cassie, are you going to join us, or what?" I called to the other room, my voice sharper than I'd intended.

"In a second," she called.

She walked out in the same band T-shirt she wore yesterday, her hair falling out of her ponytail. "Hi," she said, breathing deeply, as if she were about to take a big leap, bracing herself. "Sorry for the delay. Good to see you."

Yarvis looked back and forth from me to Cassie as he scooted to make room for Cassie on the couch, puzzled. "How are we?"

Out of obligation, I reached for Cassie's hand. It was limp in mine. "Good," I said.

"Great!" Cassie said, her enthusiasm flimsy.

"Well, good," Yarvis said, putting on an amused smile. "I'm here to check on Luke's progress. And," he said, pausing to pull out another folder from his shoulder bag, "bring you the next stage in Luke's PT, since it appears you haven't taken the time to go to the VA."

Cassie shifted in her seat, letting go of my hand to bite her thumbnail. I avoided his eyes.

"Did you find help elsewhere?" he continued.

"Yeah," I said, swallowing, hoping he wouldn't get too curious.

Cassie took her thumbnail out of her mouth, her brow furrowed. "Yeah, I mean, we're doing what we can. It threw us off when you didn't show for the first week."

Yarvis let out a whistling sigh. "And I'm sorry about that. There's only two of us for hundreds of families."

Cassie leaned forward. "*Two* social workers? For a hospital that big?"

At Yarvis's surprised face, Cassie tensed. She checked herself. She put her hand back in mine.

Yarvis continued, "Resources are scant. I've said it before and I'll say it again. I'm on your side. Veterans need to be made a bigger priority. There are serious mental and physical health repercussions for entire generations if they don't get the help they need." He leaned in for emphasis. "But you all have to at least *try*."

I looked at Cassie. Her eyes were narrowed at Yarvis. "I work a minimum-wage service job, I have to check my blood sugar eight times a day, and neither Luke nor I have the money to buy or rent a vehicle that can transport him across the river to the, uh, what's it called, the Veterans Center on South Congress. So." Her words caught. She took another breath, trying to calm herself, and put on a strained smile. "What do you recommend as far as trying?" Then, after a pause, she pushed out a sarcastic "Sir?"

Some sort of buried conditioning from a year of army training moved words out of my mouth before I could realize what I was saying. "Don't, Cass."

"Thanks, Private," she snapped.

I pressed her hand. She pressed back. She wasn't only being disrespectful to the one person trying to help us, she was blowing our cover. We weren't acting like a married couple, just bickering a little. She was on the verge of full-on fed up.

"It's all right, Luke." Yarvis looked at Cassie. "I'm sorry. I know it must be hard. I didn't mean to lecture you."

Cassie's eyes softened, though she was still breathing hard. "It is hard."

He turned to me. "Have you at least been doing your basic PT at home?"

"Yes," I lied.

I could feel her eyes on me, debating whether to call me out. *Don't push it. Please. We have to sugarcoat things so he can get out of here.*

"I'm still getting used to things," I added, resisting looking back at her.

"Yeah, well," Cassie said, sensing my thoughts. "We'll get him up in no time."

"You poor kids," Yarvis said. "You've both got dark circles under your eyes. It's going to get easier."

"I'll be right back," Cassie said. She fluttered her hands toward the two of us. "Can I get either of you anything? Honey?"

"No, thank you," Yarvis said.

I shook my head, though what I wanted was a pill. This was too much. My hand started moving toward my pocket, where I'd started keeping them in my sweatpants.

"Hey," Yarvis said, leaning close to me, snapping his fingers. I looked at him in his pool-water eyes. "What's your deal?"

"Nothing, sir. Just tired." My pulse quickened.

"Your pupils are tiny." His smoky voice was harsh. "Are you taking opiates?"

I swallowed, jerked my hand away from my pocket to my knee. "For the pain."

He raised his bushy eyebrows. "And only as prescribed?"

"Only as prescribed," I repeated, hoarse. I suddenly remembered what the surgeon said. *Pain is the alert system.* Maybe I'd fallen because there was slippage and I couldn't tell.

"I've seen kids better off than you go down a dark path. Don't do that," he said, pointing right between my eyes. Right between cloud head and regular head. "If you don't believe you're going to make a full recovery, you won't. Do it for her," he said, nodding toward the kitchen.

Cloud head almost laughed. As if Cassie would want me to do anything for her, let alone clomp around her apartment doing pony exercises. I'm pretty sure the only thing Cassie wanted was a time machine to take her forward to the day when I'd be gone.

Cassie came back, sipping water. Yarvis sat back in his chair, a smile on his face. "You know what you two need?"

"A farmhand?" Cassie asked.

"A dog."

Cassie snorted. When Yarvis got up to use the bathroom, I slid a pill from my pocket, swallowing while Cassie was looking the other way. Yarvis was right about me, but it was too late. I was already on a dark path. But I'd be fine. I'd figure out what lay on the other side of it once I got out of here.

The rest of this interview was going to get a lot more pleasant for everyone with cloud head around. Best to just ride it out, smiling. Best to just become furniture.

"Huh," Yarvis was saying, looking out one of Cassie's windows down at the street. "Wonder what that Bronco is doing."

"What?" I said, almost a whisper. I wanted the Oxy to hit me harder, to slow down the pumping of blood.

"Oh, it was idling out there when I came in, and it's still there," Yarvis muttered.

Cassie joined him at the window. "I've never seen it before."

Johnno. He found Cassie's house. I didn't have the money. Why couldn't he get that through his head? I didn't have it, and I would pay him when I did. But facts didn't matter in Johnno's chaos. I couldn't see out the window, but I could imagine his twitchy face in a cloud of menthol smoke, ready to hop out with Kaz behind him, ready to snap.

He could come up here at any time. He could hurt Cassie.

"It's leaving," Yarvis said, his voice far away.

I clung to my wheels, my wrists pulsing on my useless legs. If he came back, if he came up here and tried to hurt me—tried to hurt Cassie—all I could do was watch.

Cassie

"**M**m." Toby kissed my neck as I tried to get the notes right. "Do you have to practice? We practice enough."

"Of course I have to practice," I said. "You know that better than anyone."

After Yarvis left, Luke had started wheeling around the apartment with his phone in his lap, muttering to himself. Whenever he saw me, he seized. I'd thought about calling my mom, going over there for dinner, but instead I'd called Toby.

"You like your keyboard more than me?" he said, making a trail with his mouth to my shoulder, the tips of his hair brushing my skin. "I'm just kidding," he added, between kisses. I couldn't help wondering, *then why did you say it?*

"It's just hard to play over there right now."

"You should just live here!" Toby said, standing up.

I smiled. "Yeah, right."

"I'm serious. It's only been a few months since we got together, but we've known each other now for almost two years." He gave me a small smile.

I looked at him, unable to mask the surprise on my face.

He shrugged, clearly trying to sound casual. "We could jam all the time. All you wanted. It would be so fun."

Suddenly the room felt smaller.

"This is a great place. And I like you a lot." As Toby began to rub my neck, I said gently, "But I can't move in with you, you know that."

He was quiet then, still massaging. I had hurt his feelings. Always hurting feelings. *That's me! Mean ol' Cassie.* I remembered how kind he had always been. I knew he was just trying to be supportive, but Nora's look came back to me, her silent message.

Toby's hands dug harder, moving down to my shoulders. I dipped out from underneath his grip and stood up. "I mean, come on, Toby. As if I could just breeze over here."

He lifted his hands and left the room. I took a deep breath.

"I'm sorry," I called. "You know I have to keep up appearances with Luke."

"Of course. You have to keep up appearances with Luke. Your husband." Something banged in the kitchen. I sighed and padded into the other room. When he saw me, his face tightened further.

I paused in the doorway. "I'm giving everything I have to make a career. This is already not easy, and I can't take on anything else right now."

"If you don't want to commit to me, that's fine, but don't pretend like I'm the cause of more stress," he said, pouring olive oil into a pan. "I'm a good thing in your life. Not that bullshit you have to do with Luke. I'm real."

I stepped toward him. "I'm not saying we aren't good together. I'm just . . ." It wasn't about just keeping up the lie anymore. I was worried about Luke. He wasn't the same. And it shouldn't have bothered me, but it did. I didn't want to create a bigger gap between us than there already was. Luke and I had to get through this together. Or we at least had to try. "I just like it the way it is with us."

"I don't understand," he said, throwing garlic in the pan. "You always tell me how you're doing this for me and The Loyal, but when I'm offering to make it easier for you, you refuse."

I remembered Nora's hands on Fleetwood Friday, the choking motion. *He's going to try to lock you down.* "I'd rather no one 'offer' me anything. I'd rather make it for myself, thanks."

He turned on the gas, staring at the flames licking. "Well, good luck with that."

My capacity was full. Luke, Yarvis, the band, work, health, Mom, everything. Toby had his piece of my attention, but he wanted more and I couldn't give it to him. I had no more left.

"Don't insult my choices."

"I wasn't—" Toby started, but I was already in the living room, putting my keyboard in its case. I had a song to master.

"I have to go," I called to him. I could hear the oil searing. He didn't follow me out.

Luke

Cassie burst through the door, talking on the phone, her steps rushed. The door slammed behind her as she kicked off her Converses, her keyboard case on her back. She looked at me, probably aware, as always, that I was in the same position I'd been in when she left.

All I'd been doing was feeling. I'd been sitting here, thinking of closing Frankie's eyes. Thinking of my mom. The outline of my mom. Of everything, everyone, I'd lost.

And now Johnno was back. It could have been someone else, but even though I didn't see the Bronco last week, I'd known it was Johnno. He had not only misunderstood what *severance* meant, he also couldn't wrap his head around the fact that I couldn't give him the amount he wanted until I was discharged later this year. Time didn't matter to Johnno. Other people's lives didn't matter to Johnno, unless he was at the center. And now he was coming for mine, for Cassie's.

"I'm just saying, maybe you were right about Toby," Cassie said into the phone, and hushed her voice when she saw me. "I just don't know what we would do about the Sahara show. That's the one the Wolf Records guy is going to be at. I mean, do I throw it all away because I'm mad?"

Cassie's friend's voice mumbled on the other end.

"Right," she said, pulling the strap of her purse over her head, setting it down. "Yeah." She tossed her keys on the table. "Okay. Love you, Nora. Bye." She hung up.

I heard her start to set up her keyboard in her room.

The buzz from this dose was glorious. This was a whole new level of cloud head. And Cassie was in a fight with Toby. I didn't know why this made me happy, only that it did.

"Everything okay with you and Toby?" I called.

Cassie poked her head out of her room. "Hey, Luke?" Her voice was clipped. "Can I have a moment to myself? Without someone needing something from me?"

"I don't need anything," I said. "I just thought you might want to talk."

"Oh, all of a sudden you're Mr. Sensitive? Give me a break." She laughed, mirthless.

I felt a puffy, sticky version of regret. The words kept coming. "I didn't like how I was acting, either."

She stepped out of her room fully. The late-afternoon light caught the tips of her hair, her gold-brown eyes.

"I'm sorry," I said.

"Well," she finally spoke, quiet. "You might as well know. Toby asked me to move in with him."

"What did you say?" The words still felt distant coming out of my mouth, like someone else was saying them. Cloud head assured me they were the right thing to say.

She looked at me, her eyes red around the edges from crying. She was so *pretty*. "I said hell no."

"You didn't have to do that on my account."

"This is my home."

"I know."

She went back into her room, beginning to play scales. *Her home.*

God, what if Johnno broke in? What if he hurt her? Regular head crept back. *You couldn't do anything if he did. You're useless.*

"Cassie!" I called. My words were slurring. I didn't care. "C'mere. Please. Just for a second, and I'll leave you alone."

Cloud head began to yank my thoughts in reverse. I wheeled toward her room. I stopped.

What if I had never met her? What if I had never overheard her proposing to Frankie? What if I had never met Frankie? And if I had never met Frankie, Frankie would have roomed with someone else who could have been in the jeep with him at the Pakistan border, maybe someone who might have told everyone to stay in the jeep, and as a result, Frankie and Rooster would still be alive.

What if I had never joined the army?

What if I had never left cloud head?

What if I had never found cloud head in the first place?

What if I never needed it?

What was before cloud head?

Before, when I taught myself to change my brother's diapers and asked why the sky was blue and whether ghosts were real. When I called V100 and requested "Spirit in the Sky" for my dad. When I had a mother. When I knew how to want, and how to love. When I knew how to actually do things for people, rather than hate myself for not doing them.

Cassie finally came out, running her hands through her hair. It was down to her shoulders now. We'd known each other long enough to watch the other's hair grow.

She sat down, the heat and weight of her warming, making me feel less alone.

"I want to be better," I said, trying not to slur. "I want to help out around here."

She kept her eyes ahead, and took a deep breath. She put a hand on my back. I tried to sit up straighter. My vision was crossing.

Though she was sitting next to me, I heard her voice from far away. "You have to get your shit together."

I could. I could be a real friend to Cassie. I could protect her house. I could get rid of Johnno. I could protect my brother and his family. But I couldn't get up. All I could do was think, remember.

Come on, cloud head. Get up. You can do it. Cloud heads can do things, too. Come on, cloud head. I was sick of myself. I was sick of cloud head, I was sick of regular head, I was sick that I had even invented them. Because that's all they were. Thoughts.

One, two, three.

Get up.

Cassie

The next morning, when I walked into the living room, Luke was standing.

His hair was plastered with sweat, his sweatpants were falling off his ass, but he was up, using the back of the couch for support, shuffling back and forth, muttering to himself like Macbeth's wife.

I didn't say anything at first.

That's how Luke and I preferred it, right? We didn't acknowledge each other. At least that's how he'd preferred it until last night.

It wasn't like I was doing any of this out of the pure goodness of my heart. I was still under his health insurance, I would still get half of his severance, so it was best we kept it to practical exchanges. Me handing him damp, soapy towels through the bathroom door so he could clean himself. Him averting his gaze while I got out of the shower. It was all part of the job.

But sometimes his pain was so clear I could feel it in my own bones. At least once a day I felt it, felt him hurting so hard that it extended across the room. When he'd reach to adjust his pillow. When he'd bend to pick something up off the floor. When he was still waking up from a nightmare with a choked scream.

So now, seeing him standing like that, I couldn't help it, I started clapping.

Luke

I was panting, but I didn't care. Clutching the couch, a step. I wiggled my toes, proving I could feel the hardwood floor beneath them. I could put weight on it. It was stiff and I couldn't walk alone but I could use the muscles.

"I can't believe you got up on your own!" she said again, her smile taking up her whole face. She looked me up and down, probably so unused to seeing me upright.

Another gentle step. The floor stayed solid.

Pinching pain rather than stabbing. Pinching and poking, small, like a secret, like Jake and I used to do to each other in the grocery store line when we knew we would get in trouble if we pushed each other in public.

"Goddamn," I said, swallowing the lump that had formed in my throat.

It'd been a wave inside me when the sun had hit my eyes this morning, my mouth dry from passing out. I'd reached for my glass of water but realized I'd left it on the shelf where the records were, across the room. A chorus of *fuck, fuck, fuck* had rung in my ears, louder than usual, fueled by anger at my useless body, that I couldn't get a fucking glass, that I could feel my stomach spilling over the same sweatpants I'd worn for a fortnight.

I'd pressed so hard on my feet that I wanted the floor to fall away. Pain was there, but I'd told it to fuck off.

Fuck off, I'd said aloud on the second attempt, and I'd pressed on the coffee table, almost tipping forward until my knees caught the edge.

I'd tensed my quads like I used to when we lifted weights for football, felt them shake. Just when I thought they were going to give out, I was straight. *They* were straight.

I was up, I was up, and Cassie reached for me, taking my arm, somehow knowing I'd want to walk in a circle, around and around, away from the couch, the room its own little country.

Her steps with mine were strong, slow.

She beamed at me. My chest felt wide open.

"You don't have to stick around if you don't want to," I offered. "Do you have anywhere to be?"

"No. Here," she said, steering me toward the stereo. "Let's put on some music. What do you want?"

I didn't know at first, but then the smell of motor oil drifted toward me from another time, the vision of my dad's hands tapping along on the hood while he examined an engine. "I'd like to request," I began, and took another step with her arm now around my waist, "'Spirit in the Sky' by Norman Greenbaum."

Cassie

It was cool and sunny, so I opened the windows to the apartment and put on David Bowie's "Rock and Roll Suicide," turning it up as high as it would go. I'd decided to wait until my mother's schedule matched mine so I could tell her the band's news in person, and I had a good feeling about today. Luke had been standing on his own for a few days in a row, and was now outside with Rita, making laps around the yard.

I was nine days and a thirty-minute show away from being signed for a record deal. I couldn't wait to tell her: I was a musician, and I had proof.

When she pulled up outside, I watched her step out of her Camry wearing drugstore sunglasses, a Rosario Ferré book under her arm. I smiled, and turned down the music as she climbed the stairs.

"Who's mowing your lawn?" she was saying as I opened the door. "It's a jungle out there."

"Oh, Rita's supposed to take care of that," I said, reaching over to kiss her on the cheek.

"And you're wearing a dirty T-shirt. Same jeans for days. *Estas flaca.*"

I pursed my lips, resisting a retort, reminding myself that today was supposed to be good. To fix things between us. Still, sometimes I thought I could tell her that I won a Nobel Prize and she'd say, *Make sure they aren't using that photo of you from your goth days.*

But that was about to change.

"Anyway, Mom, I—"

"And where am I supposed to sit?" She was looking at the couch, which held Luke's pillow and blanket, crumpled and probably smelling like sweat.

My face burned.

She picked up the blanket and began to fold. "Does a nurse come?"

"Rita comes. From downstairs, on nights when I have to bartend or when I need to practice."

She set down the squared blanket, and picked up the pillow, beginning to fluff it. "Hm. And how long will you have to do that without figuring out how to pay her for real?"

I watched her work, trying to find the right words. "Well, yeah, but hopefully Luke will be better soon. And, Mom, I have something to tell you."

"Go on," she said, tossing down the pillow, a smile growing on her face.

My stomach dropped. My heart started to beat, hard. She would be proud of me. Right? "I don't think it's exactly what you want to hear, but it's good."

She pulled a strand of hair out of my mouth. "Oh, does this have something to do with your piano playing?"

A punch to the gut. "Piano playing? Mom, it kills me that you call it that. It *kills* me."

"What would you rather I call it?"

"My career."

"Your career." When I looked back at her, she was rubbing her temples, as if my lack of comprehension were giving her a headache. "All I've told you, all I've given you, out the window."

"All right, forget it. Forget it." I fought back tears, heading toward the kitchen. "You want some lunch? I'm done talking to you about this."

"Why?"

I stopped, shaking my head.

She continued, "Because you don't like what I say?"

I turned back to face her. "No, because I invited you here to tell you the best news I've ever received in my life, and I know you're not going to care because it doesn't fit into your idea of what my life should look like."

She got quiet. "So I guess you're not going to tell me you're going to law school?"

I let out a harsh breath, barely a laugh. "No. Fuck no."

"Don't curse at me."

"I might get signed to a label. Wolf Records. Do you know what that means?"

We were quiet. She sighed. "I assume it means you are putting your music ahead of your security."

No congratulations. Of course not. No acknowledgment. She couldn't even fake it.

I tried to keep my voice from shaking. "It means I might go on tour, get paid, everything."

For a minute, she looked frightened. Then she let out a breath, big and put-upon. "God help you. And God help Luke."

"Hey, Mom?" I started picking up Luke's stray clothing from the floor, stuffing each item into his bag. "Maybe, just, you know, think about what I do in the context of the larger world, instead of whatever scheme you've concocted in your little apartment."

"I fed you and raised you in that little apartment so you can throw away your education to go on a road trip."

"A road trip! Give me a fucking break." She made feel like a teenager again, like I was spitting answers back at her through my bedroom door.

"Leaving Luke behind to fend for himself. What does he think of all this?"

"Luke. He— he doesn't—mind." I couldn't really speak for Luke's thoughts on The Loyal. But that wasn't the point. She couldn't even be proud or happy for one second before questioning me, delegitimizing me. "This is not a road trip. I'm not a street musician with a hat sitting out on the sidewalk. I've been playing my whole life, and you know that."

"I know that," Mom said, quiet.

"Why do you dismiss me even when I have proof that I can do this?" I yelled loud enough that a flock of birds scattered from the ash tree out the window.

"Because I'm scared for you!" She pointed to my stomach, to my disease-ridden gut. To Luke's pills sitting on the end table, to our dirty little home. All of a sudden I could see it, the dirt, and I flushed hot with embarrassment. "I don't know how you're going to make it last."

"Your fear is your problem!"

"It's not just my problem. What will the military say? What will Luke do?"

"Luke will get severance. He has the GI Bill for when he's ready to go to school. I haven't had an episode in months, Mom. I keep my blood sugar stable. I cook. I take care of myself. My own way."

"I'm still concerned. I'm allowed to be concerned."

"Not anymore." I crossed the room, opening the front door. An invitation.

She sighed. "I'm never going to talk you out of this, am I?"

I waved my hand toward the door. "You're not going to talk to me, period, until you can respect my choices."

"Then I'll go."

I was trying to ignore my gut's panicked churning, reminding me that we had never parted this way, harsh enough not to speak.

She gathered her book, put on her sunglasses, and walked past me, a sad smile on her face. I knew she was burning inside, though. She wanted to be right. I'd wanted to be kind. I was done being kind. But she'd never not want to be right.

Mija, she'd said. *Mi hija.* Not just daughter, *my* daughter. She thought she owned me. Not anymore.

Luke

It started, as most things started for me these days, in the chair. For the exercise I had in mind, all I had to do was keep my leg straight and lift it up, but there wasn't a lot of room in Cassie's apartment to bend my good leg and spread my hands for balance. So I'd asked Rita to help me down the stairs and keep an eye on the backyard in case the pain got to be too much.

As slowly as I could, I lowered myself to the ground.

When I got there I was already breathing hard. But now I had space. I had clear vision. I had no cloud head. *Just one*, I told myself. *Just one and you can be done.*

I imagined my leg was the tree I thought it was in the hospital, when my thoughts were eclipsed by pain. It was the trunk of a tree cut down, and I was back in Buda, still young and happy, at the landscaping job with my brother. I visualized him at the other end, lifting. *Let's get this out of the way*, I said to him. *One, two, three.*

It was up two inches, and it was down.

The pain was there, but it was a calm line of waves, back and forth, lapping. This seemed to work, the practice of attaching everything my body was doing in this yard to objects outside this yard, to moments of peace.

In my mind, I was standing in the makeshift garage on the FOB, my hands resting on the door of a jeep, listening to Clark test its engine.

In my mind I was running.

Cassie

After my mom left, I had begun to pace. This was my household, I was responsible for it, and I liked it this way. Just like I liked wearing the same clothes, and I liked having my magazines scattered on the floor, and I liked that the alarm I'd set for checking my blood sugar every few hours was programmed to play "Sugar, Sugar" by the Archies.

And, yes, this was a tiny, dirty one-bedroom apartment that I paid for by slinging rail cocktails and deceiving the U.S. military, but it was mine, and there were different piles for different things.

There was the black-clothes pile. There was the not-black-clothes pile. There was the pile of Luke's clothes. There was the pile of records. There was the pile of things Luke had used or would use in the future, some of which was trash, okay, but it was convenient because he could reach it from the couch.

Yeah, I'd thought, *it did kind of smell in here.* It smelled like a sweaty human body. Which was normally fine by me, for the record. But one shouldn't have to constantly muck around in another's aura.

Fine. Fine! I would *take care of myself*, just to prove I could do it. But I would use the most toxic corporate bleach, and I would listen to Yoko Ono's primal-screaming records while I did it.

I put our clothes and Luke's blankets in the wash. I removed the trash piles in the living room and kitchen, then swept and mopped the floors, and scrubbed the sink and tub. I mopped the bathroom tile, cleaned the oven, opened the windows, and dusted the sills. I even washed my hair, shaved my legs, plucked my eyebrows, trimmed my bikini line.

Luke opened the door, flashing me a small smile. He was wearing his old sweatpants and a Buda Bears T-shirt with visible pit stains. The effort he'd been expending the last few days was now hovering around him in the form of man scent. Since he started living here, Luke had not yet properly bathed.

Well, now he would. Or, at least, he would once we got him into the bathroom.

Which is how I ended up trying not to look at his naked body as he braced himself on the edge of the tub, hands clutching either side, lowering himself into the steaming water. We had considered a shower, but we were afraid he'd slip, and none of my chairs fit under the measly tap that hung over the claw-foot tub. Problem was, I had to hold him by the chest, making sure his good leg didn't slip and splash water all over the floor, or worse, jam the injured leg against the side.

"Ow, ow, ow, fuck."

My hands were slipping across his chest. "What?"

"Just, slower."

"I'm trying." I followed the line of the water as it hit the tops of his thighs, the lines of muscle cutting his pelvis.

God, Cassie. Perv, my gut said.

I couldn't help it.

Some hidden part of my brain started shooting images of him inside of me in the motel bathroom. And again on the bed. And again on that chair near the bed. *STOP.*

Remember that this is the man who pissed himself on your floor.

Finally, he was sitting.

Oh. And he was aroused. I hadn't noticed; too busy trying not to be aroused. "Okay," I said, feeling my face flush.

"Yeah," Luke said, covering it with his hand. "Sorry. It's been a while since I, you know, was naked in front of a woman."

I shuffled around, looking for a washcloth. "It's biology," I said, my voice doing that thing that it does when I don't know what to say.

Without looking, I tossed a washcloth in the water and stood up, headed toward the door. Something tugged at me, but it wasn't like I hadn't been naked in front of a man in a while. I had no excuse.

"Is there soap?" he said behind me.

"It's in the rack hanging on the spigot."

A second later he yelled, "Fuck, ow." He sighed. "Unfortunately, I can't reach it."

"It's right behind you," I said to the wall.

"I can't."

I turned around and knelt, seeing his face strain as he twisted. In order to get it, he had to press his leg against the side of the tub.

"I'll do it," I said.

As I loaded the washcloth with soap, he rested his head on the back of the tub, breathing shallowly. He was exhausted, still wincing every few seconds. On instinct, I pushed him forward slightly, and ran the cloth down his back, to the parts it would be difficult for him to reach.

"Where else?" I said.

He opened his eyes. "Hm?"

"Where else can't you reach?"

"No." He held out his hand to take it. "I don't need you to do that."

"Just let me." I squeezed the washcloth, and the tug went lower inside me, but thank God he couldn't see that, and thank God it was just the two of us so no one else could question why I thought this would be a good idea.

He did let me. I started with his back, then up the neck, behind the ears. At first it was weird, but then it was just . . . nice. Nice to see him not in pain and, yes, nice to touch him, as it had been that night six months ago. And perhaps nicer now, since neither of us was drunk or angry or awkward.

"Thank you," he said, lulled, his silver-blue eyes disappearing under tired lids. "This is really," he started, and let out a shiver as I got close to under his arms. "Helpful."

"You're welcome," I replied, moving to his thighs, under his knees, the underside of his calves.

Suddenly, "Sugar, Sugar" started up in my pocket. Luke flinched in the water, splashing me slightly. I laughed, and stood up, grabbing my meter and test strips from the medicine cabinet, my lance and lancelets from the shelf above the toilet.

"Do you mind if I do this?" I asked, holding up the meter.

"No," Luke said, his eyes looking up at me. "I've always been curious about it, to be honest."

"Well," I said, washing my hands. "It's not that exciting."

I took my lance, poked the side of my index finger, drawing the tiniest drop of blood. I glanced at Luke. He was transfixed. I smiled.

"Now," I said, holding up a bloody finger, "I touch the edge of the strip, and we wait."

The air was quiet, thick with steam. I put a cotton ball on my fingertip.

"About 3.6. A little low." I grabbed a glucose tablet and popped it in my mouth. "Tablets for nonemergencies," I said, pointing to the bottle. "Packets for emergencies." I pointed to the box.

"Why packets?"

I hesitated, wondering how I should put this without scaring him. "In case I'm too out of it to swallow."

I heard him move around again, the water lapping. I opened the cabinet again, reaching the tiny notebook and pen I kept there to record my levels.

"You record the blood sugar in a notebook?" Luke said.

I nodded.

"I do that, too. I mean with my running times." He cleared his throat. "Or rather, I used to. Anyway, guess what?" he said. "I'm going to start physical therapy tomorrow, for real. I'm going to run again if it kills me."

I tossed the washcloth back into the water. I let out a breath. "Oh, yeah?"

"Yeah."

I glanced at his leg. The injured part was mottled brown, scarred. Just below his right knee was a single darker scar, the size of a bullet hole.

"What, you don't believe me?" he asked, snatching the washcloth out of the water to do the rest, splashing me.

I splashed him back, standing. "Actually, I do."

Luke

Jake still hadn't shown, and I was beginning to worry. I wouldn't be surprised if he backed out. We'd talked a week ago, and I'd even left my phone on just in case, but I hadn't heard from him since. I hadn't heard from Johnno, either, which was starting to make me think my phone wasn't working, or something. The air outside Cassie's house was cool. The grass was dry, the pavement wet where Rita had watered her planters. Passing cars kicked up dust and birds fluttered overhead. It was all so normal, but after weeks being cooped up in Cassie's apartment, the world felt heightened somehow, a brighter version of itself.

I'd been up, walking circles around Cassie's apartment, for days, but this was the first time I'd tried the stairs by myself, using the cane the hospital had given me.

Even so, my stiff legs were practically itching to run. I started to remember the last time, the day before Frankie and Rooster and I found out we were heading to the Pakistan border. I'd hit the track at dawn, leaving Rooster and Frankie sleeping in the little wood-paneled room, untouched air in my lungs, holding two truths at once: that everything was hard, and that everything was going to be okay.

And then it hadn't been.

The memory hooks came. If we hadn't gotten in the jeep, if I'd blocked Frankie, if, if, if. The daily desire for cloud head was rising, wanting to erase it all. I pushed it away. *Not here, not here, not now.* I'd taken only one this morning.

I'd put Rita in charge of my prescription, instructing her to stagger them out to twice a day, no matter what I asked. She understood.

Not a second later, as if to reward me, Jake turned down Cassie's street in his car. "You need a hand getting in?" he called through the open window.

I limped toward him. "Nah, it's good."

"Well, look at you," he said.

The whole drive to Buda we barely spoke, just listened to the local sports radio station's pregame analysis. It was the conference championship, they were saying. The Bears were favored to win.

We were late. Of course, precisely when I had plopped my cane onto the first row of bleachers, hauling my gimp leg like a sack of potatoes, the band director tapped his baton on the stand. Everyone rose in silence, their hands on their hearts, poised to sing the national anthem.

Thump. I had been concentrating on propelling myself to the next step, not noticing that the talking had died down. *Kerthump.*

Everyone's eyes were pulled toward the sound. "Poor guy," I heard. "Morrow's son. Veteran."

The band director, being the patriot that he was, waited until I had made a slow, rotisserie chicken–like turn to face the flag.

"Oh, say can you see," the voices began around me.

"Move to give him your seat, Carl," I heard.

Jake and I kept our eyes ahead. I didn't want anyone's seat. All I did was get shot at and come back home and sit on a stranger's couch eating pills. I didn't deserve anyone's seat. For the thousandth time that day, I wished I was cloud head. *No.*

About halfway through the first quarter, Jake and I had finally made it to the only open seats in the third row.

"You good, man?" he asked, helping to ease my lower half into a sitting position.

"Yeah," I assured him. "Just don't ask me to get you anything from the concession stand."

Jake laughed and I felt an inch of relief.

One of the Bears' post players had just dived for the ball. Out of bounds. The whistle blew.

"Good hustle," I said.

"Yeah, they're scrappy this year," Jake replied.

The game resumed.

I could barely remember what I had been thinking the other night, calling out to Cassie to watch me stand, my tongue like a dead fish in my mouth, but I remembered what I had wanted. To be better. Jake wasn't going to start talking. This was my job, without a safety net.

"Remember—" I swallowed. "It's hard to believe this is the same place I took you for basketball camp."

"Yeah, I think about that sometimes. When I go to games."

"You were good, too."

"I was all right. I had to quit to start working at the garage."

I shook my head, remembering him coming home with Dad when he was just fifteen, on the rare days I wasn't off somewhere getting high, his jeans covered in motor oil. "You grew up too fast."

"We both did." The ref called a foul on the Bears. Jake threw up his hands, groaning with the crowd. "Aw, come on!"

"Nah, not me. I was just a shithead."

"Yeah, but before that." Jake took his eyes off the game, onto his hands folded between his knees. "After Mom died."

"How could you remember that?" He was just a baby.

"How could you not?" His voice went up, thin. "I mean, I don't remember Mom. But a few years after that, I remember Dad had you walking me to day care. Walking me home."

I'd help him into his clothes. Mostly my old shirts. My Batman shirt, which I had been mad didn't fit me anymore. I had forgotten all this; it was so long ago. I shrugged. "Day care was just down the street."

The Mountain Lions missed their free throw. The crowd cheered. Jake leaned back, starting to smile. "After you walked us home you always liked to climb on the stool and get the animal crackers from above the refrigerator. And we'd sit there and watch *Power Rangers* until Dad came home."

"And then we'd act it out outside," I said. "While Dad made his terrible hamburgers."

Jake laughed. "You told me the Pink Ranger was manly. Was the most manly color. Remember that?"

"God." I laughed with him. "We were progressive as hell."

"I tell JJ that, too," Jake said, elbowing me. "I tell him that pink is fine. Whatever he likes is fine. Hailey loves that."

"I'll bet," I said. The teams took a time-out. The memories washed up, pooling around us.

"I mean, listen, Luke," Jake started, interrupted by two people getting up to go to the concession stand, muttering about the price of Coke. "You were my only person when we were little. That's what I meant to say. Dad was there, but I don't know if he ever really wanted to be a dad. He did his best. But you were there."

My throat tensed up. I looked at my shoes. The game started up again.

"And when you began to pull away, and do shit, and act out, it was like losing another parent."

The force of what he was saying was about to knock me over. I had two choices. I could try to escape through some other route, some other feeling, or I could take it. I remembered knocking on Johnno's door the day after I'd taken OxyContin for the first time. I had almost backed away before he could open it. I had almost gone back.

I turned and looked at my brother. I saw my mother's eyes in his eyes.

"I think—" I paused, choosing my words. "This isn't an excuse, but I think Mom's death hit me later. It sideswiped me."

"I know it did," Jake said, looking out on the game. He put his hand on my back for a second.

My relief had weight, had substance. "I won't do that to you again," I said, my voice uneven.

"You better not," Jake muttered. "And don't get any ideas about re-enlisting after your leg heals." Ten seconds until the first quarter was over. The Bears were behind by two points. "Mr. Purple Heart."

I looked at him. He'd probably seen it in the paper. Dad, too. I hadn't really talked about it with anyone in depth yet. Every time I thought about my own Purple Heart, I saw Frankie's bloody boots. It hardly seemed real. "We'll see."

"Come on, defense!" Jake yelled. "Here we go!"

With seven seconds left, the point guard stole an inbound pass and gained momentum down the court. Everyone around us stood, yelling, "Go! Go! Go!" Jake stood, too.

I pressed on my cane, creaking upward, my leg shooting pain. No, I wouldn't reenlist, I thought. I had other things to focus on. Staying sober, getting an education.

By the time I was standing, and could see what happened, the point guard had scored. With labor, I sat again. Instead of getting frustrated, I smiled at Jake, who helped me conquer the last inch or so.

"So, did y'all get a nurse?" Jake asked.

I clutched my cane, my lips pressed. "We should have."

Jake shook his head at me. "You made Cassie do it all by herself?"

"Her neighbor helps out. It was a decision we made together."

"Man." Jake shook his head, admiring.

"I know. She's good, yeah." I thought of Cassie's beaming face when I had started to walk the other day, her taking my arm as we circled the room. Had I thanked her for that? "She's amazing," I added, and felt the truth of my words. Even when we fought, she braced her body against mine, still fuming.

"I bet she complains, though. I'd whine about it all the time if I were her."

"She doesn't too much," I said. "Not to me, at least."

"She's a good one, Luke," Jake said, looking from the game to me for a moment. "You picked yourself a good one."

The buzzer sounded for halftime. Jake stood, stretching. "You want anything?"

Suddenly, a man in a bright orange T-shirt took the court, holding a wireless microphone. "Okay, okay, people! Who's ready to win some pizza from Gino's?"

The crowd roared.

"What the hell?" I asked Jake, laughing.

Before he could answer, a blond woman in an equally bright orange shirt accompanied the man, holding a fishbowl of red scraps.

"All of your ticket stubs were put into *this bowl*. The lucky seat I draw will get the chance to win free pizza for a year if you make a half-court shot!"

"Well, shit," Jake said, turning to look at me, eyebrows raised. I rolled my eyes.

"And the lucky seat is . . ." The woman drew a scrap from the bowl. "Row C, seat eleven!"

The folks around us turned side to side, and then, slowly, all faced me. I looked at my seat. It was me. I was in row C, seat 11. *Shit.*

For the second time that day, everyone stared. Ex-girlfriends who had gotten plump with babies, former social studies and English teachers who had wanted to flunk me, former football coaches who had failed to whip the mouth off me, former friends and parents of friends who had seen me drunk off of the vodka stolen from their liquor cabinets, all were waiting to see what I would do.

I lifted my cane, shaking my head, feeling humiliation rise in my stomach, hot and soupy. Jake tried to wave them off, smiling politely, saying, "All right, now, back off," through his teeth. "The man doesn't want to do it."

"Jake," I said suddenly, warmth rising to my face, "you gotta do it."

"What?"

"Yeah, are you kidding? You've made that shot a hundred times." Even as a kid, he could launch it from well past the three-point line, if he did it from his hip.

I pointed at Jake, and I don't know what came over me, but I began to chant. Maybe it was the army man in me, the person who loved to move in sync, who'd fall back to the privates who weren't running as fast, breathe with them, yell with them, helping them make it to the finish line.

"Jacob, Jacob, Jacob," I shouted.

Everyone caught on. "Jacob, Jacob," the whole gymnasium joined in. Jake's face turned red. He held up his palms. "All right!"

I watched him leap down the bleacher steps two at a time. I held no hardness, no anger that I would be able to go only half as fast when we left, that the pain would almost break me, that I'd want OxyContin when I got home to make it all go away.

Jake caught a bounced pass from the man in the orange shirt. *I won't do that to you again*, I'd told him. This time, I knew what terror might come, tempting me to go back, to let Oxy numb me. But I also knew that the pain of giving in to my addiction would be much deeper.

Jake looked at me. I gave him a Power Rangers stance in my seat. He dribbled to the opposite free-throw line, pressed forward, and launched the ball into the air.

Cassie

Luke sat in the front seat of the Subaru, his cane propped on the door. I reached between his legs to clear out the empty water bottles and granola bar wrappers that had accumulated near his feet. And by 'clear out,' I mean put in the backseat. "Sorry," I said, stifling a yawn.

"It's cool," he replied, laughing a little, eyeing the empty Queen, Natalie Cole, David Bowie, and Patsy Cline CD cases piled on the dashboard.

He'd wanted to go to the river, so he could keep working on his PT outside. Of course I'd said yes, and offered to pick him up later, but I was nervous, for some reason. He'd been inside for so long, sheltered from the chaos of the outside world, vulnerable and defenseless. I felt like I was releasing an injured lion back into the savanna.

When I turned on the ignition, Portishead blasted at high volume. I turned it down, giving him a *whoops* look as I reversed. "Not used to having anyone else in my car."

Except for Toby, and unless I kept the volume up high, he would talk about the music instead of just listening to it. That's why, I'd discovered, going to loud concerts with him was fun.

Luke rolled down the window. "You can keep it turned up," he said, content with his face in the breeze.

Okay, Cassie, chill. He wasn't an infant with sensitive eardrums. I turned it up, and, yeah, fine, I sang along with Beth Gibbons, because that's what I would have done otherwise. Luke nodded along, lost in his own thoughts.

When we reached the river, he guided me to a spot in the park as if he knew it.

"You've been here before?"

"Yeah," he said, not elaborating. I resisted the urge to ask him more. I didn't know why I wanted to know, anyway.

"Thanks, Cassie." He lifted his injured leg out, put the cane on the pavement, and pushed himself up, reaching a hand in to wave good-bye.

"Oh, Luke, your phone!" I said. He'd left it on the seat.

It was vibrating. He grabbed it, looked at the number, his mouth twisting for a moment in disgust.

"Eh," he said. "I don't need it. You can pick me up here, thanks." He tossed it on the car floor, out of sight.

"Okay, bye," I called through the open window.

I watched him limp away, solo against the endless wall of trees. Suddenly, I remembered: I had forgotten to get him a plant.

Luke

For five days straight, Cassie dropped me off on the trails at River Place on her way to work, and Rita picked me up after. I started with fifteen minutes of exercises. If I could get through fifteen minutes and fifteen knee raises, I'd get through twenty the next day. If I could get through fifteen minutes, I could take out the trash.

If I could get through twenty minutes and twenty ankle curls, I could get through twenty-five, and I could go to the corner store a block away and get milk and eggs and bread.

If I could get through thirty, I could practice stepping in and out of the bathtub.

After last night's training session, I'd asked Cassie to drop me off at a church down the street from her house for a Narcotics Anonymous meeting. I'm not sure if she knew why I was there, or what the meeting was for. We didn't talk about it.

Today, I was on forty. I hadn't thought of a task equivalent to forty yet. I had at least worked up the strength to text Johnno that the severance was coming soon. He'd texted back, *Cash this time, motherfucker*, which was less threatening than usual. I could enjoy the sight of the riverbank for a half hour, I guessed. Dad used to take Jake and me here whenever he had to go to Austin to see his accountant.

Now Jake was holding my cane while I leaned on a tree, bending my leg at more than a 160-degree angle. I'd called him and asked him if he could spare a Saturday to help me train. He'd said yes, as long as he could yell at me like a drill sergeant.

To Jake, I'd learned, this mostly meant adding the word "maggot" to the end of what would otherwise be encouraging statements.

"Nice work, you maggot!" he growled.

I lifted again, straining to reach the height it would take for an able-bodied person to step over a shoebox. "I'm a regular Rocky Balboa."

Jake walked up the path, searching the trees, and walked back.

"You see something?" I asked, lifting my foot through what felt like swamp mud. *There's no way Johnno would come here, right?* I swallowed with a dry mouth.

"No, nothing," Jake said, hiding a smile.

After I finished, we continued up the path. At my slow pace, I noticed the world more. The neon moss on the rocks. The white rock paths winding through the trees like train tracks. The golden retriever bounding down one of the stairways on a retractable leash.

The dog nuzzled my leg, leaping up and down on its forepaws. It ran a tight circle around me, then licked my hands. "Hey, boy," I said. "Hey, there."

"It's a girl!" a voice called down the slope.

Cassie appeared at the top of the stone steps, and jogged down, her hair flying. Behind her was her pale friend with the ponytail, Nora.

I looked back and forth between Cassie and Jake. They kept giggling, and looking at me expectantly. "What's up?"

The dog was in a triangle of delight, grinning up at each of us in turn with her big cinnamon-colored eyes, tongue dangling.

"Sorry, I meant to call you but I forgot my phone."

"You? Forgetting your phone?"

She rolled her eyes and smiled. "Luke, this is Mittens. She's yours."

"She's mine?" I put a hand on her silky head. "How can she be mine?"

"A program," Jake said. "Dogs for Vets."

"You were in on this?" I pushed him on the arm.

"Jake!" Cassie said. "You were supposed to tell him we found her at the foot of an ancient shrine, ruling over a commune of inferior dogs."

"She doesn't seem like the queenly type," Jake said, tilting his head. "Mittens is more the jester."

Mittens was currently biting a large stick, whipping it like it was a dead animal, but she kept poking herself in the side.

"Or maybe the village idiot," Nora said.

"It was Nora's idea, actually."

Nora gave me a thin-lipped smile. "Figured you could use some loosening up."

"Thank you," I said, catching her eyes. "And you're okay with this?" I asked Cassie.

Cassie's apartment was about to get a lot smaller. And smellier. I had never been much of an animal person. Not that I *didn't* like dogs. My dad just never got Jake and me any pets because "we were animals enough." And the stray dogs in Afghanistan were pretty much everyone's dogs, not to mention they usually had dead rats hanging out of their mouths. I didn't love the idea of caring for another being outside of myself, either, since caring for myself seemed hard enough.

But I guess that was the point.

Cassie bent down. "Oh, yes, I'm okay wit dis," she said, rubbing Mittens's ears. "Admit it—she's so cute. Look at that cute little face, with the eyes and the nose and the face!"

I had never seen Cassie so affectionate. With anyone, or anything. Not when she was trying to be "wifely," not on the phone to Toby, not even on the phone to her mother. I couldn't help but laugh. Mittens leaped around my knees, as if to agree.

"What?" Cassie said, looking up at me, her cheeks pink. "I think she and Dante are going to be friends."

"She could eat Dante for breakfast."

The five of us continued up the trail, me taking charge of Mittens, Mittens taking charge of her stick.

"Fingers crossed," Cassie said.

Cassie

Yarvis was back. He'd brought croissants, which I set on the coffee table in front of Luke and me while Yarvis sat across from us. We'd both showered this time. Luke wore his button-down. I wore actual pants instead of cutoffs. The apartment was airy and lemony from cleaning.

"There's nothing like fresh-baked croissants," Yarvis said.

Luke and I exchanged looks.

"Luke, you seem more awake. Cassie, how's the music life?"

"I've got to leave for practice in thirty minutes." We were doing the song I'd written for Frankie. The Sahara show was in three days.

"Well, we'll try to be prompt."

"She *will* leave in the middle of a sentence, FYI," Luke warned Yarvis.

"Yeah, so? Why is it so hard to understand that this is my work? No one would be giving me shit if I were leaving for my job at the firm. This is my *real work*."

I tempered myself, realizing I was just talking aloud to an invisible version of Mom. But Toby had started to do it, too, acting offended and hurt because I wouldn't treat him like my boyfriend at rehearsal, because he distracted me, and he pissed Nora off. He always thought I was mad at him. Then, because he kept asking if I was mad at him, I would actually get mad.

Luke shrugged. "I was just saying, honey."

"Oh." Interesting. I guess Luke wasn't passing judgment, just stating a fact. "Thanks, babe."

Yarvis checked up on Luke's PT progress—"Well, well, well," he said—then told us we had to do some sort of role-playing game before he left. When he excused himself to go to the bathroom, I turned to Luke.

"What is it with these people and their marital exercises?"

"I know," he said. "Whatever happened to the good old days of 'your daughter for two goats, please'?"

I elbowed him, feeling an ease I hadn't since our Skype days. It felt like we were old pros. Old married pros.

"Okay," Yarvis said, settling in with another croissant. "The idea is that you pretend you are the other person, and make statements of gratitude. Cassie?"

Mittens was at Yarvis's feet, tail wagging, eyes on the croissant.

"I'm Luke, and I'm grateful for Mittens," I said in a Mickey Mouse impression. He loved it when I did high voices. And by "loved," I mean he made a face like he was hearing a metal chair scrape on the ground. *If I didn't know you had such an incredible singing voice . . .* he'd said last time.

"Great. I sound just like that," Luke said, flat.

"Maybe leave out the impressions," Yarvis said. "Okay, Luke?"

Luke said, fake serious, "I'm Cassie, and I'm grateful my husband hasn't changed Mittens's name to Rambo Dog, despite repeated threats."

I rolled my eyes. "She wouldn't even *respond* to Rambo Dog."

"She would if there's bacon," Luke asserted.

"Okay, you two. Cassie?"

"I'm Luke, and I'm grateful my wife hasn't left my sorry ass," I joked. I looked at Luke, expecting him to laugh, but he was staring at his phone, brow furrowed. He did that a lot. I knew it had to do with his family, or his money situation, neither of which it was within our boundaries for me to handle. Instead, I nudged him.

"Luke," Yarvis scolded. "You're supposed to listen."

"Sorry," Luke said, tucking his phone away.

"I'm Luke," I started again. "And I let my masculinity stunt my emotions."

I wasn't joking on that one—all of his shrugging off help, his refusal to tell me what his nightmares were about—so I was surprised to see Luke smile and put his arm around me.

"I could say the same for you, honey."

We both laughed at that. He was smarter than he thought he was. When he felt comfortable, he was as observant and witty as anyone I'd ever met.

"See?" Yarvis said, smiling through a bite of croissant. "I told you it'd get easier."

Luke

"Can you catch it, Mittens?" I held a neon-pink Buda Municipal Fire Department Frisbee to Mittens's nose.

"Try to make him catch it!" JJ screamed with delight.

"That's what Uncle Luke's doing, honey," Hailey said.

"Mittens is a girly dog, JJ," Jake said, squatting next to his son. "Not a 'him.'"

"Burgers will be ready in ten," my dad called from the grill.

"Salad will be ready . . . like, right now," Cassie echoed, examining the bowl of romaine into which she had just poured Caesar dressing.

We had gathered in my dad's backyard for a barbecue. Jake and Hailey said it was my dad's idea, though I had a feeling it had been Jake and Hailey's idea.

It was sunny out, the sky was ice blue, and Mittens seemed excited about the Frisbee, wagging her tail so hard it sent her backside back and forth. I whipped the disk toward the edge of the fence until it looked like it was going to sail clean over, before Mittens leaped and snatched it out of the air.

Everyone erupted in cheers.

Pain snaked from my shin to my hip, but now that I'd started to build muscle, I just winced instead of collapsing. "Good girl!" I rubbed her velvety ears.

I hadn't seen this yard sober for three years. Mittens was trotting near the bushes where I used to hide from Jake after I drew dicks in his comic books, waiting to pelt him with pebbles when he came out the back door. I'd pee in those bushes when I came home from a party cross-faded, hoping to avoid using the toilet so I could make as little noise as possible. There were probably still cigarette butts in the soil from when I would sneak over from

Johnno's place to steal pieces of white bread or bologna or whatever else I could grab.

The last time I was here, Dad had walked in while I was microwaving a frozen burrito. He had told me to repay what Johnno and I had stolen from the garage, or he'd call the cops. It was only one or two hundred bucks. Cloud head had laughed. Dad had reached for the cordless and dialed. I'd dropped the burrito and started to run.

That's right, he'd said. *Get out. You coward.*

Johnno had already started down the block. When Dad saw that I was running to get in the Bronco, he ran after me, cordless phone in hand. *Luke!*

You've failed me. You've failed your mother. You've failed Jake.

Dad had thrown the phone, hard, breaking the skin at the back of my head. I still have a scar.

That was about a year before Jake and Hailey's wedding. It was the last time I'd heard him say my name.

Today, Cassie had rung the bell, as if I hadn't spent the majority of my life opening that navy-painted door with a karate kick, slipping off my muddy shoes, flopping on the nearest piece of furniture.

I hadn't realized my hands were shaking until Cassie, noticing, put her hand over the one that held my cane. I looked around for my brother, for someone watching us. No one was. She squeezed.

The door opened. My dad had aged, softened in a way. I hadn't noticed when I'd seen him that day at the hospital. God, when had he become an old man?

I'd held out my free hand.

"Son," he'd said, and took it.

I was trying not to make it a big deal. But I guess you could say the natural state of my face was *grin*.

While Cassie and Dad served up plates, Jake and Hailey and I watched JJ chase Mittens around the yard, launching his tiny body onto her back, trying to ride her.

"Careful, don't hurt the doggy!" Hailey called.

"Saw you and Dad talking about where you served," Jake said.

I smiled at him. "Yeah."

"Yeah," he replied, slapping me on the back.

Hailey glanced over at us. She held up her hands, sarcastic. "Whoa, hey, you two. Don't make a scene."

Over burgers, we talked about the dismal Rangers season, business at the garage, Cassie's upcoming show. Mittens begged everyone for food.

"See?" Dad said after Jake and I had teased him about how his burgers were more like little balls of meat. "Mittens doesn't care what shape it's in. She knows it tastes good."

After JJ sang us the alphabet song, Cassie told an abridged version of our city hall wedding. She did an imitation of the guy who married us, counting on her fingers in the exaggerated accent. "It was like he was listing cuts of meat, or something! We got a juicy Psalm 23, a fresh Corinthians, a fatty cut of Ephesians . . ."

Hailey and Jake were losing it. Dad started laughing, too, and I noted that as number six. The sixth time I'd seen my dad laugh, it was Cassie. Before I thought about what I was doing, I leaned my head over and kissed her on the cheek.

She kept laughing, giving me a look without missing a beat.

As the sun set, I asked my dad if it would be all right if I took Cassie up to the attic. He nodded from where he had settled in his chair, watching football. Between Cassie and the cane, the stairs took only five minutes.

"Cut my time in half," I noted.

"Don't get cocky," Cassie joked.

My father's old tin trunk sat between a box of Christmas lights and a stack of photo albums. It had been in the back of my mind for weeks now, and when Jake invited us over, I knew I had to come up here and find it. I bent gingerly to brush off dust from the top.

"What is that?" Cassie asked.

I unhooked the latches. I remembered Batman pajamas, Jake gurgling in my mother's arms, both of us fresh from the bath. The feel of the rough canvas of Dad's uniform, *Morrow* inscribed on the breast pocket. And underneath, the wooden box. Dad's Purple Heart.

I laughed to myself, holding it up for Cassie to see. She squinted from where she sat next to me on the floor, cross-legged.

"Oh, is that— Holy shit! I didn't know your dad had a Purple Heart."

Now I would have one, too. God, I couldn't believe that. I had thought it made my dad the most important man in the world.

"What'd he get it for?"

"Shot twice in the side on the Mekong Delta."

I couldn't keep the memories at bay now. "I remember he lifted up his shirt to show me the scars, and I remember touching those little pink bumps and just, like, thinking he was a superhero. Not even that. Better than a superhero because he was my dad. He was like the invincible human."

Cassie laughed.

"To survive bullets, you know? And here I was, a little baby boy, crying about a bruise, and my dad was like the cowboys on TV, getting hit and not blinking an eye. Just going about his business. I wanted to be like that."

"You *are* like that," Cassie said, touching my leg lightly.

"Of course, it's not the same," I said. I didn't feel invincible. Most of the time I felt like my skin was turned inside out. Today was one of the first days in a while when I didn't mind that it was.

"Of course not," she agreed, smiling. "It's always different when your parents do it."

"When my mom died, that's what we did. We pretended we were invincible," I said, and hesitated.

I had never talked about my mom with Cassie, but I wanted her to know. I wanted her to know everything. "We just went about our business. Didn't mourn, didn't talk about it, and it wasn't really fair."

"To you?"

"No, to her. Just letting her disappear like she wasn't also the most important person in the world."

"How old were you?"

"Five. It was ovarian cancer. I barely remember her. A lady at the church had to tell me how she died. When I asked my dad, he said something like, 'Don't worry about it. Let her be in peace.'"

"Damn." Cassie fiddled with the collar on my uniform, then looked at me. "What is it with you and your dad, anyway?"

I sighed. "It's a long story. He did the best he could."

"He's *doing*," she corrected. "Doing the best he can."

"You're right." I regarded her, realizing that even though I'd known her for only a few months, even though our relationship had been predicated on a lie, she'd seen me at my worst and she was still here. "Thank you," I said, quickly—it felt urgent, up here among all these stories, before we had to go back downstairs to the real world. "For everything, in the past few months."

She smiled, calm, unafraid. "You're welcome. You know, if you talked this much all the time, our lives might be a little easier. I might understand you a little better."

"Ha. Don't get used to it."

"I'd like to," she said, then stood, fast, embarrassed.

I busied myself putting things back into the trunk. We didn't have long before I was discharged. I knew that and she knew that, but we'd been playing married all day and there was permanence in the air. Little comments, like when she was playing with JJ, Hailey had asked if there would be a little Cassie or Luke in the future.

The ease of her taking my hand before I saw my dad, the ease of kissing her on the cheek when I was proud of her, my funny, creative, fake wife.

I knew it was all an illusion, a life we'd dreamed up out of desperation, but in that moment it felt real.

Cassie

The day after the barbecue, a couple of hours before The Loyal's last rehearsal before the show tomorrow night, I made my way to Toby's. And I was on a mission.

So the thing about Luke, the thing about him kissing me on the cheek in a fairly regular, natural way, and my recent tolerance and even fondness for the nickname "honey," and my saying *I'd like to get used to you*. So the thing about that was, I didn't know. I was pretty sure these were surface-level gestures that had been made complicated only because I had seen him naked. Combine that with a cute dog and a cute baby running around his cute family, with the cute dad making cute burgers, and bam, you've got yourself Lifetime movie feelings.

Toby, as I'd decided today, was a real person with whom I had a real thing going on. I wasn't saying Luke wasn't real, but the circumstances through which I began to care for him were not. They were fabricated. Completely. So that detracts a certain legitimacy from said caring, does it not?

But that didn't stop me from caring about Luke, and, in fact, I'll be damned if it didn't punch me right in the face with the fact that I was ready to care for *someone*. I was ready to share the space I'd built. And it should be with someone who wasn't about to limp out of my life, leaving a trail of take-out boxes and dog hair and painkiller bottles.

And that someone was Toby. Toby with the Arkansas gap in his teeth, who was an encyclopedia of music and had nimble, rhythmic hands that had been backing me up for a year now.

When he opened his door, I pulled his face toward mine.

"Um, hey," he said between kisses.

"I'm getting a divorce soon," I told him. "You know that, right? Luke and I will be divorced when he gets discharged."

"Yeah."

"I also think . . ." The words caught. "I think you and I should give the living together thing a try."

"Wait, Cassie, really?"

"Really." The way his eyebrows drooped at the ends, eyes wide, that grateful smile. He was adorable. I took his shoulders. "I mean, it just makes sense, you know? We've known each other for so long."

"And you don't have to sign a lease or anything, you know," he said.

He glanced at my hands, which were now unbuttoning his shirt. "Let's not talk logistics right now."

I unbuttoned his jeans, and they fell. It was time to show each other that we weren't going to be that boring couple who goes out to eat and farts quietly while they watch TV and meets in the bedroom where they hump each other until they fall asleep.

"We're going to live together," I said, lifting my shirt. "And sometimes," I continued, slipping off my cutoffs, "I'm going to be getting ready for work."

Toby was still standing there, jeans at his knees, watching me.

I walked past him to the bathroom. "And I'm going to want it so bad," I said, hopping onto the counter next to the sink, opening my legs. "That you're going to fuck me right then and there."

"Wait," Toby said.

I stared at him. In the twelve on-and-off months I'd been removing my clothes around him, I'd never heard hesitation in his voice.

"I feel like this is special," he said. He stepped out of his jeans and walked toward me, a soft smile on his face.

That was fine. He didn't want to dirty talk. I could still work with this. He stood on the tile, kissing me small and slow in a line, starting at my ear, down to my shoulder.

I pulled him into me by his lower back, and noticed he wasn't hard.

"I'm sorry," he said, stepping back. "Can we just take a second to talk about the timeline?"

I tried to keep the mood going, hooking my finger in his shirt, looking at him with doe eyes. "Later."

"It's also weird to have sex with you while I can see myself in the mirror." He pointed behind me. "Plus I bet this counter is really dirty."

"Isn't that kind of hot, though?"

He scrunched up his face. "Eh. I'm not drunk enough to ignore it."

"Okay," I said, hopping off.

"I'm sorry," he said, his hands circling my waist. "Is it weird that I want to just savor this without a hookup?"

"No need to be sorry," I said, trying to hide my disappointment. "It makes sense."

"We're the real deal now," he said, between pecks at my neck.

"Yeah," I said, sitting on the bed.

"Aw, damn, Cass," he said, running his fingers through my hair. "We'll try bathroom sex again." We lay together, Toby draping his arms around me. He pulled me tighter. "We'll have plenty of time," he whispered.

Luke

Once Cassie left for Toby's, I asked Rita if I could borrow her car, and drove to where Johnno used to live, hoping he would still be there. I knocked on the puke-green door, a gym bag full of cash hooked to my cane. Bass pounded from inside. Empty cans of Monster Energy and Lone Star littered the stoop. Under the peep hole, somebody had ground the letters *I C U*.

Yep, telltale Johnno markings. I pounded harder.

Kaz opened the door, a blunt hanging from his lips. I had forgotten how huge he was. I was six foot two and came up only to his nipples.

"Here," I said, and lifted the bag. I'd been saving every penny I could of my paychecks since I deployed, and I'd cashed my savings, but I finally had twenty-five hundred dollars. How I was going to find twenty-five hundred for the final payment in a month was a problem for another day.

Kaz took the bag.

"Tell him to come in here and count it out," I heard Johnno yell.

"It's all there," I called. "You know how to reach me if it's not." I was borrowing Rita's car. I had to get back so she could go to her hair appointment.

Kaz grabbed my shoulder and ushered me inside.

Three minutes later, Johnno confirmed it was all there. He lounged on the futon with the gun sitting on his belly, stockinged feet resting on the coffee table next to the pile.

When I stood up to leave, Kaz blocked my way. "We're not done yet."

"You'll get the rest in a month, like we agreed."

"We have some new *información*," Johnno said, picking dirt out of his fingernails.

"What now?"

Johnno picked up the gun, aiming it at me like a teacher's pointer. "How would you explain your situation with Ms. Cassandra Salazar, in your own words? Go."

I swallowed. My hand started to fidget on the cane. "Married."

Johnno waved the gun. "Go on."

I said nothing. I looked around the room for an answer, a weapon.

"We've been keeping tabs on you, bro. Making sure you're not going to ghost. And here comes Cassie's hot ass, so natch we're gonna follow that."

I was clenching my bum leg, hoping the pain would distract me from the fear rising up. "Do y'all just sit in the Bronco all day spying on people?"

Kaz was on his phone, muttering, "Sometimes we go to Buffalo Wild Wings. That's some good shit."

"Shut the fuck up, Kaz," Johnno said.

Kaz glared at Johnno, then back at me, and continued, "We found out where she works, and where her mom lives."

"I said shut the fuck up!" Johnno yelled. Even in the midst of dishing out threats, Johnno was such a child. "We also found out that she goes home with some other dude all the time."

Kaz commiserated. "Why you gonna let her play you like that, bro?"

Johnno held up a finger. "No, he knows."

Kaz looked at me. "You know?"

"You and Cassie are medieval-times married, aren't you? You just did it for the extra army cash. Confirm or deny."

I pounded a fist into my palm to keep from swinging my cane across his pocked face. If I did, Kaz would be on me like a bull rhino. "You didn't give me much of a choice."

"Okay, here's a choice," Johnno said, suddenly sitting up, gun swinging in his bony hands. "You either pay us fifty thousand dollars, or we report you to army police."

I stood. "You're out of your mind!" Kaz was in my face in a second, chest to chest. "I couldn't get that kind of money if I wanted to."

"That's what you say every time," Johnno said, pointing to the pile. "And then there it be."

I pointed to Johnno. "You can fuck off." To Kaz, I said, "Please move."

With a nod from Johnno, Kaz stepped aside.

"Fifty K, magic man!" he yelled after me, erupting into a cough. "Make it appear!"

"Not gonna happen, dude," I called, and slammed the door.

Once outside, my breath caught in my lungs. My vision zeroed in and out. *I C U.* I leaned on my cane, hoping I wouldn't pass out.

They could hurt me, but they wouldn't kill me if they really thought I could produce fifty K. But they'd already staked out Cassie's place, and I doubted they'd stop there. He knew where Jake lived, about my dad's garage. He wanted that money, one way or another, and I didn't have a prayer's chance of raising it on my own.

Cassie

Mom made me beans and rice, a fact of which I was made aware by her calling me to say, "I made extra beans and rice."

"Then why don't you put it in some Tupperware?" I'd responded.

"Just come over and eat it."

We hadn't spoken since the fight in my apartment. The absence of her daily texts about the names of actors she recognized but couldn't place, her voice mails summarizing the habits of her plants growing outside the duplex, her invitations to help her "wash the rich people toilets," were like little holes poked in my days. The stillness of my phone was enough at times to make me look up her name, but then I remembered she wouldn't want to speak to me, either.

She wanted to speak to her daughter the law student, maybe, or her daughter the paralegal, but not me.

When she called, I waited to answer until the last second before it hit voice mail, my heart pounding.

Now we sat in the kitchen on Cord Street over the steaming bowls of red beans and white rice with ham and *sofrito* and Sazón con Azafran. We made small talk about the dry heat, the novels she'd read recently, the new pots she'd purchased, how Tía MiMi was doing in San Juan. But everything was foreign, too cold.

I was sitting in the same chair where she used to pull a comb through my tangles until I cried. Then she'd cover her hands in coconut oil and massage my scalp until I stopped, clicking her tongue as I'd fall asleep right in the chair.

I'd dressed for the occasion. I wore a black jumper and above-the-knee socks and my law firm flats. She hadn't mentioned anything, which was her way. One should not get awards for meeting reasonable standards.

When dinner was over, I steeled myself, ready. I knew her logic. *No use in ruining a good meal with unpleasant talk.*

She poured a mug of tea for each of us. She finally cut the silence. "Does what I was saying the other day make sense?" The only other sound was the tick of her cactus-shaped clock.

I breathed in steam, trying to stay calm. "Yes, but that wasn't why I got upset with you."

"Then what was your fuss about?"

My calming breaths stopped.

She sensed this, and clarified. "I know you are always going to do what you want to do, Cassandra. You have always been very independent. So I don't understand why my opinions and advice make you so upset."

I kept my voice measured. "If you know they won't change anything, why do you say them in the first place?"

She considered, staring at the counter behind me. "Because I care."

I set down my mug. "Exactly. Me, too. That's why they make me so mad. Especially when you brought Luke into it."

"But I was just stating facts," Mom offered. "Luke *is* your responsibility . . . ," she continued.

"Mom, I know. I know. But sometimes I'm not looking for facts." I swallowed, taking her hand across the table. "At that moment, I was looking for you to be proud of me."

She suddenly looked very sad, her eyebrows knitting together.

"Luke and I, it could work out, it could not, but your support is what really matters." I pointed at her, then to myself. "You and me, we're forever."

"Oh, Cassie." A smile broke under her furrowed brows, her lips quivering.

Now it was my turn to fight tears. I wiped them away.

"I am very proud. So proud it hurts. I should—listen. Have you guessed yet, *mija*?" she asked, picking up her empty bowl.

"Guessed what?"

She held out her hand for my dish. "Who your father was?"

I handed it to her. "No," I said.

"He was a musician," she said, her back to me as she stood at the sink. I froze. *Of course. Duh. Of course.* Then she laughed. "He wasn't even that good. In fact, I can guarantee you are better than him."

I swallowed a million questions, savoring each word. Not because I cared about my nonexistent dad. But because my mom was the one telling me.

"I wish I had a picture of him but I think I burned them all."

I laughed. "That's okay," I said. She turned to me. "Really. I don't care. You're all I need, Mamita."

She opened her arms to me and I embraced her. We didn't move. "I'm sorry I don't tell you enough how proud I am of you," she said.

"Me, too. For everything," I said into her shoulder.

"I won't try to talk you into being a lawyer."

"At least for a while."

"Yes, for a while," she amended.

"So, you agree with me?" I asked, my chest tightening. "That I can actually pull this off? Because a tour and an album means money, Mom. And if I do well, I can make another album, I can even teach lessons in my spare time . . ."

"I always have believed that."

I rolled my eyes. "Ha!"

"I wasn't just worried about your ability to take care of yourself, Cassandra," she said, squeezing me. "I'm also worried you're going to leave me forever."

I brushed her head, feeling tears well in my eyes once more. "I'm not going to leave you forever."

"If you become famous at music you will. You'll move to Los Angeles or something. You tell me I should get a life, but I think I should get used to being alone. Except for MiMi."

We let go, and I looked at her brown eyes, her dimples, the lines that formed when she smiled. I took a deep breath. "Mom?"

She raised her eyebrows, sarcastic. "Yes, it is me, your mom."

Nice to know we're back to normal, at least.

"Will you come to my show tomorrow night? There's a song I want you to hear."

"Of course I will be there," she said.

I smiled big and we went back to finishing the dishes, my tense muscles falling still with the running warm water and the lavender soap smell and the texture of the thick clay bowls I had washed so many times as a girl.

I felt larger than I had when I came in, towering against the sink and the task and the counter at my hips, not only because I was bigger against this house now than I was in my memories. I felt big because my mother had said she was proud, and this time, she meant she was proud of all of me.

Luke

Something buzzed in the silence. I bolted upright on the couch. I heard the sound again, rattling the kitchen table. I felt around. My phone was on the armrest, where I'd left it. Cassie must have left hers here before she went to Toby's. The ringing stopped. I sat up and hobbled my way across the room and picked up the phone.

Five missed calls from "Mom." At 2:16 a.m. This did not seem good.

The phone buzzed again in my hand.

I answered.

"Ma'am?"

She was breathing hard. *"Mija?"*

"Ma'am, this is Luke."

"Oh. Is Cassie there?" Her voice was shaking. I sat up fully.

"She's at . . ." *Toby's* I finished silently. "She's out tonight. Is everything okay?"

"Someone has come into my house. My window is broken."

I gripped the phone tighter. "Have you called the police?"

"Twenty minutes ago. They're not here yet. I'm outside and worried the person might still be in there."

"Okay." I paused, my head racing. She shouldn't be alone. "What's your address? I'll be there as soon as I can."

I moved faster down the stairs than I ever had, adrenaline overpowering the pain. Rita hadn't said a word when I told her, just grabbed the keys from a hook near the door.

"Go," she urged.

I used Cassie's cell to call Toby's phone on the way, panic cutting through what should have been an awkward conversation. Cassie's sleepy voice immediately turned sharp as I spoke.

"I'll be right there," she said before the line went dead.

When I arrived at Cord Street fifteen minutes later, Cassie's mom was crouching next to a Camry, her keys spiked between her fingers.

"Marisol?" She jumped when I said her name.

She held a finger to her lips and pointed to the bottom floor of a duplex not unlike Cassie's, except this one was light yellow, surrounded by flowers, bushes, bird feeders. "Cassie's checking it out," she whispered.

"Oh, good, she got here?"

"Just now."

"Cassie," I called lightly.

She emerged from the side of the house, holding a baseball bat, squinted, and jogged over to me. "Oh, thank God."

Without thinking, I opened my arms. Cassie moved into them, squeezing. I could feel her fingertips trace the middle of my back as her hands clenched. "Are you all right?"

"Yep," she said, her breath on my shoulder. For a second, everything else faded.

Other than us, the street was lifeless. Kids' bikes were scattered on the lawn of the apartment complex next to Marisol's house. A streetlight flickered at the end of the block.

"I'll go in," I told her.

"I'll come with you," she offered. Cassie looked paler than usual beneath the streetlamps.

"No, you stay. Stay with your mom." I glanced back down the street. "I can't believe the police aren't here by now."

She folded her arms, shivering. "This isn't exactly a high-priority neighborhood."

Marisol handed me her keys. "Bottom floor. Biggest key. Top lock."

Cassie squeezed my arm. "Thank you."

After I turned the barrel of the lock, I pressed my ear to the door, waiting for the sound of movement. Nothing. Scooting to the side of the door, I lifted my cane, and whipped it open, bracing for a body, waiting to get a hit square in the gut, just like my dad taught me.

Still nothing.

I felt along the walls for a light switch with one hand, gripping the cane with the other. My leg was on fire, but none of it registered. All my nerves were focused on the task.

My foot crunched a shard of glass. Light from the street illuminated the rest of it, glittering, all over the floor. A large window on the east end had been smashed in. Paintings and photos hung on the wall, and there was a square of paint above a media console that was brighter than the rest of the wall. They'd taken the TV.

I paused in the middle of the room, listening for another snap of glass. If whoever was in here wanted to get out, they'd have to step loudly.

I glanced to the left. Two smaller windows had shattered, spidering from the impact of bullets. *Shit.* The intruder had a gun.

A noise filled the room. A high chime. My heart stopped.

Then I realized it was my phone. Just my stupid phone.

I glanced at it, cane still ready.

this wut u get when u dont pay, the message read.

Johnno.

The fire in my leg moved into my entire body, white, hot flames. He wasn't going to get away with this.

Sirens sounded in the distance, rapidly approaching, screeching to a halt outside the duplex.

When I came out, Marisol was talking to an officer. The flashing lights turned the walls of the house blue and then red. A few curious neighbors pressed their faces to their windows. Someone across the street opened their front door and leaned against the screen.

I limped over to Cassie. "What took them so long?"

She tucked a short strand of hair behind her ear, a shadow passing over her face. "Just be happy you're white or you'd be on the ground with a knee in your back."

I nodded, my veins still pumping. "I want to pay for your mom's windows and the TV," I told Cassie.

Cassie looked at me, confused. "That's not what I meant. You don't have to do that."

"I know, but I want to."

She shrugged, yawning, and shivered again. "I'm too tired to get offended by your pity."

"Are you cold?" I asked.

Her eyelids were drooping. "Yeah."

"Do you want me to take you home? I have Rita's car." She didn't look like she wanted to drive. She didn't look like she wanted to do anything but sleep.

"It's fine. I want to stay with my mom a little more," Cassie said, waving, as she walked away. "I'll see you later."

I hesitated, and got back into Rita's car. I kept my eyes on Cassie and her mother as I drove slowly down the street, the flashing lights cutting strobes across my vision. I watched until they were two dark, huddled specks against the night, until I turned the corner and could no longer see what Johnno—what *I*—had brought upon them.

Cassie

After the police left, Mom and I boarded up her windows. I asked her if she wanted me to stay with her, or if she wanted to come to my apartment, but she'd waved me off. "Go get some sleep, *mija*. I'm fine."

I clutched the steering wheel. My fingertips were tingling. I didn't want to wake Toby again, so I turned toward my place, stifling a yawn. The roads were empty, the traffic lights flashing yellow. My vision blurred, and a cold sweat began to work its way through my body.

Shit, I was tired. It was three thirty a.m., but it was more than that. Food. That thing I was supposed to eat. I'd forgotten my phone at home, which meant my alarms hadn't gone off. Luckily I was only ten minutes from home. I'd be fine. To distract myself, I went over the set list for tomorrow night.

Start off with "Merlin," because it's funky as hell.

"Be Still," for the romance vibes.

Straight from the harpy part of "Be Still" into Nora's drony song, "Bear Creek."

My brain buzzed and the car listed slightly to the right. I shook my head and forced myself to focus. Okay, where was I?

"Too Much."

Then slow it down with "Frankie."

"Vibes."

Crowd favorite, "Lucy."

End with "Green Heron." The song for Mom.

By the time I parked in front of Rita's, my fingers had gone numb. My forehead was cold. I needed to get inside and sit down and eat the granola bar I kept in my purse for emergencies. But just a second here, rest on the steering wheel.

Okay. I took a deep breath. *Up the stairs we go. Here we go. This is us going.*

By the time I made it through the door, I was digging in my purse for the granola bar, my knees shaking.

Luke was still up.

"Are you okay?"

I flopped on the couch next to him, still digging. "Fucking purse," I muttered. "It's a health hazard."

The shivers were getting bigger. Black started to rim my vision. *I've been so good at keeping it level*, I told my gut. *Come on.*

"Goddammit." I hadn't realized my hands had stopped digging. They were just hanging limp in the purse, cold.

"Cassie?"

My head was getting too heavy. It dropped forward. I picked it up. It dropped backward. I picked it up.

Luke got up. I heard him digging in the bathroom.

Then I didn't hear anything.

Blackness.

I felt a glucose pack on my lips.

"There you go," Luke was saying. "It's on your tongue. Move your tongue, Cass. There you go."

I felt the cool gel fall into my throat. I swallowed, involuntarily. The ceiling came into view.

"That's it," he said. "Stay with me."

"I'm here," I said, and moved my head to a more comfortable surface, which happened to be Luke's shoulder. Mittens licked my hand, warm and sticky.

"How long does it take to work?"

"About twenty minutes. I'm just going to rest here. Is that okay?"

"Absolutely. It's your couch."

"Oh, yeah," I said, and let out something like a laugh. His heart was pounding, rapid fire. "You okay?"

"Your face was just sort of . . . gone. Blank. Scared the shit out of me." He touched my head with his hands, moved them to my cheek.

I sat up to look at him.

The fear in his eyes was attached to something else, something deeper—the feeling that needs to be there in order for someone to be scared of losing someone else.

I recognized it. I had felt it that day when he left my car and went walking the first time. Fear of losing him attached to—what? Attached to what?

I laid my head back on his chest and went toward the fear. We were already there, in a way, and when you get near death twice in one night, once in fear for my mother, once in fear for myself, you don't feel like you have much to lose.

"Were you there when Frankie died?"

Luke was quiet. Mittens put her head on Luke's thigh.

"Yes."

He'd told me that Frankie'd gotten hit, that they were on the same mission, but I wasn't sure how close. I wasn't sure if it had been news, or firsthand knowledge.

Luke continued, "I guess, you mean, did I see his body?"

"Yes. That's what I mean. Is that too morbid? You don't have to talk about it." I wasn't sure why I was so curious, but I supposed there was some part of me that was still in denial, the part that saw him among faces in the street sometimes. *Are we sure he didn't just run away and find another way home?*

"It was so quiet. We were talking about fucking Pokémon cards." He paused. "Wow, I've never been able to remember what we were talking about."

"Pokémon? Really?"

"Yeah. We were riding in the jeep, routine scouting near the dam. Rooster was saying that Charizard was the best, and Frankie was arguing with him. He was saying Lugia was the best Pokémon because it was the guardian of the sea. And then bullets started to hit, and someone, I can't remember who, signaled for us to get out. Which was so stupid. We shouldn't have gotten out."

Luke's voice was passing through his chest as he spoke, to my cheek. I could almost hear the words before they came out of his mouth. "Then what?" I asked.

"Then, well. I was at the end of the jeep, toward the headlights, and Frankie and Rooster were on the sides, and I got hit in the leg, and both of them got hit."

I felt a wetness in my hair. He wiped his nose. I stayed quiet.

"I got down and pulled Frankie's body toward me to make sure. Checked his pulse. Closed his eyes for him."

I felt lucky to have last seen Frankie laughing, blowing a kiss. That I didn't have to see him that way. "That was good of you."

"Yeah. But, you know." His chest expanded as he laughed. "Those were his last words. 'Lugia is the best Pokémon because it's the guardian of the sea.'"

I laughed with him, fuller this time, now that more of my energy was coming back. "That's *so* Frankie. It's perfect."

"It is. It is." He took a deep, shaky breath. "I just wish that I had told everyone not to get out. But I was a private, you know? You were supposed to trust your captain."

I lifted my chin, looking at him. "You did the only thing you could have done."

"Maybe." His eyes had become more silver, the traces of tears still attached to the lashes. I wondered if his irises always did that when he cried.

He leaned closer. I knew why, and I knew what was unsaid. His lips found mine, soft and slow. I closed my eyes. *Safe*, I remember thinking. *I feel safe.*

Then a hunger burst through it, and I took his shoulders, pulling him closer. He didn't resist, putting his hands around my waist, pressing, pulling the fabric of my shirt into his fists.

His lips darted to my neck, to my collarbone, to the top of my breast.

I moved my leg over his while his palms fell down my back, over the curve of my ass, and then up, under my shirt to my skin. The sensation of his skin on mine shocked both of us. I heard him gasp, and I stopped.

I thought of Toby, at home, asleep, Lorraine purring on his chest. I remembered the promise I had made to him. Even then, it was a lie.

For some reason, I couldn't find the guilt where it should have been. My body couldn't yet process what we'd just done. What I'd just done. All I could think about was wanting more.

"Hey," Luke said, looking up at me.

I moved back to sitting on the couch, breaths still coming quick, brushing the back of my hand across my wet lips. "Hey."

He was trying to slow his breath, too. But nothing in his eyes held regret.

I smiled at him, surprised and unsurprised at the feeling that had announced itself in me, the same feeling I got when I found the right notes. It was new and not new, the feeling of foraging for something that was already there, never hiding, but newly found.

Luke

When I was sure Cassie was asleep, I shut off the lights in the living room and slipped on my shoes. Mittens hopped up, wagging her tail.

"Not right now, Mitts. I'll be back," I whispered.

I was buzzing. High. Clear. The opposite of cloud head.

I still had Rita's keys. I had wanted to do this right away after I'd received Johnno's text, but it was best now, now that I knew Cassie was safe in bed and he was back at his house.

I got on the highway, pushing the pedal on Rita's Volvo as far down as it could go with my left foot, my eyes out for cops. The roads were empty.

He'd gone too far. He'd taken this beyond pills, beyond money, beyond whatever ego shit he'd picked up from the street. And it might have gone on until he'd drained my pockets, until he'd sucked me back into holding for him, until he made my life as empty and ruined as his. Get up, get messed up, take out anyone who gets in the way.

But now that I was almost out of reach, I'd realized he was just playing a game. He was now just fucking with me for the sake of fucking with me. And anyone who was in my life he'd fuck with, too. If what I felt for Cassie was real, that either meant she could no longer be a part of my life or he would have to go. He and his threats and the nonexistent money he wanted.

I chose Cassie. Of course I chose Cassie.

I thought of how I had seen her tonight, wide-eyed with a baseball bat. Marisol, hunched next to her car. They should never have had to feel like that. A beast had risen in my chest, and I didn't know why, or why now, but when I thought of her sleeping, the idea of him watching her, hurting her, I wanted to eliminate him from the Earth.

I turned down his street in Buda and switched off the headlights, rolling slowly up over the curb, onto his overgrown lawn.

His door was locked. I took out one of my old, expired credit cards and slipped it through the crack, shoving bit by bit until I levered the lock out of its slot, a trick I'd learned, ironically, from Johnno.

I strode down the hall and kicked open his door, switching on the light.

He was curled in bed in his boxers, sheets tangled around his legs. He had two posters tacked on the wall, a bird's-eye view of two naked teenage schoolgirls entwined on a forest floor, and a movie poster for *The Big Lebowski*.

"Up," I said.

I waited until he'd sprung on top of his bed to strike his stomach with the cane. He doubled over.

Cassie's blank face filled my vision, head lolled back, so vulnerable, so opposite the sharp strength she had when she clipped her keyboard to its stand, when she noticed I couldn't reach something and flipped it toward me, her steady eyes as she listened to me telling her about Frankie's last moments. The idea that Johnno's pranks had sucked the core out of her, when she had done nothing to deserve it, blocked out the pain in my leg. I felt the urge to build something for her, to use my hands, to break anything in her way.

I came down on Johnno's back, his bony spine and ribs poking through his skin.

Once, twice, until he was down on the bed again.

"Number one, if you ever get *near* my family again, I will kill you. That's a promise."

In my periphery, I could see Johnno sneaking his hand under the bed. Once he had his hand on the gun, I stomped down hard, feeling bones crack. I picked up the pistol.

"Number two, I'm not paying you another fucking cent. I'm done."

I cocked it near his yellowish ear.

"Understood?"

Johnno didn't answer, breathing hard.

I pressed the barrel on Johnno's knee. "You know I'm willing to take off your kneecap. I said, is that understood?"

"Yes, you fuck," he said, his voice muffled by the sheets. "Now get out."

I wasn't about to risk the gun going off, finishing him for good, sending me into further purgatory, so I unloaded the cartridge. As soon as I did, Johnno went for my right leg, sending searing waves of pain through my body.

Before he could gain traction, I brought the gun back and whipped the front of his skull.

"Agh!" Blood spilled from his nostrils, from the cut on his head. It was a beautiful electric red. He brought a hand to his head, rolling in agony.

I backed out of the room using my cane, gun poised.

My chest was heaving as I got into Rita's car. I started the engine, reversed with a squeal, and watched Buda get smaller in the rearview mirror as the little pine tree air freshener dangled in the breeze. Sunshine crept through the cool air.

When I saw the exit for the Texas State Cemetery, I took a detour. The radio played that Bowie song "Space Oddity." I turned it all the way up, up to Cassie-level volume, until I reached the gates.

My hands started shaking. The buzz had started to wash off, the clarity. I'd never beat someone so viciously before.

I moved from the blank concrete of the highway to the quiet, green oasis. Frankie's grave was smothered. Yellow roses, white roses, daisies, carnations, chrysanthemums. Probably his mother's doing. I cleared a small path, so I could see his name.

"Hey, Frankie." I stood next to the obelisk. "I miss you, man. I'm sure you're having a good time wherever you are. And you're right, Lugia is the best Pokémon."

I sat down.

"Cassie's doing well. She's surviving. I don't know what caused you to put so much faith in either of us, but I'm glad you did. I think about you all the time. Especially lately. You had such a good head on your shoulders. You would have helped a lot of people."

I realized I had been pulling up grass as I spoke, and now I had two big handfuls. "Sorry," I said to all the souls, and let the blades catch in the breeze.

"I think I have feelings for Cassie," I said, testing out the way the words sounded.

Feelings for Cassie. They sounded good, like a song title.

"We kissed," I tried again. That sounded even better. *We.* What was I saying?

Only Cassie came out of the silence. Her black hair. Her honesty. Her voice. Her intelligence. The place where her thighs touched. The face she made when she was on the computer. The purpose I felt when I was near her. Even if it were my job to listen to her sing for the rest of my life, I would.

"What am I saying, Frankie? You're the emotions expert." I stood up and touched the top of the headstone. I guessed maybe I should speak to the woman herself.

Cassie

I woke to Mittens breathing in my face, waiting. I'd had the strangest dream. I was standing in my living room across from the futon in the late morning. The sun was shining warm through the windows that looked out on the front yard. My potted plants were gone, and instead, stalks and leaves had sprouted out of the cracks in the floorboards all around me, vines climbed up the walls, flowers drooped, resting on my bare feet. Somehow I had planted this greenery, and it was supposed to be here, warm and comforting around me.

I sat up in bed and heard music filtering in from the living room, and on top of it, a voice out of tune. The song was "Going to California" by Led Zeppelin. The voice was Luke's.

I gave Mittens a pat on the head and slipped on shorts and a tank top.

Everything in the living room was like what I had imagined, except the plants were back in their places. Somehow they seemed fuller, though. I stood still. The sun shone. Luke was in the kitchen, limping back and forth from the stove. The air smelled like fried eggs.

"Good morning!" I called.

He couldn't hear me over the music and a very exaggerated impression of Robert Plant. I tried to keep from laughing, and held up my hand for Mittens to *stay*. Luke had his back to me, poking at the skillet with a spatula.

"Good morning," I called again.

He turned to me, shirtless, startled. "Oh! Good morning. Yeah. I was just . . ."

"Making eggs?"

Luke was still an anomaly in my close quarters, too big to fit, or at least he was now that he was upright, his six-foot-plus frame in my little kitchen. And especially after last night. The memory jolted me. Our bodies, together. I wondered why we didn't stop ourselves before it got that far. Then I wondered why we stopped. I cleared my throat.

He gestured to the stove with the spatula. "Making eggs and working on some, you know. Vocal stylings."

"Very good. You should consider starting a Led Zeppelin cover band."

He laughed. "Yeah. Shed . . . Dead . . ."

"Nothing rhymes with Zeppelin," I assured him, grabbing a glass for water. "Believe me, I've tried."

I left him to the stove and caught a smile in my reflection in the bathroom mirror. I was thinking about the recent uptick of his interest in music. Today was not the first day he'd started by putting on one of my records. He was just as he said he was, a straight classic-rock fan, but I could put on something rock-y but obscure and get a curious glance out of him.

We emerged at the same time, me with my face washed, him from the kitchen with two plates.

He sat, I sat. Over-easy eggs, still steaming, and avocado on toast. The last time we were here, we were holding each other. He'd revived me. He'd cried into my hair. Now his elbow touched mine only on occasion, balancing the toast to his lips, trying to get the crumbs to fall on the table rather than all over his leg brace.

"What are you gon' do t'day?" he asked, his mouth full.

I laughed. "Eat eggs and avocado."

"Oh, yeah?" He took another bite. "That sounds pretty good."

"What are you doing?"

He swallowed. "Eat avocado and eggs."

"Huh, who knew?"

Mittens trotted in, tongue out. We moved our plates out of her reach. I stood, paused the Led Zeppelin, and put on Xenia Rubinos's "Hair Receding." A crease rose between his eyebrows, his mouth slightly turned up, listening.

"I knew it," I said.

"What?"

"I call this look your new face." I pretended to frame him with my fingers.

"My new *face?*"

"Your *new* face. It happens every time you're exposed to something outside of your comfort zone. It's the song, and I can tell because of this." I reached across the coffee table to touch the crease between his brows. "You got it when I put on Dirty Projectors, too. And when you ate sweet potato fries."

He touched the spot, too, and shrugged, looking at me. "I bet I get it a lot around you."

"Hey!" I sat back down beside him, an inch closer than I had sat before, and gave him a small push. He didn't scoot away.

"It's not a bad thing." He glanced at me, smiling.

"No, it's not." We were quiet for a while, finishing our breakfast.

Our breakfast. The plants were flourishing even though I'd been so busy with the band. Because he'd watered them. I thought of my dream and felt a rush of gratitude. He'd asked what I was doing today, and I realized I just wanted to be here, or anywhere, anchored in peace, knowing Luke was there, too. I'd tried not to name it last night. I could tell myself I had been too tired, too confused, too torn up from talking about Frankie, wanting someone's comfort.

"Are you okay?" Luke asked beside me. I nodded, unable to look at him right then. Looking at his hands.

Because here we were, wide awake and well fed, and I knew I hadn't just wanted to be held by anyone last night. I wanted to be held only by him.

Luke

Beside me on the futon, Cassie curled her knees into her chest. The flash of her lower back under her tank top, her calm breath, the waving black strands of hair falling on the back of her neck—it all kept pressing, pushing some tender part of my chest out into the open. Since I'd come back from the cemetery I still hadn't figured out how to broach the subject of what she meant to me, what we meant to each other, let alone what to say. I'd tried to get some sleep before she woke, but I couldn't. So I'd taken a shower. I had put on her music, letting it loop quietly, realizing I'd learned the words. I'd made her eggs and avocado toast.

And now I just wanted her to lean into my arms, against my bare skin, and stay there indefinitely. I didn't want to reach out to her without knowing she wanted me to, without knowing that what happened last night was not just a fluke because we were both so exposed, so vulnerable.

"Can I ask you something?"

She nodded, her chin still against her knees, her eyes ahead.

"When we were talking last night . . . ," I began.

She suddenly adjusted her legs, shifting to face me, her gaze set on mine. I didn't break it.

But now that she was listening, not just listening, but listening for *something*, there was so much to say. There'd be no way I could say it all without messing it up. I started slow. "Talking about Frankie meant a lot. And I didn't get a chance to thank you."

"It meant a lot to me, too," she said. "And—"

"And—" I echoed, almost on top of her. We paused, waiting for the other, and burst out laughing.

"You go," she said.

"No, you," I said.

"Well," she said, then swallowed. "I was thinking about what I said at your dad's barbecue. I mean in the attic. When I said if you talked this much all the time, our lives might be a little easier."

I remembered what had taken root that day, the day I showed her my dad's medal. "Right."

"And you have, lately."

"I've tried."

"You're different," she said. Then she shook her head, holding up a hand. "Not that you were bad before," she added.

"I was, though."

"What do you mean?" she asked, quick.

Another step toward the truth. I realized I had stopped breathing. Honesty was a new sensation. It wasn't unpleasant, but it still shocked me, bit by bit. Like descending into a cold pool. I was probably making that *new* face Cassie pointed out. I tried to relax, to breathe again.

"I was just in this for the money, and now I'm not." The truth, lapping harder. Refreshing. Cleansing. Wishing I could take her hand.

"Yeah, yeah," she said, sitting straighter, nervous. "Yeah," she repeated. "Me, too."

My heart skipped.

I saw her eyes glance at where her phone lay dead on the coffee table. She was thinking of Toby, probably. Trying to tread carefully. She brought her eyes back to mine. "Now that we're better friends," she continued, and the word "friends" felt like a stab, though it shouldn't have. "I can't help wondering why you needed the money. I mean, the real reason you were in debt."

"Right." This part of the truth was harder, cracking ice. The feeling of Johnno's bones under my foot. His crumpled form on the bed. "I'm sorry. I should have told you a long time ago."

"That's okay," Cassie said, quiet. "You don't have to tell me now. But sometime."

"No, I want you to know," I said, and hoped I didn't look like I was in as much pain as I felt. Here was the rotten core, the snake in the water that didn't belong with all the other sweet, cool facts. I wanted to tell her that I loved her, not that I was even worse than she could have imagined. I was a criminal. Even before we played this marriage game, I was an addict and a thief and a terrible son, a terrible brother.

"You can tell me," she said, and held out her hand, palm up, on the futon between us. I took it and tried not to grip too hard.

If I was going to tell her the truth, that I was paying for pills that I flushed down a toilet, then I'd have to tell her I was too addled to understand what I was doing, and then I'd have to tell her that not two days before I flushed the pills, Johnno had kicked me awake because I had washed down some crushed-up Oxy with beer and "it didn't look like you were breathing," and then I'd have to explain that it wasn't a big deal because I regularly smashed Oxy into a powder and either sucked it up my nostril with a straw or put it in my drink, and that I'd been doing it for years.

And then she'd wonder why, and I'd have to say I wasn't sure, all I knew is that I felt better as cloud head at Johnno's than I did in my own home, because I was pretty sure my dad hated me, and she'd ask why I thought my dad hated me, and I'd have to say I didn't know, but I knew what hate felt like more than I knew what love felt like, and I was pretty sure what I had for her was love, so if she could look past all that, it would be great.

"Luke?" She squeezed my hand and let go, her eyes full open, still on mine.

"I owed money to an old friend from my hometown," I said. The guilt grew but I couldn't bring myself to force the right words—the real words—out. To see her eyes shutter, feel her hand pull away. "I . . . I lost something of his that was incredibly valuable. And I couldn't pay him back for a long time, and so he started to charge interest. And it really added up."

It wasn't a full lie, at least. Cassie nodded, thinking. "What did you lose of his?"

"I was working for him, selling . . . medical supplies." I looked away. Cassie wasn't dumb. The honesty had felt so good, and now it was ebbing away. "And it was really embarrassing to have lost it, like, so dumb. So, so dumb how much money I owed. So I don't like talking about it."

"I get it," she said, and put a hand briefly on my knee. "No further questions, Your Honor."

"But it's paid back now," I said, not ready for her to move on, to get up and forget that we were getting somewhere.

She kept moving, slow, a smile almost hidden, and stood. Maybe someday when we were further away from all this, when the blood from Johnno's nose wasn't fresh in the drain, and when Cassie didn't have a million other things to think about, like her mother's safety, like the show at the Sahara she'd been rehearsing for for months and the stupid pseudoboyfriend who was tagging along, I would tell her everything, start to finish. If there was a "we."

"Cassie," I said, and resisted the urge to ask her to sit down again, her thigh close to mine, and we wouldn't have to kiss, just sit, and I would run my hand down her back.

She turned, taking her hair out of its ponytail, and I was overcome. "What?"

"Your show's going to be great tomorrow."

A smile grew as my gaze traveled her face. But I had trouble smiling back. Cassie deserved the truth, and sooner or later I'd have to find a way to come clean. Even if it meant losing her.

Cassie

The day of the show, I went with Luke to River Place. While he did his physical therapy, I walked Mittens through the trails, up and down the hills, letting her sniff every leaf and root and footprint she wanted to. After breakfast yesterday, Luke had fallen asleep immediately. I'd gone over to Nora's to practice, and Toby had asked me to stay at his place. I'd said yes too quickly, worried he'd sense my hesitation or feel my guilt. As conflicted as I felt right then, I was glad to get out of my apartment. I couldn't work out my feelings for Luke very well while he was around, because the feelings themselves were too big. I needed space away from him to identify them, to wonder when they'd come, what to do next.

But the feelings had followed. They'd followed me to Toby's, where I lay awake next to him, and today, through the trails, thinking about the day I'd first given Luke Mittens. How his face changed, softened. How I'd catch him speaking to her and everything inside me would become all warm and syrupy. When I'd tried to think about the future, somehow I could think only of him now.

The trails ended. We circled back to the green where Luke waited. My stomach did jumping jacks.

"Who's got the cutest face?" He bent down and rubbed his nose to Mittens's. "Who's the cutest? Hello," Luke said to me, grinning, scratching behind Mittens's ears.

I could barely get a word out before grinning back. "Hi."

We walked to the car together, and drove home with the windows down.

I walked behind him up the steps, slow, and when we got through the door, Luke turned to me. "Cassie, can we talk?"

My heart pounded. "Yeah! Yeah. I'm glad you— Yeah, we should definitely talk."

I tossed my keys on the front table and headed toward the couch. Before I could sit, he touched my arm. I stood, waiting, my face on fire.

"I want to tell you something. I've been wanting to, but I just couldn't . . ." He shook his head and took a deep breath, as if steeling himself. "I have to be completely honest with you."

"Okay," I said, letting out a nervous laugh. "Should I be scared?"

"No, not scared, I think, but I'll understand if you're upset," he said, his voice dropping, deep and more serious than it had been in a long time. I folded my arms. "I told you I owed money to a friend from my hometown. And that's true, but it wasn't the whole truth."

I nodded, braced, waiting for him to go on. I wasn't stupid. His explanation had been vague, and it had been vague on purpose. I assumed that was for my benefit. He was my business partner, not my confidant. At least not until a few days ago.

Luke searched for words, and when he couldn't find them, he looked me straight in the eyes. "He was my dealer."

I felt my eyes widen. "Dealer of what?" I said.

"OxyContin. Or any other opiate I could get my hands on. Vicodin. But mostly Oxy."

I'd known in the back of my mind that his mood swings weren't natural. He'd been struggling to stay sober this whole time, tempted by the very drugs that'd been meant to help him through. I remembered that day he had given me earplugs, how his head had lolled on his shoulder.

"How long?"

His face contorted, trying to keep back tears. I reached out to squeeze his arm, his shoulder.

"Sorry." He pushed on his eyelids. "This is hard. It was just recreational when I was a teenager. Then two years ago I realized I was addicted. But I couldn't stop. So I got clean and joined the army, and . . . here we are."

"Why didn't you tell me right away that you were sober?" I searched myself for anger, for a feeling of betrayal that he hadn't leveled with me. But as I stared at him, at the way his hand gripped his cane, the stiffness of his leg, the way his shoulders hunched as if bracing himself, I couldn't find it. All I found was a man who'd been through hell.

"I didn't think you would want to . . ." He made quote marks with his fingers. "*Be with* a person who got involved in that kind of stuff."

"You mean be married to you?" I smiled.

"Yeah."

"Well." The jumping-gut feelings returned. "I wish you'd been honest with me . . ."

He smiled back, reluctant, then bigger. "You're not upset?"

"I'm not happy, but hell . . ." I shrugged. "I was no stranger to recreational drug use in college. It could happen to anyone. Especially with opiates. That stuff . . ." I sighed. "I don't envy you." I swallowed. "So what now?"

"I gave him all the money I owed, and now we're done." Luke stepped closer.

For some reason, I began to get uneasy. Maybe it was a delayed reaction. Or maybe that he had started to talk about his dealer again. I still didn't know the whole story about that, and I wasn't sure I wanted to just yet.

I had meant "what now" with his sobriety. And mostly, I had meant "what now" with us.

"He *used to* be my dealer. Key words, *used to*. So, yeah, I plan to stay sober. Sober as a . . ." He looked for the phrase.

"Sober judge?" I said, trying to smile, opening and closing my hands, trying to shake off the feeling that something had wound tight around me. "I can't totally dive into it with you before the show, but I want to know more. And help you."

"Of course. I just . . . wanted to tell you. Anyway." He paused, shaking his head. The sensation wound tighter, for some reason. "He won't bother anyone anymore."

I wanted to reach out to him, to give him a hug, but something wasn't sitting right. The way he phrased it made me pause. "What do you mean, 'anyone anymore'?"

Luke's mouth dropped open, and he closed it. All of the composure of his confession had left his face. He hadn't meant to say that. He began to stammer. "Well, like, you and me . . ."

"What?" There was something else he wasn't telling me. Then it hit. There was a reason why his eyes had flashed with anger after he left the duplex two nights ago. Why he had offered to pay for the TV. My insides were a tidal wave. "No. No. Wait, really? No."

"What is it?"

"I think I'm going to puke," I said.

I could feel him stepping closer. "Cassie."

"Don't come any closer." I felt my hands form fists. I resisted the urge to hurl them at his chest. "Did your *dealer* fuck with my mom? Did you bring that on my mom? Tell me the truth."

Luke tried to hold my gaze, but couldn't. He lifted his hands to his face. "Yes, that was him," he said, hollow.

"My mother!" I shouted. My beautiful mother, my heart, my only family, huddled on the ground near her car. Her pajama pants getting dirty in the street. Shifting into Spanish when she spoke to the cops, because that kind of fear was too deep for her second language.

"It's done now, though," he continued, putting his hands down. "Trust me."

"How am I supposed to trust you?"

He spoke quieter now. "I took care of him, Cassie. I mean it. You're safe. That's my first priority, especially now."

"I don't care."

Now. He was talking about what happened yesterday, and the night before, and long before that. The feelings that had grown for him, that I was ready to give. I'd fallen for every single lie out of his mouth. I'd blinded myself.

"I know I can't change what I did, and I take full responsibility for it."

A laugh built in me, hard, spiked. "You can't offer to pay for a TV and expect everything to be fine." My mother's windows, broken. Her bare feet, cut.

"I didn't know he would do that. I fucking almost killed him last night, Cass."

I stayed quiet.

"And I didn't like doing it, but I would do it again. I would do anything for you." Another look of shock. He hadn't known he would say that part, either. He was staring at me, barely blinking. I could hear him breathe. "If you want to forget about what we have and never speak to me again and be with Toby, fine. But you have to at least know that I have real feelings for you. That's why I'm being honest with you. I'm telling you everything. When we kissed the other night, I meant it."

"Don't," I said. I was so angry, my words caught in my throat. He was trying to smooth it over. Trying to distract me from my anger. And on this day. The most important day of my life. "I have to go do soundcheck."

I headed toward the door.

Then I paused. I kept my voice cold, staring at the floor. "I want you out, Luke. Don't come to the show. Don't come back here. I'll contact you about a divorce."

"Wait," I could hear Luke say. It was one of those moments when his pain crossed the bridge, and I could sense his agony. I bolted down the stairs away from it, and shut the door.

Luke

I refused to accept this. I stood under the ash trees across the street from Cassie's house shortly after she and Toby had left, my packed army bag on my back, Mittens's leash in one hand and my cane in the other, and knew this was not how it was supposed to go.

Maybe she didn't have the same feelings I had for her, maybe she was scared out of her mind, but this wasn't the end. Hell, maybe she and I weren't even meant to be friends after this, but we had both fought too hard to build these new lives just for them to be knocked down by Johnno.

And those new lives were forever going to be connected, I knew that. I didn't know how. I didn't know when. But they would be.

So, yeah, maybe I was being delusional.

That's one of the great things about having an addict's brain: We are fantastic at fooling ourselves. We could fool ourselves all the way until the end.

For instance, right now, I had started to think it would be a good idea to be cloud head.

My heart had just been ripped out, leaving a gaping hole.

Cloud head was good at filling holes.

But then I thought of Jake. I thought of what I'd done to him when I had succumbed to Oxy the first time, when I'd tried to escape.

Today was not unique in the grand scheme of things. Every day was hell, if you were paying attention. Every day would rip a new hole, maybe two, maybe three. Knowing this full well, sometimes I started to think that the rest of my life would be like bailing out a sinking boat. Once you stopped the leak that came from one pain, another hole would open.

But at least now I wasn't alone. "Right, Mittens?" I asked her, giving her a scratch on the head.

Mittens barked.

"And where should we go now?"

I didn't know. There was nowhere *to* go, at the moment, just the street stretching before us. Maybe if I started moving, maybe if I went around the block, Cassie would be waiting for me when I returned, and I could take her into my arms and we'd go from there.

I dropped my bag next to the tree, and leaned my cane against its trunk. I looped Mittens's leash around my hand so she couldn't get too far, made sure my shoes were tied, and started walking.

I walked fast, putting full weight on my injured leg. The same amount of weight I put on the other. Every step was a new hole and it hurt like hell.

But then it didn't. So I moved my legs faster. I added bounce to my step. My heart carried blood to every ending and back in an instant. My bones did not break. Everything was working as it should.

The body is a miracle, did you know that, Mittens?

House after house passed, and the pain was there, but I was there, too.

Mittens galloped beside me, her tongue flopping.

My throat was raw and my lungs burned from lack of practice, but I felt awake, alive.

I didn't need to attach the pain to other objects, other scenes far away where I had found peace. I found peace here.

I was running.

Cassie

"Check one," I called to the empty bar, late-afternoon light hitting the dim neon and gilded walls. Any other day this would be a triumph, imagining my music hitting the bodies that would fill the tiled floor. But Luke's shocked, bitter face haunted me. Drugs and threats and my mother's broken windows. Luke drawing my leg across his lap. A drop of drool falling from his opiate-slack mouth. His nightmares. His calisthenics. The way his big hands flopped to his sides when he told me the truth. Everyone who he had lied to, everyone I knew and didn't, following him like ghosts everywhere he went. I had brought poison into my home. The memory of Luke's lips on mine sent a chill through my bones, the kind of staticky, tipping feeling I got before my blood lacked sugar, or the feeling I used to get when I couldn't make rent.

But my rent was paid, and I had checked my levels in the bathroom.

"Cassie?" Nora was saying. "Up, down? That sound good to you?"

My keys loomed white, anonymous. I pressed a chord, and a surge of power leaped through my fingertips. He could walk through the door any second. I was scared that he would, scared that he wouldn't. A man's laughter across the room made me jump. Just the bartender, setting up. The door behind him swung back and forth, then shut. Why was I disappointed it wasn't Luke? Of course it wasn't Luke. I closed my eyes against the image of him laughing. I imagined him lying on the floor in front of me, motionless. Good. *Stay where I can see you. So I know you aren't out there, where you'll hurt me again.* I pressed another chord to drown him out.

I turned my head to where Nora stood, waiting behind me. "That sounds great."

The hours flew, the lights went off, the neon clicked on. People were arriving, and I stayed in the corner, playing silent chords on my thighs so I would have something to occupy my flighty hands.

Nora asked me questions. No, I wasn't that nervous. I was nervous, but not that nervous. Yes, I wanted to go on. I wanted to helm this block of concrete like a raft into space. Yes, I was pleased with the lighting. I liked how it looked like we were in the middle of a giant blood orange. How many did I think were out there? Oh, I didn't know. It sounded like it was at capacity, that was for sure. Yes, I'd heard from the Wolf Records guy. His plane had landed earlier today. No, I didn't know what he looked like.

Oh, shit, was I not saying any of this aloud?

The realization seemed to click on the sound. For me, and for the world. It rose in an electronic din, like that Dolby sound bite they play at the beginning of movies in the theater.

"Sorry," I said to Nora, who had now dragged me into what appeared to be a supply closet. "I'm all out of whack."

"Cassie, thank God, you were just, like, *silent*," she said, her plump lips dark purple and sensuous, like two plums. "You look like one of those women who dies of consumption in the 1800s. Are. You. All. Right."

"Yes, I—" I began, but with the sound turned up, some of the emotions had started to trickle back in. I bit my lip to keep it back until the show started.

"If you're not, we don't have to do this," Nora said.

"Oh, yes we do," I said. We did. This was a chance to leave all the bullshit behind. And you know what, fuck it. If I thought the dissolution of the fake marriage would stop me from playing the biggest show of my life, I didn't deserve a record deal. Control was overrated. I played because I loved to play, that was it. If I wanted control, I wouldn't be here. Regardless of what happened, we had worked too hard to let it go now.

I pulled her close by the collar of her long, black sheath dress. "I'm ready. You ready?"

Nora took me by the cheeks, and planted a huge purple set of lips on the spot right between my brows, which I didn't wipe off.

We left the closet. I checked in with Toby, who winked, banging out his warm-up. So far I'd been able to avoid him. I had no idea what to say to him, how I felt. Had no idea what would happen to us. But all that would have to wait.

From the wings, I scanned the crowd. There, in the corner, her bag clutched on her lap, her navy Crocs perched on a bar stool, sat my mother. Rita turned around from the bar with two glasses of white wine, handing her one.

I caught Mom's eye. Her calm smile stopped my shivers, my doubts. This would be the first show where Mom wouldn't want me to walk offstage and be someone else.

Nora picked up her bass, drawing three deep-end-of-the-pool notes.

I stepped up to the keyboard. Whatever intro music they were playing at the Sahara had ceased, and the crowd began to bellow.

My heart had just been ripped out, leaving a gaping hole.

But sometimes that just meant more room for the music.

"Ladies and gentlemen, thanks for being here," I said into the mic, the keys' soft weight against my fingertips as familiar as the Casio I had as a little girl. I looked straight into my mother's smiling eyes. "We're The Loyal."

Luke

When I finished, red faced and humming with a cocktail of endorphins and excruciating pain, Mittens and I walked the rest of Cassie's block.

As I approached, I noticed two figures standing near the ash tree where I'd left my bag and cane. Two men in identical suits.

The endorphins dissolved. Now it was just pain. Pain and knots in my gut.

A few feet from me, the taller of them flashed a badge.

CID, it read. I recognized it. Dad used to have the same one, I remembered that now. My heart raced. *Johnno.* He really had reported us. The other shoe had dropped.

"Are you PFC Luke Morrow?"

I thought of saying no. I thought of testing my running skills again, of having a few more minutes of freedom before they took me. Some wall had been knocked down. I almost felt like laughing out loud, though there should have been nothing to laugh at.

I tried to keep my voice from cracking. "I am."

"We're going to need you to come with us."

"For what?" I asked, but I knew.

"You're under arrest."

I couldn't stop my eyes from darting across the street, toward Cassie's house. If she were here, we might be able to talk them down, to show them we weren't a fraud in the way they thought we were. We could come up with another story together. But the Subaru was nowhere in sight.

I let go of Mittens's leash to hold my hands up, and said, "Sirs, can I drop my dog at my neighbor's place?"

Mittens looked back and forth between me and the men like they were her new friends, her tongue still hanging out.

The tall one nodded.

I scrambled in my pockets for the extra key, remembering Rita was at Cassie's show right now. Where I should have been. Where I wanted to be. Mittens looked at me knowingly for a moment as I shut the door, then turned and ran back into the house. I felt my muscles relax, beyond relax, and fall into bone tired. For the first time since I was nineteen, since before I met Johnno, I wouldn't have to look over my shoulder. That was it. Johnno had done his worst. Mittens was safe, Rita was safe, Cassie was safe, and they were safe because they were away from me. The dirt was out of their corners, drowning me. It was messy and awful and too much at once, but I didn't care. I didn't want to be floating above my life without any consequences anymore, because up there, I was missing everything. The bad and the good.

This part, the part where the tall officer was picking up my bag as the short one put a firm hand on my back, happened to be bad.

But inside the bag he held, there was no pill bottle. It was in the trash, in the house of a woman across the street. Everything was flowing around me, the pavement, the ash tree, the sweat that still fell in drips from the exertion, the cold handcuffs on my wrists, the good, the bad, I was in it.

I let the CID lead me to their car.

Cassie

"Holy shit, Cassie." Nora had latched herself to my back, muttering repeatedly as we exited the stage as one strange, sweaty creature. "Holy shit, holy shit, holy shit."

We had even done an encore. I had nothing left. They had it all.

You could still hear the crowd, even from back here.

Toby had jumped into the crowd at the end of the set, greeting a friend. Now he wove through the edges of the mob, his gap-toothed grin bobbing over screaming head after screaming head. He held my shoulders and we rocked back and forth, laughing. And yet I couldn't be in his arms long enough without my throat seizing, thinking of Luke.

His image was a stone I kept choking on. That asshole. *That fucking asshole. He wasn't here.*

"They want to sign us," he said into my hair.

I unlatched and looked up at him. "What?"

"What?" Nora repeated. Her eyes were glued on Toby.

"They want to sign us," he said louder, making a circling motion with his finger. "My friend heard him talk to the owner of the Sahara. They may even have us start opening for one of their bigger bands right away."

"On tour!" Nora screamed. "We're going on tour!"

"Is he still here?"

Nora and Toby held each other's hands, hopping in a circle, chanting, "We're going on tour, we're going on tour, we're going on tour."

I had to laugh.

"Quick, get your phone!" Toby said, ignoring my question, shuffling me toward the greenroom. "He may call right now."

Not a minute after Toby said it, the phone began to ring. I smacked Toby and Nora on the arms, pointing.

They stood with their arms around each other, looking at me.

"Hello?"

"Cassie?"

That did not sound like Josh van Ritter's New York voice. It sounded like a Texas voice. A Texas voice, beat down.

"Yeah?" I said, moving away from the eager onlookers.

"It's Jacob Morrow. Senior. Luke's dad."

"Hi," I said, my blood suspended.

"I have some bad news. Luke's been arrested."

That fucking asshole, I thought, and immediately burst into tears.

Luke

The official charge was larceny and fraud. They held me overnight, in a room about the same size as the one I shared with Frankie and Rooster at Camp Leatherneck. A bench with vinyl tacked on for sleeping. A toilet sticking out of the wall. A hallway where officers passed, glancing in my direction under their crew cuts and dress blues on their way to somewhere else.

I fell into a deep sleep, deeper than I'd ever slept, losing track of whether it was morning or evening.

When I woke, I taught myself to tell time, as I'd done at Cassie's. The rounder, balding officer who brought a circular yellow rubber thing that was supposed to be eggs meant it was around nine in the morning. The dark-skinned officer with glasses who brought me a bologna sandwich with stale corn chips meant it was around noon.

They must have forgotten dinner. No one passed but a jowl-faced officer who was playing on his phone and didn't notice I was in the cell.

I made up rules for myself for after I got out, whenever that would be. *Meetings twice a week. Bachelor's degree, not associate's. Finish a book every week.* And the last one, the one that would be the hardest, that I would constantly reverse in my head for every selfish reason, but knew I couldn't break: *Leave Cassie alone.*

Finally, shortly after the balding, rounder one brought the third yellow rubber thing, they told me that the court-appointed attorney would be arriving later that afternoon.

I was used to the way business was handled in a place like this: I had about three questions max before they lost their patience or felt I was challenging their authority, and after that I had to shut up and operate on their terms.

First, I asked about Cassie. Had they taken her in, too?

"No information is available at this time, Private."

Second, I asked when the hearing would be.

"I will let you know."

I knew what the third question should be, but I was hesitant, knowing it might be wasted. It was highly doubtful Dad would drive to Austin just to watch me fuck up again. But if the arraignment was soon, and if no one posted bail, I could be detained up until they moved me to prison. I didn't know when I would have the chance to speak to him. I wanted to explain. I wanted him to be here.

Cassie

We sat on the covered porch at Mozart's, waiting to work out the details of a record deal that might be just a myth. I had left The Loyal show in a haze, the details Luke's dad gave me written on my hand with a Sharpie while lying down backstage at the Sahara. Jake had told me it was best to keep my distance until after the arraignment, unless they called me in. And depending on which way Luke pled, they might do worse than that. Arrest. Last night, I had told Nora and Toby about the arrest. I told them that I didn't feel well and went home, locking the door and lying in darkness, not sleeping.

Now we'd meet Josh van Ritter of Wolf Records. Two fates: one good, one bad. Two waves poised above my head. I didn't touch my tea.

Shit was hitting the fan. I didn't know what lay beyond that. I didn't know what consequences I would face. I didn't know how this worked. I didn't know when, or if, I would be called. Would I be called? Or would they take me, too? Would they yank me away in front of my friends, cuff me, and let them watch as I took everything they'd wished for into the back of a squad car?

"Any word?" Nora asked, reaching across the table to rub my hand, sipping her coffee.

"Nothing yet," I told her. No news. I had texted Jake the next morning, got nothing back.

Luke had put his minimal possessions in his bag, and cleared out. Mittens had wandered the apartment all night, sniffing the corners, looking for him. Every time I dozed off, I woke up to the sound of her claws on the wooden floors, and waited to hear his weight creak with hers, his quiet mutters. My mind circled around him. He was gone. He was gone and I hated him and I had forgiven him fully. I hated him because I had forgiven him, and I wanted to say sorry for hating him. Under it all, I missed him. I missed him and he was a liar and I hated him and I missed him.

Toby swung his arm over the back of my chair.

A cop car passed. I flinched.

Josh approached us with a latte in hand, big glasses over friendly eyes and a beard. He looked vaguely hungover.

"Hi, Cassie! I looked for you after the show," he said, sitting down, offering his hand.

I waved it off. "I was fighting off something before we played, and then it hit me," I lied. "Sorry about that. Don't want to get you sick."

"No problem," he said, introducing himself to Toby and Nora, who wore smiles to their ears.

"Right." Josh set his hands on the table. "So I don't have much time before I have to catch my flight, but you all have it going on, let me make that real clear."

"Thank you," I said, and some of the excitement from last night came skipping back, making me sit up a little straighter.

"We're wondering if you can bring that kind of energy to, say, twenty shows, rather than one."

"Totally," Toby said.

As I was about to assure him, a text came through on my phone. I jumped. I didn't check it, not wanting to be rude, but I knew it must be from Jake.

Josh continued, "We're thinking you'd be a great fit with Dr. Dog. They've got a sixties Brit pop sound, you've got a more modern, edgy take on that. More minimalist, more female dominated."

"We're so down with that," Toby said. "They've always been a big influence."

"Absolutely," Nora said. "Right, Cass?"

"Yes," I said immediately, trying to keep hold of the dual feelings that had risen in my chest, trying not to let the facts catch up with me. There was the ecstasy that all our hard work had paid off, that we could go on the road and play for strangers, that I had the talent and work ethic to make it happen.

Then, tearing that happiness apart, there was the possibility that I had destroyed every last bit of our new lives before they began.

Nora reached for my hand under the table.

I took her hand in both of mine, grateful, squeezing hard.

"So." Josh stood, pointing at me. "I'm sorry you're sick."

I mustered a smile.

"We'll talk when you're better. But in the meantime," he said, opening his hands to all of us, "look for an e-mail from me with the contract. Plan for a week or so from now, when Dr. Dog swings through Galveston. Okay?"

"Okay!" Nora said, trying to be cheery, shaking his hand again.

As he walked away, I looked at the message from Jake. *Luke and Dad meeting with lawyer today, will keep you posted if they decide to charge him*, the message read. "Shit."

I showed it to Nora and Toby.

Toby said, slowly, "Well, we have to at least assume the good before the bad." He drummed on the table, ecstatic. "Also, hi. That man walking away is about to give us a *record deal*."

I couldn't get anywhere near to the good Toby was talking about. I started to think about what "jail" actually meant. What it meant to Luke, what it meant to me. Punishment. Loneliness. Cut off from everyone. His agony, reaching across toward me. Between my bandmates, over the lukewarm tea, I started to shake.

"Let me go get you some more hot water," Nora said, her brow furrowed. She stood and went inside.

"Come on, Cass. That would be Luke's trial, not yours," Toby said. "Right?"

"We're married. It's going to be my trial eventually, T."

Toby shook his head with a confident smile. "He's worse, though. His dealer? I mean, that's some shady shit. You could probably even spin it so he manipulated you."

My hands clenched. "I would never do that to him."

"Think about it, though." Toby swallowed. He reached over to brush away one of my tears. "I mean, we're about to go on tour, Cass."

I pointed to the text on my phone. "There might not even be a band to go on tour. Because *I* lied. I'm a fraud, too."

He searched for words, eyes narrowed in confusion, leaning toward me. "You're just going to give yourself in?"

"I'm not giving myself in," I snapped. "But I am being honest about what's happening here."

"All right, be honest, then," Toby said, smacking the table. "Be fucking honest."

I threw my hands up. "What? What do you want me to say?"

"You're in love with him!" Toby yelled, his eyebrows raised.

Nora had arrived between us, holding a small teapot. She bit her lip, and set it down gently.

Toby let out his breath slowly. His face turned softer, sadder. He tucked his hair behind his ears, and leaned back. "You're freaking out because you are. I always knew that you were," he said. "All that time. I just tried to ignore it."

All the breath was knocked out of me. I couldn't say yes, but I couldn't say no, either. And the person who was most relevant to that sentiment was completely out of reach.

Suddenly, I was so tired I could barely hold my head up. I picked up the teapot, and poured some steaming water into my cup. I could feel Toby's gaze on me. I looked at his sweet, sad eyes.

"I'm so sorry," I said, and meant it.

His jaw was still clenched. "I can't fucking believe this," he said. "I need a drink."

Nora came between Toby and me, and put her arms around our shoulders. "First, we're going to get food for Cassie. Then we're going to The Handle Bar. But no matter what happens, this band is going to get through this. We're going to be sad together, and we're going to celebrate together."

"We're going to do both?" I asked, trying not to cry.

"Both," she said.

Luke

I sat in another room about half the size of my cell, a room with metal walls and nothing in it but a table and two chairs. When the door opened, I kept my eyes on my cuffed hands. I smelled motor oil and salt, sunflower seeds. I looked up.

"Well," Dad said, sitting down across from me, one limb at a time. "You're not supposed to have visitors."

"No, sir."

"But I told them I was former CID and I would likely be posting bail, and they let me through. They do this sham marriage shit too much anyway. Waste of money."

We had the same sitting method, I'd noticed. Both of our injuries were on the right-hand side. "You don't have to post bail. I just wanted—"

Dad waved his hand, his face stern.

I stopped. "Thank you."

"Jake contacted Cassie, as you requested."

I felt something burst inside me at the sound of her name. "What did she—?" I began.

He held up a hand. "But we told her not to come until she has to."

"Yes, sir. So they didn't arrest her."

"No. Not yet, at least."

"Fucking Johnno." I bit down on my tongue, tasting blood.

He folded his hands, waiting for an explanation. Too long of a story. It was always too long of a story. Nothing simple. Nothing good.

He squinted at me, thick brows knit together, perplexed. Puzzled as to how I could have possibly originated in his household, I imagined. From his DNA. "Do you know what disappointment feels like, son?"

"Yes, sir." *Every day.*

"No, I often wonder if you do. I don't think you ever did. Because if you did, I believe you wouldn't inflict as much of it on the people in your life."

He was going to get up and walk away, again. He was going to wash his hands of me for a second time. I couldn't let that happen.

"I do know," I said. "And I am disappointed. I made a mistake."

"One mistake isn't the problem, Luke. It's that you set yourself up for a life where doing something like this is acceptable. When your life is a series of mistakes, mistakes are no longer mistakes. They're just your life."

"Dad," I said, my hands balled in fists. *I need you.*

"I thought you'd changed."

"I have. I'm talking to Jake. I'm going to meetings." I thought of the life on the ground I'd chosen, the consequences. I had nothing to lose. "Mom's death really messed me up, Dad." I took a breath. "And I've missed you. I love you."

He cleared his throat, putting his hands in his pockets. "You'll get a dishonorable discharge, I expect."

"Just as long as nothing happens to Cassie."

"Nobody can guarantee that."

"Maybe not, but I can try."

Dad paused. "What do you mean?"

Just then, the lawyer entered. A man about my age, of Asian descent. Thick, black hair cropped over plastic-rimmed glasses, dress blues. "My name is Henry Tran, and I'm with the United States Army Trial Defense Service."

He shook both of our hands, and sat down next to Dad, across the table from us.

"So," he began, running his eyes down a piece of paper. "You stand accused of entering into a contract marriage in order to fraudulently collect BAH and FSA pay, in violation of UCMJ Article 132."

For a minute, we were all silent. Dad opened his mouth to speak, but I spoke first. "We were married. That's it. That's all anyone has to know."

"I agree, Private Morrow. The Department of Defense's official stance is that marriage is a personal, private decision, and 'why' some-one chooses to enter into a legal union is not a court issue." He held up his hands in quotation marks. "The issue is usually whether you can provide the necessary legal documents to the service proving that you're married."

My face burst into a smile. Dad looked at me from across the table, frowning. I ignored him, holding out my fingers one by one, thinking of Frankie, his goading, his insistence on closing every loophole. "We have an official marriage certificate. We have photographic evidence of the proposal. We have witnesses that saw us before and after the wedding as a couple . . ."

I glanced at Dad. He was looking at the lawyer, his eyebrows raised. I don't think he realized how very committed I was.

Henry spoke slowly, considering. "Could the prosecution collect significant evidence that the marriage coincided with a time of finan-cial need?"

I swallowed. They could. They could dig. They could see how my bank account went rapidly up and down as I paid Johnno, mostly down. They could see that Cassie got fired. But if I could stop them from doing this before the investigation got that far . . . I put a hand flat on the table, leaning forward. "They could, but it wouldn't be relevant. If they bring up evidence, I will testify that I married her because we loved each other and we wanted to help each other out. It's not up to the court to determine 'reasons for marriage,' that's what you just said."

Dad shifted in his seat. I couldn't tell, but he might have given me a small, almost imperceptible nod.

"Beyond that, the angle they may take here is 'intent to deceive.'" Henry cleared his throat. "The phone call included mention of adul-tery on the part of Ms. Salazar. This would detract from the legiti-macy of claims of love or support."

I heard Kaz's voice, saw Johnno sneering. *Why you gonna let her play you like that, bro?*

"If I don't—" I choked on the words. I tried not to wince at the thought of Cassie and her drummer embracing. "Whatever anyone saw, if I don't consider her adulterous, then she wasn't adulterous. And I will testify to that, too."

I felt Dad's gaze on the side of my face.

I kept my eyes on the lawyer, and continued. "Cassie was there for me while I was in Afghanistan and she cared for me, day and night, when I came home injured, and we have proof of that. She was my wife in the ways that mattered, and she was an amazing wife."

A discerning look passed over the lawyer's face, and he picked up the case folder again, flipping through the papers. After a minute, he put the folder under his arm, and nodded. "Private Morrow, the hearing will likely be in a few days." A small smile grew. "I advise you to keep hold of the words you just said. I advise you to list to me any witnesses of the authenticity of Ms. Salazar's commitment, and vice versa. And I advise you to plead *not guilty.*"

After I told him about Rita and Jake and the photos, Henry reassured Dad and me that, depending on how motivated the prosecutor was, he would likely not even have to use them. He stood. Before he exited, he looked back and forth from Dad to me. "I've defended cases like this before. From what I can see, you share something very real."

A micro version of the warmth I'd felt when I kissed Cassie two nights ago spread under my skin. It wasn't over yet, but it was real. Even a stranger said it was real.

Dad turned in his seat to look at the doorway, and we heard footsteps down the hall. He turned back to me, speaking quietly, deliberately. "You did a good thing. When you said you would testify. You didn't bring her into this. You didn't even bring up the possibility."

"Yes, sir. I want to keep her out of trouble."

He lifted his chin. "You care, huh."

"Damn right." The words came quickly, sure. I had never felt more sure of anything.

"Okay," Dad said, standing. He looked down at me under his brows. "Let's get you out of here."

There's a photo of my dad from the day Jake was born, holding the little wrapped purple potato like a football. The long line of his mouth had become crooked with joy and awe. He's looking up at my mother, the photographer, with dewy eyes.

I had a strange thought once, that my dad, through no fault of his own, hadn't had one of these moments at my birth. That was why I continued to disappoint him, because we never connected, and I never knew what he wanted from me.

But when we glanced at each other as he left the room, I knew one of two things was true: that either I had been wrong all along, and we had had one of those moments to bond as infant and father and we had just forgotten; or, because I'd never witnessed such a look on his face—a look of surprise, sympathy, admiration, a look that said *you are capable of great things*—today, I had been reborn.

Cassie

I was sitting on my floor, my possessions scattered around me. When my phone rang with Luke's name on the screen, I froze. It rang again. I couldn't answer it.

I hadn't heard anything since the text from Jake yesterday. Now Josh van Ritter had made good on his promise to e-mail us. We'd head out for our first stop, Galveston, tomorrow. Next to me was a travel coffee mug, two pairs of underwear, some Bruce Springsteen records. All stuff I had collected from Toby's. Over his bourbon, my soda water, and Nora's advice, I'd finally told him that I had slept with Luke. When we'd parted, we'd exchanged a cold hug. It would get better.

I would get better, at least, if I wasn't put in jail. The phone buzzed, and Luke's name appeared again. The vibrations hammered the floor like a woodpecker.

What if the investigation was deeper now? What if he was calling me to say the police were on their way? Guessing was worse than knowing. I answered.

"I'm downstairs," he said.

My heart jumped into my throat. "It's open," I said, and seconds later, I heard his heavy footfalls on the stairs. I tried to keep myself from shaking.

If we were now both charged with fraud, he could be bringing news of prison, or some abstract version of prison I had been visualizing for two days. Either way, I would be living with people who wanted to hurt people, people who were stuck and angry and beaten down by the world. No, I would not be living with them. I would become one of them. The Loyal would be dropped from Wolf Records before we could even play one song. Nora and Toby, screwed out of their big chance. And every other part of my identity—my music, my friends, my mom—would be stripped from me and, considering how difficult it was for felons to get jobs, might never be returned. *I should push past him now,* I thought. *I should run.*

I opened the door. At the sight of him, tall and clean, everything inside me seemed to float. He had lost the tension that was always there since I'd known him, the line in his forehead and between his eyebrows, this feeling of *get me out of here.*

"Hey," he said.

"Hi."

Our voices were hushed, though they had no reason to be.

"Can I come in?" he asked. Messages passed in nanoseconds. We were back in Frankie's Lexus, scoffing at the absurdity of the eye contact exercise. We were across from each other at city hall, holding sweaty hands while the orange-shirted officiant rambled through the Serenity Prayer. We were in his dad's backyard, laughing at JJ trying to climb on Mittens's back. What did we do to each other? What did we do?

"Depends."

"What do you mean?"

I sputtered, embarrassed. "I mean, what's happening? With the charges?"

He smiled. "I can explain here, or I can explain inside. Whatever you want."

"Come on," I said, and stepped aside. We landed on the futon.

"How was the show?" he asked, as if he had just dropped in for a friendly chat.

It was magic, I wanted to say, *I wish you could have been there,* but the words couldn't get past the pulsing fear. "It was great," I pushed out. "Luke, what's going on?"

He scooted to face me. "The lawyer said I have a case. He said it's almost a sure thing. I'm pleading not guilty."

"Not guilty," I echoed. "Wait, you keep saying *I,* not *we.* Am I not—?" I began. "Okay, start over. How did they know to arrest you in the first place?"

His look of triumph faded. "My old dealer."

"But why?" I asked, sharp. Then, softer, I added, "Don't leave anything out."

Luke nodded at me, eyes intent on mine. "Of course."

He began with how he'd met this man, Johnno Lerner. How they'd been something like friends, until Luke wanted to change his life. How Luke flushed pills down the toilet. How he ran from his debts and thought he could keep on running to Afghanistan, until Johnno found him. And then Luke found me.

"And that's what I focused on in the conversation with the lawyer," he finished. "You know, like, a marriage isn't up to what people think it should be. It's up to the people in it. And even if we look at what's official, like 'in sickness and in health, richer or poorer,' et cetera, we did all that. We were good together. We took care of each other." He looked away, almost pained, and with a short breath he added, "So that's everything. The lawyer said that we have a shot. That it sounded very real."

"And he told you to plead not guilty."

"Yes," Luke said. "You probably won't even have to testify. But if you do—"

"The story is that we really care for each other."

He took a breath, struggling. "That's the story."

We sat in silence. We'd had so many silences, but this one felt different. Maybe it was the first silence we didn't have to break by lying. To everyone, to each other. Or maybe there were still lies. I didn't know. I didn't think Luke was lying now, or when he told me he had feelings for me. But, then again, I didn't think he was lying when he told me he owed money to "a friend from his hometown," either. And now, if I said in a court of law that everything we had was real, would that be a lie? I answered my own question.

"I would come in, though," I said, quiet. "If they need me to. I would testify that it was real, too. Or at least, it became real," I amended.

"That testimony would certainly help," he said.

"Will you let me know the minute you know the time and date?" I would need to make sure that I could drive back from wherever we were on tour. We were sticking around in Texas for a while.

Luke nodded. The room was so silent, I could hear him breathing.

"What now?" I asked.

"Well, we can't get a divorce until after the hearing," Luke pointed out. "Obviously."

"Oh," I said. I hadn't even thought of the divorce. For the minutes he'd been here, it had seemed like old times. Like the days when we were working together.

"I mean, that's what you want, right?" Luke tilted his head, the line in his forehead back.

What did I want? I wanted to be careful. My feelings were huge and twisted and rushing inside me like rapids, and they were going to tip out if I didn't tread slowly. I couldn't let them knock me over.

"I don't know," I said, staring at the wooden floor. "What do you want?"

Luke swallowed. "I don't know."

Before I could stop myself, I said, "I liked what we had. Or rather, what we had minus the lying and pissing of the pants." Luke let out a small laugh. I looked at his lips. "And I guess you would have to take out the kissing."

"So you want to be friends?" Luke asked, slow.

My insides, still floating, dropped an inch. "Yeah, but—"

"You can't have your cake and eat it, too."

"I can't eat cake, period. I have diabetes."

Luke's calm broke into a real laugh. I giggled with him.

"And how are you and Toby?" he asked, trying to be casual.

"Uh," I said, with a quick look at the objects strewn on the floor. "Toby and I are done."

"Oh. Sorry."

When I caught his eyes, there might have been a look of hope on his face, a hint of a smile, then he brought it back. He shook his head. "As far as our relationship," he started, and stopped. He seemed to have to force out the words. "I'm barely stable. The most important thing is that we stay safe and healthy, and I think that means you go on with your life, and I go on with mine." He smiled for real, and I couldn't help thinking that this one was wasted. It was a tragic thing, what he just said. "We'll probably be better off."

"Probably." My insides slipped another inch lower.

His gaze locked on mine, those blue eyes rimmed with black. Then they dropped to my lips. "We'll just have to see," he said. "Right? After the hearing."

"Right."

All of Luke's stammering and all the vague truisms about staying safe and healthy and him going on with his life, me going on with mine, were a far cry from what he said two days ago. Maybe he was regretting it. Maybe he was angry, considering the last time I saw him, I had kicked him to the street.

And yet he'd said that stuff about our marriage being real, the stuff I wanted to put on pause forever, and turn over, and make sure that we were feeling the same thing.

And what was that thing? Could I stand that he lied and feel what I was feeling at the same time? Was it just brought on by adrenaline, by the extreme? *Should I tell him I forgive him? Do I?*

"Oh, guess what?" he said, bursting my thoughts, his eyes wide and happy.

"What?"

"My family is having a little Purple Heart ceremony for me. Tomorrow. They wanted to make sure they got it in before the arraignment. You know—" He paused. "Just in case."

"That's wonderful." I smiled at him. He smiled back. My skin got warm.

"Yeah, Yarvis will be there. It's going to be really small. But nice." He looked shocked. "Do you want to come? I mean, if you want. I would love for you to come." He cleared his throat. "I mean, I would like that a lot."

I could feel my face flush warmer, this time out of discomfort. "We're going to Galveston tomorrow," I said. "On tour. We got a record deal out of the show last night."

"No!" he almost yelled, more animated than I had seen him in a long time. "Cassie, that's amazing!"

"Yeah," I said, letting a grin break through my nerves. "Yeah, it's kind of the shit."

His phone buzzed. He looked at it, and looked at me. "Jake's outside with JJ in the car seat, so."

I stood. He stood, slow.

"I'm sorry I probably can't make the ceremony."

"No, no worries," he said, his voice deep, restrained. "I'll just see you . . ."

"At the hearing?"

"Yeah."

My hands twitched at my sides. His made fists. We walked side by side to the door, and he braced on his cane as he stepped down.

On the stairs, he looked back at me for a long minute. I didn't break his gaze. "Bye, Cass."

"Bye, Luke."

The hole in my chest was back. My ears followed the steady rhythm of his footsteps growing fainter. Tension in every muscle released at the hope that we were going to beat the charges, balled up again at the thought that he might not want to see me anymore, and released at the memory of his calm words, his conviction, his determination to make this right.

"Hey!" I heard, muffled, from below.

I panicked, dashing to the door, my heart racing. He was looking up at me, waiting, his chiseled arms resting on either side of the door frame at the bottom of the stairs, now open to the porch.

"What?" I said, laughing a little. "You scared me."

"Sorry. I forgot to tell you. I did it!" he called up the stairs. He gestured toward his injured leg, where he had leaned his cane, and I gasped, knowing what he meant.

He nodded. "I ran. I went running!"

But before I could congratulate him, the door was closed, and he was gone.

Luke

A string held me to that room, where she was still sitting, wearing that silly white button-up shirt that looked nothing like the soft T-shirts she normally wore, stumbling over her words, looking at me like she had never looked at me before. Hearing that she was open to something new afterward, maybe not as friends, maybe not as husband and wife, but just whatever we were, was almost too much to take.

I reminded myself of the rules I had come up with after being arrested. *Leave Cassie alone.*

She was feeling warm toward me now because she was coming off the wake of the news that we had a chance to beat the charges. But it was just one day I had been good to her. Soon she would remember everything that came before that, that I had messed up her life. Whatever she was feeling now, she would have time to reconsider.

And yet when the sun hit me outside as I walked to where Jake idled near the curb, a hard bright diamond bouncing off the hoods of parked cars on Cassie's street, tinkling piano sounds drifting from her open window, I waited until the last possible moment to open Jake's car door. I savored the seconds when Cassie was still a few hundred feet away, wanting me.

Cassie

The next morning, I stopped the Subaru outside my mother's house, and got out, standing on my old street. I knocked on the screen door. When there was no answer, I let myself in.

"Mom," I called into the dim light that shone through the east windows, almost tinted green from her plants.

She came out into the living room, her reading glasses dangling around her neck. I didn't say anything. Instead, I wrapped her in my arms and squeezed.

"Will you comb my hair?" I asked into her shoulder, too relieved to see her to feel embarrassed about making a request I hadn't made since I was a teenager. "Once before I go?"

"Of course," she said.

I sat in the kitchen, staring at the cactus clock, her fingers on my scalp giving me shivers of warmth. "I'm leaving behind a mess."

"Oh? You mean your apartment?"

I laughed. My laughter stopped at the first yank of the comb. Automatic pain tears gathered in the corners of my eyes.

"Sorry," she muttered. "Just getting out this big one."

"That's okay," I said. "No, not just the apartment." She yanked again. The tears flowed freely. I took a deep breath. "So. About this marriage thing."

I told her what I'd realized about Luke. About sleeping with him, and immediately meeting and falling for Toby. About the injury, Frankie's death, and about how hard it was to fake that we loved each other. Until it wasn't.

By the end, she had made my hair into a sleek, damp curtain. Every time she'd paused the comb as I spoke, I wondered if she was going to throw it down and smack me on the back of the head. She didn't, though.

"And now I'm confused, Mom. I know I made mistakes, but I've learned so much. And I haven't lost sight of my goals. And Luke and I, I don't even know what that's supposed to look like, but we have something very deep, you know, and— Will you say something?"

She was quiet. I turned around in the chair to face her, looking up at her dimpled face, her eyes traveling my face.

She put her hand on my chin. "Ay, *mija*. If you're asking me for advice, this is the first time I have nothing for you."

"Nothing?" I felt a smile grow, despite a jump in my gut. "From the judge of all judges?"

"No. This is a rotten pickle." We laughed. "And you know what? After our fight, it feels pretty good to say, okay, Cassie, you're the woman now. Take care of your own pickle."

She was right. If I wanted my independence, I'd have to take it. The good and the bad.

"All I have for you is sorry," she continued. "And I know you think you had a fake marriage and did it for the money, and I know I've been hard on you, but hearing you talk just now, well, it sure sounds like something real to me."

Something real. Even to Mom. I smiled at her. "Really?"

"Of course. You took care of him. He took care of you. Even though you both had it harder than most. You've grown up."

"But next time . . . ," I began, wondering what I meant. Next time I would mess this up royally? I didn't like putting it that way. I didn't want there to be a next time. "Next time we're in any trouble we've got to help each other out, first and foremost."

"I like that idea."

I got up. I had to get on the phone with "Young at Heart" again, figure out how to finally get that state-sponsored health insurance, and then it was time for my last practice before we went on tour.

"Call me from the road."

"I love you, Mom."

"*Te amo*, Cass. Play well."

• • •

An hour later, it was time for Fleetwood Friday. A very special Fleetwood Friday, Nora and I had decided, full of good-luck rituals and silver confetti and candles. We draped the concrete walls of her basement in a gauzy fabric we found in the bargain bin at Goodwill on North Lamar. We hung strings of beads from the pipes. Before we signed the contracts we had printed out and set in the middle of the floor, before we rented the U-Haul to load up, before we started our new lives as professional musicians, we'd play whatever we wanted, for the hell of it, for hours on end. We'd play *Rumours* all the way through, in whatever wonky, champagne-soaked way we felt like.

Nora had brought three bottles of champagne, one for each of us. We popped them, swigged, and got set up.

"Should we begin?" Nora said. "Or did you two need a moment?"

I looked at Toby, who rolled his eyes, testing his bass drum louder than necessary. "We'll probably need a few moments at some point," I said. "But not now."

Nora raised her eyebrows, not able to hide her pleasure.

"We'll be fine," Toby called over his beats. "Come on, let's just play."

I lit a joint and let it hang from my mouth while I played, Marlon Brando style. I started to forage for the notes that said *Yes, we'll be fine. I'll be fine.* Of course, I couldn't find them. There was another, stronger feeling that was taking priority. The Loyal would be fine, but would I? Would Luke?

Toby banged out a couple of triplets to move it along. Nora plunked a minor string to act as the spine. Without words to carry us over the brink into our new lives, the sorrow of what was behind us and the joy of what lay ahead, we played together instead.

Luke

"Ready, Mittens?" What a stupid question. I was poised with the neon-pink Buda Municipal Fire Department Frisbee; her snout was raised, eyes glued, tail wiggling. Of course she was ready.

"Go!" I launched it high, almost wishing it would sail over the fence this time.

Mittens beat it at an angle, leaping like a wonder dog.

My wonder dog. I would miss her.

We were in my dad's backyard. Jake and Hailey would bring JJ out in a second, once they got the brownie stain off his suit. Dad was standing next to Lieutenant Colonel Yarvis in his old uniform, hands clasped in front of him, watching Mittens run around in circles. I was wearing my uniform today.

It was weird to have it on again. I wore it at my graduation from boot camp, for special events at the base in Afghanistan. In the dorms, at Frankie's house, on planes—this uniform had hung next to Frankie's.

His family had received their Purple Heart in the mail.

"We're back!" Hailey said, JJ in a piggyback ride. "Don't kick Mommy's dress, please," she cooed.

"Okay, Yarvis, I'm ready when you are."

Turns out soldiers who were under investigation could still receive the Purple Heart, just not in the fancy army-sanctioned ceremony. That was just fine with me. All things considered, I wasn't really one for official ceremonies.

I just wished Cassie could be here.

We gathered in the middle of the lawn. Dad lifted JJ from Hailey's back.

"Wait," Jake said. "Let me grab the camera."

We stood, quiet, JJ making cooing noises. A motorcycle rumbled by. Someone across the way was having a barbecue.

Yarvis looked at me. "You given any thought to what you want to do after you beat this thing?"

"I'm not sure yet," I told Yarvis.

I glanced at my dad, who was staring off into space. Though he'd agreed to be here, to host us, I feared he was doing it only because Jake had asked him to.

Every word he had spoken to me since I was released was clipped, laced with the possibility that I could fuck up again any minute. *Do you have any "conflicts" for the afternoon of the gathering Jake has planned for you? Do you know what disappointment feels like?*

But that was to be expected. No matter how little faith he had in me now, he had the capacity for more. Everyone did. I wouldn't give up.

I turned to Yarvis again. "You said y'all only have two social workers for hundreds of families, right?"

Yarvis nodded. "Regretfully."

"Well, maybe you could use one more." It was an idea that had been sitting in the back of my head since I sat in the holding cell.

He patted me on the back, grinning. "That sounds like a fantastic idea," he replied.

"Maybe I could work with vets who struggle with addiction."

Yarvis agreed again, naming some programs and schools I should check out. Dad kept his gaze forward, but I could tell he was listening.

"Okay!" Jake said, jogging back from his car in a suit, holding his camera.

Yarvis cleared his throat, and brought a small square box out of his pocket.

"The Purple Heart is given to soldiers wounded or killed in the line of duty. It is a symbol of courage and sacrifice. Today, we award Private First Class Luke Morrow, active—soon to be inactive—member of the United States Army Thirty-fourth Red Horse Infantry Division."

Yarvis took the medal out of the box and handed the box to Hailey, who teared up. "Though off the battlefield, Luke, let's be honest, you can be kind of a dumdum."

Jake snorted, covering his mouth.

"It doesn't take away the courage you showed in combat. I'm proud to present this medal to you today."

He pinned it to my uniform. Jake and Hailey clapped and I couldn't help but smile as I looked down at it. A gold heart hung from a purple ribbon, etched with Washington's silhouette. It signified sacrifice, pride. Hard work. Even as my life exploded around me, this proved that there had been good, at least for a little while. And that maybe, one day, there could be good again.

"Yay!" JJ shouted. "Let's eat more brownies!"

"Okay, okay, gotta get a photo. Yarvis, do you mind?"

Jake handed him the camera. We moved closer together—me on one side, then Hailey, Jake, and my dad, facing the sunset behind the house.

"I want to stand by Grampy," JJ said.

"Okay," my dad said. "Right in front of Grampy." JJ moved. "And Luke?"

I turned my head. His medal was pinned next to his sewn name, Morrow, just like mine. It glinted in the sun. Dad stepped to the right, making a space between him and Jake.

"Why don't you come stand over here, next to me?"

Cassie

I'd found it. Frankie had sent the wedding footage from city hall so long ago, and I'd downloaded it, thinking that someday when it was all over I'd remix a sample of the hilarious orange-shirted of-ficiant for a song. That part when he said, *Jewish, Christian, Muslim, Pagan, I got 'em all.*

I sat on my bed. After Fleetwood Friday, everything had felt like a dream: signing a contract, loading Toby's drums into a U-Haul trailer that we'd pull with my car until we could afford a tour van, calling the lead singer of Dr. Dog to introduce ourselves.

I had thought about calling Luke upward of twenty million times after we had met up yesterday. But I didn't know what I wanted to say. Part of me was still mad that with the hearing and the feelings I was wrestling with, I had forgotten to be more angry at him. There'd been no guarantee that my mom was okay except his word, and the fact that so far, no one had messed with her. I guess I had to trust him.

And part of me was still sitting across from him, seeing how he tried not to be disappointed that I couldn't make the Purple Heart ceremony. And it wasn't just guilt. I wanted to be there. But when he had said it would be just a small thing, with family, I probably wasn't included in that anymore. His sweet nephew, his funny brother and tough-as-nails sister-in-law, his father, whose wall was thick, but once you were in, you were in. I liked them. I wanted to see them, to say sorry for the trouble. To tell his father, especially, that his son was a good man. A brave man.

But of course I couldn't call Luke and tell him this.

People in the social media age don't just call people and tell them their feelings. Instead, they look at photos and videos of them, and convince themselves of how they *should* feel, right? Sure. I didn't have any photos of Luke, but I had the video of our city hall wedding.

I pressed Play.

Frankie had forgotten to press Record at first, I remembered that now. He didn't catch the part with the prayers. We'd had to start again.

The officiant looking pointedly at the camera, opening the Bible, pretending he was doing this for the first time.

As you embark on this marriage, God grant you both the serenity to accept the things you cannot change, the courage to change the things you can, and the wisdom to know the difference.

Can't disagree with that, I had said.

A shot of our hands, Luke squeezing. Me trying not to laugh.

Every shot of the ceremony was weaved with my memories of what would come after it.

Do you, Cassie, take Luke to be your partner for life? Do you promise to walk by his side forever, and to love, help, and encourage him in all he does?

Goddamn, that was good! Luke had exclaimed when I played it for him over Skype, one of the first displays of enthusiasm I'd ever seen out of him. *She will leave in the middle of a sentence, FYI,* he'd told Yarvis, and I thought he was making fun of me. But no: *I was just saying, honey.* He was accepting me. Accepting that my work came first. Never trying to swallow me.

Me opening my mouth to say *I do*, but being interrupted. Luke glancing sideways.

Do you promise to take time to talk with him, to listen to him, and to care for him?

The image of his back as he entered Mom's house, cane lifted, ready to protect us. Holding the glucose pack to my lips, letting my head fall on his shoulder. His slumped form as I washed his back in the bath, surrendering. He'd always remembered to thank me. Every time.

Will you share his laughter, and his tears, as his partner, lover, and best friend?

The feeling of his tears falling onto my head as we sat on the couch, into my hair, before we kissed. The feeling of safety. The feeling of making him laugh, even when we were sitting stiff on my futon, discussing the possibility of being convicted of a crime. Our crime.

I do, I had said.

I do, Luke had said.

By the power vested in me by the state of Texas, I now pronounce you husband and wife.

The thick second of staring at each other in the eyes.

Go on and kiss her, son!

I'd kissed him. I thought it was just his lips that I'd liked.

Ow! I yelled. *Fuck!*

I laughed out loud on the hotel bed, watching my enraged face try to yank my hair out of his buttons.

What happened?

Luke laying a hand on my head.

We'd come so far since then. So much had happened. And we had come out with scars, with strength.

I rewound the footage to the beginning.

. . . the serenity to accept the things you cannot change, the courage to change the things you can, and the wisdom to know the difference.

The courage to change the things I could. We still had a couple of hours before we needed to hit the road to Galveston.

I found my keys.

Luke

Strange to find myself back on Dad's lawn, feeling differently than even just weeks ago, when I was here with Cassie. I felt as if I had been chewed up and spit out, but tougher for it. Less static. Less of the elephant-on-the-chest feeling. Less doubt, even when I thought of Cassie, and came up with only questions. That was how this worked, I was realizing. Big questions had only small answers, barely answers at all, more like fractions of answers, and you just had to hope that one day those fractions would come together to form something passable.

Dad and Jake were approaching from the cooler, fresh beers in their hands.

"And then Luke starts chanting," Jake was telling Dad. "And the whole crowd is like"—he made the airy, loud whisper that people make when they're imitating crowds—"*Jacob, Jacob, Jacob.*"

"I mean, it's a year's worth of Gino's," I said, letting out a laugh. "Big moment. Lot on the line."

"Except Gino's pizza tastes like cardboard soaked in grease," my dad said.

Jake shook his head. "You just like undercooked dough, is your problem."

Dad made a *pff* sound, and sent a sunflower seed rocketing a little too close to Jake to seem accidental. Jake put up a forearm to block it, laughing.

We were quiet again, watching JJ make a nonsense-sound-filled circle around Hailey, who was sitting in the grass, sipping a beer.

Jake pulled his phone out of his pocket, stared at it, and began texting furiously.

I looked back at JJ. Though I was hopeful about the charges being dropped, I was planning for the worst, where Cassie was concerned. I was resigned that no matter how I ended up, wanting Cassie from a distance and knowing she'd never want me was the most manageable way to think. My method: I could think of things that I liked about her, and then replace them with some very concrete, tangible elements in the present moment.

Thing: I missed the way her car smelled. Replacement: The fresh-cut grass. Remnants of Dad's meatball burgers on the grill.

Thing: I missed the way she shuffled around her wood floors in her socks, not bothering to pick up her feet because, as she said, "It's fun, it feels like ice skating." Replacement: The sound of Jake snorting to himself as he looked at his phone. A casual moment. A kind of moment that I had taken for granted.

Thing: her singing voice. Replacement: I didn't have one yet.

Jake cleared his throat. "Hey, uh. Luke."

"Yeah," I said.

"You're gonna wanna check around the house."

I shot him a puzzled look, but he just shrugged. I made my way across the yard, and squinted beyond the back door. A car was pulling into the driveway. A beat-up white Subaru, to be exact.

Cassie

I texted Jake when I got close to Buda. That way I couldn't back out. I sped, making the twenty-minute journey in fifteen, and each time I thought about turning around, I pressed the gas more.

What was I going to do, run into his dad's backyard and give him a Hollywood kiss?

Here's looking at you, kid.

God, they were going to think I was crazy. I was going to solidify every stereotype about emotional women that ever existed. Crazed, illogical, blind to the rules of society. Rules like speed limits and whether a relatively random woman could just waltz into someone's private property and declare love.

I was just a woman with something to say.

I just wanted him to know. That's all. He could do whatever he wanted with it. I fucking helped him take a bath, for God's sake. The least he could do was hear me out.

I slowed down as I approached, and parked in the driveway. I took a deep breath, and got out. As I came around the house, my hands were shaking.

"Hey," I called when the backyard came into view, shielding my eyes from the sun.

Luke's mouth was hanging open. He was wearing his dress blues, looking handsome and distinguished and unapologetically happy. Jake was covering his face, trying not to laugh. Luke's dad was looking at me like I was a crazy woman.

Fuck 'em.

I approached Luke. He was still smiling. That was a good sign. I could hear Jake and his wife muttering to each other.

"Hi," I said, stuffing my hands firmly in my pockets.

"Hi," he said.

Well, this was it, the *fuck it* moment. I motioned to a corner of the yard. Luke met me near a patch of bushes.

"I'm sorry I missed the ceremony," I started. "I just needed to come anyway. Because after we talked, I thought a lot."

"Yeah, me, too," he said.

My heart lifted. "Really?"

"Really." He swallowed. "But go ahead."

I pressed tighter into my pockets. Holding myself together. I stared at the grass below my feet. "I know it doesn't make a lot of sense for us to, you know, be involved after everything that's happened. But I need you to know that—" It felt wrong to say this to the ground. I looked up at him. "I love you."

His eyebrows raised, those long lashes blinking in surprise over the blue-gray eyes. He wasn't responding. *That's okay. At least I said it.* And yet.

"And I don't mean it in a shallow way, you know, like, *in love*, like what someone would say in a Disney movie, or what teenagers say to each other so they can have sex."

He laughed.

"I mean it without a doubt, like the old people who hold hands on the street. I care for you, I will always care for you, I love you, and I will wait for you, if that's what we need to do."

"Cassie, I—" he began, taking a deep breath, and looking past me.

Just say something. I looked back down at the lawn. My old friend, the lawn.

"I love you, too."

My eyes snapped upward.

He reached out his hands, hesitant, and put them on my shoulders. "I love you."

"Really?" My heart expanded, flooded with light.

"Really."

We moved together at the same time. I wrapped my arms around his neck, meeting his open mouth with mine, pushing into his lips with a sure kiss, a relieved kiss, a kiss with his still hands on my ribs, his fingertips sliding around to my back, mine brushing his chest, exploring in a way we had never gotten a chance to before.

"So no matter how the hearing goes, we're going to do this?" he asked when we let go.

"No matter how it goes," I said. "And we're going to win. Well, we're going to fight it hard, anyway."

"Damn right, we are," he said, wrapping an arm around me, pressing, holding.

I looked over at his family, and gave a feeble wave. Jake and Jacob senior turned away, pretending to fiddle with the grill. Hailey hid a smile behind a cough, and JJ stared unabashedly, a toy car dangling from his hand, forgotten.

I turned back to Luke, and looked at the time. It was five. We were going on at nine. "Shit." I smiled at him. "I gotta go play a show."

"Okay."

We headed side by side toward the driveway, skipping every other step, making good time. He took my hand as we walked. My eyes pricked hot, wet.

"Cassie," Luke said suddenly.

"Yeah?" I said through my tears.

"I don't know what we're going to do, or how this will work, but I love you," he said. I let go of his hand, and got into the car. He added through the window, "And then we'll go from there."

I nodded at him, unable to speak. As I backed out of the driveway, Luke waved. I waved back.

Luke was right; we didn't know what we'd do. We knew we were no longer the worst things everyone once thought of us. We weren't criminals or addicts or liars or cheats, but what came after, we didn't know. But maybe we didn't have to know. We'd love each other, first and foremost, and then we'd go from there.

Acknowledgments

Thank you to Lanie Davis, Annie Stone, and the entire team at Alloy Entertainment. Thank you to Emma Colón for her time and her sharp eyes on the outline. Thank you to Aimee, Ondrea Stachel, and Kim Ross for sharing their experience with diabetes. And finally, big thanks to Kyle Jarrow for the inspiration, and to Emily Bestler for putting *Purple Hearts* out into the world.

CPSIA information can be obtained
at www.ICGtesting.com
Printed in the USA
JSHW062027230822
29593JS00002B/2

9 781501 136498